HER REBEL HIGHNESS

DAUGHTERS OF THE DYNASTY

HER REBEL HIGHNESS

DAUGHTERS OF THE DYNASTY

DIANA MA

AMULET BOOKS • NEW YORK

Images are used courtesy of the following: Jacket and page ii, center image, Mercedes deBellard; center image background, aphotostory/Shutterstock; bottom left, JayKay57 (Getty/157473098). Page iii, clockwise from top left: Portrait of a seated woman, Portrait of a Chinese aristocrat of Canton, both courtesy Musee des Arts Asiatiques-Guimet, © RMN-Grand Palais/Art Resource, New York; Mercedes deBellard; Qianlong; Yongzheng (courtesy of the Metropolitan Museum of Art).

Cataloging-in-Publication Data has been applied for and may be obtained from the Library of Congress.

ISBN 978-1-4197-4998-8

Book design by Chelsea Hunter

Printed and bound in U.S.A.
10 9 8 7 6 5 4 3 2 1

ABRAMS The Art of Books
195 Broadway, New York, NY 10007
abramsbooks.com

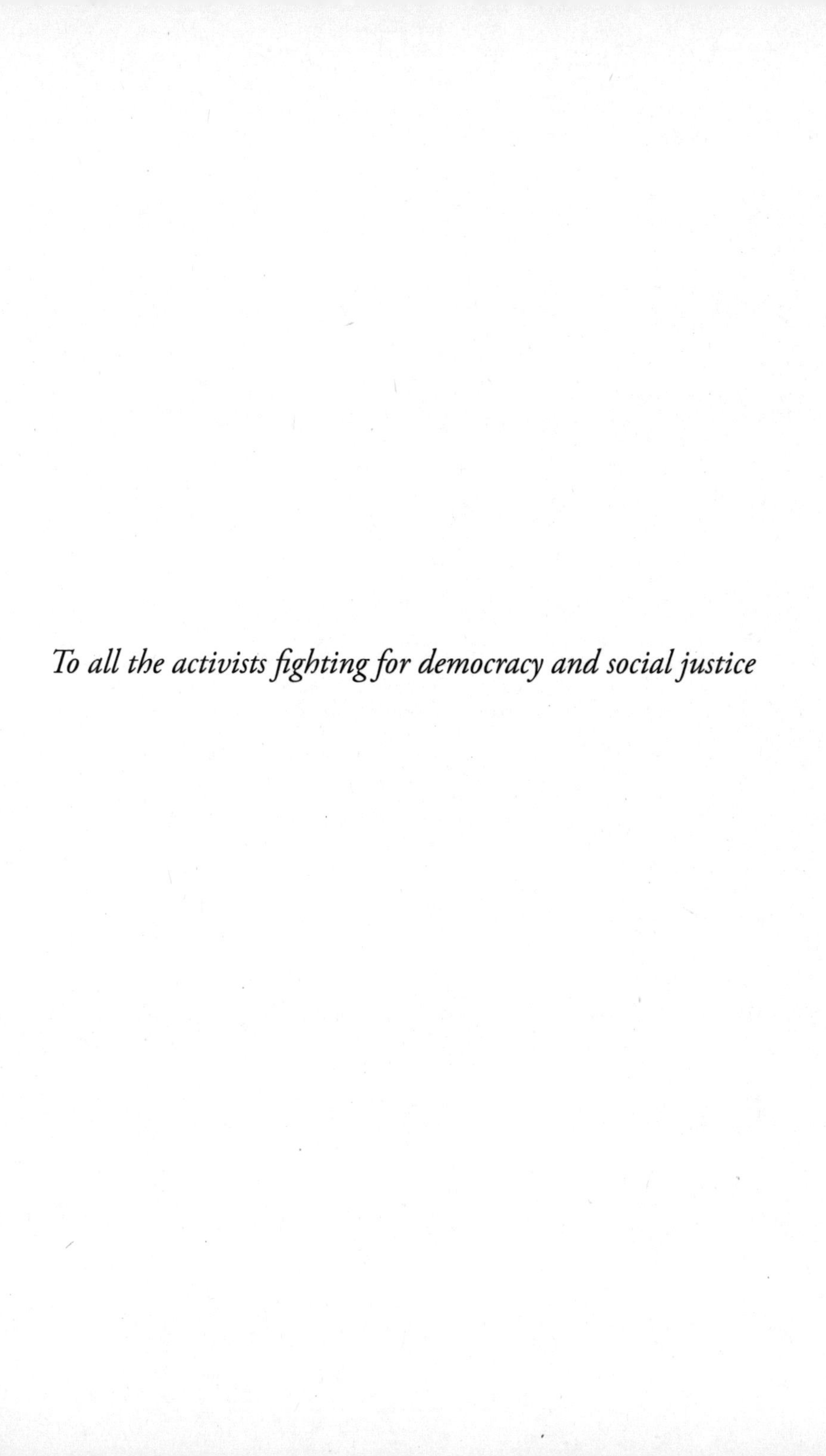

To all the activists fighting for democracy and social justice

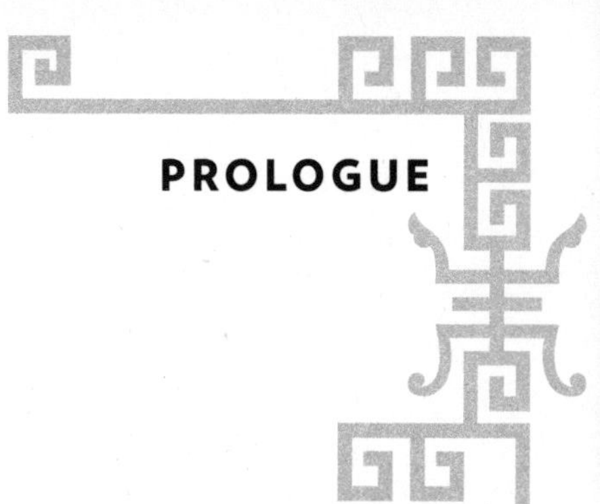

PROLOGUE

Luoyang, Eastern Capital of the Tang Dynasty, Seventh Century

Who *is* she? The strange girl, a little older than Princess Taiping, is wearing a plain gray tunic, her back ramrod straight like she knows Taiping is watching her. Even her short, ragged hair seems stiff and tense as she disappears into the artist studio behind Wan'er.

Wan'er exits and comes to Taiping after escorting the girl into the Illustrious Artist's presence. The Illustrious Artist has a name, but Taiping can't remember it. Her royal mother told her when she commissioned the portrait, but then Wan'er came up with the "Illustrious Artist" nickname, and now she can't, for the life of her, remember the actual name.

Wan'er probably knows. There isn't much Taiping's best friend, secretary to the empress, doesn't know. For instance, she knew that Empress Wu had bestowed a priceless gift—a gift only the most exalted in the empire could hope to receive, and one that even Taiping's older brothers have not received—on Taiping, her only daughter: the invitation to sit for a portrait. And now the empress has given this unheard-of gift to a commonplace girl with no connections. What reason could there be for so great an honor? The only possible explanation is that this girl must be an artist of some kind. Her mother *loves* supporting female artists. *Too bad I don't have an artistic bone in my body.*

"Princess Taiping," Wan'er says slyly, "you're early for your sitting. Two hours early."

Taiping rolls her eyes, because of course Wan'er knew nothing would keep her away. She's never met a secret that she didn't need to uncover. And a secret to do with the empress, her mother? Impossible to resist. "Who is she?" Taiping demands.

Wan'er narrows her eyes. "Believe it or not, I don't know."

"Then find out."

"I don't know if that's possible."

Taiping snorts in a decidedly un-princess-like way. "That's hard to believe. You can do anything." Three years ago, Wan'er was a palace slave. She should have been raised to be a lady, but both she and her mother had been condemned to slavery for her grandfather's treason against the empire. But then Taiping's mother discovered one of Wan'er's poems and was so impressed that she decided to test Wan'er further. The empress asked her to write an essay on the spot, and she performed so beautifully that the empress named Wan'er as her personal secretary. She was only thirteen at the time, the same age Taiping was.

Wan'er laughs. "Anything but pry a secret from your mother."

"Well, if anyone could, it would be you. My mother thinks the world of you." You'd think Taiping would be jealous. Actually, when Wan'er was first promoted to royal secretary, she *was* jealous. Taiping's essay writing is competent but not gifted. And her poetry? The less said about that, the better. But Wan'er is so luminous and spirited that no one can resist her charm. And her elevation in station three years ago meant that finally there was a girl in the palace with a high enough status to be a companion to a princess. Since then, they have been inseparable.

Except now they are to be separated.

Wan'er steps closer to her. "Forget the new girl. She's not important. I'd rather focus on getting you out of this marriage."

Taiping's heart goes cold. The empress wants to make a political alliance by marrying Taiping to her cousin, and no amount of tears or tantrums will change her mother's mind. Officially, it's Father who arranged for the engagement, but everyone knows who the real power behind the throne is. These days, her father, Emperor Gaozong, doesn't even physically sit on the throne anymore. He just lies in bed and lets Mother make the decisions. Like this one to marry Taiping off to her cousin.

From what she knows of him, Shao isn't a bad sort. But it would mean leaving Wan'er with her quick wit and bright eyes.

Dread squeezes Taiping's body. "I'll run off to the Taiping Temple before I marry Shao!" A few years ago, her mother named a Taoist temple after Taiping and made her the abbess just to have an excuse for refusing an offer of marriage. So why is her mother pushing this marriage with Shao now?

Wan'er shakes her head. "We both know you're the temple's abbess in name only. How many times have you actually been there?"

She thinks of the cool bamboo floors under her feet and the laughter of girls floating through rice-paper walls as they debated politics and read Taoist scriptures aloud to each other. "Enough times." Enough to know that the temple could never shelter her from her mother's will. Enough to know that warmth and peace could never be hers. But that's fine. Because Wan'er is here. As long as Taiping has her, she doesn't mind losing the temple.

Echoing her thoughts, Wan'er says, "Besides, running off to a temple means leaving *me*."

"You could come with me," she says suggestively.

"Your mother would never let me go. I am her right hand." Wan'er says this with a mixture of resignation and pride. But if Taiping knows her—and she does—it's mostly pride.

Then Wan'er clasps her hand, and a thrill goes through Taiping at the feel of Wan'er's blunt fingers on hers. With her heavy build and square jaw, Wan'er is a great beauty, though her looks are inferior to Taiping's—or so the courtiers say. It's true that Taiping takes after her mother, whose strong features and ample body are considered the ideal of beauty. But she thinks Wan'er is even more beautiful. It's the wicked intelligence in her eyes, the way her whole face lights up with mischief. Or passion.

A smile spreads over Taiping's face as she looks toward the beaded curtain. Wan'er isn't the only mischievous one. "I don't want to be late for my sitting," she says innocently as she smooths down the heavy brocade of her yellow gown.

Wan'er doesn't bother to point out again that Taiping's sitting isn't for another two hours. She just shakes her head. "Your curiosity is going to get you in serious trouble one day."

She's one to talk, Taiping thinks. Wan'er is already following her.

Taiping slides open the wooden lattice door, and two faces turn toward her. The girl's face is steady and composed, but the young artist's face is pale and shocked. Both incline their heads.

"Princess," the artist exclaims, head still bowed. "Forgive me, but I did not think it was time for your sitting."

A twinge of guilt hits Taiping. Even bright young artists worry about offending royalty. "It's not time yet," she says reassuringly. "I'm just satisfying my curiosity." Her eyes are already drifting to the mystery girl.

The girl's head is also inclined, but that head looks drastically different from how it did before. She's wearing a wig, intricately arranged with jeweled hair pins and precious strings of glittery beads. And her gray tunic has been replaced by a red dress embroidered with peonies, a blue-green sash, and a matching filmy scarf around her shoulders. But her high-court outfit isn't the worst offense. Hot anger rises in Taiping at the sight of a blank parchment spread before her on a low table. And she has a quill in her hand. *How dare this common girl pretend to the accomplishments of the ladies of the high court?*

The girl raises her head, and whatever she sees on Taiping's face makes her put the quill down. "Princess."

"Your name?" Taiping asks coldly. In her heart, she knows she's not being fair. But it's one thing to share her mother's favor with

Wan'er and a different thing completely for a stranger to walk in and take the place of a princess. *Her* place.

"My name is Si." She inclines her head again, and Taiping can't help but notice how gracefully she does it. The girl is not classically beautiful. She's slight, with a face too delicate for beauty, and she certainly doesn't have Wan'er's lively charm. But the watchful intensity on her face *is* interesting.

"No family name?" Wan'er asks.

"No, my lady." Si doesn't offer any other information.

Taiping eyes the elaborate wig pinned to those short, uneven strands. Her hair looks like it's growing out, and it makes Taiping wonder if Si is a former nun. Unlike Taoist nuns, Buddhist nuns are required to shave their heads. "What temple do you come from?"

"Ganye Temple."

A chill creeps over Taiping. That was where her mother, a consort to Emperor Taizong, was consigned after his death. They're not supposed to talk about it, but the late emperor was also the father of her own father, Emperor Gaozong. Although her mother never mentions being a consort to Emperor Taizong, she does talk fondly of Ganye Temple. In her heart, she's still a Buddhist. Which is why it still rankles that she made Taiping a Taoist nun for political reasons. And now the empress has brought a girl with no beauty or obvious talent from her beloved Buddhist temple to the palace.

Head still lowered, Si says, "Princess, with your permission, I will change back into my own clothing and take my leave."

Taiping ignores her request. Besides, if her mother wants this girl's portrait, then Taiping had better not get in the way. Well, any more than she has already. But that doesn't mean that she can't ask questions. "Why are you here? Why did the empress invite you?"

Si raises wary eyes to her face. "I don't know, Princess."

She's lying. Despite Taiping's preoccupation with an unwanted marriage and her impending separation from Wan'er, her interest is completely hooked. This is a mystery she *must* solve.

CHAPTER ONE

Beijing, 1989

This is a mystery I *must* solve.

Books are haphazardly stacked on my nightstand, and papers are strewn all over my elegant rosewood writing desk, spilling onto the floor. On my artist's easel, I've hung my new paintings: portraits of two unknown Tang dynasty court ladies.

Who were they? Unfortunately, I have little chance of ever finding out for sure. Almost no one has seen the originals because they disappeared before my birth. In fact, there's only one person living who *has* seen them. My mother.

I look critically at the portraits I've tried to re-create from my mother's descriptions. One lady is wearing a yellow gown, and the other is wearing a red one. I'm impatient to show my mother my latest attempt, but I know what she'll say: *No, that's not the right shade of yellow. No, the faces are all wrong.* She's said all that before and more.

The only thing I've gotten right is Wu Zetian's red imperial seal on the back of each painting.

Muttering under my breath, I scan the four sheets of thick cream paper covered in calligraphed characters on my desk, but I ignore the pile of history books on Wu Zetian, the only female sovereign of China. There's nothing more the history books can tell me about Empress Wu, my ancestress.

But these Tang dynasty poems might help me get a better sense of who the ladies in the two missing paintings were. They've given me half the answer already. The poems aren't the originals, of course. They're all copies.

I figured out a long time ago that I'm a decent artist but not a great one. That's why I've turned all my energy to studying art rather than creating it. Other than copying the calligraphy of the poems and painting the two portraits over and over again, I don't do any art myself. But being an art historian is something I can succeed at. Something I *will* succeed at.

Looking at the copies I've made, I have to say that I'm also a damn good forger. Not surprising, since I've been studying the calligraphy of these poems ever since I could read.

Not the copies. The originals.

The poems are part of Wu Zetian's secret art collection of women artists. In her time, Empress Wu was a great patron to women in the arts. And all that art and history has been passed on from daughter to daughter since the Tang dynasty until it reached us: Ma, Jun, and me. We're the last living direct descendants of Empress Wu Zetian through the matrilineal line. We're the keepers of her dynasty.

I glance at one of the poems. This is actually a known poem by Wu Zetian about an imperial visit to a park, written in Wu's own hand. It's relevant only because it confirms that the other three were *not* written by her. I set Wu's poem aside and pick up the three poems that are more important.

Taking these poems, I sit on my silk love seat and spread them on the low, carved table in front of me. The first poem is an ode to Princess Taiping. Each character is a miracle of boldness and elegance. The lüshi form is perfect. The complicated tonal conventions of this type of Tang dynasty poetry are followed exactly. Read aloud, the poem *sings.* Only one woman was accomplished enough to write a poem of this caliber: Empress Wu's own secretary, Shangguan Wan'er. Actually, "secretary" is a bit of a misnomer. "Prime minister" is a better description of her role as the politician second only to the empress during Wu's reign. In fact, Shangguan Wan'er was probably the first prime minister of China.

I look at the second poem on the table. It's also an ode to Princess Taiping but amateurish in comparison to Shangguan's poem. The one fascinating thing about the second poem is that it uses all fifteen of the characters that Empress Wu modified during her reign. But this clever gimmick isn't relevant to solving the mystery of the two ladies. What's important is that both poems describe Princess Taiping as wearing a yellow dress.

There's no doubt in my mind that the lady in yellow is Princess Taiping, the only surviving daughter of Wu Zetian. And since Empress Wu's art was passed on from daughter to daughter, that would make Taiping my ancestress too. I've always felt a connection to the princess. Maybe because she was the first daughter in a long line of daughters who guarded Wu's legacy. She must have loved this art too. It would have been dangerous back in the Tang dynasty to be the keeper of art by women. It's dangerous now for a different reason.

Taiping is the reason I have to re-create these portraits. There aren't any known images of the princess in existence, and it makes me physically ache to think of her image lost and forgotten forever. Not if I can help it.

And while I'm at it, I'll try to paint the other lady back into existence too. Whoever she is.

That's where the biggest mystery comes in. No matter how many times I've scoured the history books, I can't find any mention of a lady high enough in Empress Wu's favor to be included in her art collection. Except for Shangguan Wan'er, of course. But it's clear from my mother's description that the two portraits were done by the same artist with even the same backdrop, and it's hard to imagine anyone, even Wu's personal secretary, being important enough to merit the same treatment as the empress's royal daughter. Plus, Shangguan was supposed to be beautiful, and my mother has described the lady in red as slender, which doesn't fit the standards of Tang dynasty beauty.

Who is she? Second only to my desire to bring Taiping's image back into existence is my obsession to find out who the mystery lady is. *Too bad no one wrote a poem about her.*

Reminded, I turn my attention to the third and last poem. It's the one that fascinates me the most because I believe that it was written by Princess Taiping. The whole poem is as inept in the lüshi form as the second one is, but Taiping's poem has a feeling of heavy sorrow and dark prophecy that the other poems lack. I can't figure out what this last poem has to do with the lady in the red dress, but I have an unshakable feeling that it's the key to that mystery.

Out loud, I read, "'The sun has set below the border of mountains—'"

"Lei." My twin sister is standing in the doorway to my bedroom and fidgeting. Jun never fidgets. She's never anything but calm and composed. But now she's tapping her foot against the floor. "Can I talk to you?"

Curious, I say, "Sure, what's up?"

"I need your help."

My ears perk up even more. Jun doesn't ask me for help often. To be fair, my brand of help usually gets one or both of us in trouble. Like the time I signed her up for the school singing competition and forgot to ask her first—which, in retrospect, was a *big* mistake. It's a shame she froze up onstage, so no one got to hear what a beautiful voice she has. I scoot over on the love seat and pat the space beside me, trying not to look too eager. "Of course!"

Gingerly, she sits next to me. "You know how worried I am about the Gaokao?"

The National College Entrance Examination in two months is a big deal, and Jun's been hitting the books even harder than she usually does. After all, the best colleges in Beijing take only students with the highest test scores. And it doesn't help that colleges have unofficial quotas, so the number of women admitted is much lower than the number of men. In other words, women have to score higher on the Gaokao to get into college. Naturally, I don't say this out loud. "You'll do fine," I assure Jun.

"*You'll* do fine," she retorts. "You study half as hard and get grades as good as mine or better." Jun's right, although I'd never admit it aloud in a million years. She keeps talking. "I knew I needed help, so I hired a tutor. Yanlin is a college student, and he got high marks the year he took it."

I look at her sharply. Come to think of it, Jun *has* been looking suspiciously dreamy-eyed lately. "Can I assume that this Yanlin is cute?"

"Cute?" she says faintly. Her red cheeks say it all.

I roll my eyes, because Jun can't keep a secret to save her life. At least not from me. My twin sister and I don't keep anything from each other. "So this is the reason you've been wandering around the house in a daze all week!"

"I don't even know how he feels about me!"

"Of course he's smitten with you," I say loyally. "He'd have to be crazy not to be!"

"He just thinks of me as the clueless girl he's tutoring."

"Then you get him to see you as more." A slow smile spreads over my face. "And I have the perfect idea for how to do that!"

Jumping up, I press the play button on my mint-green imported boom box. As the opening chords of Cyndi Lauper's "Girls Just Want to Have Fun" float through the air, I seize Jun around the waist and start dancing her around my room filled with hand-carved rosewood and bright silk pillows as well as Western tech like my boom box. "You invite him to a historical event happening tomorrow night!"

"Lei!" Jun exclaims. "Ba forbid us to go!"

Ba is an old-school Communist Party official who thinks a Western-style nightclub is the beginning of the end (although he has no problem with foreign luxuries). If he'd had his way, the

Communist Party would have never lifted the ban on commercial dancing spaces like it did just recently.

But there's no way my father is keeping me from going to the very first nightclub in all of Beijing on its opening night. "Please, Jun," I say. "I've already got it worked out so I can be at Club Flash tomorrow night."

"You mean you're going to sneak out." Disapproval stiffens her voice.

"You know it." I give her my best entreating smile. "Come with me? Yanlin would love to be invited to the hottest event of the year, and it's the perfect way to get those sparks flying!"

Jun looks torn but shakes her head. "Yanlin won't be able to get on the guest list."

Interesting. That means he's not part of our usual upper-class social set. And it could also explain why Jun's so hesitant to get involved with him. My parents have made it clear that they want us to date the "right" kind of boy. Good family, good prospects. In other words, *boring*. I'd always thought my straitlaced, rule-following sister would date only someone our parents approved of, but maybe I was wrong. Maybe I'll like her new guy. "No problem. I'll get all three of us on the guest list." I'm not about to let my parents *or* Jun stand in the way of her happiness. "Get ready for a night of romance!"

She twirls the end of her braid around a finger. "I don't know . . ."

I can tell she's weakening, but before I can say anything more, a knock sounds at my door.

"Come in!" I call out, irritated at the interruption when I was this close to convincing my sister to break a rule. For her own good, of course.

The door opens, and it's our mother.

I rush to the door, Jun's romantic prospects forgotten for the moment. "Ma! Just the person I wanted to see!" I drag her over to my easel. "What do you think?" I demand. "Am I getting closer?"

"Yes," she says, barely glancing at the portraits. "The imperial seal looks good."

That's because I've actually seen Wu Zetian's seal. It's stamped on the back of every painting and poem in her collection. It took me years to become good enough at brush painting in ink to replicate the seal, but now you can hardly tell the difference between the original stamp and my ink-and-brush copy. I'm proud of that accomplishment, but that's not the kind of feedback I need from my mother.

At my groan of frustration, Ma smiles and takes a closer look. "This one," she says, pointing to the lady in yellow, "had a heavier face." She holds up a hand against the barrage of questions she must know I'm about to hit her with. "I need to talk to you both."

"Oh?" Frantically, I search my conscience, but I've been almost as proper as Jun lately. After all, I need to rack up some goodwill points in case I get caught sneaking out to Club Flash tomorrow. But our mother said she needed to talk to *both* of us, and I'm sure Jun hasn't done anything wrong. Not yet, anyway.

"What is it, Ma?" Jun looks attentively at our mother.

"Not here," she replies. "Let's go downstairs."

My eyebrows rise and Jun's forehead wrinkles. Why is Ma being so cagey?

We follow our mother out of my room and down the wide marble staircase with gold railings. Even after four years, I'm still not used to living in a mansion with gold finishings everywhere. Not to mention six bedrooms, four bathrooms, two sitting rooms, a library, a media room, a game room, and a greenhouse.

I assume Ma's going to bring us into the main living room or one of the sitting rooms for our talk, but she leads us into the library and shuts the door. The library is the only room in the house that she won't let the cleaners touch. Unlike other families of high-level Communist Party officials, we don't have live-in servants. And it's all because of what's hidden in here.

Ma takes out a key from the chain around her neck. Jun and I have duplicates of the key, but I'm the only one who uses mine on a regular basis. In fact, I'm wearing it now like a locket around my neck. I can't remember the last time I've seen Jun use her key. Ba doesn't even have a key that I know of. And Ma uses hers only on special occasions.

Ma is unlocking the metal panel on the wall hidden behind a family portrait. She presses a button, and a large bookshelf slides open to reveal a set of stairs. The last time the three of us went down to the secret lower level of our Beijing mansion was New Year's Day. Why is Ma taking us here now, in April? OK, something seriously weird is happening.

Jun and I look at each other, but she seems as puzzled as I am. Ma doesn't explain herself as she descends the stairs, with us following in her wake. There are no gold railings on these stairs because no one is meant to see this space except for us. In fact, when Ba was having this house built for us, Ma's one request was this hidden subbasement.

It's where we keep the secret gallery of Wu Zetian's art collection.

CHAPTER TWO

At the bottom of the stairs, Ma flicks on the dim lights to reveal vivid paintings and calligraphy scrolls on the walls, ornaments in glass cases, and statues mounted on marble pedestals. As always, no matter how many times I've seen this, my breath catches in awe. The best thing about our new home is that we can finally display Wu Zetian's art, even though it's only for ourselves.

I've made sure to come here every day since we moved into this mansion. Even in our old house, when all the art was packed in crates and crammed into a locked room, I used to sit among the crates and just breathe in all the history in the air. Ma likes to tell me that she used to do the same when she was little. *Her* childhood home also had a hidden room. But that one must not have been hidden enough. Because when she was around my age, the unthinkable happened.

Ma waves a hand at the black lacquered chairs that look like they could be antiques from the Tang dynasty (they're not, but still super expensive). "Sit down."

Jun promptly sits, but I settle myself on the carpeted floor. I hate those hard, slippery chairs; I can never get comfortable on them. But the chairs are the only thing I dislike in this room. Everything else I love. No, that's not enough to describe my passion. I'm willing to give my life for the art in this room.

And that's exactly the kind of commitment required of us, the keepers of Wu Zetian's collection. There's a good reason her art is in our basement rather than a museum.

"What are we doing here, Ma?" I ask.

Ma paces the room, walking past a small statue of Wu Zetian, who ruled briefly with her own Zhou dynasty, interrupting the great Tang dynasty. There's a bigger statue of Empress Wu in the Longmen Grottoes in Henan Province. If anyone saw this small statue of Wu Zetian, they would assume it's a copy of it.

They would be wrong. The statue in the Longmen Grottoes is actually a large-scale copy of *our* statue.

At last, Ma sits down on a chair next to Jun. "I want to talk to you both about why it's important to keep this collection secret."

My brow furrows. My sister and I already understand why Wu Zetian's art has to be hidden. It's a history that everyone knows—the Cultural Revolution, which started in 1966 and lasted for a decade. Deng Xiaoping, the leader of the Community Party, was a product of that bloody time. And so were my parents. Why does Ma feel like she needs to explain this?

"I was your age when the Cultural Revolution started," Ma says. "You need to know what it was like to live under the violence of the Red Guard."

Despite myself, I shudder. The Red Guard was a militarized student group that raided homes, beating and jailing anyone found in possession of bourgeois art—anything that wasn't state and Communist Party approved. As for priceless Tang dynasty art from the private collection of the most reviled royal, the most hated woman in all Chinese history? That could have gotten our entire family beaten and jailed at the least, killed at the worst.

"Lei, are you listening?" Ma asks sharply.

I sit up, folding my legs under me. "Of course!" Just because Jun is sitting on a chair all proper and I'm not, Ma thinks *I'm* the one not listening?

Ma's face softens. "Of course you are." She knows how important this is to me. How I would do anything to protect the ebony-framed paintings, statues, jade jewelry, and scrolls of poems surrounding us. Our legacy.

"We're lucky," Ma says, "that we were able to keep our secret during the years of the Cultural Revolution that the Red Guard was allowed its reign of terror. But we still lost something important."

"The two portraits of the Tang dynasty court ladies!" I scramble to my feet and blurt out, "Did the Red Guard take them?"

"Lei," Jun says, "Ma has told us many times that if the Red Guard knew her family had those paintings, they all would have been arrested and sent to a labor camp."

"Yes," I say impatiently, "but what if one of the Red Guard stole them for his own gain?" My excitement quickens as I explain the theory that's been brewing in my head for months. "Maybe he didn't report Ma because he didn't want anyone to know he was keeping such priceless art for himself!" And that could mean that those paintings are still out there, whole and intact. I can't bear to think of the alternative: that they were burned with so much other classical art. That's what the Red Guard did during the Cultural Revolution. Burn the art they pillaged.

"It's possible," Ma says, but the hopeless look in her eyes tells me she doesn't really believe that the paintings survived.

Oh, right. There's a reason I haven't shared my theory before. Because it makes Ma sad to talk about those paintings. But then again, *she's* the one who brought them up in the first place. "I think it's time we start looking for the missing paintings," I say quickly, before I lose my nerve.

Jun gasps. "Lei!"

"I know! I know!" I've already anticipated my family's reaction. "Searching for the paintings will bring unwanted attention, and we're supposed to keep the art secret because if the Communist Party found out we were hoarding dynasty art, we'd be in big trouble. But China is changing! Look at the student protesters—"

"Enough, Lei!" Ma has turned pale. "Don't forget the Red Guard were also students."

Except it's completely different this time. That's the argument the independent, left-leaning newspapers are making, which is what

I've been telling my parents all week. The student demonstrations springing up at colleges all over the city are in response to former Communist Party leader Hu Yaobang's death nearly a week ago. Hu was a popular progressive politician among young people and was ousted from political power two years ago, largely for his refusal to quell the student protests back then. Now, his widow is laying the blame for his ill health and death squarely on the party that discredited him. That was enough to spark protests on college campuses and at Tiananmen Square in support of Hu and his call for democracy.

In other words, today's peaceful protesters are speaking out *against* government authoritarianism, which is the exact *opposite* of the Red Guard, who brutally enforced state-mandated control. But my parents won't listen to me. The terrible memories of the Cultural Revolution are still too close.

"We have to hide the art," Jun says, sounding like the older sister that she is. "It's our duty."

That stings. Just because she's the oldest and will inherit the art and the responsibility of being its guardian doesn't mean that I don't know how dangerous our inheritance is. But I also know how wonderful and beautiful it is. We are descended from Wu Zetian, the only female ruler of China. And from Princess Taiping, who risked everything to preserve her mother's legacy.

Always the peacemaker, Ma says gently, "Your sister understands her duty. Isn't that right, Lei?"

"Yes." I shiver in the coolness of the basement, the temperature perfectly calibrated to preserve the art surrounding me. It's exactly how I feel in my privileged life of imported luxuries and elite schools: stuck in cold storage. *I have to break out.*

My acute awareness of wealth is why I'm going to join the student revolutionaries. The students' fight to make our country more equitable has fired up my passions, even though it's money and status like mine they're fighting against.

My throat constricts at the thought of my parents finding out. It would be their worst nightmare. I haven't even told *Jun*. It's not like me to keep anything from my twin, but my tongue seizes up every time I try to tell her. What if she thinks my commitment to the students' cause is a passing interest, like my infatuation with shoulder pads or the band A Flock of Seagulls?

But it's not like that at all. My determination to join the protests is real. The students are fighting for a more open and free China. If they succeed, our country can be a place where Wu Zetian's art is no longer dangerous. A place where *who I am* is no longer dangerous. The only thing more important than hiding Empress Wu's art is fighting for a world where we don't *have* to hide it.

I can't help but say this out loud. "We shouldn't have to keep this gallery a secret! The world should know about Wu's legacy: a brilliant collection of art by women. Think about it. This is a Chinese feminist revolution in art. It would make it impossible for Western countries to consider us backward or repressed."

Jun shakes her head. "It doesn't matter what the rest of the world thinks. We have to make sure no one finds out about *this*." She gestures at the art surrounding us, sparing only the briefest glance at the walls vibrant with paintings and the glass cases filled with carved jade and painted vases. "Empress Wu's art is dangerous to our family—that's why we have to keep it secret!"

My gut twists painfully. When my sister looks at the bold lines of calligraphy or the intricate stone carvings, does she even see their beauty? Or does she just see the danger they represent? Yes, Jun will be a faithful guardian of our inheritance. But it will be out of duty, not love.

"There's more to it, Jun." Ma's eyes are shadowed. "We keep this gallery secret because our job is to protect our family *and* the art—something I failed to do because I didn't value what I guarded enough. You must understand that in order to avoid my failure."

My sister flushes. As far as rebukes go, Ma's is pretty mild, but Jun isn't used to being criticized. After all, she's the *good* daughter. Jie Jie, the older sister, who does everything right. And I'm Mei Mei, who definitely does not do everything right. But according to Jun, I get away with everything just because I'm younger (by minutes, but still . . .).

"That's why there *is* one person you can and should tell," Ma says. "The man who will join you in guarding it. I trusted your father to help me protect our secret, and that's why I married him."

Oh hell. If this is our mother's way of telling us that she's picked out our future husbands or something archaic like that, I'm going to throw an *epic* tantrum.

"Your ba," she says softly, "risked everything to protect me. He was a Red Guard, you know."

Jun and I both nod. Of course we know. It's a legend in our family, our parents' great love story. Ba broke his oath to the Red Guard by protecting the art he had sworn to destroy. All because he fell in love with the heiress of a dangerous legacy. It certainly wasn't because he appreciated Wu Zetian's art. In fact, I can't ever remember him coming down to the gallery, and he hardly even mentions it. If there's anything my father is afraid of, it's what he brought into this gold-and-marble mansion to hide.

A chill passes through me. It's terrifying to think about what would happen if anyone found out that Ba, a high-ranking Communist Party official, was hiding imperial art in our basement. The Cultural Revolution officially ended thirteen years ago, but Ba says it will take decades more for our country to heal from that monstrous time.

Ma stands up and gestures for me to take her vacated chair. Reluctantly, I sit and immediately start squirming. I've never mastered Jun's skill of being still.

"I brought you two down here to tell you that I've made a decision." Then she pauses and presses her hand to her forehead.

Alarmed, I leap up. "Ma, why don't you sit back down?"

"I'm fine. It's just one of my headaches." She sinks into my offered seat with a small sigh. "Come sit next to me, Lei."

I sit back down, and on the other side of Ma, Jun looks on with worry in her eyes. The same anxiety licks at my stomach. Ma's migraines seem to get worse with every passing year. She's had these headaches ever since I could remember, but she usually lies down in her darkened bedroom until they pass. If she's in the middle of a migraine now, why is she still up and insisting on this mysterious meeting? Cold touches my heart. What is this all about, anyway?

Our mother takes a deep breath, and a strange anxiety lurks in her eyes. "Lei will be the one to inherit Wu Zetian's art collection."

What?! I couldn't have heard right. Jun is supposed to inherit! She's the oldest, so she should be the guardian of Empress Wu's art . . . But could all this really be mine? I feel dizzy with guilt.

Jun turns pale but says nothing.

Ma looks at my sister, worry creased into her face. "Jun, I know you're the eldest, but Lei's study of art makes her the right choice to be the keeper of our legacy."

I wonder if Jun also hears what's under Ma's words: *Lei is the one who loves this art.* And if so, will that make Jun feel better about our mother's decision? Or worse?

"The money, of course, will be divided equally between the two of you," she continues.

Well, there's certainly more than enough money to inherit. Under Deng Xiaoping's economic policies, old Communist Party members like my father have made money hand over fist. That's how he was able to build this mansion.

But money isn't my passion. Art is. "Jun can have my share of the money!"

"Don't be ridiculous, Lei." Slowly, the color comes back into Jun's face. "I'm not taking your half of the money. You'll need it if you're going to be . . . guardian of Empress Wu's art."

She's right, of course. Ba has drilled it into us that the only things keeping our secret and family safe from discovery are money and power. That's why he's worked so hard to give us both. Money that we will inherit. Power that I will get by rising in the Communist Party and that we both will get by marrying well. Of course, a position in the party won't get me an exemption from a "good" marriage. Not that our parents have ever said that in so many words. But my sister and I know what's expected of us.

A heaviness tugs at my heart because I don't want that path anymore. The feeling has been building for a long time, but when the students began to march in the streets, denouncing the corruption of the Communist Party and calling for an end to censorship, it set my soul on fire. I hate how the party tells us what to think and makes it dangerous to have our own ideas. I hate how the art I love is banned. I hate my life of secrets. And joining the party would make me complicit in everything I hate. That's when I knew I couldn't follow in Ba's footsteps. I just haven't told my parents yet. Ma won't mind, but Ba is a different story.

Ma smiles at us. "My two daughters. I couldn't be prouder of you both."

"But, Ma, why . . ." I lick my dry lips, not sure I want to hear the answer to my question. "Why are you deciding this now? Is there something you're not telling us?" And does it have to do with the headaches that keep her isolated in a dark, quiet room for hours at a time?

Jun and I exchange concerned glances, and for a moment, I'm in sync with my twin again. But then she looks away, and the connection is broken.

"No. Everything is fine," Ma says reassuringly. "It's just that you're both going to college next year. I felt it was time to figure out your future." She touches my sister's knee. "Jun, you're learning the charity work I do. Someday, you'll take over for me as a leader in society."

I try to keep my face blank, but . . . that sounds like pure hell. I might not want to join the Communist Party, but the high-society circle Ma inhabits makes my skin crawl. My sister, on the other hand, seems right at home there. Jun has always been like a mini-Ma, which makes our mother's decision to give me the guardianship of Empress Wu's art even more mysterious. *Poor Jun.* This must be killing her.

Except there isn't even a trace of resentment on my sweet sister's face. But she's sitting a little too stiffly on her chair, and she doesn't react to Ma's words about her future.

Ma pats my arm. "And you, Lei, will study art here in Beijing."

Wait a minute . . . that's it? No future as a "leader in society" for me? Not that I want the socialite path being carved out for Jun, but I *do* have ambitions. "What about after college?" My chin lifts. "I want to study abroad."

I've been trying to convince my anti-Westernization father that a top-rate international education would be good for my future, but I didn't think I'd have to convince Ma too. She's supposed to be planning for Jun's future, not mine. That's the way it's always been. My sister is set to follow in Ma's footsteps, and I'm destined to follow in Ba's. Has that changed now that I'm going to inherit the art?

I *do* want the art. Badly. But I also want to see the world. I breathe deeply to calm the turmoil in my body. Then I glimpse Jun's closed face, and for the first time I wonder if my sister's predetermined path chafes her as much as mine does.

Ma's mouth purses. "Where would you go, anyway?"

I shrug as if I haven't already made a list. "The United States, maybe. France or Germany. Hong Kong, definitely."

She snorts. "Hong Kong doesn't count as going abroad! Besides, it will convert back to China from British rule in eight years, and you can go then. See, you don't need to study abroad, Lei. Everything you want is here."

That's . . . not quite true. Yes, my family and Empress Wu's art are both here. But I want to share Wu Zetian's legacy with the world. And I can't do that if I'm trapped in Beijing, keeping watch over a hidden basement. Still, it has always been my plan to talk Ma and Jun into revealing the art and Wu Zetian's true history one day. Maybe that day is closer now that *I* am going to inherit the art.

"I'll take care of our inheritance. I promise." I might not be as responsible as Jun when it comes to most things, but I'm serious about this.

Ma smiles. "I know you will, Lei."

I still can't tell what Jun is thinking, and that bothers me because I *always* know what my twin is thinking. But beneath my concern for Jun, a fierce joy is humming in my soul.

I am going to be the keeper of Empress Wu's dynasty.

CHAPTER THREE

"Just pick an outfit, Lei!" Of course Jun's already ready in a pink dress with lots of filmy layers, with minimal makeup and her hair arranged in a complicated braid. Her face is flushed with excitement, and she looks beautiful.

I whirl around on the cushioned stool of my dressing table to face her. "A little patience, please!" I can't believe I'm the one telling Jun, of all people, to be patient. I want to tease her about it, but after finally talking her into my plan to meet Yanlin at Club Flash, I'm not about to stir up her doubts now.

Hesitantly, Jun says, "Lei . . ."

I know exactly what she's about to say. Jun is always sacrificing her own happiness to do what everyone else expects of her. *Nope. Not this time.*

Ignoring her, I turn back to the mirror and fluff up my teased hair. "You know I go through a minimum of three clothing changes before making up my mind. Standard operating procedure for me." The big joke in my family is that Jun beat me out of the womb by six minutes because I was still deciding on how to make my entrance. Screaming and crying, apparently. Jun, on the other hand, was a preternaturally calm baby.

She's not calm now. Her face wrinkles as she points to my electric-blue off-the-shoulder dress. "That's number four already."

"OK! I'll pick something." I jump up and shimmy out of the electric-blue dress. Hastily, I put on a black tulle miniskirt and sequined lace top. "Decision made!" Only the threat of Jun backing out could motivate me to make up my mind so fast. Then I touch the green jade of the pendant nesting between my collarbones. Decision *almost* made. "Should I wear the necklace? It doesn't really go with the Material Girl vibe I've got going here."

"I'm wearing mine," she says, pulling her pendant out to show me. Hers has "jie," the character for "older sister," carved into it.

Mine has "mei," the character for "younger sister," carved into it. Together, they form the word "jiemei," *"sisters."* Ma gave us these pendants on our sixteenth birthday, and mine is almost as precious to me as the art downstairs. But the necklace doesn't fit my outfit's look, so I take it off and put it into a tray in my jewelry box. There's only one other item in this tray: a chain with the key to the hidden art gallery. The key and the pendant are the two pieces I wear almost daily.

Jun tucks her pendant beneath her dress and sinks down on my bed. "Lei, what if we get caught?"

I shrug on a black trench coat and belt it around my waist. "Why would we get caught? We've got an ironclad excuse for going out tonight." I told our parents we're going to study with friends. Nothing suspicious in that. Everyone our age is doing these late-night cram sessions this close to the Gaokao.

"I suppose you're right."

To distract Jun from her worry, I say, "Tell me about Yanlin."

It works. Her expression softens. "Well, he's in his first year at Beijing University."

Wait. Beijing University? That's not only my dream college but also the hotbed of the protests. "Is Yanlin a student protester?" My pulse races at the thought. I haven't quite figured out how to join a dissident movement organized by college students, but if I had a connection . . .

"Of course not!" Jun shakes her head. "Yanlin is far too practical to get involved in anything like that."

"Practical. I see." Maybe this boy is boring after all.

"If you're done getting ready, we can go to the club, and you can see for yourself what he's like."

She has a point. I grab my sequined purse. "Race you to the door!"

I bolt out of my bedroom and down the hallway, hoping Jun will break character and chase after me, but of course she doesn't, so I'm the one who gets Ma's full-on glare as I double-time it down our marble staircase.

"Sung Lei!" she thunders from the bottom of the stairs. "Stop at once!"

"Sorry, Ma," I say breathlessly, slowing as I make my way down the stairs.

"You're too old for such careless antics, Lei. You could have hurt yourself. Can't you be more like your older sister?" she asks as Jun sedately descends the stairs and joins us.

There's no sting in her words. Ma has said more times than I can count how much she loves having two such different, unique daughters. I throw my arms around her. "I couldn't if I tried," I say cheerfully.

"Silly girl." But she returns my hug.

"Hi, Ma." Jun's not the hugging type, but she greets our mother with a smile.

Ma surveys her approvingly. "You look simply lovely, dear." Her tone turns into exasperation as she switches her gaze to me. "You, Lei, look . . ." Words apparently fail her. "What are you wearing under that coat, and why does the hem need to be so high?"

I grin. "To show off my 'skin golden in the pale moonlight,' of course!"

"That's my daughter—quoting Tang dynasty poetry," she says dryly, "and wearing so much makeup that your natural skin, golden or not, is completely covered up."

Not fair. I'm not even wearing blush! Just some pressed powder, black eyeliner, and cherry-red lipstick. And I *did* decide against the top with the plunging neckline.

Ma shakes her head. "No one who sees you would guess you have such a sharp brain under all that sprayed hair." It's not like Ma to keep up her criticism of me, and Jun casts her a look of surprise.

Ignoring the pinprick of hurt, I shrug. "Then I'll just have to prove them wrong."

Ma sighs. "I'm sorry, Lei. I shouldn't take my bad mood out on you."

"Headache?" I ask sympathetically.

She shakes her head. "No. It's just this planning meeting for the cancer fundraising event."

My eyebrows draw together. Why would that put her in a bad mood? Ma usually comes back from those sorts of charity events in good spirits. Unless . . . "Was Mrs. Xu there?" I swear that woman lives for spreading gossip. "Did she say something?"

"She just passed on some information"—her mouth tightens—"about *that woman*."

No need to ask who she means by *that woman*. Liu Yuan has been after my mother again. Ma won't say what started Mrs. Liu's vendetta, but it's been going on for as long as I can remember.

"Don't worry, Ma," Jun says soothingly. "She can't do anything to you. I don't even know why Mrs. Xu bothers with her. Mrs. Liu is a nobody, an upstart social climber. But no matter how much she flatters Mrs. Xu, she'll never become a member of our society!"

Wow. It's not like my sister to be so catty, but Mrs. Liu brings out the worst in all of us.

Ma sighs. "Actually, the Women's Fundraising Society is considering Liu Yuan for membership. She just got a job as a reporter. She might not have the wealth or party connections usually required for membership, but being a journalist for the *Beijing Mirror* has its own cachet."

My jaw drops. "The tabloid?"

"No one reads that garbage," Jun says, careful not to meet my eyes. She knows I have a subscription to the *Beijing Mirror*. Then again, I have a subscription to several of the independent newspapers that have sprung up lately, especially the ones that are sympathetic to the student demonstrators. But the *Beijing Mirror* isn't political. It's just mindless gossip about celebrities and society's elite, which is why people eat it up like candy.

I shut my jaw with a snap. "Um, yeah," I say. "Jun's totally right. No one reads the *Beijing Mirror*." I make a mental note to throw out the stack under my bed so Ma doesn't accidentally find it. At least I don't have to worry about the newspapers (like the leftist *World Economic Herald* out of Shanghai) that Ba wouldn't approve of. Ba has always been proud that I have my own mind, even if my politics are more liberal than his. Not that any of the liberal newspapers come right out and criticize the government. It's just that the independent papers don't toe the party line as much as the state-run *People's Daily* does. Obviously, the *Daily* is the only paper Ba trusts.

Ma gives us a small smile. "I'm not worried for myself," she says. "I just don't want her to go after my daughters." She means me, of course, because Jun wouldn't do anything that would make *her* fodder for gossip.

Ba wanders into sight at that moment. *Uh-oh.* Why isn't he working late as he has been all week? It's been a tough week to be a high-ranking Communist Party official, with the student protests happening in the past few days. Tuesday was the worst for Ba. He didn't even come home, just stayed at the Central Office all night. That was when Beijing University students spontaneously rallied on campus around midnight and marched the entire ten miles to Tiananmen Square.

I wish I could have been there.

But with the government finally honoring Hu Yaobang with a state memorial tomorrow, the protests will probably die down soon. Maybe that's why my father is home tonight. Disappointment shoots through me. On the one hand, I'm glad my father, who's been looking haggard and grim all week, is finally getting a break. On the other, I'm also 100 percent on the students' side. And now I've missed my chance to join them. My gut twists. Wanting to be a part of something my father is against feels weird.

"Shen," Ma says, "I was just telling Lei that she wears too much makeup." But her tone is lighter now, with its usual blend of resignation and amusement.

"Listen to your mother," Ba says absently. He's got bigger things on his mind than how much makeup I wear. Plus, crazy big hair and bold makeup aren't unusual for me, even if I'm just headed to a Friday-night study session. Jun, on the other hand . . .

Ba's gaze sharpens on her. Her makeup is minimal compared with mine, but her face is usually bare, and she typically wears a simple skirt and blouse to go out. "You look very nice, Jun." His voice is deceptively mild.

A frisson of anxiety starts up between my shoulder blades. I should have told my sister to put a coat over her fancy pink dress, and I would have, if I'd known Ba was going to be home.

"Thank you, Ba," Jun says. Fortunately, she doesn't seem to have picked up on the danger, or else she would have never sounded so calm. In fact, she's such a novice at lying that she'll probably crack and spill everything if she thinks our father suspects what we're up to.

"We have to go," I say as casually as I can. "Our friends are waiting for us."

"Who's going to be at the study group tonight?" Ba's attention is on me now, and it's a good thing too, because my sister's eyes are widening in panic. *She doesn't have a ready answer.*

"Ai, Chen, and Chunhua," I reply without missing a beat. You have to be on your toes if you're matching wits with my father. He's the smartest person I know.

"Ah." He relaxes a bit. "I know their parents." Damn right he does. I gave him the names of three girls who happen to be daughters of big-shot Communist officials. "And where," he asks, "are you meeting?"

It's tempting to tell him that we're meeting at one of the girls' houses, but what if he calls her parents to check up on us? Also, I need a plausible explanation for Jun's fancy dress, so I take a risk by giving him a half-truth. "We're getting dinner in Sanlitun first." The Sanlitun neighborhood is full of popular restaurants. It's also where Club Flash is located.

"Sanlitun," he says in distaste. "All those businesses and hotels catering to Westerners."

"Well, it makes sense with the foreign embassies there." Unable to resist needling him, I add, "And isn't opening up China to foreign investors part of Deng Xiaoping's economic policies that have helped us make so much money these past few years?"

A familiar argumentative gleam comes into his eyes. "Deng is being crafty in his economic policies. And the Westerners hate us for it! If they had their way, they'd pry China open and suck us dry. That's what they mean by 'free market.' Keep that in mind when you join the party."

My stomach twinges. I was ten years old when I asked him why women aren't leaders in the Chinese Communist Party. He told me that I could be one of the first, and ever since then, he's been not so subtly nudging me toward that goal. Ma, of course, thinks my dream of becoming an art historian is best suited for the task of safeguarding Wu Zetian's collection. Ba is fine with that, but he wants me to be a leader in the CCP too. He tells me that if I want a more equal world, I'll need to change the party from the inside.

Except a career in the CCP is the *last* thing I want. "The protesters are speaking out against Western exploitation too," I say defiantly, "and they aren't asking for a capitalist 'free market.' They just want an equal distribution of wealth." And this mansion of gold and imported high-tech gadgets is about as far from "equal distribution of wealth" as you can get. Hu Yaobang's progressive ideas have always been popular with young people, but in the wake of his death, his proposed policies have gained even more momentum—including freedom of the press and economic reform, which are two things Ba is passionately against and I'm just as passionately for.

"Lei," my mother says, "I told you not to bring up those protesters!"

"No, let her talk." Ba's always ready to go a couple rounds with me on politics, except his expression is more serious than usual. "I want to hear her defense of these dangerous young radicals."

Is it radical to want the CCP to live up to the ideals of communism? Look at where we live! How is this equality? But for once, I keep my thoughts to myself. I'm on a mission to infuse some adventure into my sister's life, and I don't have time to debate politics with Ba. Better wrap this up. "We need to go, but if you really don't want us to go to Sanlitun," I say, "I could suggest that we all meet somewhere else."

This makes Ba pause, just as I had hoped. The unfamiliar hardness eases from his face, and I can practically see the gears turning in his head. He thinks we're meeting the kids of his colleagues, and he doesn't want to risk being seen as behind the times—especially now. "That's not necessary," he says at last. "Have fun, but don't forget to study." Then he glances at Jun. "How's the tutoring going?"

Great. Ba almost never asks Jun about her studies, but of course he would take an interest at the *worst* possible time. I try sending a telepathic message to my twin: *Don't panic! He's just asking about tutoring. He doesn't know you're going to meet Yanlin tonight.*

But Jun actually seems to perk up under Ba's attention. "It's going well!"

"That's nice." He doesn't wait for a response before turning to me. "Lei, I don't have to tell you how important it is to do well on the Gaokao, do I? You have to get a top score to get into Beijing University."

"Don't worry." I wince to see the light in Jun's eyes dim. Would it kill Ba to have expectations of her too? "Studying with our friends will help *both* of us get high scores."

"Good." He pauses. "Why don't we add a little incentive?"

Not this again. I hate how he's always offering financial rewards for academic achievements.

"Ten thousand renminbi for a third-tier score, twenty thousand for the second tier." A slow smile spreads over his face as he watches me. "And fifty thousand for placing in the first tier."

Whoa. Despite myself, my jaw drops. This is *extra* generous, even for Ba. The average annual salary in Beijing is only six hundred. It's no wonder the protesters are angry about the income disparity between Communist Party officials and common citizens.

Ma glances at Jun and her lips press together. She's probably wishing that Ba wouldn't keep pitting us against each other in academic competition. Especially since I always win.

Jun is carefully not looking at anyone as she fiddles with the strap of her white leather purse.

"Lei," Ma says, "I've been meaning to ask if you're applying to the Central Academy of Fine Arts."

It's an obvious effort to change the subject, but I still blink in surprise. Ma has never suggested that I apply to CAFA before. Does this have anything to do with my new role as future guardian of Empress Wu's art?

Ba's smile fades. "CAFA doesn't offer anything but fine arts. At Beijing University, Lei can get a degree in whatever she wants and take some art classes."

Ma's eyes flare up. "And what if fine arts *is* the degree she wants?" My parents hardly ever disagree, but this is starting to look like one of those rare exceptions.

If I don't nip this in the bud, Jun and I will never get out of here. "I'd have to take a separate practical art exam in addition to the Gaokao to get into CAFA," I say quickly, "and I wouldn't make the cut."

I'm not just saying that to keep the peace between my parents. CAFA has about a four percent acceptance rate, and the practical exams require students to produce art in several mediums over just two days. Then the art is judged on a set of rigid and conventional criteria. Somehow, I don't think the admissions committee would be impressed with my one trick of painting the same pair of Tang dynasty ladies.

The fire goes out of Ma's eyes. She knows I'm right. But why did she even bring up CAFA? I wonder if she secretly wanted to be an artist herself. Of course, she wouldn't have been able to—not growing up in the time of the Cultural Revolution, when art was so dangerous. But if anything, art is too safe these days in China. Students at Chinese art colleges are discouraged from any kind of risk or innovation, which is *definitely* not me. I'd rather study dangerous outlawed art than create tame art. "Sorry, Ma. I don't think I'll be applying to CAFA."

Ba looks triumphant, and normally, I'd at least pretend to consider CAFA, just to mess with him. But not tonight. "We should get going," I say again.

"Of course." He waves us on. "Don't keep your friends waiting."

I try to recapture my excitement about Club Flash, but my mood has soured. I should be trying to join the protest movement, not going to an upscale club. Still, it feels weird for a rich girl like me to demonstrate for class equality. And then there's my father.

Letting me go to Sanlitun is one thing. Letting me go to a protest is a totally different story.

CHAPTER FOUR

Even though it's not even eight, Club Flash is packed by the time we arrive. The club is staying open only until midnight. The bars serving foreign expats at international hotels don't close until two in the morning, but the proprietor of the first Chinese-owned Western-style bar/club is still feeling his way. Maybe he's worried that Beijing's young people won't want to stay out all night drinking and dancing. But I'm pretty sure that we'd have no trouble partying for as long as the club stays open.

Disco balls hang overhead, and colored lights bounce off shiny black surfaces. Popular American music like Pet Shop Boys, Depeche Mode, and Madonna blast through big speakers, and the vibrations shake the floor. Jun looks around nervously, but I'm jittery with eagerness to dive into this new world.

Then the unmistakable sound of English being spoken penetrates my bubble of happiness. "Jesus. Is this what passes for a nightclub in China?" A white guy in his twenties, wearing a tight black T-shirt and even tighter black jeans, is looking around with a sneer.

My stomach twists as I see the club through this foreigner's eyes: the tables and chairs pushed to the edges to make room for a dance floor, the few people gamely trying out their moves. Worse, I see it through my father's eyes, and I know what he would say: *Why do you young people try so hard to imitate Westerners? Don't you know what they think of us?* Anger surges through me. I'm not going to let this guy tarnish my excitement. Club Flash might not be up to his standards, but it's *our* nightclub, the first one in Beijing, and we have the right to be proud of it.

His companion, an Asian girl in a short black sheath dress, says, "It's not that bad, Chris."

He laughs and plants a kiss on the Asian girl. "Really, Anna? We wouldn't be caught dead in a place like this in New York or any big city in America. The only good thing about the nightlife in China is that there's no drinking age. But we could get a drink at the bar in Dad's hotel instead of this dive."

Americans. It figures. In some ways, I get where Ba is coming from. The problem with foreign capitalists is that they come here on business trips with their snooty kids who look down their noses at everything. And of course it makes sense that Chris is into Asian girls. *All kinds of white guys catch "yellow fever,"* I think bitterly.

He's still talking. "Look at what these people are wearing! It's like they're at a costume party. I mean, who is that girl trying to be? Asian Madonna?"

With a start I realize he's talking about *me*. To Jun, I say in Mandarin, "He doesn't think we can understand English." Doesn't he know there's a foreign language section on the Gaokao? Most of us pick English from the foreign language options, so nearly everyone at this club can understand and speak English.

Anna casts an anxious look at me. "Shh, Chris. People can hear you."

Ah. Chinese American. And she knows enough Mandarin to understand what I said.

"Be nice, Lei," Jun warns. She senses that I'm ready to tell off this white guy. But I remind myself that I'm here to play matchmaker for my sister, not start a fight. So I'm going to overlook his rudeness.

Then Chris speaks again. "So what? They can't understand me."

Slowly, I count backward from ten as the heat rises in my chest.

"See? Asian Madonna's not paying any attention to us." His gaze swivels to Jun. "Hey, I think those two are twins. Get a load of the one in the pink dress. Who wears an outfit like that to a *nightclub*? Does she think she's at a high school prom?"

Jun flushes bright red at his words.

That does it. No one insults my sister. An angry haze clouding my brain, I march right up to him. Planting my feet in their tall, lace-up black boots (OK, I kind of see his point about overkill in my outfit, but that doesn't matter right now), I say in English, "Hey, if you think this club isn't good enough for you, then why don't you leave?"

His mouth gapes open, and Anna looks mortified. "I'm sorry you feel that way," he says stiffly, "but you shouldn't eavesdrop on conversations that are none of your business."

Oh, right. Like he wasn't talking so loudly that the whole club could hear him. In fact, people are starting to stare at us and edge closer. There are a lot of familiar faces in the crowd, and it would be nice if someone else would jump in, but the only sound is the poppy beat of a Tears for Fears song. Fine. I'm on my own. "It's my business when you make fun of my sister." I jab a finger at Chris's chest. "And who are you to judge us in your wannabe Goth but secretly prep boy costume?"

He takes a step closer to me, his face all red and sweaty. His girlfriend is plucking at his arm now, but he shakes her off. "Now, see here—"

"Leave my sister alone!" Jun's black eyes are flashing, and her face blazes with protective fury. My big sister is downright *awesome* when she goes ballistic.

But Chris doesn't budge, and he's so up in my face that I can smell his icky testosterone. "You two can take your little twin whore and virgin act and piss off!"

Oh no, he didn't! Unfortunately, I'm so worked up that I can't remember any English curse words at the moment. Maybe if I stomp on his foot with my big boots (which, I decide, are not overkill after all), he'll get the message—no translation needed.

I'm saved from any rash actions when a young Chinese man in jeans and a button-down shirt strides over to us and roughly pulls

Chris away from me. "That's enough." He speaks calmly but with such authority that Chris doesn't immediately react. "You're not welcome here. So leave." Giving him a little push toward the exit, the stranger releases his grip.

Chris rubs his shoulder and glares at the newcomer. "Who the hell are you?"

I'm wondering the same thing. This guy isn't flashy, but he's cute enough that I'd remember if I'd met him before. Maybe the club owner's son?

But he merely replies, "I'm their friend."

That's when I notice my sister gazing at him with starry eyes. This must be Yanlin. *Nice going, Jun!* But much as I appreciate the help, I can handle this on my own. "Listen—it's Chris, right?"

He nods sullenly.

"Well, Chris, let me give you a little hint. Opening night at Club Flash might not seem like a big deal to you, but it's the social event of the year in Beijing. All the tabloids will be covering it." That could be true, actually. But I take a sharp detour from the truth by pointing to my friend Chunhua, who's a high school senior like me and definitely does *not* work for a tabloid. Lowering my voice, I say, "She's paparazzi."

His eyes grow alarmed as his gaze flickers toward her. Chunhua raises a quizzical eyebrow at me, but I just smile and wave. He turns back to me, face tense. "She doesn't look like she works for a newspaper."

"Oh, she doesn't. Not directly anyway. The tabloids love to pay teenagers for scandalous pictures." I lean in, and he pulls away just enough to let me know I'm getting under his skin. "So what will your father think of you appearing in the papers? That won't be good for Daddy's business interests in China. Especially if the picture is of an angry girl throwing beer in your face."

On cue, Yanlin snags a bottle of beer from an onlooker and hands it to me. It's official—I approve of this boy. The round contour of cold glass feels good in my hand, and it feels even better when Chris visibly pales. My voice lowers to a purr. "I can just see the headline. 'Chou lou de mei guo ren.' "

He eyes the beer bottle nervously. "What does that mean?"

"Ugly American." I pass the beer back to Yanlin without taking my eyes off Chris. "That's you, asshole. Now leave."

"Come on!" Anna urges, pulling on her boyfriend's arm. Her eyes meet mine then, and she blushes. In Mandarin, she apologizes. "Dui bu qi."

I reply in the same language. "You don't actually like this creep, do you?"

The red in her face deepens, and she doesn't answer.

"Fine!" Chris snarls. "They can have their cheap, knockoff club." Still muttering under his breath, he lets her lead him out.

Should I go after Anna? Technically, she's American, but she's also Chinese. I should pull her aside and tell her that she could do better than Chris. Tell her that she could stay—that she belongs with us.

But then people start coming over, and the moment is lost. Now that the Americans are gone, casual friends and acquaintances are loud in their indignation.

"Who does he think he is, coming into our club and insulting us?"

"Waiguoren!" Everyone knows the word "foreigner" said in *that* tone means Americans.

"That American is full of shit." My friend Chunhua wraps a glow-in-the-dark bracelet around my wrist. That still leaves her with half a dozen bracelets for herself and big orange plastic earrings that clash jarringly with the teal minidress she's wearing. "Lei, you look awesome."

"You too," I say. I mean it. We *all* look great.

A new song blares over the speakers, and this time it's a Chinese rock ballad. "Nothing to My Name," by Cui Jian, a hot young performer who's also arguably China's first modern rock star. It's about a boy addressing a rich girl who dismisses him for being poor. Cui released the song a few years ago, and I've been dying to go to a concert of his but just haven't managed to sneak away to attend one. *Someday.* But I'm glad it's being played at Club Flash with all the American pop songs. I love "Nothing to My Name" for its catchy beat, as powerful as any American import, but also for its roots in traditional Chinese ballads. That's who we are. Young people aching with desire to make something new without losing our past.

I peer around again at the small, dark interior of the club. And this time, I'm not seeing it through anyone else's eyes. So what if we're trying to create an American club scene that doesn't really exist? Yes, Club Flash and our fashion sense are based on pirated VHS tapes of Hollywood movies. But Hollywood has been creating a mythical China for years. At least *we* know our America is a fantasy. Americans mistake their fantasy for reality.

"Foreigners!" Jun mutters. She doesn't seem to notice the people surrounding us. She's glaring at the doors where the American couple has just exited.

Yanlin touches Jun's arm. "Are you OK?"

Her expression smooths over. "Thank you so much for stepping in, Yanlin."

"No problem." He smiles back at her. *Good. His eyes are all soft and gooey too.* "You look beautiful."

My sister glows under his obvious admiration, and an unfamiliar feeling creeps up on me. If I didn't know any better, I'd think that it was envy. Not because of Yanlin, specifically, but because of the infatuation that has clearly consumed them both. I give myself a stern shake. Jun's the romantic, not me. I've got more important things to do than lose my head over a boy.

I'm about to sneak away and leave them to it, but Jun pulls me to her side. "This is my sister, Lei."

"A pleasure to meet you," he says with a smile.

"Lei is the one who got us all on the guest list," Jun adds.

His smile deepens. "Then I'm *really* glad to meet you. Thank you."

"You're welcome." I'm definitely glad I dragged Jun here tonight. My first impression of him is good, but it's still my job as the pesky younger sister to grill him. "So, Jun tells me you're studying business at Beijing University."

"That's right."

Jun tries to head me off at the pass. "Yanlin has been—"

"Are you a protester?" I ask.

"No." His pleasant demeanor doesn't slip, but is that a tightness in his voice? "I'm sympathetic to their cause, but I have no wish to be involved." *Ooh, I sense a story there.* More lightly, he adds, "Maybe I just don't have what it takes to be an activist. It seems that when they're not protesting in the streets, they're rallying on campus at all hours of the night. I don't know when they have the time or energy to study and take classes."

"So the protests aren't over?" Excitement makes my voice rise. "The students are going to keep demonstrating?" Maybe I haven't missed my chance after all.

"Actually, according to a flyer I saw, there's a rally on campus tonight."

"Really?" I say as casually as I can, hoping Jun doesn't notice the catch in my voice. Normally, she can always tell when I'm up to something. But luckily, she seems to be too focused on Yanlin to pay her usual attention to me. "Where do they hold these rallies?" I try to imagine where a crowd of dissident students might gather. "By the dorms? Or in one of the gardens?"

"I've seen them meet behind the instructional buildings near the West Gate, so I suppose they'll be there tonight."

"Will they keep meeting after tonight?"

"I don't know." He gives me a measured look. "As I said, I'm not a part of their movement."

I still think that there's something he's not saying, but I can't just come out and ask him what he's hiding.

In this awkward pause, a voice calls out, "Jun! Lei!" A young, attractive guy in a shiny blue suit comes rushing over. Chua Qiang. The American would've had a field day with *that* suit. But Qiang makes it work. He's so full of brash charm that he can pull off nearly anything. Anything but getting his heart's desire, that is.

"I just heard about what happened with that rude foreigner!" Qiang's gaze locks on to Jun. "I can't believe you actually came out to a nightclub!" Poor Qiang has been in love with my sister ever since I can remember. And shiny suit aside, he's exactly the kind of boy my parents would want for her. Like ours, his family is well connected to the Communist Party and he has a solid future ahead of him, and if he's not quite as boring as my parents might hope for, he's got the money to make up for it. "I wish I'd been here. I would've thrown him out!"

"I wanted to do exactly that," Jun says fiercely. "One day, I'm going to have enough money to buy a bunch of clubs that foreigners like him will be dying to get into. And he'll be banned from them all."

I look at her in surprise. What happened to my easygoing sister? Yanlin looks taken aback as well. Qiang just beams at her.

Then she smiles as if she hadn't just sworn to get petty revenge on someone she'll never see again. "Fortunately, Yanlin got rid of him."

Hey, I was the one who kicked his ass to the curb! But Qiang's crestfallen face floods me with pity and makes me forget my indignation. "Come on, handsome, let me buy you a drink," I say, leading him away from the lovebirds.

Qiang comes along, but he keeps peeking back at Jun. "Who's the guy?"

"Uh, Jun's tutor." We come up to the bar, and I order him a beer and myself a cocktail. How am I going to explain Yanlin?

But Qiang doesn't need to be told. "So that's Jun's new guy." He takes a large swallow of beer, face grim. "He's not right for her."

I glance over to where they're standing. People are eddying around them to get to the dance floor, which is finally starting to fill up. They're oblivious to it all, and Jun laughs at something Yanlin says. "She seems happy," I say gently.

Qiang's eyes follow mine, and he all but slams his bottle on the bar. "All that guy sees is how pretty and sweet Jun is, but he doesn't really know her."

"Well, she *is* sweet. And pretty too, if that doesn't sound vain coming from me."

"Yeah, but Jun's more than that." He shakes his head. "You don't see it either. How ambitious and strong she really is."

My hackles go up at the implication that I don't know my twin sister. Then I remember her saying that she wants to be rich enough to stick it to arrogant foreigners like Chris. Maybe I don't know Jun as well as I think I do.

Glumly, he says, "I don't have a chance, do I?"

You never had a chance, I think sympathetically. Jun is fond of Qiang but has never taken him seriously as a romantic prospect. "Look, maybe it's time you moved on. Lots of girls would love to date you." It's true. Big, attractive, and fun—Qiang's definitely a catch.

"Including you, Lei?" He tries to work up a flirtatious smile, but it falls flat.

I bump his hip with mine. "Sorry, Qiang. You know what I'm like."

That gets his attention. "Yeah, I do. You've left a trail of broken hearts from one end of Beijing to the other. A guy goes on a few dates with you, gets his hopes up, and then you're gone."

I laugh. "What can I say? I'm not the relationship type."

"Nah, I don't believe that. You're like me. I love to flirt and have a good time too."

"And your point is what, exactly?" I take a sip of my drink, letting the sweet tartness wash away the bitter tang in my mouth. For some reason, I don't like the direction of this conversation.

"All I'm saying is that when you fall . . ."

"Go ahead." My voice is flinty. "Finish that thought."

He smiles. "You'll fall hard. Wait and see."

Qiang leaves Club Flash after he finishes his beer, and I'm left in a strange, unsettled mood. I dance a couple of songs with some girls I know, and I'm laughing as loudly and shaking my butt as much as anyone else. On the outside, I'm having a great time. But I'm thinking of what Qiang said.

When you fall . . . you'll fall hard.

Qiang's full of shit. I'm not like him. I don't *want* to be like him. Look at where love has gotten him—heartbroken over my sister, who's chosen someone else. And he's not the only one. Look at all the stupid mistakes people make just to be in a relationship. Anna with that smug white guy. My friends who focus more on boyfriends than anything else. No thanks. I'll save my passion for art. I'm not saying I'm planning a life of celibacy or anything. I just don't ever want to be a fool for love.

But everywhere I turn, there are couples making out in dark corners or grinding on the dance floor. I told Jun that it would be a night of fun and romance, and it looks like I was right. I'm down for fun, but romance? Not so much. I scan the room for my sister, and she and Yanlin aren't making out, but they're sitting at one of the few tables in the club, and the way their heads are pressed together seems way more intimate than if they were actively groping each other or kissing.

Uncomfortable, I turn away. I'm happy for Jun, but I don't need to see this. I should get back on the dance floor or get another drink and flirt with one of the boys trying to catch my eye. But my skin is prickling with heat, and I'm getting breathless from the stuffy air inside. It's not a problem with the club. No, the problem is me. I'm just not in the mood to party. I'm sure I'll be back to Club Flash many more times and that it will be great.

But tonight something is calling me. Something more than the strobe lights and laughter of Club Flash. I've got to get out of here.

On the way out, I stop by the table where Jun and Yanlin are in deep conversation. "I have a headache," I lie, although I probably will get one if I stay any longer. "I'm heading home."

Reluctantly, Jun tears her gaze from Yanlin. "Oh, I'm sorry you don't feel well! Should I come with you?"

Yanlin makes a motion to stand. "I can escort you both home."

"No. Absolutely not!" I wave him back into his seat. "You two have fun. I'll be fine!"

"Well, if you're sure." Jun's already turning back to Yanlin.

"I'm sure," I insist, scooting away fast before Jun's conscience tells her she should come with me.

My friend Chunhua intercepts me before I get too far. "Leaving already?" she asks, adjusting a large color-block purse across her body.

"Yeah, I'm not feeling well," I say. "Oh, by the way, my parents think that Jun and I are studying for the Gaokao with you and some others tonight, so forget you saw us here at Club Flash, OK?"

"No problem." She winks. "I never saw you." One of my favorite things about Chunhua is how discreet she is. Unlike the rest of what I call the CCP Brat Pack (kids of Chinese Communist Party officials), she can keep a secret. But even then, I've never been tempted to tell her my big secret, about Wu Zetian's hidden art and my imperial bloodline. As for the other CCP Brat Pack kids, I try not to tell them anything at all. Actually, Chunhua is the only one in our social group whom I think of as a friend.

The bracelet she gave me has lost all its brightness, so I toss it into a nearby trash can. "Listen, do you have any more of those glow bracelets that you haven't used yet?"

She laughs. "Sure." She unzips her purse and hands me a few unused bracelets.

I slip them on and head toward the exit. "Thanks, Chunhua!"

Using the club's hospitality phone, I call a taxi. I have to yell over the music to make myself heard, and I hope the dispatcher was able to get the address. On my way out, I snag my trench from the coat check, but I don't really need it—not on this warm April evening.

My spirits lift once I'm outside. The bright lights of the Sanlitun neighborhood and the mild spring breeze make me throw back my head and take in this ineffable feeling in the air. It's as if the city is holding its breath, on the cusp of some great change. My body tingles. I'm not in the mood for a club, but I do want *something*. To be a part of something bigger than myself.

My taxi pulls up to the curb.

"Where to?" the driver asks as I hop into the back.

I think of what Yanlin said. *Actually, according to a flyer I saw, there's a rally on campus tonight.* "Beijing University."

CHAPTER FIVE

The campus is quiet. And dark. After all, it's ten at night. Anticipation makes my heart pound as I crack the glow bracelets Chunhua gave me. They cast an eerie, pale light, but it's better than nothing. *Behind the instructional buildings near the West Gate.* I know exactly where that is, and my favorite spot is on the way. In fact, it's the reason that Beijing University is my top pick of colleges.

Using the dim light of my glow bracelets, I walk down the stone path between the lush green spaces and ornate red-pillared buildings side by side with monochrome modern buildings. The campus, located on the former site of the imperial gardens of the Qing dynasty, is gorgeous. But that's not why I want to go here.

It doesn't take me long to reach the construction site of the future Sackler Museum of Art and Archaeology. Arthur M. Sackler was a rich American who had acquired the largest collection of ancient Chinese art in the world, which he then donated to the Smithsonian. You'd think I'd feel nothing but bitter resentment toward a man who took our art to be displayed in a foreign museum. But I'd rather have all that art in an American museum than destroyed in the Chinese Cultural Revolution. And then there's the offer Sackler made five years ago: to partner with Beijing University to build the first Western-style museum in the country, a teaching museum located right on the grounds of the university. Best of all, the museum means keeping our culture and history *in* China. This is the kind of foreign investment that even my father can't object to.

The museum is slated to open in a few years, and I want to be a student here when it does. A pang hits my heart. It would be hard to study art history here . . . and stay quiet about the art we guard. My family knows my dream is to study art history at Beijing University. But they don't know about my deepest, wildest desire: to bring Wu Zetian's art collection into the open. An electric vision of the future shoots through my body. One day, the art will be displayed in a place like the future Sackler Museum instead of our basement. Then the world will finally know Empress Wu for who she really was. Not a power-mad woman clawing to the throne with one scandalous deed after another, but a brilliant visionary who uplifted women artists and their work.

I give myself a mental shake. I didn't come here to daydream about the future of Empress Wu's art. I came to find a rally.

Holding my arm out in front of me to light the path, I follow it deeper and deeper into the heart of campus until bigger clusters of buildings come into view. Indistinct voices float toward me as I get closer to the instructional buildings, and my heart starts beating faster. Could this be it? Behind the dim outlines of blocky gray buildings, there's a soft glow cutting through the darkness. My breath comes short and sharp as I pick up my pace.

And when I round a bend to find an open square, I see them.

Hundreds of students are clustered together in an area that's lit with flickering battery-powered lanterns. No one seems to have seen me arrive. They're all too engrossed in listening to a young man with a megaphone yelling about how the rich get richer while the poor get poorer.

A rush of excitement makes me dizzy. I have to get closer. This could be my chance to be a part of this movement. *Like they're going to let a high school student join them!* Impatiently, I shrug away this thought. Cold practicality has no place on a night like this, when the very air is heavy with the promise of revolution. Anything could happen.

But nothing is going to happen if I hide in the shadows. Gathering up my courage, I inch closer. I'm being as stealthy as I can in my mega boots, but it's not quite enough. A girl with a stocky figure and short hair turns around. Frowning, she nudges the boy next to her, and he turns. He frowns too. Then they leave the rest of the crowd and walk toward me.

Uh-oh. I've seen friendlier faces on Ba's dour Communist Party comrades. Hell, I've seen friendlier faces on Ma's cutthroat socialite acquaintances.

Still, I muster up a bright smile and say, "Hello."

The girl is looking me up and down, and her expression grows even warier.

My spine tenses. *Oh shit.* It's such a warm night that I never bothered to belt my coat over my black tulle miniskirt and tight, sparkly top. And then there's the row of neon glow bracelets stacked on my arm. I might as well be wearing a sign that says "Party Girl."

"Who are you?" the girl asks frostily.

"A better question, Yawen," the boy says, "is what she's doing here." He rakes me over with a scornful look.

"My name is Lei." Anger whips through my voice. "And I'm not here to spy, if that's what you're implying!"

The boy laughs. "Of course not. The government wouldn't send a girl to spy." Yawen grimaces, but the boy continues: "Go home. This is none of your business."

"Why not?" I ask sweetly. "Don't you allow girls in this movement?" The men at this rally outnumber the women by *a lot.*

"Not spoiled little rich girls." His voice rises, catching the attention of a few other protesters at the edge of the crowd.

Unbelievable. "That doesn't answer my question. Why aren't there many women here?"

"There are fewer women at the university," he mumbles with a defensive hunch to his shoulders.

"That's exactly the problem!" I shoot back. "Only twenty percent of the student population at Beijing University are women."

One of the other protesters, who has detached himself from the crowd, arrives in time to hear this. There's nothing out of the ordinary in his lanky frame, his thin, serious face, or the shaggy black hair falling to the nape of his neck. So why do I suddenly feel all breathless?

With an effort, I tear my gaze from the newcomer and return my attention to the first boy. "So, I'm going to ask again. Aren't women welcome at this protest?"

Yawen puts her hands on her hips. "Answer her question, Rong. I've been thinking we need more women, actually, both at the university and in this movement."

"There are lots of women involved," he says defensively.

"You might be missing the point, Rong," the newcomer says quietly. "Women are involved, but mostly in support roles so far. We need female *leaders*. Yawen is right. And so is . . ."

He looks at me inquiringly, but my tongue has turned to mush. It takes me a moment to realize that the silence has stretched on for far too long and that he's still looking at me expectantly. What was the question? Oh, that's right. My name. I swallow to clear my throat. "Lei."

"Lei," he echoes slowly, like he's savoring the single syllable. "We need voices like yours." His dark, brilliant eyes are intent on mine. Does he feel the current running between us too? "I'm glad you're here. I'm Delun."

Delun. Beautiful name. Thankfully, I don't say that out loud. In fact, speech doesn't really seem to be an option right now. My body hums with an awareness of his long, tapered fingers and those full, sensuous lips so at odds with the rest of his scholarly appearance. Mentally, I shake off these thoughts as if they were a swarm of flesh-eating ants. I don't need this kind of distraction in my life.

Then Delun smiles, and his whole face is transformed as if he were lit from within by a brilliant blaze. But the smile fades as he glances at my outfit, and an unreadable emotion flickers in his eyes. "Are you a student at Beijing University?"

Trying to be subtle, I pull my trench coat closed. What made me think it was a good idea to skulk around campus in a fancy nightclub outfit? Especially at this *very* tense time, politically speaking. *Don't freak out, Lei.* I can show him that I'm not an empty-headed girl with frivolous interests.

But then my mother's words echo in my head. *No one who sees you would guess you have such a sharp brain under all that sprayed hair.* Cold seeps into my body. Am I really going to hide who I am just to impress a guy?

I let my coat fall open and jut out my chin. I've never sought anyone's approval, and I'm not about to start now. So what if I like cool clothes and dancing? That doesn't mean I can't commit to more serious causes. "I'm a high school student. But I want to go here in the fall. And I want to join the student protest now."

Delun's eyes are hooded. "I see."

Rong, whose presence I'd almost forgotten, snorts in derision. "Fat chance! You need pretty damn high scores on the Gaokao to get in."

"Especially for a woman, right?" I ask without missing a beat. "Because the quota system means I'll have to beat out all the men who score lower than I will." Deliberately, I look him up and down. "Luckily, I don't think that will be too hard."

As Rong glares at me wordlessly, Yawen cracks up. "You know what? I like you!" This girl is blunt, has no sense of fashion, and has the loudest laugh I've ever heard. *Yeah, I like her too.*

"As far as I'm concerned, you can join us!" She gives Rong's arm a fond squeeze. "Anyone who can take my boyfriend down a notch gets my respect."

"It's not up to us to decide who joins," Rong says huffily, and turns to Delun. "What do you think? You're one of the leaders."

My skin burns with indignation. Two boys are deciding my fate as if I'm not here. Not exactly my favorite thing. But as much as I hate to admit it, I also want to hear what Delun has to say.

Delun shakes his head. "It's not up to me either, Rong." He stares at me so long that it borders on rudeness. At last, he blinks as if he's coming out of a trance. "I don't doubt that you can get into school here, Lei, but why is it that you want to join our movement?" His voice remains courteous, but I'm not fooled. He thinks I have no idea what the protest is about and that I'm just a rich girl looking for a temporary thrill.

Irritation steals over me. He wants me to prove myself. Fine. "I don't think it's right that our government overthrew a feudal system during the Communist Revolution only to create a new upper class now." *Even if my family is among that upper class.* "We shouldn't have invaded and colonized Tibet either. And I don't like the government's repression of free speech or the unequal opportunities for women."

"Way to go, Lei!" Yawen pumps a fist in the air, and even Rong looks reluctantly impressed.

"Good answer," Delun says, face impassive.

There's no judgment in his voice, but my face grows hot. I believe in what I said. But I had responded as if I were answering one of the Gaokao practice questions. Textbook perfect. And that's not good enough for this boy with his sharp, brilliant eyes and quiet intensity. He wants more. He wants to know if the fire inside me is as fierce as his own. *Yes. Oh yes.* I want more too. I want to take down the system that turned family and friends against each other and sent the Red Guard into the night to destroy art and artists during the Cultural Revolution. The system that keeps us silent with fear. My father may think the only way to protect us and our secret heritage from the aftershocks of the Cultural Revolution is to participate in the same dangerous web of corrupt power that threatens us, but he's wrong, and I want to show him that. Heat races through my veins. I want to burn it all down.

And . . . I want to see if this mild-mannered boy can match me. I want to spark against the steel under that diffident surface—because I'm steel too.

Sudden shivers seize my belly. What am I thinking? Rong said that Delun is one of the leaders. That means he's as much a revolutionary as the students who tore down the old-world order during the Cultural Revolution. He would never accept me into the movement as I am. And I'm not just talking about my love of fashion and fun. I am the keeper of Empress Wu's art and her descendant. The imperial heritage in my basement and in my blood would have been more than enough for the Red Guard to drag me out into the streets and make me kneel on broken glass during the Cultural Revolution. And this boy might be just as dangerous as the Red Guard.

A wave of panic closes over my head, pulling me under, so there's only one thing to do: come out swinging. "Do you ask everyone why they want to protest?" I demand. "Does the people's movement have gatekeepers now?"

Unexpectedly, Delun smiles at that, and my traitorous body melts when a dimple winks out from his left cheek. "As I said, it is not up to me or anyone else to decide who joins." His body tilts toward me as if he can't help himself. "So why don't we just call it curiosity on my part?"

"Or we could call it none of your business."

"Fair enough," he says evenly.

"You say you want women in the movement, even as leaders," I say, "but maybe you'd prefer women who wear a Mao suit, not a cocktail dress. And if the wrong kind of woman rises to power—like Jiang Qing, Madame Mao—she's demonized."

Rong makes a strangled sound and Yawen gasps.

Oops. Defending a woman who used the Red Guard to torture and murder her political enemies during the Cultural Revolution isn't exactly the way to make friends. "All I'm saying is that Madame Mao wasn't the *only* one who did terrible things. And look who got the brunt of the blame for the Cultural Revolution." Not Mao, that's for sure. No, it was his actress wife, who loved Hollywood films and fashionable clothes, who went to trial. I'm veering dangerously close to a criticism of Chairman Mao, and I expect Delun, revolutionary that he is, to blast me for my blasphemy.

Instead, Delun's face turns thoughtful.

It's Rong who speaks. "Jiang Qing and the other Gang of Four were tried for their crimes. She's in Qincheng Prison where she belongs, and she's lucky the party commuted her death sentence so she can spend the rest of her life in more luxury than she deserves!" Qincheng is a maximum-security prison labor camp. During the Cultural Revolution, many political dissidents were sent there, but today, it's where corrupt party officials are imprisoned. Reportedly, the higher your rank, the better your accommodations and privileges are. For example, instead of working on the Qincheng farm like the other prisoners, Jiang is allowed to make dolls in her cell.

"I'm not defending Jiang Qing," I say, "but she was the only one nicknamed the White-Boned Demon in the Gang of Four and the only woman. That's not a coincidence."

I'm still looking at Delun and barely paying attention to what I'm saying in response to Rong.

"And then there's Wu Zetian." My breath catches. *Oh hell.* I'm usually careful not to mention my ancestress.

"Empress Wu, the only female sovereign ruler of China?" Yawen asks curiously. "What about her?"

"Another woman who rose to power and was demonized for it," I say feebly.

"Another woman who murdered her enemies, you mean," Rong snorts. "Except Wu is the worst. Even Jiang Qing didn't murder her infant daughter like Wu did."

That's a lie Confucian historians tell! Heat rises in my throat. Like Jiang, Wu might have done awful things, but every history of her has been written by men. And the history in my basement tells its own story—beauty, art, and a passion to preserve what other women created. But it's not like I can tell them that.

"Male historians see powerful women as dangerous," I mutter finally. "And men are afraid of dangerous women."

"That's what I've been telling Rong!" Yawen's mouth quirks up. "He needs to get it into his head that the Communist Revolution overthrew that tired Confucian patriarchy and replaced it with socialist equality for women!"

"I guess I have a thick head," Rong says unrepentantly, but his look is tender when he looks at Yawen. "Don't give up on me, OK?"

"Never," she declares, snaking her arm around his waist.

"Yawen," I say, "I think we're going to be friends."

She grins. "You bet!"

I turn to Rong. "Truce?"

He shrugs. "Sure, since you're friends with my girlfriend now."

That just leaves Delun, staring at me with his intense eyes, the dark wings of his hair framing sharp cheekbones. It's easy to know what to say to Yawen and Rong, but I don't know what to say to this boy. It's an unusual feeling for me to be at a loss for words, and I don't like it.

"You should come with us tomorrow," Delun says abruptly.

"Tomorrow?"

The crowd roars with sudden approval at something the speaker is saying.

"Come on!" Yawen says, tugging at Rong. "They're announcing the plans!"

The two of them rejoin the crowd, but Delun stays with me. "Tomorrow, we're marching to the Great Hall of the People at Tiananmen Square, where the state is holding Hu's memorial service." His eyes search mine. "It will be a demonstration of our resolve." Is it my imagination, or is there a double meaning in that statement? Is he testing *my* resolve?

It doesn't matter. Earlier this night, I was disappointed that the protests would be over before I ever had the chance to join. Except now I have that chance. This is why I felt so restless at Club Flash tonight. I'd told Jun that the opening of a Western-style nightclub would be a historical event. But for me it was the wrong event. *This* is the history-making moment I've been waiting for. "I'll be there."

"Good." He hesitates and then adds, "You were wrong, you know."

"How so?" My breath comes short and fast. I knew this boy was too good to be true. But I'm hoping that he's not just another condescending boy who will judge or try to change me.

He says something, but the crowd is clapping and cheering now, so I can't hear him. "What?"

Delun takes a step forward and puts his head close to mine so I can hear him better. His warm breath on my ear sends shivery feelings through me. "I'm not afraid of dangerous women."

CHAPTER SIX

I wake up the next morning with a giddy feeling in my heart. I'm not sure how I'm going to sneak out of the house and get to the demonstration at Tiananmen Square today, but I'll figure something out. I have to.

Jumping out of bed, I get dressed and then race to Jun's room and pound on her bedroom door. Without waiting for a reply, I open the door and scoot into her pink-canopied bed with her. While my room is a riot of bright colors overflowing with paintings and books, hers is decorated in pale pink and white, with all her books neatly shelved and everything in its proper place.

She sits up in bed and rubs her eyes. "What time is it?"

"Early." I'm bursting with eagerness to tell her all about last night, but I know she has news herself, so I ask, "How did it go with Yanlin last night?"

A dreamy expression replaces her sleepy one. "Oh, Lei, it was so wonderful! Can you believe he likes me too?"

I snort and pelt her with a pink satin pillow. "I told you that he'd be crazy not to like you!"

Jun puts her hands up to defend herself against the pillow, but she's still smiling. "What do you think of him?"

"That he'd be a good father for my niece," I joke, fingering my jade pendant with the character for "mei" engraved on it.

But Jun answers seriously. "I think he would be. Now what about *my* niece?" She reaches over to her nightstand for a black velvet jewelry box and takes out her own necklace with the character for "jie" carved into jade. She fastens the necklace around her neck. "Don't forget our promise."

"Oh, Jun! We made that promise when we were *ten*!" We got the pendants for our tenth birthday, and we promised each other that Jun's pendant would go to whichever of our daughters was older, and mine would go to the youngest.

"It's important to think about the future," she says calmly.

"A future that might not happen!" I throw up my hands. "Who knows? We might not have children, or we might both have sons." Ma gave us those pendants the year after the one-child policy went into effect. Maybe she meant her gift to be a good luck charm, because with the one-child policy, Jun and I have only one chance each to have a daughter, and Wu Zetian's legacy is meant to be passed on daughter to daughter.

"One of us had better have a daughter," she says grimly.

I might be the most passionate about Wu Zetian's art, but sometimes I forget that my twin also wants to preserve our legacy. "Jun," I say hesitantly, "if you have a daughter and I don't, or if your daughter is the eldest, she can inherit Wu Zetian's art." This is the closest I've come to mentioning Ma's decision the day before yesterday to make me the heiress of Empress Wu's art.

Jun looks away. "Daughter to daughter, remember?"

My mouth sets. "That's a dumb rule. In fact . . ." My voice trails away as a brainstorm hits me. "There's no reason we can't share our inheritance! And our daughters can too!"

Jun looks doubtful, but I put my hand over my heart, palm covering the cool jade. "If we both have daughters, they will inherit our pendants and share in the guardianship of Wu Zetian's art. I promise."

Jun's mouth curves up in a smile. "And you said our promise at age ten was silly."

"Promise!" I demand. "Promise that our daughters will grow up like sisters. Think about it, Jun! This way, there won't be any jealousy between them because they'll share the legacy that we give them."

"I promise." Her eyes are shining.

Satisfied, I squeeze her in a big hug.

Laughingly, she says, "Lei, cut it out!"

Releasing her, I reposition myself at the edge of her bed. "Now that our inheritance is settled, let me tell you about my night!"

Her eyebrows rise. "Weren't you in bed with a headache? It was late when I got home, and everyone was already asleep."

"Yeah, we should get our stories straight before we talk to our parents." Uneasiness seeps into me. "Make sure to say that we both came home from the study session after they were already in bed, so they won't know that we didn't come back together."

"Lei, where were you?"

"I went to Beijing University to see if I could find the protesters, and I found them!" I give a little bounce at the edge of her bed. "The students are going to march to Tiananmen Square for Hu's memorial service. And I'm going with them."

Jun bolts upright. "What? You know Ba will be furious!"

"As if I'd tell him! Look, we can say we're going to another study session today. I'll go to the demonstration at Tiananmen Square, and you can go hang out with Yanlin."

But even the mention of Yanlin doesn't distract my sister. "What are the students going to do? I've heard what Ba says about them. Are they going to riot?" Her voice goes small. "Will it be dangerous?"

I wave a dismissive hand. "Don't believe what Ba says or what you read in the state-run newspapers, Jun! These are peaceful protesters. They just want their concerns to be heard."

"That doesn't mean it will be safe for you to join them!" Suspiciously, she asks, "Why are they letting a high schooler join them, anyway?"

I grin wickedly. "You know how persuasive I can be."

She just gives me a sour look.

"Remember what Yanlin said?" I ask, switching tactics. "He's sympathetic to the student protesters. So, if your own sister and your boyfriend both think well of this movement, can't you trust in it?"

"Yanlin also said he didn't want to get involved!" Jun shoots back. "Maybe you shouldn't either. He has good reason to stay away from these student demonstrations, and so do you."

I'm momentarily diverted. "Last night, I got the feeling that Yanlin was hiding something when we talked about the protesters." My eyes fix on the way she's suddenly absorbed in plucking at her flowery pink bedspread. "Did he tell you what it was?"

"Actually, yes."

"Well, what is it?" I demand.

A furious pounding on the bedroom door interrupts whatever answer Jun could give. "Lei! Jun!" our mother's voice thunders through the door. "Are you both in there?"

Jun and I exchange startled looks. Heart beating fast in anxiety, I call out, "We're both here, Ma! What's wrong?"

The door slams open, and it's *both* our parents standing in the doorway. It's hard to say which one of them looks angrier, but if I had to choose, I'd say it was Ba.

His face is pale, and his hands are clenched by his sides. "I'll tell you what's wrong," he grates out. "I just got off the phone with a comrade from the Politburo. The *Beijing Mirror* was about to print an article."

Uh-oh. Anxiety squeezes my lungs. My words to the American last night echo coldly in my head. *Opening night at Club Flash might not seem like a big deal to you, but it's the social event of the year in Beijing. All the tabloids will be covering it.*

"The article was going to say that many of Beijing's young socialites were in attendance at Club Flash's opening night—including you two," he continues, confirming my fears. "After I expressly forbade you from attending."

Jun pales, but I leap into the breach before she can say anything compromising. "The article was wrong!"

Jun gives me a startled look, which Ba doesn't see because his attention is on me. But Ma's gaze is sharper, and her mouth settles into a thin line as she takes us both in.

"Are you saying you weren't there?" Ba demands.

"No," I reply, my nerves twisting into knots. "*I* was there. But Jun wasn't." I'm not about to let her get in trouble for something I talked her into. "People can't tell us apart. You know that. Some kid at Club Flash must have taken a picture of me and sold it to the paparazzi, who assumed we were both there. But Jun went to the study session. I was the only one who went to the club."

Ba turns to Jun. "So you covered for your sister. That means you lied to us."

"I'm sorry," she whispers.

"Jun," our mother says, "you're the older sister. You have to set a good example."

She hangs her head. "I know."

"It was my fault," I insist. "I asked her to cover for me."

Ma gives me a dry look. "I know." *Oh shit. Does she know Jun was at the club with me?* "You both need to be more careful."

I let out a silent breath of relief that Ma's not going to pursue her suspicions about Jun.

But she still has more to say. "Remember what I said about Liu Yuan?" she asks. "*She* was the one who wrote the article. I told you that she wouldn't be above using my daughters to hurt me."

Jun grips her bedspread with both hands.

"It was just a story about a nightclub opening," I mutter.

"This time, yes." Ma comes over to the bed and sits next to me on the edge. "But next time, it could be more damaging rumors."

"Rumors of what?" *Why does Mrs. Liu hate our family so much?*

"That's none of your concern," Ba says coldly. "You are in enough trouble as it is without looking for more."

"Will it be a problem that the *Beijing Mirror* is going to print our names in an article about Club Flash?" Jun asks worriedly.

"No," Ba says firmly. "I've made sure your names don't appear in the article."

Good. Mrs. Liu doesn't know who she's messing with. Ba's position in the Politburo makes it easy for him to kill a tabloid story.

Then a queasy feeling invades my stomach. True, Mrs. Liu is a mean-spirited woman who has it in for my mother. But she's also a woman whose story has been buried by a powerful man—the way Wu Zetian's story was buried by Confucian historians. It was only last night that I was talking about the unfairness of women's stories being rewritten by men. So how can I be OK with Mrs. Liu's story being suppressed by my father?

And what if . . . this isn't the first time he's doctored the truth to serve his own purpose? I stare at him, and my throat goes dry. "You've done this before, haven't you, Ba?"

He spears me with a hard look. "What do you mean?"

The awful suspicion grows stronger. A few weeks ago, Ba had a reporter from the *People's Daily* over for dinner. At the time, I thought it was strange, since Ba had privately called him a spineless toady. But now I'm starting to understand. "Is that why you invited Mr. Su to our house?"

"I invite many people to dinner. So?"

Yeah, except that for my father, dinners aren't friendly social events. They're an opportunity to advance a political agenda. A reporter like that would be useful for Ba to have in his back pocket. "Mr. Su was pretty upset about being passed over for promotion and top assignments at the *People's Daily*. He seemed to think you could do something about it." And then they went into Ba's office and closed the door to talk over drinks. "Mr. Su was in a much better mood when he left, wasn't he?" *Stop talking, Lei. You don't need to get in more trouble!* But I have to find out if I'm right. "It's interesting," I say doggedly, "that a couple days later there was a story in the *People's Daily* painting the student demonstrators as thugs and criminals."

"I fail to see your point, Lei," he says icily.

Ma's lips tighten, and Jun's face scrunches in worry, but I'm focused on Ba. My stomach heaves. We've always disagreed about freedom of the press, but it's still shocking that my father could be capable of such corruption. The article didn't have a byline, but I *know* Mr. Su wrote it. It can't be a coincidence that a story fitting the party narrative came out right after Ba did Mr. Su a favor. "You bribed him to slander the protesters."

"What if I did?" Ba scoffs. "The protesters hate us and would destroy us if they could."

"But what he wrote about them wasn't true!" My heart burns as I think of Wu Zetian, slandered by male historians. And we, the keepers of her legacy, have been silent about this long-standing injustice. Sometimes I wonder if Empress Wu's real legacy isn't just the art but the truth of her story. If so, we've failed her.

"Don't be naive," Ba says scathingly. "Journalism isn't about telling the *truth*, if there is even such a thing. It's about controlling the narrative." He glances at Ma and Jun, who are watchful and silent. Then he turns back to me. "You should know how important it is to control what stories are told. Think of what could happen if the wrong story about our family got out."

"The story about the protesters wasn't about protecting our family," I say hotly. "It was about protecting the party!"

"Mr. Su serves the party, and so do I." He makes a sweeping gesture with one arm. "Look around you! The latest electronics. Pretty clothes. Where do you think all these comforts come from? The party rewards loyalty. That's how it works, and *you* have benefited from this system. Remember that the next time you feel compelled to defend those dangerous young upstarts."

My heart goes cold. Every story my father might have manipulated, every corrupt person he might have bribed—it's all gone to maintain this wealthy lifestyle. Shame overcomes me.

"And that's not all," my mother says quietly. "You're the keeper of Wu Zetian's dynasty, and that means you need to understand the threats against us. Your father's status in the party keeps the protesters and paparazzi from uncovering our secret. But if they unearthed what we're hiding and who we are"—she shudders—"your father would lose his position for hoarding bourgeois art and harboring us. We could even be arrested and sent to labor camps."

"The party lets us have this mansion and wealth," I say stubbornly, "so how can it condemn us for our inheritance from Wu Zetian?" But I already know the answer. It's one thing to accrue wealth under party-approved economic policy. But to stash away a secret collection of dynastic art that the party has decreed counterrevolutionary? *That* would ruin us. And then there's who we are. China's revolutions, including the Communist Revolution, were fought to overthrow the last traces of imperial rule. Yet here we are, descendants of those long-dead dynasties.

Ba shakes his head. "If you think you're safe just because the Cultural Revolution ended thirteen years ago, think again. The ruthless men who cut their political teeth on the lessons of the Cultural Revolution are still in power. And I've been in too many locked-door meetings with those men to believe that the old hatred of imperial decadence is gone."

"It's hypocritical!" I cry out. "The party is fine with its highest officials making more money in a month than most people make in their lifetime, but it's afraid of *art*?"

"Art," Ba says sternly, "is a symbol. And symbols are dangerous."

He turns to leave, and I look to my mother for support, but she's following my father out the door.

My whole body starts to tremble with anger. I'm tired of the secrets that keep us silent and afraid. If I go to the demonstration, it could expose us to both the Communist Party and the protesters. My father could get in trouble and lose his job. We could lose Wu Zetian's art. My family could be denounced by the same students I want to join. *Everyone* hates us for who we are and what we're hiding.

But there's a determination in me that can't be doused. If I turn my back on the student movement, I'm no better than my father, coldheartedly spreading lies to protect his life of privilege and damn everyone else. The thought of being like that makes my skin crawl. But can I really risk my father's career, the art I love, and my family to go to the protest?

But I already know the answer, and my belly burns with conviction. *Yes.* That's exactly what I'm going to do.

CHAPTER SEVEN

My parents forbid me from stepping foot out of the house for the rest of the weekend and warn Jun that she's responsible for keeping me in line. Then Ba heads back to the Central Office, and Ma gets ready to attend one of her charity planning meetings.

That leaves just me and Jun. She gets out of bed without looking at me. "I'm going to take a shower."

"Wait, Jun." I always hate it when my twin is angry with me, especially since it doesn't happen often. "I'm really sorry. I shouldn't have made you go to Club Flash with me. Please don't be mad."

"I'm not mad! If it hadn't been for you, I wouldn't have been brave enough to make the first move with Yanlin, and nothing would have ever happened." She ducks her head. "And you covered for me about being at Club Flash. Thank you."

Relief pours over me, spiked with confusion. If Jun's not mad, then why is she acting so weird? "What's wrong then?"

"Why do you think something is wrong?" She belts a robe around her pajamas and sits down at her dressing table to run a brush through her hair.

"Because I know you, that's why!" I toss a pillow at her, which she easily dodges. "Now spill."

Her eyes meet mine in the reflection of the mirror, and there are dark shadows beneath her eyes and a tense set to her jaw. "It's Yanlin."

"He obviously likes you, so what's the problem?" That's when I remember that Jun was about to tell me what Yanlin was hiding before our parents interrupted us. What the hell is Yanlin's secret? And why does my sister look like her puppy just died?

Jun turns on her stool so she's facing me. "The problem is that Yanlin and I shouldn't be together."

I blink in surprise. "That makes no sense."

"It's because of who our parents are." Slowly, she says, "Yanlin's mother is Liu Yuan."

My jaw drops. "What?!" That horrible, scandal-spreading woman is Yanlin's mother?

Jun's face crumples. "When Yanlin answered my bulletin board ad for a tutor, he didn't know who I was," she says miserably. "It wasn't until I told him my name in our first phone call that he knew. He agreed to be my tutor but was too embarrassed by his mother's actions to confess that he was actually her son. But last night, he felt he had to tell me."

At least Yanlin came clean. But no wonder my sister is worried. "Oh no, Jun!" It would have been hard to sell our parents on the idea of a penniless student in the first place, especially with the highly eligible Qiang waiting in the wings—but the son of Liu Yuan, the woman who's giving our mother so much grief? No way.

She nods glumly. "Our parents won't let me date Yanlin."

"Maybe you can just introduce him to our parents as a student at Beijing University. They'll be impressed by that."

"You know they'll ask who his parents are!"

"Then lie," I say flatly.

"I suggested that," she says, surprising me, "but Yanlin won't go for it. He won't lie to our parents or his. In fact, he wants to tell both sets of parents that we're dating each other."

Yanlin seems like one of those incurably honest people who can't help but tell the truth. *Poor Jun.* "What are you going to do?" I ask. "If he tells his mother that you two are dating, it will get back to our parents." Between Ba's work at the Politburo and Ma's socialite circle, the two of them know everything. Case in point—our presence at Club Flash last night.

"I know," she says. "I was barely able to convince him not to tell his mother, but he doesn't like the idea of sneaking around." She sighs. "I don't like it either, but I don't see what choice we have."

"Do you know why Yanlin's mother is out to get ours?"

"No idea," she replies.

"Well, did you ask Yanlin?"

"No. It seemed to be a sensitive issue."

"Jun!" My sister's utter lack of curiosity never ceases to amaze me.

"He'll tell me when he's ready," she says.

"OK." I stand up. "There's nothing you can do about this feud. The question now is how you feel about Yanlin."

"What do you mean?"

I give her a measured look. Jun's always been the good daughter. Is she willing to go against our parents' wishes to get what she wants? I hope so. "If you think this guy is worth it, then I'll help you see him without our parents finding out."

"He's worth it." There's no hesitation in her voice, and she looks less gloomy. "Thanks for helping me, Lei."

I grin at her. "Don't thank me yet. This isn't going to be easy."

"I'll do whatever it takes to be able to see Yanlin."

"And one more thing," I say, remembering my plans to sneak off to Hu's memorial. Now that I'm in trouble for sneaking off to Club Flash, it's going to be *much* harder to get to that protest. "You're going to have to cover for me today."

"Seriously?" I ask. "*That's* your best impression of me?"

Jun is sitting on the curved gray velvet couch with her legs crossed at the ankles while I pace the living room. Getting her to sound like me when our parents inevitably call to check up on me is starting to seem impossible. Classmates and acquaintances are one thing, but it's a totally different thing to fool our parents. We'd never be able to pull it off in person, but I thought Jun could successfully impersonate me over the phone. Now I'm not so sure.

"I'm trying!" she says.

I sigh. "I know, but you sound so guilty." I stop pacing so I don't wear a groove into the luxurious tufted rug decorated with cream peonies. "They'll know at once."

"That's because I *do* feel guilty!" She tugs the end of her braid, which she always does when she's feeling nervous. "Why do you need to go to that demonstration today, anyway?"

"We've been over that already." This demonstration is where I have to be—a compulsion as strong as the one to understand and guard Empress Wu's art. I want to live in a China where Wu Zetian's legacy is known, and if the student protesters are shaping a new China, then I need to be a part of that.

But none of that will convince Jun.

"Think of this as practice," I say to her. "If you want to keep our parents from finding out about Yanlin, you've got to get better at . . ."

I pause as I search for a word that won't make Jun dig her heels in. *"Lying"—nope. "Deception"—not better.*

"Not feeling guilty," I say at last.

She straightens up on the couch. "Let's try again. I'm ready." She tugs her braid again.

And don't touch your braid. It's a sure tell that you're lying. But I don't say it out loud. Our parents won't be able to see her over the phone, so there's no point in making her feel self-conscious.

I maneuver around the glass-topped coffee table to stand in front of her. "It will probably be Ma who calls." I'm not sure which parent I'd prefer. In general, Ba is better at sniffing out a lie, but Ma knows us better.

She nods. "Got it."

"When you answer the phone, joke a little about her charity committee meeting."

"Joke?" Jun's forehead wrinkles.

"Yeah, you know," I say impatiently. "Ask her to bring home some of Mrs. Wan's mooncakes." Mrs. Wan used to make the most amazing mooncakes—just the right amount of flakiness on the outside and complex sweetness on the inside—and we always looked forward to Ma bringing some home to share with us. Then Mrs. Wan started to go on diets, but instead of giving up the mooncakes, she made this awful version without butter and the barest pinch of sugar. Everyone in the committee hates those mooncakes but is too polite to say anything. "Go ahead," I say. "Pretend I'm Ma and try saying it."

"Can you bring home some of Mrs. Wan's mooncakes?" Jun says dutifully, not a breath of irony to be found in her voice.

"Gah!" I grab fistfuls of my hair. "Jun! We *hate* those mooncakes!"

"Then why did you tell me to ask for them?" She looks just as exasperated as I feel.

"It was supposed to be sarcastic!"

"I'm not good at sarcasm." *Obviously.*

"OK. Forget the mooncakes." I take a breath and cast around for something Jun can say to convince our mother that she's me. "Ask Ma if Mrs. Xu has any new gossip."

"Lei!" she exclaims. "It would be mean when she's so worried about Mrs. Liu and the *Mirror* article! I would never do that."

"But *I* would." And *mean*? Who does Jun think I am—a careless child stomping over everyone's feelings? "I'd joke about the gossip to let Ma know that it's not the end of the world. I'd say it like this." I put my hand on my hip and cock my head to the side. "So, Ma, does Mrs. Xu have any new gossip? There's got to be *something* juicier than the boring news that I was at Club Flash last night." I straighten my posture. "See? Then Ma will laugh, and I'll have shown her that I'm on her side, laughing about it all with her."

Jun stares at me so long without speaking that I start to feel uncomfortable. Then she stands up, putting her hand on one hip and cocking her head exactly as I had. Her mouth even twitches into a sly smile. I didn't know that I smiled like that. Word for word, she copies what I said—and she nails it.

Chills crawl up my spine at the eerie precision of her impersonation of me. I swallow hard before I speak. "That was good."

"You really think so?" she asks eagerly.

Relief warms me to hear Jun sound like herself. "Yes. That will fool Ma for sure."

Worry clouds her expression. "What if it's Ba who calls?"

Then be ready to riff on economic reform and international trade laws. Right. "It won't be Ba. He'll be too busy with the behind-the-scenes politics of Hu Yaobang's state memorial service." I smooth down my denim jacket over my red-striped T-shirt and jeans. My hair isn't curled today, and I'm wearing just a dab of lip gloss. No one can accuse me of looking like a party girl this time. "Speaking of Hu's memorial service," I say, "I should get to the demonstration."

Jun's face goes tight with concern.

"Don't worry," I see breezily. "It's a state funeral—what could happen?"

CHAPTER EIGHT

The morning's family drama has made me late. By the time I got out the door, my new comrades had already marched from Beijing University to Tiananmen Square.

Now the gray stone-paved square is crowded with protesters, and I have no idea how I'll even find Delun, Yawen, and Rong. But for a moment, I forget about finding them and just take in the awe-inspiring scene before me. The familiar Tiananmen Square I know has been transformed. Demonstrators have erected a huge portrait of Hu Yaobang at the foot of the gray obelisk that is the Monument to the People's Heroes and surrounded his black-and-white image with colorful wreaths of flowers.

I push through the crowd to get closer to the monument, intrigued by the art display that's been erected there. Art as protest is totally my thing.

Students are shouting for reform and carrying protest signs, and I'm dizzy with astonishment to be among them. There must be at least a hundred thousand protesters here.

From what Delun had said, I thought there would be a few thousand students at the most. I had no idea the demonstration would be this big.

And neither did Ba. It's not often that my father is wrong. He's going to be furious.

I glance toward the western edge of Tiananmen Square, at the imposing facade and many columns of the Great Hall of the People, where the official state funeral is happening. Ba and his cronies are inside, probably having conniptions over what's happening out in the square.

Distracted by thoughts of my father and the other CCP officials, I accidentally bump into a girl with a sketchbook. "I'm so sorry!" I say. "I was trying to get closer to the portrait of Hu Yaobang, and I guess I wasn't paying attention." I slow down to take a breath. "I hope I didn't ruin your drawing."

The girl pushes her glasses up her nose. "It's OK." Her eyes travel over me, and sudden doubt hits me. Did I make a mistake with my outfit? It's true that my matching denim and brightly colored T-shirt don't exactly blend in as well as I had hoped. Everyone else is dressed in mostly neutral colors like this girl, in khakis and a white button-down shirt. But I don't own khakis, and all my button-down shirts come with an ascot, practically screaming "high school uniform." Yeah . . . no. T-shirt and jeans were the best I could do.

And . . . maybe I'm worrying over nothing.

The girl is smiling as she shows me the blank page of her sketchbook. "As you can see, I haven't started yet. I was just standing here, waiting for inspiration."

"I'm Lei," I say, relieved that my clumsiness didn't ruin some great masterpiece. "Are you an art student then?"

She nods. "I'm Heng." Then she gestures toward the portrait of Hu. "You said you're interested in the painting. Are you a student at CAFA too?"

"No, I'm applying to colleges this year, and I'm planning to study art history." Excitement makes my breath catch. "But do you mean it was CAFA art students who did this portrait? Were you one of them?"

"Oh no!" She blushes. "I mean, yes, it was students at CAFA who did the portrait, and yes, I go there, but I'm not a painter. I'm a sculptor." She smiles again, her cheeks still slightly pink. "You should consider applying to CAFA. Many of us are here at this protest."

I shake my head. "I appreciate art, but I'm not an artist myself."

"There are many ways to be an artist." Heng scribbles something in her sketchbook, tears out the page, and hands it to me. "Here's my number. Call me if you want to talk more about art."

I take the paper, fold it carefully, and tuck it into the pocket of my denim jacket. "I will. Thank you!"

She closes up her sketchbook. "I don't think inspiration is coming to me today," she says wryly, "and I should go meet my friends anyway."

We say goodbye, and I'm left with my spirits brightened by the encounter.

Then my attention is caught by the sound of someone speaking through a megaphone by the Monument to the People's Heroes, so I continue making my way through the crowd to hear better. At last, I get close enough to see who the speaker is.

It's Delun.

Everything around me seems to freeze except for this young man in a starched white shirt and fire in his eyes.

In stark contrast to his burning eyes, Delun's voice is calm and steady. "Freedom. Equality. Are these just words, or are these truths worth fighting for?"

The crowd cheers, and I hear Rong's boisterous voice chanting, "Delun! Delun!"

Yawen cheers and flashes Delun a peace sign.

"Then this is a moment where we must act," he continues. "Hu's death cannot be the end of what he stood for."

My body strains toward him although I don't need to be nearer to hear him. His words bloom into the square with crystal clear perfection.

"This is the people's movement, and such a movement can grow beyond its start."

The crowd bursts into applause again, but my throat is too full of a strange new emotion to cheer with them.

That's when Delun spots me.

My breath stops. The people and noise melt away, and I forget that I'm in a crowded public square. For a heartbeat, it's just the two of us.

He breaks our locked gazes to look out over the crowd, and I can breathe again. *What the hell is happening to me?* It's not like me to get all light-headed over a boy.

"We cannot be gatekeepers for the people's movement," Delun continues, echoing what I'd said to him last night. "This must be a revolution for everyone. Women, the poor, ethnic and religious minorities—we must fight for the rights of all. While growing beyond our beginning, we cannot forget where we started. If what we mean by freedom and equality is a capitalist open market so the few of us who attend elite universities can rise to the top, then we will have betrayed our socialist roots."

His conviction resonates in my soul like a clear, sonorous bell. And at the same time, a chill steals over my body. Delun isn't just a student demonstrator—he's a leader in the revolution. If he is dangerous to me because of the secret art I'm safeguarding . . . then I'm just as dangerous to him. Because my father is trying to crush this revolution.

Delun hands the megaphone to a new speaker, but I don't hear what the other person is saying. All my attention is fixed on the young man parting the crowd to get to me.

He comes to a stop before me. "So, what did you think?"

"No gatekeepers for the people's movement, huh? I remember saying that last night." Mentally, I kick myself. Why do I always have to go on the offensive with him?

He reddens. "You made a good point," he says. "I hope you don't mind that I borrowed it."

"No, I don't mind." I smile. "I'm glad that you liked what I said." He visibly relaxes, and I add, "I like what you said too—about women's rights and how fighting for freedom doesn't mean embracing capitalism without question." The strange thing is that Delun and Ba aren't that different in their commitment to socialism and their wariness of capitalism.

"It amazes me that Americans see democracy as synonymous with capitalism, and communism as synonymous with authoritarianism!" His face lights up as he speaks. "I think it's a failure of the imagination to be unable to conceive of a socialist democracy, but to be fair, it's a failure of the imagination our Communist Party seems prone to."

I blink in the face of his passion and intelligence. I've always had a thing for geeky boys, but Delun is the embodiment of a fantasy I never even knew I had: a smart political activist who's not afraid of dangerous women.

Delun keeps talking politics, and I could listen to him all day, but he stops and smiles sheepishly. "I'm sorry, I must be boring you. I talk too much."

"I'm not bored. And you don't talk too much. I was watching as you spoke. People listen to you because what you have to say is important."

He shakes his head. "There are far better speakers than me." Before I can respond, he points to the woman taking the microphone now. "Look!" he says. "*She's* a gifted speaker."

The woman who has caught Delun's attention seems to be a bit older than me and is wearing a white button-down shirt like so many of the students. What is striking about her is the calm charisma she exudes. Her small frame, sideswept bangs, and round face should make her seem too young to be an activist; instead, she looks like a woman in charge.

And then she starts speaking. "Here is where we make our last stand!" Her words ring through the square. "If we fail now, we will lose our country! Do we want a country of corrupt officials and government repression? Or do we want a country where the people live free from fear? I know which one I want. We must fight for freedom!"

I get what Delun means. People listen to Delun because of his knowledge and the clarity of his ideas. People listen to this woman because it's impossible not to. Her words and passion electrify me, and if I hadn't been committed to the students' cause before, I would be now.

And yet Delun's thoughtfulness makes him just as compelling to me.

"See what I mean?" he says to me after she finishes to thunderous applause.

"Yes," I say, but I have to swallow my unease. When the woman spoke of *corrupt officials and government repression*, I know she meant men like my father. It's true that he is a high-level official who supports policies like government control of the press. But Ba is also a man of honor and principle. How can he be the enemy the students are fighting? Then I remember the *People's Daily* story my father orchestrated. OK, maybe Ba's honor is more flexible than I had thought. Trying to ignore the conflicting snarl of feelings about my father, I focus on the magnetic boy facing me. "She's amazing."

"If anyone should be a leader of the movement, it should be her," he says. "As much as we should have leaders, that is."

I look at him in surprise. "Aren't you a leader yourself?"

His smile is self-deprecating. "I'm just a political science student who talks too much and overthinks everything. I'm no leader."

"The crowd cheering for you seemed to disagree. Like it or not, a movement needs leaders, and your comrades seem to have chosen you."

His bright eyes bore into mine. "I can't stop thinking about what you said last night."

I gape at him, flabbergasted. "Me?" I said a lot last night, and as far as I can remember, none of it was earth-shattering. In fact, it may have bordered on offensive.

"What you had to say was so different and unique," he replies. "I'm worried that an official leader will reduce our message to one voice, one vision. This movement needs many voices, sometimes in opposition to each other, or we risk replicating the authoritarian government we're fighting against."

"Yes, that makes sense."

One eyebrow lifts. "I thought you were going to argue with me."

"Why?" I ask archly. "Just because I've argued with you about almost everything else you've said?"

Delun laughs at that. "You have your own mind. I respect that."

"So you're not going to grill me again about why I want to join the movement?"

"Sorry about that." His expression turns wary. "I guess I was surprised that someone like you wants to be a part of all this."

My face heats up. "You don't know me."

"You're right," he says quietly.

Tension stretches between us as the demonstration goes on around us. It's as if we're in our own bubble, facing off against each other.

At this moment, Yawen rushes over, giving me a hug. "Glad you showed up, Lei!" she says. Then her eyes shift between us. "Whoa. I'm sensing some serious sparks here."

I choke at that, and Delun turns bright red. "Ah, I should . . . I need to . . ." He turns abruptly and hurries away without bothering to finish the thought.

"Yawen," I say furiously, "there's nothing going on with Delun and me! I'm here to join a revolutionary movement, not hook up with a guy!"

She shrugs. "Who says you can't do both?"

"I do," I say grimly. Bad enough that my father and our family's wealth are a big part of what we're fighting against. The last thing I need is a silly schoolgirl crush to complicate things even more.

CHAPTER NINE

The following Friday, I'm jogging down the sidewalk outside of my high school and calling out over my shoulder, "Thanks again, Jun!"

"This is the last time!" she shouts after me.

It's what she said yesterday, and anxiety slithers into me. Jun's been covering for me so I can sneak out to Tiananmen Square after school, but she's obviously getting cold feet about lying to our parents. I'll have to figure out a way to convince her to keep helping me.

I flag down a taxi and clamber into the back seat, telling the driver, "Tiananmen Square, please."

"Tiananmen Square, huh?" The driver is young, not much older than me, and his eyes meet mine knowingly in the rearview mirror. "You're doing a good thing! It's about time someone took on the government."

Feeling like an imposter, I squirm on the bamboo-covered seat. I don't deserve praise for sneaking away from my privileged life for a few hours a day to protest.

The driver doesn't seem to notice my discomfort. He grimaces as he pulls away from the curb. "They keep saying the people are the backbone of the country, but our backs are breaking! I'm working twenty-four-hour shifts with a few naps in the cab. And I *still* make barely enough to get by."

"That's terrible." Guilt burrows deeper into me. What would he say if he knew about my obscene wealth? "Workers' rights are at the top of our demands," I say weakly, but this talking point sounds glib in the face of his real-life injustice.

"Yes!" He bangs the steering wheel with a fist, and we veer alarmingly, but he gains control without seeming at all fazed by nearly sideswiping another car—which is now blaring its horn at us. "Look at me. I failed the Gaokao, repeated my last year of high school so I could take it again, and then failed a second time! Ba said we couldn't afford for me to keep studying and not working. So here I am."

I feel worse and worse. I don't have to choose between studying and working, and if I need help with the Gaokao, my family can afford tutors. "It's criminal that only about twenty percent of all students who take the Gaokao get into college." *Ugh! The last thing he needs is for you to quote statistics at him.* Desperate to say something more useful, I offer, "You should come protest with me. I'm Lei, by the way."

"I'm Guang," he says, "and thanks for the invitation, but when would I have time?" He smiles wryly.

Shame rises into my throat. "Of course. Sorry." It was thoughtless of me to ask him to join us when he had just told me about the long shifts he works.

"No worries."

I fall silent for the rest of the ride.

Guang pulls up to the square. "We're here," he says.

I pay the fare and then hesitate. It doesn't seem right to give him just this paltry amount. Even though it's not common to tip, I tear a sheet of paper out of my composition notebook and fold it around some extra renminbi bills in order to make it seem more like a gift and not like a tip. "Thank you," I say, handing him the money and hoping it won't offend him. "It was nice to meet you."

He accepts the paper-wrapped bills without looking at them and smiles. "Nice to meet you too."

I stand on the curb and watch the taxi pull back into traffic. I hope Guang's shift is ending soon.

As I turn toward the square, a wave of noise washes over me. Thousands of young people fill the square, bright-faced and loud.

Yet something has changed for me. I still feel inspired by the sight of so much passion and commitment, but I have to face a hard truth.

Delun was right to question my motivations.

I felt constrained by the path of prestige and success that my parents have laid out for me, and I thought that the movement was a way for me to choose a different path.

But I was wrong.

Most people, like Guang, have no choice or say in their future. This movement is not a way for me to break free from my family's expectations of me. I know why I'm here now, and it's not to choose a different path for *myself.*

I'm fighting for *all* of our futures.

Thousands of boisterous students are cheering, and Tiananmen Square crackles with youthful energy. Some are carrying signs and shouting. Some are blasting music out of boom boxes and dancing. Some, like me, are listening to speakers.

The demonstrations at Tiananmen Square have been steadily increasing in number of protesters and intensity for the past week. Unfortunately, my attraction to Delun has grown with equal intensity. He's just so darn smart and surprisingly funny and hot . . . but I can resist temptation.

Besides, it's not like he's falling all over me. He treats me with the same friendliness as he does Yawen and Rong. Except that sometimes, when we're talking, he gets this look in his eyes. *Nope. Not going there.*

Delun finishes his speech to loud applause from the crowd and bright camera flashes from the reporters. He hops off the makeshift stage and makes his way toward Yawen, Rong, and me.

"Great speech!" Rong enthuses.

"Love the part about the danger of embracing capitalism!" Yawen says.

"Thank you." Delun smiles shyly.

I start to add something when another flash goes off in the corner of my eye, making me turn. A vaguely familiar figure is taking pictures of the crowd, and for some reason, the sight fills me with dread. Where have I seen him before?

"Lei," Delun says, "are you OK?"

But I can't respond. With a lurch of my stomach, I recognize the mysterious man with the camera: Mr. Su, the reporter from the *People's Daily*. Or, as Ba calls him, the spineless toady.

My blood freezes. "I'll be right back," I say abruptly.

Ignoring my friends' questions, I push through the crowd toward Mr. Su. Is he here to write another slanderous story about the protesters? I don't know how to stop him, but I have to try.

He's still taking pictures of the crowd and doesn't seem to notice me moving toward him. When I reach him, I say angrily, "You're the one who wrote that horrible story about us!"

With a start, he turns toward me. His beady eyes blink rapidly. "I know you!" He wipes a sheen of sweat from his forehead. "You shouldn't be here. If your father knew—"

My chest constricts. I'd been in such a hurry to confront him that I didn't even consider how he could expose me. "Are you going to tell him?"

His gaze becomes calculating. "Maybe. Unless my silence is worth something to you."

Is he seriously trying to blackmail me? *Oh, hell no.* When I was little, I used to crawl under tables or sit in a corner with a book, quiet as a mouse, whenever Ba had his comrades over for a drink or dinner. One of the most important things I learned from those gatherings is that Ba never, *ever* gives in to blackmail or bribery. And I'm my father's daughter.

"Really?" I ask with false sweetness. "You want to be the one who tells my father that his daughter is protesting Communist Party authoritarianism and corruption? Then you're braver than I thought."

His face goes ashy pale. "No! You've mistaken my meaning! I won't say a word, but others might not be so . . . cautious."

"What others?" I ask sharply.

"You think I'm the only one here working for the party?"

"The reporters?" I ask, my heart beating faster.

"Nah," he says. "Not them. I'm talking about the people the Politburo sent here to get pictures and take down names."

"Spies." My voice is flat, and the pounding of my heart has become an earthquake.

His voice drops. "Listen, the party is making a list, and shit is going to go down. This could follow you for the rest of your life. I'm talking about getting blacklisted from jobs." There's sympathy in his voice now. "You're in your last year of high school, right? If you don't leave now, you can forget college."

I stare at him in horrified disbelief.

"Come with me," Mr. Su urges. "You don't belong with the rest of them. It's not too late to save yourself."

No way. My comrades need to know about the danger they're in. My spine stiffens. "I'm not going to leave the others." Repulsed by his suggestion, I take a step backward—and bump into someone's chest.

"Is everything all right?" Delun asks, looking at me with concern. *How much did he overhear?*

Mr. Su's eyes glitter, and he points his camera at Delun.

Without thinking, I lunge forward and put my hand over the lens of his camera. "No. You're not taking a picture of him or anyone else!" I might not know who the other spies are, but I can stop this one. Quickly, I pop open the back of the camera and yank out the roll of film.

"Hey!" Mr. Su yells as the brown film unfurls, the incriminating images fading to nothing in the light.

Turning to Delun, I say, "He's a party spy. He's making a list of us for the CCP, and there might be others."

Delun doesn't stop to ask me how I know all this. "Get out," he says sternly to Mr. Su, "and don't come back."

Mr. Su blanches. "You'll regret this!" Then he scurries away.

My gut wrenches as Mr. Su's ominous warning rings in my ears, but I couldn't just abandon everyone else to save my own skin.

Delun is watching me with an odd expression on his face.

"What?" I ask. "Why are you looking at me like that?"

He swallows hard. "You didn't leave. You knew the risk, and you stayed."

My face burns. "Oh, you heard that." *You don't belong with the rest of them,* Mr. Su had said, and he's not wrong. I could walk away from this protest at any time and return to my sheltered life, trusting my father to erase any repercussions. The others don't have that privilege. "I couldn't leave," I say softly.

Delun holds my gaze, his eyes dark and intense. He's standing so close that the heat of his body burns my skin.

A deep awareness of him vibrates in my bones, and my breath goes short. "Delun . . ."

Then he closes the gap between us and kisses me.

My body bursts into flame. Without thinking, I clutch his neck and seek out the angles of his mouth, electrified by the force of the kiss.

Then Delun breaks away, and I'm left breathless and disoriented. "I'm sorry! I don't know what came over me. It's just . . ." He runs a hand through his hair, making it stand on end. "I've been wanting to do that since I met you."

With a slow-motion finality, my heart thuds to my feet.

Damn that Qiang. He was right.

When you fall . . . you'll fall hard.

But in some ways, Qiang was wrong—I'm not falling at all. I'm flying.

Then Delun says, "Even though I shouldn't."

Ouch. Coming back to earth *hurts*. "Why not?" I demand, even though I had been thinking the exact same thing for the past week—that I shouldn't give in to the attraction between us. But that was before the most scorching-hot kiss ever.

Delun seems like he's choosing his words carefully. "We barely know each other."

Except I *do* know him. My attraction to Delun isn't just physical. I'm drawn to his integrity and passion in a way I've never felt before. *So now what?*

There are only two choices: Get the hell away from him (clearly the smart choice) or lean into this dangerous attraction (clearly the insane choice). But I was the one who encouraged Jun to take a risk with Yanlin. Can I be less brave than my twin sister? *OK, we're doing this.* Forget all my silly proclamations against romance. It is *so* on now.

My heart in my throat, I move closer to Delun, who sucks his breath in sharply. *Nice to know he isn't unaffected.* "Would you like to get to know me?"

His eyes widen. "What do you mean?"

I steel my nerves and ignore the churning of my stomach. "I'm just wondering if you were telling me the truth when you said you weren't afraid of dangerous women."

"I was telling the truth." He looks intrigued.

"Good." I smile as if my insides aren't a quivering mess. "Because I'm asking you on a date. Do you want to have dinner with me tomorrow?"

In the silence that follows, my heart forgets how to beat.

Then Delun takes in a lungful of air like he's about to dive into the deep end of the pool. "Yes."

CHAPTER TEN

"Are you sure Maxim's is a good idea?" I ask for the thousandth time. Jun and I are in the back of a taxi, on our way to a restaurant to meet up with Delun and Yanlin. "I did tell you that Delun is a student activist protesting class inequality, right? I don't think a five-star French restaurant is really his thing."

"Who *wouldn't* love Maxim's?" Jun's face is shining with anticipation. "Trust me. I've taken care of everything." She looks lovely and radiant in a peach-colored dress.

I opted for a purple velvet sheath dress with puffy short sleeves tonight. "All right," I say doubtfully. Technically, the double date was *my* idea, but Jun lost no time in taking over all the arrangements. She's been dying for another real date with Yanlin, but he felt uneasy about sneaking behind our parents' backs. That's why I suggested that we all go out together, making it seem less datelike. Plus, I hoped Jun would be more willing to help me go to the protests if she thought there was a guy involved. But now I'm having second thoughts. What if this double date gets awkward and weird?

I fiddle with my puffy sleeves. "It's just that my very first date with Delun is going to be with my twin sister and her new boyfriend, who happens to be the son of our mother's archenemy."

"You didn't tell Delun that, did you?" Jun asks sharply.

"Of course not! It was just a joke." Great. Now *Jun* looks nervous. "You're right," I say quickly. "It's going to be fine. Delun and Yanlin are both students at Beijing University, so they'll have lots to talk about. You'll like Delun too."

"How do you know I'll like him?" Worry lines crease her forehead. "You met him a week ago—*you* barely know him."

"Not true," I say. "Yes, it's only been a week, but you can get to know someone pretty well under intense circumstances." I don't tell her about his calming influence when tempers flare among the other leaders or the quiet integrity that has earned him the respect of all the protesters. And I definitely don't tell her that he's one of the leaders.

She sighs. "At least you're not grounded anymore. I don't know if I could cover for you after school *and* over the weekend again."

I roll my eyes, because Jun didn't even have to pretend to be me when I went to the demonstration at Hu's memorial last weekend. Our parents got their signals crossed—each of them thought the other was going to call home to check up on me, so neither of them did. It was probably for the best, but a part of me was curious to see if Jun could pull off being me.

"So does Delun like you back?" She's not asking to be mean—my sister is incapable of that.

But her question cuts right to my heart. Because I didn't ask *her* if Yanlin liked her back. Doubt hardens in my stomach. Maybe Delun agreed to this date only because he was too nice to turn me down. "I don't know," I say shortly. That kiss certainly wasn't out of niceness.

Jun's eyes are round in surprise. "I'm sure he likes you back. I don't know why I asked! I just thought . . ." She twists her fingers in her lap and looks genuinely distressed. "You're usually so sure of yourself, but you don't seem to be this time. I wondered if you like him because you're *not* sure of him."

"A challenge, you mean?" No, that's not it. It's his sharp mind—and his respect for *my* mind—that has me in a knot of anticipation for our date. "Trust me, I'd love to be sure of him."

"You are smart, beautiful, and kind," Jun says firmly. "Any guy would be thrilled to date you."

It feels odd for Jun to be the one to reassure *me*. But not unpleasant.

Then she smiles slowly. "You really like him, don't you?"

The taxi pulls up at the curb of the Chongwenmen Hotel. I pay up and hop out before I have to answer.

Jun follows me, her eyes sparkling. Her interest in my love life and anticipation of her date with Yanlin seem to have eroded her anxiety.

The hotel doorman, dressed in vibrant red, opens the door for us, and we go up to the second floor of the hotel and enter Maxim's Beijing. This is the restaurant our family goes to when we're celebrating birthdays or any important event.

The restaurant opened to great fanfare six years ago. It's a branch of Pierre Cardin's Maxim's de Paris—the first overseas branch. According to Ba, the profits are shared by Cardin and the Chinese government, but it was Cardin who spared no expense in decorating the Beijing restaurant to mimic the art nouveau aesthetic of the original French one: glass ceiling, gold-gilded mirrors, Western art murals, and Tiffany-style lamps. If you didn't know better, you'd think you were dining in a restaurant in Paris. That's probably why Jun thought it would be the perfect romantic spot for a date. But worry crests over me again. Not that I had any hope of hiding my wealth from Delun after showing up to the first demonstration in an imported designer outfit, but Maxim's is more than just a dead giveaway. It's announcing my upper-class status with gold and crystal and everything but a five-piece band.

A hostess in a smart black-and-white uniform greets us. Jun gives her our names and asks if Delun and Yanlin are here yet.

"Yes, miss," she replies, "and as you requested, I informed each gentleman on arrival that it is a prix fixe dinner that has already been prepaid."

Worry flutters in my chest. Any meal here is sure to be expensive, so I guess it's good that Jun made sure it's already paid for. As the hostess leads us to our seats, I whisper to Jun, "Good thinking."

When Jun and I turned fifteen, our parents opened a checking account for each of us and gave us a generous monthly allowance. The price of dinner tonight won't make a dent in either of our accounts, but that wouldn't be true for most of Beijing's residents. Our family does come here pretty often, but the majority of the clientele are tourists or people from foreign embassies. For the most part, locals can't afford to eat here. It's a sure bet that neither of our dates would've been able to afford dinner easily. Another pang of anxiety shoots through me.

Delun and Yanlin stand up as we approach. Delun is wearing another one of his white pressed shirts with a black jacket and tie. My heart flutters madly.

Then Delun drops his gaze and frowns at the snow-white tablecloth and gold candelabra with its slender candles emitting a soft glow. "Thank you for dinner," he says stiffly.

"Yes, thank you," Yanlin echoes. His face looks tense too.

My sinking feeling grows stronger. Coming to Maxim's was a mistake. If we were here with Qiang or one of the guys I usually date, we'd all be insisting on being the one to cover the bill. It's the polite thing every Chinese person does even if the bill is prepaid. The fact that Delun and Yanlin aren't even making a token offer to pay means that they *really* can't afford this place.

"You're welcome." My face burns even though it wasn't my choice to eat here.

"It's nothing," Jun says quickly. She's looking at Yanlin, so she doesn't see Delun wince.

But I do see—and I understand his reaction. Because for Jun and me, it *is* nothing to drop two hundred renminbi per person on a meal when the average monthly salary for someone living in Beijing is only about fifty. Squirming in realization that this date is only going to confirm Delun's worst fears about me, I mutter, "Let's sit."

Jun and I sit down across from our respective dates. I introduce Jun and Delun, and they each say something about being glad to meet the other. Then Yanlin and I say how nice it is to see each other again.

At that point, we run out of things to say.

Normally, I have no problem in any social situation, but this time, my throat is clogged with the paralyzing fear that I've just blown everything. And that if I open my mouth, I will only make everything even worse.

Our awkward silence is interrupted by a waiter who arrives to pour us champagne. I glare at the bubbly froth in my flute, wishing I had at least thought to ask the waiter to skip such an obvious sign of bourgeois wealth. If we were someplace like the United States, I could say that Jun and I are only eighteen and can't drink. But of course there's no drinking age in China.

Delun lifts his flute and says, "A toast to Lei and Jun. Thank you for this dinner." That's all he says, but he smiles at me.

My chest grows tight with gratitude, because he's putting aside his pride to give me this kindness. "Thank you for joining us tonight." I lift my own champagne. "Ganbei."

"Ganbei!" everyone says, and we all drink up.

Conversation flows more easily after that.

Jun looks between Yanlin and Delun. "Do you two know each other from Beijing University?"

Yanlin nods. "We had a class together last year. English, wasn't it?"

"Yes," Delun confirms. "It was taught by an American. She was a good teacher."

Yanlin laughs. "Of course *you* would think highly of her."

What does Yanlin mean? Did Delun have a crush on this American? Unreasonable jealousy spurts through me.

"Because she was the first foreigner to tell us of a socialist movement in America? You're right that I appreciated that." Delun turns to me. "You would have been interested in what she told us about socialist feminism in the U.S. It's too bad you won't get her as a teacher if you go to Beijing University next year. She wanted to get back to the United States before her first grandchild was born."

"I would have liked to meet her." My voice is bright with relief. It's true that I'd like to meet an American socialist feminist.

"I liked her too, actually," Yanlin says. "It was interesting to learn about American activism."

"Speaking of activism," Delun says, "I'm surprised you haven't joined the students' movement."

A shadow passes over Yanlin's face, but the waiter arrives at that moment with our starters: a tiny scoop of caviar nestled in fromage blanc on thin toast.

Jun and I unfold our white napkins to reveal glittering silverware. "No chopsticks," I say. "Sorry."

"That's OK." Delun eyes his plate like he's not sure what to do with this microscopic portion of foreign food.

Jun doesn't help matters when she says, "It's an amuse-bouche."

"A what?" Delun asks.

"It's French for 'amuse the mouth,' " she explains.

"Oh." The bafflement on his face would be funny if it weren't for the fact that with every passing moment, it's probably becoming clearer and clearer to him that we're from two different worlds.

"It's just fish eggs and cheese on bread," I say shortly, and Jun casts me a look of surprise. I don't blame her. I'm not usually this on edge. But it's not every day that I watch my dreams go up in smoked caviar.

Delun pops the amuse-bouche into his mouth.

"What do you think?" I ask, throat dry with anticipation.

"My mouth is amused," he replies, deadpan.

I relax a little when I see how determined he is to take everything in stride. Maybe there's hope for us yet.

Delun turns to Yanlin. "I'm sorry, it's none of my business whether you participate in the protests or not. I hope you don't mind my bringing it up."

"Not at all." Yanlin pauses as he chews his food, but it's such a small portion that it doesn't take him long before he finishes. "I do support the protests, but my . . . family history makes me wary of becoming a revolutionary."

"I see." Tactfully, Delun changes the subject by talking about a classmate they both know.

Jun's face tenses, and she picks up her fork even though there's nothing for her to eat with it. After a beat, she puts it down again. It's clear my sister isn't going to ask the hard questions.

So it's up to me. Normally, I'd let it go. But an uneasy suspicion is crawling into my stomach. Because we also have family history that makes me afraid of becoming a revolutionary. We're barely thirteen years past the end of the Cultural Revolution, and its bloody consequences still reverberate through our lives. "The Red Guard?" I ask Yanlin quietly.

Jun kicks me under the table, but strangely, Yanlin's face loosens. "Yes." It's as if he's been holding on to this past and is relieved to finally let it out.

"Was someone in your family part of the Red Guard, or a . . ." I can't quite ask him point-blank if the Red Guard had dragged a family member out into the street to kneel on broken glass and be beaten for some bourgeois crime—like owning classical art.

"Victim?" he finishes for me. "Both, actually. My father was part of the Red Guard"—Yanlin's face shutters down—"until they turned on him. He spent years in a prison labor camp, and he's never really recovered from the . . . reeducation he endured there."

"Oh, Yanlin." Jun reaches across the table and grips his hand.

Delun looks sympathetic, but unsurprised.

I feel sick to my stomach even though I know the "reeducation" happened to many, especially at the start of the Cultural Revolution. No wonder Yanlin wants nothing to do with another revolution. "I'm so sorry." I can only hope that Yanlin's father was one of the rare Red Guards who refused to participate in the looting and beating. Like

Ba. It was why Ma trusted him with her secret and her heart. Groping for something to say, I add, "Our father was a Red Guard too."

I'd hoped to convey some kind of understanding with that information, but Yanlin's expression turns to granite. Jun hisses softly in pain, and he glances down at their clasped hands; his is white-knuckled. "Sorry." He lets go of her hand and looks at me. "I know your father was a Red Guard."

My jaw drops. This time, Jun doesn't kick me. She must think that even *I* wouldn't be rude enough to ask more questions.

Unfortunately, she underestimates my curiosity. "How do you know that?"

Here comes my sister's kick now, swift and hard.

Yanlin's voice is as cold as ice. "Our fathers knew each other during the Cultural Revolution. They were best friends."

CHAPTER ELEVEN

What? My head whirls with questions. Yanlin's father and my father used to be best friends? Then why is his mother going after mine? *What is going on here?*

Jun is staring at him in disbelief.

"Too many terrible things happened during the Cultural Revolution," Delun says somberly. "I'm sorry about what happened to your father." He hesitates as if he's not sure if he should say more. "I promise that today's movement remembers what the Red Guard did. We remember that they were students too. And we won't make those same mistakes."

Yanlin nods. "I appreciate that." He glances over at the waiter bearing down on us. "What's the next course?" he asks as if he has nothing on his mind but food.

And as if he hadn't just dropped a conversational bomb in the middle of the dinner.

"French baked snails," Jun replies, giving me another kick under the table.

For once, I hold my tongue. Relationships were . . . complicated in the time of the Cultural Revolution. Neighbors, friends, siblings, parents, children—everyone turned against each other. Everyone was afraid. And behind the fear, the looting, and the beatings, there was always the Red Guard.

Somehow, dinner limps on.

By the time dessert arrives, a chilled raspberry sorbet, I'm wishing dinner would hurry up and be over already. Definitely a first for me at Maxim's. I'm so caught up in my glum thoughts that I'm not paying attention as I take my first bite of the sorbet. The frothy tart sweetness bursts onto my taste buds. "Mmm. Oh, so good!"

My face flushes. I'd forgotten that I'm incapable of eating this particular dessert without making embarrassing moans of pleasure.

Delun's eyes are locked on me, and inexplicably, his cheeks redden as he catches me noticing him. He ducks his head and concentrates on his own sorbet without so much as glancing at me again.

I eat my sorbet in determined silence. No matter how meltingly good this is, I won't make a peep. But seriously, it's a crime to eat a culinary masterpiece like this without *some* kind of appreciation. Plus, Delun's cheeks have returned to their normal color, and he's so cute when he blushes. Daringly, I emit a small "Mmm."

Instant red cheeks. And Delun won't meet my eyes. Interesting.

After dessert, we head downstairs, continuing the stilted conversations that got us through the meal. It's not until the doorman in his posh red uniform opens the door that it hits me. This is it. Delun's about to leave, and I'll have blown my chance with him! Beads of perspiration form between my shoulder blades. *Get it together, Lei. Think of a way to spend more time with him.* But my brain is frozen.

Jun glances at me and then at Delun. "Yanlin," she says, "will you take a walk with me?"

"Of course." He smiles hugely even though he can't possibly be excited about exploring the Chongwen District. Other than Maxim's, there aren't many places to go in Chongwen, the smallest of Beijing's districts. The only thing going for it is that it's close to Tiananmen, the heart of the city. It's obvious that Yanlin doesn't care about his surroundings—he just wants to spend time with Jun.

Glad *someone* doesn't want to see the date end. Unlike Delun, who probably can't get away from me fast enough and return to the encampment at Tiananmen Square. Still, I'm relieved that the night isn't ruined for my sister.

Apologetically, Jun says to Delun, "I don't feel comfortable leaving Lei out here by herself. Would you mind waiting with her?

We'll be back in about half an hour." *Jun, you wonderful, genius sister! I owe you.*

"Of course," Delun replies so promptly that hope swells in my chest.

I look at my sister with heart eyes, and she smiles smugly.

Jun and Yanlin leave, and for the first time, I'm alone with Delun—with nothing to say. Nerves prick at my skin and make my hands clammy.

"So, you like Western food," he comments, shifting from foot to foot.

"I do." I know he's just making small talk, but it feels like a rebuke. Suddenly, I'm tired of walking on eggshells around him, constantly worried about looking shallow and spoiled. "And I like Chinese food too, but there isn't a restaurant for what I wanted tonight—" I break off abruptly.

"What is it that you wanted?" His eyes are intent on mine.

I wanted to take you to a restaurant so romantic that you'd fall head over heels for me. But I just ended up making a complete mess of things. Frustration rises in me. It figures that the first time I cared enough about a boy to *try* would be the first time I totally bombed a date. But there's no way I'm going to say all that to Delun.

Instead, I say, "It's not fair that all the nice restaurants in Beijing are foreign ones, meant for foreigners or rich Chinese like me! And even the not-so-nice hot spots are foreign. I mean, people our age go to KFC for a big date!" Kentucky Fried Chicken is a recent import from the West, and its affordable prices and convenient location right next to Tiananmen Square have made it a popular hangout for the protesters as well as any other young person.

Delun's lips quirk up. "I see your point."

"I want more choices—nice restaurants that Chinese people can afford, serving *our* food." I throw my arms out. "I want a Beijing duck restaurant there and a noodle shop over there. I want places where people our age can go and have *fun.* I'm sick of people thinking that good food is a Western invention! We have a long culinary history—since when did good food come to mean Western decadence?" But I know the answer to that: 1966, the start of the Cultural Revolution. "The West takes our food and art, and the Cultural Revolution taught us that those things are elitist and wrong. But I won't be satisfied with bare restaurants and stripped museums."

A woman in khaki slacks and a shapeless blouse walks by and gawks at me.

I'm used to it. There aren't a lot of women who dress like me. Not too long ago, we were a country clad in beige or drab green. Bright colors were seen as counterrevolutionary, and it's only recently that the local stores started selling brighter colors. Not that they sell anything like the imported clothing I wear. I glance down at my purple velvet dress. Ironically, my father's elite status in the Communist Party is what allows me to shop at stores normally available only to foreigners. "We rejected our colorful past—literally—during the Cultural Revolution. That woman who passed us probably thinks I'm a foreigner." My chin lifts. "But I'm not. I'm proud to be Chinese, and I'm not trying to mimic foreign ways, if that's what you're thinking."

"No. I'm not thinking that at all." He had been silent during my speech, and I don't know what to make of it.

I tap the toe of my patent leather pump against the ground. "Then what *are* you thinking?"

"I'm thinking that you are a brilliant woman with startling ideas." Delun takes a step closer to me, making my heart thump madly. "I've never met anyone like you."

"Oh." That's a *good* thing, right? His nearness is seriously affecting my ability to form a coherent thought.

He speaks so softly that it is almost a whisper. "You're a complete mystery, Lei."

Worry cools the heat pooling in my stomach. "There's no mystery about me." *Nothing to see here, folks. And I definitely don't have a centuries-old art collection in my basement.* I hate that the threat of discovery is always present.

"Here you are, wearing velvet and eating caviar—and protesting in Tiananmen Square with the rest of us. Why?"

"Why fight to burn down my charmed life, you mean?" I ask, hoping he doesn't notice how shaky my voice is.

"It's not just that. The way you talk about the Cultural Revolution . . ." His voice trails off, and he starts again. "There are officials in the Communist Party who were imprisoned or exiled during the Cultural Revolution. The party is afraid that our student movement is the start of a second Cultural Revolution, and it will do anything to stop us." His eyes darken. "So that's the mystery. Why does a teenage girl hate and fear the Cultural Revolution as much as those powerful old men? And why aren't you afraid of *us*?"

The words he doesn't say linger between us: *Why aren't you afraid of me?*

I take a deep, unsteady breath. The truth is that I *am* afraid—of him. Delun is one of the student leaders. The Red Guard were students too. If this student movement becomes a second Cultural Revolution like my father and his comrades fear, then Delun could be the one breaking down the doors of my house and burning the Tang dynasty paintings and poems of my legacy. He could be the downfall of my family.

But I can't believe that. "Do I need to be afraid?" I meet his eyes squarely. "Is this a second Cultural Revolution, Delun?"

"You've been demonstrating shoulder to shoulder with us for a week now." His expression is hard to read. "What do you think?"

"My father once told me that the Red Guard was being used by Mao and the Gang of Four to get rid of political opponents."

Delun gives me a sharp look, no doubt remembering my father is a former Red Guard, but he doesn't interrupt me.

"All that art and history destroyed—and it was just a cover for the real mission of purging enemies." Bitterness tightens my throat, but then I look at Delun, at his open face and clear eyes, and the hard knot in my body eases. "You and the other students aren't tools being used by unscrupulous leaders. You are fighting for freedom based on conviction and integrity. So, no, I don't think this is a second Cultural Revolution."

"Good. Because it's not." His face looks strained. "But there *is* danger. Lei, you have a good heart, and I know you want to be involved in this movement . . . but you have so much to lose."

For a panicked moment, I think he knows about Wu Zetian's art and my imperial heritage, even though that's impossible. "How do you know how much I have to lose?"

He takes a step backward, and his eyes flicker over me. "An upscale foreign restaurant. Your stylish dress. I wondered before, but it's obvious now." He takes a deep breath. "I knew you had money, but only a daughter of a high-ranking Communist Party official has access to luxuries like this."

My stomach drops. "So you're judging me based on what my father does."

"No." He shakes his head. "It's just that a girl like you has more to risk than someone like me."

"I can't be the only protester with a father in the Politburo."

"True. And I think that's one reason the government is torn about what to do with us. Quite a few high-ranking officials have sons and daughters in the movement and are sympathetic to our cause."

"Well, there you go." No need to tell him that my father isn't one of those sympathetic party officials.

"But I don't think that's your situation."

What the hell? It's just my luck to fall for a mind reader.

"How do you know that?" My voice is defiant, but I'm shaking on the inside. I should have known that a relationship with Delun was doomed. I'm hiding too many damn secrets from him already.

"Just a guess."

Good. He doesn't know anything for certain.

He peers at me for a moment and then asks, "What does your father think of your going on a date with a poor student leader of a protest movement?"

My mouth hangs open for a second before I snap it closed. I think of my father's determined rise through the ranks of the Communist Party, all to protect my mother's secret. And now I'm risking that secret by starting a relationship with a young upstart revolutionary. So how would my father react if he found out? *He would kill me.*

"You didn't tell him about me, did you?" Delun smiles sadly. "You should quit now, Lei. You've had your adventure, and someday you can tell your children that you once spent a week protesting with a rabble of revolutionary students in your youth."

Anger and loss punch me in the gut. "If you think that I'm just a bored rich girl looking for a temporary thrill, then why did you even agree to come here tonight?"

"Because I couldn't help myself," he says wryly. "The most intriguing and exciting girl I've ever met asks me on a date, and I'm supposed to say no?"

The most intriguing and exciting girl. I should be over the moon. And I would be . . . if I didn't know what was coming. My heart contracts painfully. "But you're saying no now, aren't you?"

"I have to."

I had expected this. But his words hit me with a bone-thudding force. How could rejection from a boy I hardly know hurt this much?

His eyes drop. "You and I are from different worlds, Lei. It would be better if we don't see each other again."

"Fine." A jagged ache in my throat makes my voice hoarse. "Don't worry, I've never been one to chase after a boy, and I'm not about to start now."

My body throbs with disappointment, but I can't let him know that. I've got my pride, after all. And joining the protests was never about him anyway, I remind myself.

"But I'm not going to quit the movement just because you told me I should go home and file this moment away as something to tell my future children." My voice grows stronger even though the backs of my eyes burn with tears that I can never let him see. "I'll be demonstrating at Tiananmen Square like before. We can ignore each other if you want, but you're not going to stop me from doing what I believe in."

"I'm not questioning the strength of your belief. I just don't want to see you get hurt." He falls silent, body stiff, like he's holding back a torrent of words. At last, he says, "Lei, please stay away. It's for your own good. And I should walk away from this too. For both our sakes."

My muscles tighten, and I want to scream, but instead, I force myself to smile. I can't let him see the hurt bubbling under the surface. Better for him to think I'm just a vain and heartless flirt. "Don't be so dramatic, Delun! I'm hardly heartbroken."

"Oh." He stands with his arms hanging awkwardly by his sides.

I force myself to sound light and unconcerned. "Like you said, we're from two different worlds."

"I did say that." Delun doesn't sound happy about it. He looks past my shoulder. "Here comes your sister and Yanlin. I'd better go." He hesitates. "I guess it was presumptuous to think someone like you would be seriously interested in me."

"Someone like me." I'm already raw with pain, but I can't seem to help myself. "What's that supposed to mean?"

"Just that I'm a poor student, and you are . . ."

My spine tenses. "I'm what?"

"Gong Zhu." *Princess.* He says it gravely, with no mockery in his voice. "Strong and beautiful. A leader."

I gape at him, my mouth dry with shock. *Oh shit.* If he feels that way about me, maybe he doesn't really want to end this. Then my own damnable words thunder in my head. *I'm hardly heartbroken.*

His mouth twists up sadly. "Goodbye, Gong Zhu." This time, "Gong Zhu" sounds like an endearment.

Nausea spreads through my gut as I watch him walk away. I have the awful feeling that I've just blown my chance with Delun with my pride and thoughtlessness.

What have I done?

Luoyang, Seventh Century

W*hat have I done?*

It was nothing but stupid pride that made Taiping push Wan'er away. But she can fix it. She has to. Standing outside her bamboo-and-rice-paper door, she calls out, "Wan'er! It's me, Lingyue. Please let me in." It's a good thing there aren't servants around to hear her, the imperial princess, using her personal name and imploring a former slave girl to let her into her room.

Wan'er slides open the door. Her face is impassive. "Princess Taiping."

Oh no. Her heart falls to the floor. Wan'er never calls her by her formal title when they're alone. In fact, she makes fun of it. *Princess of Great Peace, my ass,* she likes to say. *You're more like the Princess of Great Mischief.*

Taiping had *definitely* been a princess of mischief tonight. "I'm sorry about the poetry contest," she says as she enters Wan'er's chambers. It was the height of vanity to hold a poetry contest and order the contestants to write an ode to her. But if Taiping is being honest, her true purpose had nothing to do with vanity and everything to do with petty vengeance.

All week, she's had to sit for portrait sessions, sweating in a heavy yellow dress and pretending to play a zither. She's used to uncomfortable clothing. But the zither? That just added insult to injury. Not only did she have to follow Si in the portrait sessions, but she had to be painted with an instrument she can barely play. It's just another reminder that she doesn't have any *real* artistic talent for her mother to be proud of. Her only hope is that Si's blank parchment was as much a useless prop as her zither.

That's why Taiping set up the competition between Si, an untutored Buddhist nun, and Wan'er, the shining literary light of the court. She wanted to humiliate Si, to show her how little she belonged among accomplished ladies of high learning.

Wan'er closes the door. "It's not about the contest and you know it."

Taiping lowers her eyes. "I know." The memories of the contest make her stomach clench. At first, her plan to embarrass Si seemed to go beautifully. Wan'er performed as admirably as she always does. She regularly beats grown men of the court in these poetry competitions, so what chance did Si have? None. And Si's poem seemed to exceed Taiping's wildest dreams for her failure. It was even more childish and devoid of all poetic literary conventions than she had hoped. Understandable triumph filled her as she pronounced Wan'er the victor and gloated over Si's failure.

But it had all gone wrong the moment Wan'er picked up Si's silly, clumsy poem. Wan'er's face froze for a moment, and then she began to laugh in delight. "You've made a mistake, Princess Taiping," she declared. "Si is the true winner." Then Wan'er handed her the poem, and Taiping was so angry that she didn't understand what the upstart girl had done until Wan'er explained it.

Mother had recently made a major decree—a modification in the way certain characters are written. Her enemies whisper that she changed the language to glorify her own importance, but to her face, it's all honeyed praise. Yet, not even the smoothest flatterer at court was as clever as this rustic novice.

Si's poem used all fifteen characters that the empress had changed.

In other words, Si turned a poem that was supposed to be an ode to Taiping into an ode to her *mother*. To her utter annoyance, she couldn't even tell if Si meant to insult her. But that wasn't the worst part. What *really* made her blood turn cold with anger was that this upstart girl was smarter and more interesting than Taiping gave her credit for. Si had certainly gained Wan'er's attention . . .

Wan'er interrupts her painful thoughts. "You just can't stand to be contradicted." She wouldn't have dared to say that in front of anyone else, but she's never been afraid to tell Taiping hard truths when they're alone.

"It's not that," she protests. It's true. She wouldn't have minded being contradicted. But the light of admiration that flooded Wan'er—that was supposed to be just for her. Certainly not a nobody of a girl who somehow managed not only to charm her mother but also her beloved. "I suppose it was clever, what Si did," Taiping admits, "but your poetry is more than clever. You write from deep study of literary craft and heavenly inspiration. Your poem was brilliant. *You're* brilliant."

"Oh?" Wan'er's eyes harden. "And I suppose it was my *brilliance* that made you say what you did? In front of everyone."

Taiping's face flames in mortified recollection. *A former slave girl should not presume to question a princess.* "I shouldn't have said that."

"No, you shouldn't have." There's no give in Wan'er's expression. "You should remember why my mother and I were relegated to palace servants in the first place."

Taiping winces. Wan'er is skirting the thing they never talk about: how the empress accused Wan'er's grandfather, a high court official, of insurrection. And how that charge cost her grandfather and father their lives. Wan'er and her mother, a former court lady, were spared, but they lost their high place in court and were forced to serve as palace slaves. Small wonder Wan'er is angry with her. Shame burrows into Taiping—how could she be so awful as to remind her of what Taiping's family did to hers? "I'm so sorry."

"Sorry?" Scorn drips from her voice. "There's no need to feel sorry for me. I've proven my worth to Empress Wu a million ways and restored my family's standing. And I did it with nothing but my wits. I am the empress's right hand now." Her eyes glitter coldly. "No one, not even you, my princess, will take that power and prestige from me now."

Taiping's breath catches at her beloved's daring. It is dangerous to challenge her mother's imperial authority as directly as Wan'er does now. *Someday, her reckless ambition will get her in serious trouble.* But she pushes away that disquieting thought. "Yes, you've earned your place. By my mother's side . . . and in my heart."

"I love you, Lingyue," she says, and Taiping's heart swells. Then agony flashes across Wan'er's face. "But I can't be with you if I'm afraid of you, afraid of what you will do to your enemies."

She will never be in danger from Taiping. Not now. Not ever. "I'm not my mother," she insists. Rumors of what her mother has done to her enemies could give the most hardened soul nightmares.

Not that Taiping believes the more gruesome of the rumors. Like her mother ordering her enemies walled up until they were half dead, then having their limbs hacked off before throwing their bodies into a pit to drown in wine. That's what her mother supposedly did to the two ladies accused of murdering her infant daughter—Taiping's older sister. She has no doubt her mother put them to death for such a crime, but the barbaric method of execution is nothing but slander.

"Your mother did what she had to do. It's hard for a woman to stay in power, and I don't believe most of the gossip anyway. That's not what I'm talking about." Wan'er takes a deep breath. "I'm talking about the two of us. I need to believe that we're equals and that we want the same thing."

"We do," Taiping says eagerly. She takes Wan'er's hand in hers. "I love you, and I want us to be together."

Wan'er's face brightens like the sun, and Taiping can see why her brother has nicknamed her "Shining Countenance." She runs her thumb across Taiping's palm, making her shiver with desire.

"Good," Wan'er says. "Then tell your mother that you won't marry your cousin."

Disbelief constricts her throat, and she snatches her hand away. "What? You must be joking."

Wan'er says nothing, just looks at her with her unwavering dark eyes, and Taiping realizes that she's serious.

How can she ask her to do such a thing? Yet, Taiping has already come too close to losing her beloved's faith. Now Wan'er is giving her a chance to regain her trust and prove her love, and she'd be a fool not to take it. "Very well. I'll refuse this marriage and every other marriage proposal afterward."

Wan'er's eyes glitter with triumph. "That is all I've ever wanted. For you to choose me." That's not true. She wants power as much as she wants Taiping. But who can blame her? Wan'er climbed to power after seeing half her family executed and enduring the humiliation of palace servitude. Of course she needs power to feel secure.

Taiping smiles as if it is nothing to disobey her mother, the empress who rules China in all but name. As if it isn't dangerous. "I'll break the engagement," she says. "I promise."

CHAPTER TWELVE

Beijing, 1989

Jun is quiet and edgy all through our cab ride back home, but I'm too absorbed in my disappointment with Delun to ask her what's wrong.

Our parents are asleep when we get home, and I head for my room without attempting to debrief our double date with Jun. All I want to do is sink into the soft pillows on my bed and have a good cry.

But Jun follows me into my room. "I need to talk to you, Lei. Come downstairs to Wu Zetian's art gallery with me."

That cuts right through my self-pity. Jun never goes to the art gallery unless our mother takes us there. I take a closer look at her pinched face. "What is it? What's the matter?"

"I'll tell you downstairs."

She isn't denying that something is wrong. My body tenses. Did she and Yanlin have a fight? But why does she want to go to the art gallery to talk about that? This doesn't make sense. Better find out what's going on. I grab the key from my jewelry box and follow her downstairs.

We enter the library and descend the stairs behind the bookcase in silence. Jun waits until we're standing in front of the stone statue of Wu Zetian before speaking. "Yanlin told me who Delun is." She stares straight ahead at the statue without looking at me.

Confusion washes over me. "What do you mean?"

"You told me that Delun is just a regular student protester—one of thousands!" She turns to me, lines of worry etched into her face. "But he's really one of the leaders, isn't he?"

A cold lump forms in my stomach. I don't blame Jun for being upset. I might not have lied to her, but I certainly kept something important from her, and I've never done that before. "I'm sorry I didn't tell you, but it doesn't really matter." With a heavy heart, I'm about to tell her that Delun and I are through, but she doesn't let me.

"How can you say it doesn't matter?" she cries. "Have you forgotten who it was that burned classical art during the Cultural Revolution? Who it was that dragged the owners of that art into the street to be beaten and imprisoned? The Red Guard were leaders of a student movement too!"

"It was over twenty years ago when the Red Guard were at their peak and did their greatest destruction!" I protest. "Anyway, Delun and the others aren't anything like that." Delun might not want anything to do with me, especially after I pretty much told him that he was just a meaningless flirtation. But I'll still defend him with my last breath.

"Yanlin doesn't agree with you."

Surprised, I ask, "Did he say Delun and the student protest movement were like the Red Guard and the Cultural Revolution?" That's not how I read Yanlin.

"No," Jun admits, "but you heard him say that his own father was a victim of the Cultural Revolution. He has good reason to be wary of this movement. And he knows the students behind the protests. He says the leaders are so passionate about their cause that they will let their followers drown in blood before they back down. Yanlin thinks this will all end in tragedy."

"Yanlin's own father was a Red Guard. Our father too," I remind Jun. "Not all the Red Guard were bloodthirsty fanatics."

"Then make Delun prove it," she says immediately. "Like our father did when he gave up the Red Guard for Ma. Make him leave the protests to prove he's not a fanatic!"

I couldn't do that even if I wanted to. And I definitely don't want to. My sister needs to understand how wrong she is. "This is a different time! Not a single protester I've met has said anything about looting and burning art or beating up and imprisoning the rich."

"It's not a matter of being rich and owning one or two classical paintings!" She throws her arms out. "Look around you, Lei. Look at what we're hiding! Our ancestor's dynasty."

Despite myself, I look around at the glowing colors of landscape paintings, the cases of glass filled with carved jade and painted vases, and the scrolls of poetry. And then there's the stone statue of Wu Zetian, the template for her Grand Vairocana Buddha statue in the Longmen Grottoes. It was her seventeen-meter-tall answer to the Confucian principle that women could not rule. My ancestor drew upon her Buddhist faith to cement her divine right to rule. Now, her serene Buddha's face seems to reproach me. By joining the protests, I am fighting against my own inheritance. Who I am. Not just the keeper of Wu Zetian's legacy. I *am* her legacy.

Jun's voice rises. "The Communist Party hated the old imperial power so much that they started the Cultural Revolution to destroy whatever was left of the dynasties. And that's just *art*. What do you think they will do to *us*, the last direct descendants of Wu Zetian's dynasty?"

Pain hits me in the gut. If there's anything the Communist Party and the student protesters have in common, it's their united hatred of our country's imperialist history. And the last remnants of China's most despised monarch, a woman who dared to seize the imperial throne, lies in our basement and runs in our veins. For as long as I can remember, my goal has been to show all this art in museums and share our history with the world. But Jun is right. "We've hidden it for this long," I say, my heart heavy. "We can keep on hiding it."

Jun's face softens with something that looks like pity. "Delun seems like a nice guy, but have you considered how dangerous it would be for you to get close to a revolutionary leader committed to bringing down imperialism?"

"That won't be a problem." I'm fighting to keep my voice from shattering. "He's not interested in me." And even if he *had* been interested, I let my pride destroy any chance I had with him.

Her jaw drops, but she recovers quickly. "Good."

Hurt rises in me. "Gee, thanks for your sympathy."

She flushes. "I just meant that it's good that you won't be going to the protests anymore. It's better this way."

I'm seriously getting tired of people telling me what's best for me like I'm some child careening into disaster. First Delun, and now my twin sister. "I'm not protesting because I have a crush on some guy, Jun! I'm protesting because I believe in this fight!"

"But do your comrades know who you are?" She comes closer to me. "You are a direct descendant of royalty. Heiress to priceless outlawed art. What will those students do if they find out that *you* are everything they're protesting against?"

My bones turn to ice. *They will feel betrayed.* It already feels hypocritical enough to be a rich girl protesting the very class structure that fills my closets with trendy clothes and allows me to live in a mansion. But a girl with imperial blood? Already, I can see the hurt and shock on my friends' faces. "They won't find out."

"Does this mean you'll stop going to protests?"

"I'd do almost anything for you, Jun." I take a deep breath. "But not this. A change is coming, and I need to be a part of it. I have to fight for a better world—for all of us. It's not fair that we live a life of ease and luxury when others work themselves to the bone just to survive." I think of Guang again, who has to sleep in his taxi during long shifts.

She contemplates me in silence, and I fidget under her gimlet stare. At last she says, "You're the one that Ma made the guardian of Wu Zetian's art. Will you betray her trust by putting us in danger? Because that's what you're doing." *Low blow, Jun.* Then she goes in for the kill. "And what do you think Ba will do if he finds out about your protesting? If he finds out about Delun?"

My breath whooshes out of me as if she'd punched me in the gut. Ma has hinted that Ba used his standing as a Red Guard more than once to protect her and her secrets during the Cultural Revolution. Ba himself has said that this powder keg in our basement is what drove him to higher and higher echelons of the Communist Party. There's nothing he wouldn't do to protect his family. Nothing to stop him from bringing down all his amassed power on anyone who threatened us. My heart stops. He would crush Delun. "You wouldn't dare tell Ba."

"Mother didn't make me the guardian of our legacy," she says coldly, "but that doesn't mean I won't do what I must to protect our secret."

I stalk away from her, my vision a red haze. Jun lets me go without a word. She'll let me stew in my rage and hope I come around to her way of thinking. *Keep dreaming, sister.* I have no intention of giving up the protests. And I don't really believe that she'll rat me out to our parents, especially Ba. But the fact that she made that threat makes my blood boil.

By habit, I end up in front of the wall containing the three poems I've painstakingly copied. As an excuse to keep my eyes averted from Jun, I start to read the poem I'm sure was written by Shangguan Wan'er as an ode to Princess Taiping. But despite its flawless mastery of form, it fails to keep my attention. My emotions churn in my chest, and even the last poem with its prophetic despair can't hold my interest.

Strangely, the other ode to Princess Taiping, with its odd use of fifteen crucial characters, *does* pull at me. Because it reminds me of my legacy. Those fifteen characters are written in a way that no one ever sees today. In fact, those forms existed at only one time in history: during Wu Zetian's reign, including the period that she renamed the Wu Zhou dynasty.

But she did more than reshape a dynasty. She changed the way certain characters were written and ordered her subjects to use these new forms. Fifteen of them. The sun and moon and heavens for the empress's personal name of Zhao, which means "to shine." A circle as the character for a star. Some might think Empress Wu was motivated to make the changes out of vanity, but I side with the scholars who argue that Empress Wu was making our language more female-centric. Unfortunately, it was a short-lived change. After Wu's death, those characters reverted to their original forms.

Now the characters exist only in this poem.

All because an unknown poet used all fifteen of Wu's characters in an ode to Princess Taiping. But it's more than an ode to the princess. It pays homage to the empress, a woman powerful enough to change language itself.

Can I really jeopardize the most lasting evidence of my ancestress's power? This room is not just an art gallery. It is where we keep the brilliant creations of women who dared to change their world. And I am just one in a long line of women who have guarded this legacy as dynasties have fallen and new worlds have formed. It doesn't matter what I think I'm fighting for with the student movement. My greatest calling is this. Keeper of Wu Zetian's history.

Nothing is more important.

I turn back to Jun. "I'll quit the protests," I say. "I promise."

CHAPTER THIRTEEN

I squirm at my desk as Teacher Hong drones on and on about some dates in history that she says might be on the Gaokao. Automatically, I take notes, but my focus is shot.

It's been five days since I made my promise to Jun.

And I'm already weakening. Even though Delun isn't the reason I joined the movement, I can't stop thinking of him. Did he think that I joined because of him? *Of course he does.* And now that I've stopped going to the protests, it will just confirm his assumption that my commitment to the cause wasn't that deep. *Great. That's just great.*

It doesn't help that my life is filled with the same meaningless nothing as before. Ma announced this morning that she's dragging Jun and me to a charity dinner tomorrow night. Well, dragging *me* anyway. Jun actually enjoys these events—she'll happily follow in my mother's footsteps as a high-society matron someday. I hope Yanlin knows what he's in for.

Things between Jun and me are not back to normal. There's a new tension that has never been there before, even though we're being perfectly nice to each other. Too nice. It's like we're afraid of what will burst out if we crack this unnaturally polite facade.

My friend Chunhua taps me on the shoulder, interrupting my thoughts, and passes me a note. Jun carefully ignores this illicit activity. Normally, she'd be casting me warning glares. Not that Teacher Hong is going to come down on us today for passing notes. The whole class is on edge and whispering about what is happening.

This morning, our father told Jun and me to stay away from Tiananmen Square, and I'm sure my classmates got similar warnings from their parents. Today is May 4, the anniversary of the 1919 anti-imperialist student-led protests, which also took place in Tiananmen Square. That's why the students have promised a huge demonstration today.

I'd give anything to be there. Anything except breaking my promise to Jun and turning my back on my responsibilities as guardian of Wu Zetian's art. I keep repeating to myself the two reasons I shouldn't run off to Tiananmen Square after school: *You promised Jun. You are the guardian of Wu Zetian's art.*

And then I read the note that Chunhua, whose father is a high-ranking Communist Party official like ours, gave me. *I heard that the university students have decided to end the walkout and return to their classes tomorrow.*

I almost fall out of my chair in shock. *What?! So that's it?* It will be over soon, and I'll have missed my chance to be a part of the greatest protest movement of my lifetime. And more important, how can the students give up without achieving the change they fought for?

Restless energy fills my body, and I feel Jun's gaze on me as I furiously scribble a note to Chunhua to find out more. But it's no use. My friend doesn't have any more information.

By the time school is over, I'm so antsy to join today's demonstration at Tiananmen Square that I want to crawl out of my skin. I'm definitely not looking forward to three hours of Gaokao study with Jun and our friends. But Jun will know exactly what I'm up to if I announce that I'm ditching our study session again—the way I did all last week to go to the protests.

Bright sunlight hits my face as we exit Beijing No. 4 High School, more commonly known as Sizhong. Our prestigious school has the distinction of being located in the Imperial City section of old Beijing, and I usually love the campus, with its mix of modern and imperial architecture, but with students protesting at Tiananmen

Square for equal access to education, my high school feels like just another status symbol setting me apart from Delun, Yawen, Rong, and the others.

As Jun and I reach the edge of campus, she turns to me and the rest of our friends. "Bye, everyone. Have a good study session."

Surprise overtakes me. "Aren't you coming with us?"

"Today is Thursday," she says, as if this explains everything. And actually, it does. Thursdays are the days Jun meets Yanlin for tutoring sessions. Fate has handed me a gift.

"Right. Have a good session," I say, careful not to sound too cheery. The last thing I need is to raise Jun's suspicions with a break in our coolness toward each other.

As the others say goodbye to Jun, my body practically vibrates with excitement. I can sneak off to Tiananmen Square one last time, and she'll never know.

"Ready to go?" Chunhua asks. We're meeting at her house today.

Ai and Chen both say that they're ready, but I don't respond. My stomach is churning as I wrestle with temptation and caution. My friends are already pissed at me for missing all of last week. They're not going to be happy with my ditching them again.

Jun climbs into the back seat of a taxi, and all the ways this can go horribly wrong race through my head. But the taxi hasn't even disappeared into the distance before I've made up my mind. This is my last chance to find out what's happening with the movement before it's all over.

I turn to my friends. "Sorry, I'm not going to be able to make it to our study session today."

When I get to Tiananmen Square, I'm surprised by how many people are here. And there are some who don't look like college students. Older people. Workers. *The people's movement in truth.* My heart expands with pride to be part of this. Who cares if I'm shaking with nerves to see Delun again? This is more than me. I push my way through the crowd, shouts ringing in my ears and the heat of many bodies making me feel light-headed. At last I reach the Monument to the People's Heroes, hoping (and dreading) to find Delun, Yawen, and Rong in their usual place.

Yawen and I spot each other at the same time, and an unexpected jolt of happiness hits me. I didn't know how much I had missed her until this moment. "Hey, stranger!" I call out, a big grin on my face.

With a shriek, she shoves her way through grumbling protesters and grabs me in a bear hug. "Lei! I wondered what had happened to you!"

"I was busy with school," I mumble, embarrassed that I had stayed away so long.

"That's right. I always forget you're still in high school," Rong says without a trace of the condescension he had toward me when we first met. "It's good to see you again."

"You too, Rong!" And I mean it. Although I haven't known Yawen and Rong long, they've somehow become my friends.

My stomach clenching in anticipation, I glance past Yawen and Rong, but I still don't see Delun.

"Hello, Lei." The familiar voice hits me with the force of a tsunami.

Heart slamming into my ribs, I do a slow spin until I come face-to-face with a pair of serious eyes that do odd things to my breath. *Delun.* "Hello yourself." I wince at how flat I sound.

The smile starting to form on his face fades away at my less-than-warm greeting. Awkwardly, he says, "I should have known you'd ignore my advice to stay away from the protests."

"But why would you tell her to stay away?" Rong asks in bewilderment.

Yawen's eyes dart between us. "Come on, Rong," she says, tugging at his sleeve. "Let's leave them to talk on their own." The two of them disappear into the crowd as if swallowed.

No! Don't go! My palms go hot and slippery with sweat. The last thing I want is to be left alone with Delun. Well, not exactly alone, since we're surrounded by tens of thousands of people. At least the protesters are loud, and their cheers and chants allow us the chance to talk without being overheard. Not that anyone cares about our drama.

Delun speaks first. "What's the real reason you stopped coming, Lei?"

I don't know how to respond. He won't buy my half-assed excuse of being busy with school. "It doesn't have anything to do with what *you* said." *Ouch.* Can I be any more defensive? But anything is better than letting him know how much he hurt me.

"I said a lot of things," he says wryly.

He did say a lot of things—and not all of it was bad. *Intriguing. Brilliant. Strong and beautiful. Gong Zhu.* I almost tell him a few not-so-bad things too. *Nope. Don't you dare flirt with him, Lei.* "I don't have to answer your questions."

A shadow passes over his face, and my heart twists. How did we come to this? My reunion with Delun is a thousand times worse than I could have imagined.

"Of course you don't," he says, painfully polite.

The silence between us lengthens uncomfortably, and I feel like I'm being eaten up from the inside. "I'm going to find Yawen and Rong," I say, desperate to escape. "I'm sure you have a speech to prepare for or something."

"I already gave my speech."

I'm sorry I missed it. But I don't say it aloud. When was the last time I was this tongue-tied around a boy? Never. At least Delun is acting as stilted and unnatural as I am. I'd hate to be the only one to be feeling this. Whatever *this* is.

"Lei," he says, and then stops. He swallows visibly and tries again. "Tomorrow the student walkout will be over."

My stomach drops. After today, I won't see Delun again. Everything changes now. Sweaty bodies crowd me, but I don't mind. I'd stay here forever if I could. But I can't. This movement will be over soon, and I'll have lost my chance to be a part of it. Suddenly, I wish I hadn't stayed away for a week because of Jun's fear. "I know. You're all going back to classes tomorrow." Why is he telling me this? Just to twist the knife in my heart harder?

"But we'll continue to fight for reform," he says in a rush. "There's a student union meeting Saturday night to discuss what we should do next."

My brows lift. "You've formed a student union?"

Student unions are illegal. According to Ba, they will only feed the fears of Communist Party officials, but even that sobering thought doesn't keep my body from flaring into hope. Maybe I can still play a meaningful part in this movement after all. And maybe Delun doesn't want our time together to end either.

"Are you asking me if I want to come?" Painful hope charges through my body.

"A student union is still against the law, but it won't be as dangerous as protesting out here." He looks around the square, where student protesters in armbands are keeping watch for military intervention.

I should respond with seriousness and discuss what this new stage in the movement might mean. But giddy from the possibility that all might not be lost, I sidle up to him and murmur, "You sure know how to ask a girl out." *Dammit, Lei!* No. Flirting.

He flushes bright red. "I . . . um . . ." he stammers.

I have to get it through my thick skull that he doesn't think of me that way. "Relax, Delun." I step away, putting some distance between us. "I know it's not a date." Technically, a student union meeting isn't a protest either, so I can keep my promise to Jun. Except I've already broken it by being here. "I should get going."

He doesn't comment on the fact that I just got here, or that I haven't actually replied to his invitation to go to the student union meeting on Saturday.

But as I turn to leave, he says softly, "It's good to see you again, Lei."

CHAPTER FOURTEEN

Everyone but me is in a good mood tonight.

Ba is actually humming as Ma adjusts his tie. It's Friday night, the day after the massive May 4 demonstration, and the student protesters have largely returned to their classes. Ba and his comrades are breathing a sigh of relief. They wouldn't be so complacent if they knew about the formation of the student unions. But all they're worried about now is making sure that Mikhail Gorbachev's state visit, in just over a week, goes off without a hitch. Gorbachev isn't just the leader of the Soviet Union. He's the leader of a sister communist country, and Ba and the rest of the Politburo were in a panic when it looked like the student protests might disrupt his visit.

Ma is happy because tonight's charity dinner, with the proceeds benefiting cancer research, is her baby. She's worked hard for months to organize this, and tonight she gets to reap the fruits of her labor with her family by her side.

Jun has been glowing since her "tutoring session" with Yanlin yesterday. Plus, she likes going to charity events with Ma. She's so content with her world that she's starting to forget this weird polite distance we're maintaining.

"You're able to pull off the most outrageous looks," Jun says wistfully as I descend the last few steps of the stairs to join my family in the living room.

My spirits lift to hear genuine admiration in her voice. "Thanks!" I preen in my minidress with its fitted black velvet bodice and polka-dotted hot-pink satin skirt. "Obviously, you're my twin, so you could pull this off if you wanted, but you look gorgeous as you are."

She smooths down the skirt of her lacy baby-blue dress and beams. For a moment, it feels like things are back to normal between us.

Ma shakes her head when she sees what I'm wearing, but she just says, "Now that we're all here, let's get going." Apparently, she's decided getting into an argument with me about my attire isn't worth the risk of being late.

Ba smiles at us both. "I'll have to beat off your suitors with the two of you looking so beautiful."

I manage not to wince visibly. Because Ba might *literally* beat off Delun and Yanlin. Not that Delun is my suitor. Far from it.

My parents have hired a limo tonight, so we're all in the comfortable back seat. On the way to the banquet room at Beijing Hotel, Ma and Jun gossip about the other ladies of Ma's charity organization while Ba talks politics with me. He's been so busy lately that we've fallen out of this habit. Honestly, it's not a habit I'm ready to pick up again. How am I supposed to discuss the student movement like it's nothing but a topic for political debate?

"Despite General Secretary Zhao's inexplicable softness in dealing with the protesters, this mess is finally over," Ba says confidently.

At the mention of the protesters, Jun darts a concerned look in my direction, but she doesn't need to worry. It's not like I'm going to blurt out that I went to the demonstrations. And I'm certainly not going to tell Ba that the students are holding a meeting tomorrow night to plan next steps. In fact, I still have to figure out a way to get to that meeting.

Ba is looking at me expectantly, and I rouse myself to reply. "You don't really believe what Premier Li says, do you? That the students are trying to overthrow the government?" The premier is technically second in power to Zhao Ziyang, the general secretary, but Li's opinion about the protests seems to be the prevailing one at the moment. And of course neither of the men is the *real* leader of the country. That would be Deng Xiaoping. He might not have an official title anymore, but everyone knows he's the unofficial head of state and holds all the power.

Ma says to Jun, "I hope the caterers remember that I put lobster on the menu. Mrs. Xu was so snide about there being no lobster at the last dinner!"

"You checked the menu twice. I'm sure it's fine," Jun answers calmly, but I have the feeling that she's still paying anxious attention to Ba and me.

"It doesn't matter what I believe," Ba says. "It only matters what Deng Xiaoping believes, and Li has convinced Deng that the protests will lead to chaos and violence if they're not nipped in the bud."

A chill steals over me. "I read the editorial in the *People's Daily* last week," I manage to say. It was basically a long, rambling conspiracy theory about the demonstrations being a plot to overthrow the socialist government in favor of a capitalist one. At the time, I had dismissed it as utter nonsense, but now anxiety congeals in my gut as I wonder what deep fears were behind that editorial.

Ba gives me an approving nod. "You're quick on the uptake. That editorial was based on what Deng said in a Politburo meeting." He looks off in the distance, an absent smile on his face. "I have to hand it to Li. It was smart of him to wait until Zhao was on a state visit to North Korea before calling that meeting. It gave Li free rein to convince Deng of the true danger of those young counterrevolutionaries."

Delun's words come back to me. *The party is afraid that our student movement is the start of a second Cultural Revolution, and it will do anything to stop us.*

"And what was your role at that meeting, Ba?" There's an edge in my voice that I can't hide. "Were you with Li, stoking Deng's fears to pit him against the student protesters?"

I have not only Ba's full attention but Jun's and Ma's as well. My twin is wringing her hands, no doubt remembering that *she* was the one who covered for me last week when I was sneaking off to Tiananmen Square.

Ma's thoughts are harder to read. She's peering at me intently with her mouth pressed tight.

Coldly, Ba says, "When you go to Beijing University next year, Lei, I hope you will be smart enough to stay away from the protesters."

Sorry, Ba, that ship has sailed.

I'm saved from replying when the limo pulls up to the hotel. The chauffeur opens our door for us, and we all file out, silent and tense in our fancy clothes.

Speaking for myself, I'm definitely *not* ready to party for charity.

Once inside the hotel's lavish banquet room, Ma and Jun are swept off by some ladies in Ma's social circle, and Ba goes off to find his cronies in the Politburo. Normally, Ba invites me to join these conversations, but not tonight. Clearly, my reproof in the limo still rankles.

I'm relieved to be left alone until I realize that I don't know what to do at these events without Ba. The tables are all set with white tablecloths and red runners, but no one is sitting at them yet. This is the predinner mingling portion of the event, except there's no one for me to mingle with.

I could join Ma and Jun. But standing awkwardly by myself is better than wading into the dangerous conversational waters with society matron gossips.

Then I see a familiar figure standing by the bar—and gazing at Jun with naked longing.

"Still mooning over my sister?" I say as I approach Qiang.

"Always," he replies without looking away from Jun.

I should remind him about Yanlin and tell him that it's a lost cause, but pity stirs in my heart. After all, I know what it's like to want someone who doesn't want me back. "You should go talk to her."

"My mother is over there."

I peer over at Mrs. Chua, who's in Ma's charity circles. She's a sweet-faced woman, wearing a pleated floral lace dress, but I'm not fooled by her innocent appearance. Like all Ma's friends, she has the shrewdness of a fox. "Are you going to let a little thing like your mother stop you?" I tease.

"I'd go over and talk to Jun if I thought it would do any good." He tears his gaze from her at last. "Would it do any good?"

"Sorry, Qiang," I say soberly. "I'm afraid there's nothing you can do."

"I don't suppose fake dating you would make Jun jealous enough to take notice," he says, making a feeble attempt at a joke.

I laugh and am about to tell him that my sympathy goes only so far—and that's when inspiration hits me. My mouth curves up in a slow smile. "A date. That's not a bad idea." He grins back, certain I'm joking, but I'm dead serious. "Tomorrow night," I say. That's when the student meeting is happening.

"Wait, what?" A startled expression comes onto Qiang's face.

"You don't need to be there," I explain, "but I have somewhere I need to be tomorrow."

"And you think that if I pretend to be with you, it might make Jun jealous?"

My conscience won't let me lie. "Probably not," I admit.

Qiang fixes me with a piercing look. "You went and fell for some guy, didn't you? And for whatever reason, your parents don't approve."

If only it were that simple. But how do I explain how the student movement has changed me? I've gone from happily living my privileged existence to fighting for the destruction of its very foundation. It's not just Delun whom my parents wouldn't approve of. It's this new person I've become. Squirming, I mutter, "It's complicated."

"Right." Skepticism laces his voice. My hopes plummet, but then he says, "Ah, what the hell? OK, I'll be your alibi. You can buy me a drink to seal the deal."

“It’s an open bar,” I reply with a smile.

“In that case, I’ll get the drinks,” he says promptly.

I laugh. It’s too bad that neither Jun nor I is into Qiang. The Sung twins clearly have inconvenient taste in men.

New arrivals are making heads turn, and my stomach goes icy with shock when I see who’s getting all the attention. *Speak of the devil.* Mrs. Liu has just entered the banquet room . . . with her son in tow. Yanlin.

CHAPTER FIFTEEN

It's no wonder Mrs. Liu and Yanlin have caught everyone's attention. They're the only ones who don't belong to this elite circle of Communist Party officials and their high-society wives. But they certainly *look* like they belong. Yanlin is dapper in a perfectly fitted suit, and his mother is wearing an elegant floor-length black gown. At another time, I'd be hounding them for their fashion hook-up. But now is not that time. My gaze flies to Jun. Predictably, she's turning as pale as milk.

"What's *he* doing here?" Qiang mutters.

Good question. But the better question is what his *mother* is doing here. It must have been a strain on her income to afford the price for this charity dinner. Unless she's covering the dinner for the *Beijing Mirror*. Yes, that's it. Surely, she didn't make all this effort just to get to Ma.

Even as I think this, Mrs. Liu is heading in Ma's direction with a determined gleam in her eyes. Yanlin looks unhappy as he follows her.

"Excuse me," I say distractedly to Qiang, and make a beeline to Ma and Jun.

I reach them a bare moment before Mrs. Liu and Yanlin do. Jun grips my hand, and suddenly, the lingering tension between us is gone. Right now, the only thing that matters is standing by my sister's side and supporting her.

The ladies surrounding Ma have stopped chattering, their faces avid with curiosity as they watch Mrs. Liu approach. In contrast, Ma's face is grim.

"Mei," Mrs. Liu says as soon as she reaches my mother.

I'm shocked to hear her use Ma's personal name.

Ma doesn't seem fazed by Mrs. Liu's familiarity and responds in kind. "Yuan." Politely, she turns to Yanlin. "And this must be your son?"

"Yes." Her voice is steely. "I thought my son should meet the family who betrayed his father."

Whoa. This woman is seriously demented.

"*Ma,*" Yanlin says, clearly scandalized. "That's *not* why I came."

Bending down, he says something in his mother's ear too low for me to hear. But my guess is that it's some variation on *I came to stop you from causing a scene in front of the girl I'm secretly dating.* Except that he probably left out the part about Jun. Not that their relationship will be a secret for long, especially if he and Jun keep sneaking not-so-subtle glances at each other.

Yanlin straightens and says firmly, "I *thought* we were here to make peace with the Sung family." His eyes go to Jun again, but this time he doesn't look away.

His mother snorts. "Not a chance."

Yanlin opens his mouth, but Jun is shaking her head at him. Again, not subtle. His mouth shuts, and his jaw tightens. It couldn't be clearer that he wants to proclaim his love for her in front of everyone, and equally clear that Jun doesn't want him to do it. Still, it's good to know my sister's boyfriend is willing to stand up for her.

Mrs. Liu is so focused on Ma right now that she might not notice what's going on underneath her nose, but Ma spares a glance at Jun before returning her attention to Mrs. Liu. "Yuan, this is a charity dinner," she says repressively. "Such wild talk is not fitting here."

Mrs. Liu's eyes glitter with malice. "I have another reason for being here."

"I hope it is to enjoy the food," Ma says calmly. "The lobster is delicious."

My mother's cool poise is impressive. Me? I'm more the scratch-her-eyes-out type. Jun, who knows me well, tightens her grip on my hand.

"Girls," Ma says to us, "we should go to our table now."

Mrs. Liu's hand shoots out and grabs my mother's arm. "Don't you dare walk away from me!"

Anger rises in me, hot as bubbling lava. The only thing stopping me from yelling at Yanlin's mother is the knowledge that Ma would kill me for speaking in such a way to my elder.

Ma just stares icily at her until she removes the offending hand.

With a visible effort, Mrs. Liu pulls herself together. "I came here tonight to warn you." She steps closer to Ma and lowers her voice. "I know who you are, Mei. I know what you're hiding."

Shock roots me in place, and Jun's fingers in mine are ice cold. *No.* She can't possibly know that we're descended from Wu Zetian or what we've inherited from her. She must mean something else. She *has* to mean something else.

"What did you say?" Ma's voice is shaking, all her calm gone.

"You heard me." Triumph lights up her face as she looks around at the listening ladies, their perfectly lipsticked lips hanging open like they're brightly colored fish waiting to gulp down her every word. "And I have proof too."

"Proof?" my father says coldly. He's come up on us so silently that no one noticed him before.

Yanlin goes very still, and a fleeting look of terror crosses his mother's face.

Formless dread writhes in my stomach as I think back to what Mrs. Liu said. *I thought my son should meet the family who betrayed his father.* And then there's what Yanlin said at our ill-fated dinner. *I know your father was a Red Guard. Our fathers knew each other during the Cultural Revolution. They were best friends.* It all leads to one very awful conclusion: that my father refused to help Yanlin's father when he was beaten and imprisoned by the Red Guard. But why wouldn't Ba come to his friend's aid? It makes no sense.

Ba doesn't do much to allay my fears. "Think very carefully, Liu Yuan, before you threaten my family again. And if I were you, I would watch what I write for the *Beijing Mirror* in the future. The press has had too much license to print their lies, and it's time the government took a firmer hand in this." His voice is taut with suppressed menace. "You know what I will do to protect those I love."

My heart thuds against my chest. I don't recognize this fierce stranger threatening Mrs. Liu, the *Beijing Mirror*, and the freedom of the press in general. It's becoming harder and harder to see him as the father who has encouraged me all my life to think for myself, and frighteningly easy to see him as the shadowy authoritarian figure that the student dissidents are fighting.

"That will do, Shen." Ma takes Ba's arm. "It's time we were seated." Uncharacteristic anger threads through her voice as she addresses her gawking friends. "Well? What are you waiting for? Go on and find your seats!"

"Come on," Yanlin says to his mother. "Let's go." His eyes slide to my sister, and he takes a step toward her.

But Jun sweeps past him without a word, still holding my hand and dragging me after her. My sister is leaving a trail of broken hearts in her wake tonight. First Qiang and now Yanlin.

As we go to our seats, my father says in a low voice to our mother, "I *could* take care of this, you know."

"No, Shen," Ma says. Then so quietly that I almost miss it, she adds, "Not again."

It's late when we get home, but that doesn't stop me from following Jun to her room. Shutting the door firmly, I ask, "What's going on, Jun?"

She goes to her bed and hugs a pink pillow to her chest. "I should break up with Yanlin."

I join her on the bed, take the pillow from her, and hug her tight. She snuggles up to me, and my neck grows wet from her tears. I kiss the top of her head. "Do you love him?"

"What a thing to ask! Of course I love him, but it's no use," she says, sniffling. "His horrible mother is making threats to Ma and spreading nasty rumors about Ba. How can I stay with him?"

Are we so sure that those rumors about Ba aren't true? But I keep my unsettling suspicions about our father to myself. "If you love Yanlin," I say stoutly, "then you shouldn't break up with him."

She takes her head from my shoulder and looks at me like a lost child seeking reassurance. "What if his mother knows we have Wu Zetian's art? Or that we're descended from her royal bloodline? Or that while Ba was rising in the party, we had all this forbidden art in our house? If she knew any of that, she could destroy us!"

I understand Jun's fears. It would be a disaster if Mrs. Liu found out that Ba had betrayed the ideals of the Communist Party and the Cultural Revolution by protecting Ma instead of arresting her and burning her contraband art. His entire career as a party official would be toppled by this revelation, and who knows what would happen to us without Ba's Politburo protection?

But I've had time to think about it, and I'm convinced that Mrs. Liu is bluffing. "How would she know about the art we're hiding?" And the less said about my *other* fear, the better—that our father had abandoned his former best friend to torture and imprisonment. Logically, I know that the Red Guard had done those things. But I just can't believe my father was capable of such unspeakable betrayal. "Think about her threat, Jun. It was pretty vague. She was just fishing for something to spook Ma."

"Do you really think so?" she asks eagerly. Then her face clouds over. "But why does she hate our mother so much?"

"Our parents and Yanlin's parents clearly all knew each other when they were young," I say carefully. "Maybe Mrs. Liu is jealous because Ma and Ba are better off than she and her husband are." I do believe this, but I'm also starting to believe there's more. My stomach turns. Better not say anything to Jun. The last thing I want is to infect her with my suspicions.

Jun thinks this over in silence, but at last she shakes her head. "It doesn't matter. It's too dangerous to get close to Yanlin when his mother is out to destroy our family. I can't risk her finding out about Wu Zetian's art."

I reach out to brush away a tear still clinging to her cheek. "Jun," I say softly, "don't give up on Yanlin because of your fears."

And suddenly, I realize I don't just mean my sister. I wish someone had said that to me about Delun. Specifically, I wish *Jun* had said that to me. But instead, she had told me to give up on both Delun and my commitment to the protest movement.

Unaware of the swelling resentment in my chest, Jun smiles at me tremulously. "Thank you, Lei. You always know what to do." She doesn't seem to notice that my hand is limp when she grasps it. "I won't break up with Yanlin. Like you said, there's no need."

I smile back at her, cheeks straining with the effort. "By the way, you'll never guess who I'm going on a date with tomorrow."

She seems a bit surprised at the sudden change in subject but recovers quickly. "Who?"

There's nothing but innocent curiosity in her voice, and I should feel guilty about lying to her. But I don't. In fact, there's an unfamiliar bitterness spreading through my heart. *She should have supported me with Delun.* "Qiang."

Her eyes widen. "Really?" she chokes out, and petty delight sneaks through me. It's obvious she's struggling to tell me that Qiang has been hopelessly in love with her for years. As if I didn't know.

In the next moment, shame stings me. What am I doing? This is my sweet big sister who wants nothing but the best for me. I feel bad about misleading her, but she's never been into Qiang, and besides, she has Yanlin now. But lingering guilt makes me say, "I know he used to have a crush on you. Are you OK with this? We're not serious or anything."

Relief lightens her face. "Oh, good. Of course I'm OK with this." As if in afterthought, she says, "It's too bad you're not serious about Qiang. You'd make a good couple."

"That's not in the cards," I say. "I'm just looking forward to an interesting night tomorrow." And I am—but not in the way I've led Jun to believe.

CHAPTER SIXTEEN

A *hunger strike?* Surely I didn't hear that young man at the other end of the long table correctly. "He can't be serious," I whisper to Delun.

"I'm afraid he is," Delun says grimly. He's sitting next to me in the common room of one of the dorms, where for the past two hours a dozen or so students have been discussing what they can do to keep the momentum of the protests going.

"If the leaders call for a hunger strike, I'm in," Rong says stoutly.

"Oh, you're all hot air," Yawen says, but her eyes are worried.

The man who suggested the hunger strike pins her with a hard look. "Anyone who's not willing to make sacrifices for the cause shouldn't be here."

Yawen flushes, and anger on her behalf sweeps through me. Rong is glaring at the man, but none of us seems to know how to respond.

"Bo," Delun says as calmly as usual, "we must not turn against each other. No one should be shamed into participating in a hunger strike. And we haven't even decided on a hunger strike yet. We have to consider the possible backlash." This is the kind of thing Delun has been doing for the past two hours: deftly defusing tension and injecting reason. No wonder I'm smitten.

"General Secretary Zhao is on our side," Bo says. "He'll succeed in convincing the Politburo to listen to our demands!"

I should say something, *but* my hands are sweaty with nerves. After all, I'm just a high school student in a roomful of college and graduate students. But I also have information they need to know.

"Zhao isn't the one calling the shots," I say, and all eyes swivel to me. My heart pounds, but I force myself to continue. "The Politburo met last week when Zhao was out of the country. At that meeting, Premier Li convinced Deng to come out against the students."

"How do *you* know all that?" Bo's voice is filled with contempt.

Suddenly, I feel self-conscious in my belted royal-blue dress. I would have worn something less conspicuous if I hadn't been pretending to my family that I was on a date with Qiang.

"Lei has given us useful information, and we'd be stupid to ignore it, Bo," Delun says. For once, there's an edge to his voice.

His support makes me all warm and giddy. And it gives me the strength to speak up. Staring down Bo, I say, "Delun is right to be afraid of a backlash. The hunger strike will only confirm Deng's worst fears. He's afraid that the students are fanatics. It's *his* words that were in that *People's Daily* editorial last week."

I half expect Bo to ask how I know *that*. But whatever he was about to say gets lost in the explosive reaction to my news.

"I suspected it all along!" a student says. "Wasn't I telling you that the other day?"

"That devious Li!"

"What should we do then? Gorbachev's visit is only a week and a half away! We will have the world's eyes on China. This is the time to act!"

The debates rage around me, but I'm not paying full attention. I'm looking at Delun, who is pale and withdrawn. *What is he thinking?*

And then my stomach lets out a loud rumble. My face flames up. *Great.* Of course my empty stomach would make itself known in the middle of a discussion about a hunger strike.

Delun seems to come out of his abstracted thoughts and raises an eyebrow at me.

"I didn't eat much," I say sheepishly. No need to explain that I couldn't eat dinner because my family thought Qiang was taking me out for a meal.

Delun's mouth quirks up in a smile, but instead of responding, he stands and addresses the group. "We've been talking for hours, and nothing will be gained from making a decision when we're all tired and on edge. Let's get some rest and meet again tomorrow."

Bleary faces look back at him, and everyone murmurs agreement. Even Bo.

"Come on," he whispers to me as we all stand and leave the room. "I still owe you a meal."

Surprise fills me, but I'm more than happy to go with him. Yawen and Rong look at us curiously as we break away from them, and Delun calls out, "We're going to get something to eat." I expect him to invite them along, but he doesn't.

They wave at us, and Yawen smiles knowingly. *Sorry, my friend, but there's nothing going on between Delun and me.* Unfortunately.

"Where are we going?" I ask. "The campus cafeteria?"

"I think I can do better than that."

Daringly, I ask, "I don't suppose you're taking me to Maxim's?"

He laughs as we walk past the pagodas and statues on campus. "Not even close."

Thankfully, we can joke about that disastrous date. But I'm not foolish enough to believe that all our tension is suddenly gone. And he's definitely not taking me on another date now. *He just didn't want my unnaturally loud stomach to interrupt the meeting again,* I tell myself firmly.

"Where are we going then? KFC?" It's probably where I should have taken Delun instead of Maxim's. But again, this isn't a date.

"It's a surprise," he says mysteriously.

Oh. That does sound a *little* datelike. My stupid heart skips a beat.

Delun leads me to a bus stop and bows with a flourish. "Your carriage, Gong Zhu." He knows I've probably never been on a bus in my entire life, but there's not a hint of self-consciousness in the way he presents our means of transportation.

I can't help myself. A laugh of sheer delight pops out of me. I spread the full skirt of my dress and dip into a Western-style curtsy straight out of a Hollywood movie. "Thank you, kind sir."

When a bus arrives at that exact moment, it seems like magic. And it's a different kind of magic when Delun helps me up the steps of the bus by taking my hand. The instant he touches me, my flesh goes hot, and all my breath gets compressed into a small square inch of my chest. His pupils are dilated with an emotion that I don't understand, and he releases my hand only to pay our fare. My head is dizzy with possibilities, but I can't let myself think that this is something it isn't.

All the seats are taken, so we're jammed together in the narrow aisle, holding on to a strap hanging down from the ceiling of the bus. We're standing so close that I feel his body heat through the thin fabric of my dress. My skin prickles at his nearness, and my stomach contracts with an unfamiliar feeling. Delun swallows and looks out the window. We spend the entire ride not looking at each other and not talking about the fire practically sizzling in the small space between us.

After half an hour of heated silence, Delun tells us that we've arrived. This time, he doesn't take my hand to help me down the stairs of the bus.

He gestures to the red gate in front of us. "Our destination is near Dongzhimen."

The East Straight Gate was one of the old city's fortifications, and if we're here, then I have a good idea of where he's taking me. Excitement rises through me. "Are we going to—"

"Ghost Street," he finishes. "The best and cheapest snack street in the city."

I grin. "I've always wanted to come here."

As we approach the street lit up with red lanterns and crowded with people, I ask, "So, what's the best food stall?"

"Seriously?" His eyes widen in mock horror. "Don't you know that a question like that could start a riot? Sword duels have been fought to protect the honor of one's favored food stall." He pretends to look around in paranoia. "It's not worth my life to have an opinion on that."

I'm doubled over in laughter at this point. "OK! Then which one is *your* favorite?"

Surprisingly, the teasing light fades from his eyes. "Oh, you wouldn't like it."

I put my hands on my hips. "Delun, I made you eat with a fork at a restaurant where tiny bread with tinier fish eggs was actually one of the courses. The least I can do is go to a place that you choose this time."

"When you put it that way, I guess we can give it a try." The light is back in his eyes, and it makes me absurdly happy. I don't care where he takes me or what I'm served—I'll eat anything.

But it's not a place serving fried snakeskin or pickled pigeon hearts that he takes me to. We stop at a stall where a man is scooping steaming soupy rice out of a metal pot into bowls.

"Xi fan?" I ask, trying to keep my voice neutral. I mean, I'll eat it, but I'm a little surprised that this is his favorite food. It's just so *plain*.

"Yeah," Delun says enthusiastically. "This place has the best toppings."

It's true that tantalizing smells of spice and fried goodness are wafting from this stall. Now we're talking. I peer at the menu, and when I'm asked what toppings I want, I rattle off my order while Delun beams like some benevolent deity granting all my wishes.

Delun carries our loaded tray to a small table, and we dig in.

Oh, wow. Like every other Chinese person, I've had xi fan before, but not like this. Not this creamy. And seasoned with garlic and sesame oil and topped with scallions, pickled black turnips, and fresh ginger, with a side of perfectly salted duck eggs . . . well, this is pretty much heaven. "This is *amazing*," I mumble through a mouthful of food. "I can see why this is your favorite."

"Glad you like it." He takes a bite of his own food. "Growing up in my village, I had xi fan every single day because it was all my uncle could afford. I never thought I'd want to eat it again when I came to college in Beijing." He smiles. "But I found myself missing it. I guess it's comfort food for me."

My heart twinges to hear him talk so casually about how his family couldn't afford to feed him much beyond xi fan. "So you grew up with your uncle?"

He nods. "My parents died in a car accident when I was young, so my uncle took me in."

"Oh! I'm so sorry." Another stab at my heart. All these things that I didn't know about Delun.

"It was a long time ago," he says quietly.

"Your parents would have been proud to know you got into Beijing University." He must have had sky-high Gaokao results to beat out the Beijing applicants because that's what it takes for someone from a small village to get into universities in Beijing. And to think I had lectured him about the low rate of women who get admitted to the university.

"I'd like to think so." His gaze goes inward for a moment. "But I wonder what they would think of me boycotting my classes and jeopardizing this opportunity of a university education that they never had."

"But that's why you're involved with the protests, isn't it? You're fighting for people like your parents—for everyone—to have the same opportunities." Gently, I say, "I think your parents would have been very proud of you."

"Thank you." He ducks his head and chews for a few minutes without speaking. When he looks back up at me, his eyes are dark and intent. "Do you know how amazing you are, Lei?"

"Who, me?" I say in surprise. "There's nothing special about me. I've been handed everything I've ever wanted on a silver plate and have never had to fight for anything." It's only as I say this that I realize how true it is. I've never known sacrifice or met a hardship

I couldn't charm or buy my way out of. Shame suffuses me. No wonder I pushed Delun away. Not because my pride was hurt that I couldn't have him, but because I couldn't have him on my own terms. He challenged me in a way I've never been challenged before. But at the first sign of difficulty, I gave up on him.

But Delun is shaking his head, rejecting my evaluation of myself. "You could choose to live a life of luxury without bothering with these protests. Instead, you're taking every risk to fight with us. And you don't even know how incredible you are."

My throat clogs with a hard lump. To be seen in this way by a man I adore—it's almost too much.

In a lighter tone, he says, "Tell me about yourself, Lei. What did you do before you were sneaking off to protests? You can't have spent all your time eating baked snails at a French restaurant."

I smile in gratitude at this change in subject. But my relief is short-lived. It's not like I can tell him that I spend my spare time trying to re-create Tang dynasty paintings stolen from us during the Cultural Revolution. I compromise by saying, "I study art history. It's what I want to do in college and why I want to go to Beijing University." But I say nothing about my determination to show Wu Zetian's art in the museums of a country that might be on the cusp of embracing its history again.

Delun listens closely and asks questions to draw me out. It is *so* lovely to be given his full attention.

"What about you?" I ask. "You told me that you're studying political science, but that's all I know."

"It's such an interesting study," he says seriously. "Take Hong Kong. China is saying that there will be a 'one country, two systems' policy when Great Britain hands over Hong Kong to Chinese rule in eight years, but I don't think it will be that easy. Can you imagine?" His face becomes animated as he talks. "One city governed under capitalism and a democracy of sorts, and every other part of China under communism and authoritarianism. But it's not just a difference of political structure or even ideology. It's a fundamental tension between cultures. For example, Hong Kong's primary language is Cantonese, but the party has insisted on Mandarin as the country's official language. That will be a seismic shift, considering that even the smallest change in language is radical."

I nod. "Like Empress Wu's change of fifteen characters."

He beams at me. "Exactly. That's a perfect example."

Daringly, I say, "I think Empress Wu made those changes to emphasize female power."

His eyes grow thoughtful. "Interesting. Can you tell me more?"

I explain my theory willingly as he asks questions and makes insightful comments. If I had thought his attention was wonderful, then it's pure heaven to have his respect. My father was the only man to take me seriously before Delun.

The thought of my father pierces my happiness like a sharp needle. I look around and realize that we've eaten all the food and have been talking for hours with disregard for the time. "I should be getting back home."

Delun checks his watch. "You're right. It's late. Will your parents be worried?" He frowns. The mention of my parents seems to be a cold reality check for him too.

No, they won't be worried, because they think I'm out with the highly eligible, parent-approved Qiang. "It's fine, but let's find a pay phone so I can call a taxi."

He walks me to a pay phone, and I call the taxi service, only to be told that it will be a twenty-minute wait. I tell Delun, and he nods gravely like a patient being given bad news.

What happened to the ease that we felt with each other just minutes ago? I suppose that when all is said and done, we still live in different worlds.

It's gotten colder, and I rub my mostly bare arms. The short, puffed sleeves of my dress that looked so cute when I was getting dressed don't seem like such a good idea now.

Delun takes off his jacket and starts to drape it over my shoulders, but he stops when I rear back like a startled horse. "Sorry," he mumbles.

"It's OK. I'm just . . ." But what can I say? *I'm afraid I'll shatter with desire if you so much as touch me*? That will drive him away for sure. Especially since it's true. "I'm not that cold."

He puts his jacket back on and takes a deep breath. I'm reminded of when he agreed to our first date, like he knew exactly what a bad idea it would be. "I tried to do the right thing," he says. "I told you to stay away from the protests. And from me."

"I remember." My heart is beating so fast that it feels like it's going to fly out of my chest.

"That week you didn't come to Tiananmen Square—I looked for you all the time, thinking you were somewhere in the crowd and I just had to find you." He pauses. "But I never did, so each day ended in disappointment. Until you finally came. And I knew—as soon as I saw you again, I knew I'd made a mistake. In walking away from you."

My breath is knifing into my throat. Who knew that such intense joy could feel like pain?

"Lei, I know I'm probably nothing but a diversion for you—"

"No." With an effort, I unlock my voice. "You're wrong. You have no idea what you are to me."

The look Delun gives me lights up my whole body.

I'm not cold anymore. In fact, I'm burning up. I take a step closer to him. "I don't need your jacket," I say shakily. Then I do what I've longed to do since I first saw him. I reach up and touch his cheek, running my fingers over his rough stubble and hot skin. His breath catches, and his reaction makes my body tighten with building pressure. "But I need you."

Then Delun is kissing me with a hunger matched only by mine, and I'm lost to the world.

CHAPTER SEVENTEEN

On Monday after school, I'm staring down a wall of pleated plaid skirts and pressed white shirts, facing off against Jun, Chunhua, Ai, and Chen. Or at least that's what it feels like.

"What do you mean you're meeting with a tutor?" Chunhua's forehead scrunches up.

"You don't need a tutor," Chen says, envy leaking into her voice.

"Yeah," Ai chimes in. "You got the highest score of all of us on the Gaokao practice test last week!"

Jun is markedly quiet, but her eyes bore into me like she can see the lie curdling in my stomach.

"Jun has a tutor," I point out, "and no one is giving *her* a hard time about it."

The girls turn to look at my sister, and she flushes. "I'm only seeing my tutor on Thursdays." She frowns at me. "How often are you going to be meeting with your tutor, Lei?"

Damn. She suspects that I'm ditching the study group to meet Delun. But I have no choice but to brazen this out. I throw back my shoulders. "Every day."

Jun's nostrils flare as if she can sniff out my deception. "You're meeting with your *tutor* every day?"

"Yes." Guilt zings through me. I'm not used to lying to my twin.

Chen huffs out her breath. "Fine! If Lei isn't going to be a part of our study group, then I'm out!"

Ai nods. "Me too. I'd be better off getting a tutor than staying in a group without Lei."

Chunhua clears her throat, looking uncomfortable. "Lei, are you sure? I mean, my parents wanted to hire a tutor to work with me, but I said I'd rather be in a study group. *This* one."

More guilt hits me. It's my fault that the group is breaking up. "You all should keep meeting!" Sweat dampens the starched collar of my shirt. "You don't need me."

Chen snorts. "Says the only one of us who's sure to score in the first tier."

"No one is guaranteed to score in the first tier," I protest. It's true. No matter how well I've done on the practice tests, it's still possible to choke over two days of intensive test taking. Besides, a ridiculously small percentage score high enough to get into even the tier-three colleges, much less the tier-one colleges like Beijing University.

And the Gaokao is the *only* standard for admission into college. No wonder my friends are freaked out. I look at them: Chen is glaring at me, Ai is biting her lip, Chunhua is frowning in confusion. And Jun staring at me with her hooded, suspicious eyes. I used to be just like them. The Gaokao and getting into a top-tier college used to be the center of my life too. But the protests have changed all that now.

"Who is your tutor, anyway?" Jun asks, her expression hard and challenging.

"I guess that would be me," a voice booms from behind me. *Right on cue.* Yawen slings an arm around my shoulders. "These must be your friends." Her mouth splits into a huge grin as her eyes go to Jun. "And this is your twin! She looks just like you! Except for the hair, of course."

Jun touches the end of her signature braid. "Actually, Lei wears her hair in a braid sometimes," she says coolly.

"Really?" Yawen's eyebrows rise. "I've never seen her hair like that."

I elbow her subtly. She's not supposed to know this much about me.

"But we just met," she says hastily, taking her arm off my shoulders. "So what do I know? I'm just Lei's tutor."

Smooth, Yawen. Real smooth.

"*You're* Lei's tutor?" Chen's gaze rakes over her, no doubt taking in her unfashionably blunt haircut and wrinkled shirt.

"Are you a university student?" Ai asks doubtfully.

Anger rises in me. How have I never realized how stuck up my friends are? "She's a student at Beijing University. You know, a *top-tier* college." I don't have to add that Yawen had to score higher than most of the top-tier boys to beat the quota system.

Respect creeps into Chen's face, and Ai's eyes widen.

"Damn straight," Yawen says loudly. She must have noticed that she's not exactly getting a warm welcome from my friends. "I'm just about to graduate with a degree in engineering."

"That's wonderful," Chunhua says firmly.

There's a reason I consider Chunhua to be my best friend in this group. Other than Jun, of course. Although I'm not sure where Jun and I are right now. Eyeing her warily, I say, "Yawen and I need to get going."

The others say goodbye, but Jun stays silent.

Grabbing Yawen's arm, I practically sprint away with her, but I can feel my sister's accusing eyes boring into my back.

Once we get out of earshot, Yawen says, "Whew! What's up with those friends of yours?"

"Sorry about that. They're . . ." *Entitled, arrogant brats*? Except for Chunhua. But what does it say about me that Ai and Chen's snobbery has never really bothered me before? ". . . intense."

"Hmm." It's all she says, but heat rises into my face.

"Thanks for agreeing to be my cover."

"No problem," she says cheerfully.

We take a taxi to the square, and when we get there, the sight of so many protesters makes my heart lift. Workers like Guang, the taxi driver I met, have joined the movement, adding their voices with shouted slogans and cardboard signs. But I wonder what kind of sacrifice of time and sleep they've made to be here.

"So none of your friends know that you're part of the protests?" Yawen asks, interrupting my thoughts. "Not even your sister?"

"Jun probably suspects," I say as we walk into the square. I hate breaking my word to Jun, but I don't know how to explain to my sister how necessary it feels to be part of this movement to change our country for the better.

Before we wade through the crowd, I pull a white shaker-stitch sweater out of my backpack and put it on. There. That's the best I can do to hide my schoolgirl uniform.

Yawen laughs. "You still look like a high schooler." A teasing light comes into her eyes. "But at least you're not wearing that black sparkly thing you had on when I first met you!"

"Shut up," I say with mock grumpiness, but I'm smiling. It's hard to imagine that I had crashed a rally in a nightclub outfit and glow bracelets only a few weeks ago.

"I take it that your sister doesn't approve?" Yawen asks as she guides us around a group of students arm in arm and singing along to the tinny strains from a boom box.

To say Jun doesn't approve would be an epic understatement. "You could say that." I keep my voice neutral.

She gives me a sideways glance. "I guess you and your sister really are different."

A sense of loyalty makes me say, "She's just trying to look out for me. She feels the protests are dangerous."

Yawen's face turns uncharacteristically somber. "Yeah, I get that."

"Thinking about Rong?" But of course she is.

"He's just so impulsive!" she bursts out. "Saying he'll join a hunger strike! It's just like him to leap into something without even talking to me about it first."

"He might change his mind." I get chills at the thought of Rong starving himself.

"Ah, who knows? You're probably right. He's always been a big talker." But her mouth is puckered in worry.

"You've been together a long time then?"

"Since our first year at college. At first, I thought we were both too outspoken and strong-willed to be a good match. But Rong never had any doubts about us. I guess we're destined to become one of those old bickering couples." She visibly shakes off her glum mood and grins at me. "Like you and Delun."

"What?" I gape at her, but I suppose she *did* see us leave the meeting together on Saturday. "Delun and I don't bicker," I say weakly.

She rolls her eyes. "I didn't mean that you two fight the way Rong and I do! Actually, no one fights like us, and that's probably for the best. But you know what I mean!" She punches me in the arm, probably harder than she meant to.

I wince and surreptitiously rub my arm. Yawen isn't exactly small and delicate.

"Come on! I know you two are together. Admit it!"

"Fine!" I can't help the big smile that spreads over my face. "I guess we are."

"I knew it!" she says. "I've never seen Delun as energized as when you're around. When you disappeared from the protests, it was like a light had gone out in him."

My throat tightens. "I'm sorry I ever left." I straighten my spine. "But I won't abandon the movement again."

Her eyes are full of confidence and trust. "I know."

CHAPTER EIGHTEEN

That Saturday the hunger strike starts.

Delun is grim as we work side by side to set up the encampment in Tiananmen Square for the hundreds of students who are going on the hunger strike. We've been together for a week now, and it's the strangest relationship I've ever known.

Instead of dates, we attend planning meetings. Instead of flirtatious banter, we talk on the phone deep into the night about our fears and hopes for a new China. Instead of long hours of making out, we steal kisses whenever we can. Hot, steamy, mind-blowing kisses—so, there's that.

And as much as we talk about our country's future, we never talk about *our* future. Maybe because neither of us truly believes we have a future together. My heart twinges. But I still wouldn't trade this time with him for anything.

Delun and I aren't participating in the hunger strikes. And neither is Yawen. But Rong is. It turns out that he *was* serious about doing this. He and Yawen are arguing in loud, fierce voices.

"This is crazy!" Yawen insists.

"I support your decisions," Rong says. "Why can't you support mine?"

"Because it's a stupid decision!"

His reply is too quiet for me to hear, and the rest of the argument takes place in low voices.

"Will Rong be OK?" I ask Delun as I fold the last of the blankets and place it in the tent.

"I don't know. Rong has never known what it's like to have an empty belly."

I remember what Delun told me of his childhood in an impoverished village. He probably knows what it's like to go hungry.

"Rong is tougher than he seems." I'm trying to convince myself as much as Delun. Despite our rocky start, I'm now quite fond of the boisterous, impulsive Rong.

"I don't know if any of them will be OK." With a vigorous snap of his wrist, he shakes out the blanket he just folded. "I wish this hunger strike wasn't happening."

Surprised, I ask, "If you're against the hunger strike, why didn't you speak against it at the meetings?"

"I'm not going to tell someone else how to protest." Worry flickers in his eyes. "But maybe I should have spoken up."

"There were plenty of people arguing against the hunger strike, and that didn't stop anyone." I take one of his hands in mine. "We don't need another leader telling us what to do and think. We need a leader who respects people's right to make their own choices. We need *you*."

He grips my hand tightly. "I don't know how I became a leader. And I sure as hell don't feel like I have the aptitude to be one."

"You're a good leader exactly because you don't feel entitled to leadership." Jokingly, I add, "But I hope you're not confessing your doubts to anyone else."

"Only you," he says seriously. "You know all my deepest fears, my most daring dreams."

My heart turns over, and I let go of his hand. I *do* know all those things about him. But my deepest fears and most daring dreams all revolve around Wu Zetian's art, and I'm still keeping that secret from him.

Delun's attention is caught by approaching foreign reporters. "It looks like the leaders in favor of the hunger strike were right. They did say that starving students in the square two days before

Gorbachev's visit will draw the attention of the world." He glances at the blanket spilling over his arms and carefully refolds it. "I think I'm at the end of my usefulness here."

The bleakness in his eyes worries me, but he's right that there's not much we can do here. I give his hand another squeeze and ask, "Should we say goodbye to Rong and leave before the reporters descend on us?"

He nods, and we walk over to Rong and Yawen. At least they seem to have stopped arguing. Yawen is staring down at Rong as he sits cross-legged on the hard ground, a stubborn set to his jaw. In contrast, Yawen's face has none of the exasperation I expected to see. There is nothing but tenderness in her eyes as she gazes at Rong.

Delun clears his throat. "Rong, we're going now. Do you need anything?"

"No," he says shortly, as if daring Delun to try to talk him out of his decision.

"OK," Delun says.

"Bye then," I say awkwardly. After a beat when no one else says anything, I ask, "Yawen, are you coming with us or staying?"

She sits down next to Rong. "Staying," she says, a muscle jumping in her jaw.

His expression softens, and he puts his arm around her. "Thank you."

I turn my head as we're leaving. My last view of them is of Yawen leaning on Rong's shoulder with his face turned toward her. A lump forms in my throat for no reason at all.

"What time do you need to get back?" Delun asks as we leave Tiananmen Square. I've already told him all about deceiving my family into thinking that I'm studying with a tutor after school and going on dates with Qiang on the weekends.

"I've got another few hours. I told my parents that Qiang was taking me to the Great Wall on a day trip."

"Oh," he says, his forehead creasing.

My body tenses. He hasn't said anything, but I know he's not thrilled about me having a pretend boyfriend to hide that I'm here, with him.

More lightly, he says, "We won't have time to go to the Great Wall, but how about Zhongshan Park?"

"Chuang Delun, are you asking me out on a date?" I tease.

He smiles at me. "We've only had two official dates so far. And after the first one, I told you that I didn't want to see you again. I'd like a chance to improve my record."

It would be nice to have something as normal as a date with Delun. "No arguments here." I link my arm through his. "Let's go to Zhongshan Park."

The park is between Tiananmen Square and the Forbidden City, so it doesn't take us long to get there. Ancient cypresses line the paths of what used to be an imperial garden, and the bustle and brightness of the city are replaced by a lush green space. One would never know that Zhongshan Park is in the middle of a metropolitan city.

"Anywhere in particular you want to go?" Delun asks. The strained lines around his eyes are gone, and he looks more relaxed than he's been since the hunger strike was decided on.

"Yes, actually." I lead him off the shaded path and across a paved courtyard. Excitement quickens my pace. I haven't been here in a while, but I know exactly where I want to go.

A tiered pavilion with crimson columns comes into view. The Lanting Eight-Column Pavilion. It was built by Emperor Qianlong of the Qing dynasty to commemorate the lost *Lanting Xu*. But Qianlong was not the only emperor who revered the *Lanting Xu*. Emperor Taizong, my ancestor and Wu Zetian's first husband, was obsessed with all the lost works of Wang Xizhi, *especially* the *Lanting Xu*. Empress Wu didn't share Taizong's passion, preferring to sponsor the women artists of her time. But I have a fascination with lost art, and that includes the original *Lanting Xu*.

Reverently, I trace the calligraphy on one of the columns with my finger. "Do you know the legend of the *Lanting Xu*?" I ask Delun.

"The 'Preface to the Orchid Pavilion Poems,' by Wang Xizhi?" he asks, watching me curiously. "Yes, I know it."

"Can you imagine what it would have been like to be Wang Xizhi at the Orchid Pavilion Gathering?" The celebrated calligrapher couldn't have known what would come out of his invitation for forty-two of his buddies to join him for a poetry drinking contest on a spring day during the Eastern Jin dynasty. "I would have loved to be there—an artist on the brink of inspiration. And to have my moment of perfect creativity become one of the most famous pieces of Chinese calligraphy!"

"You do calligraphy?" Delun asks, his eyebrows quirking up. "I knew you studied art, but I didn't know you were an artist yourself."

"I'm not." My hand falls away from the faded, but still beautiful, calligraphy on the red pillar. I think of the elegant characters of the three Tang dynasty poems on the wall of our basement. "I just copy superior works of art."

Delun points at the pillar I had been touching. "These are copies too," he reminds me. "It's too bad the original was lost long ago, but at least copies of the *Lanting Xu* still exist. And we're fortunate that Emperor Qianlong of the Qing dynasty had the most famous of the copies inscribed here, on these columns."

I shake my head in frustration. "You don't understand. The original calligraphy of the *Lanting Xu*—it was said to be so exquisite that it was touched by the heavens. Wang himself, when he tried to re-create it sober, failed to capture the beauty of the original."

"So you're saying that great art . . . requires that you be drunk off your ass?" he says dryly.

"Argh!" I throw up my hands. "It's useless to explain it to you!"

"I won't accept any denials." He's grinning at me in open amusement. "You're clearly an artist."

I shoot him a mock glare. "Because I have an artistic temperament?"

"Because you're passionate." The teasing look on his face turns serious. "About art. About your beliefs."

About you. My face burns, and out loud, I say, "I just wish the original *Lanting Xu* had survived."

"Who knows? Maybe some descendant of Wang's has it stashed in an attic somewhere."

I just about choke at that.

Delun grips my arm. "Lei, are you OK?"

"Sorry," I gasp. "Something just went down the wrong way." Yeah, like the inherited art from my ancestress. "What were you saying?" I gabble, clutching my scattered wits together. "Right—the *Lanting Xu*. You know, it *was* actually passed down through generations of Wang's descendants until it was inherited by a Buddhist monk."

"Really?" He sounds intrigued. "I didn't know that. What happened to it then?"

"Emperor Taizong of the Tang dynasty had an imperial agent track it down and steal it from the monk." Not exactly my proudest legacy, to be descended from an art thief. "And as if that weren't bad enough," I say, "Taizong had the original *Lanting* buried with him at his death, so it was lost to everyone. All because of the selfish whim of an emperor."

"But copies of the original still exist." Delun looks around the pavilion.

"That's because Emperor Taizong had the most celebrated calligraphers of the court make copies of the *Lanting Xu*," I say dismissively, "but it can't make up for taking the original to the grave with him."

"I don't know," he replies thoughtfully. "Wang Xizhi wrote the *Lanting Xu* to be a preface to the collection of poems written in a fleeting moment of artistry. Most of the poems never gained any fame, and they weren't meant to. They were meant to celebrate camaraderie and pleasure."

Delun's words make me wonder what moment in time the third poem in Wu Zetian's collection—the one full of grave, prophetic sadness—commemorated. Softly, I recite the last four lines of the *Lanting Xu*.

> **We commemorate the people and art we create today.**
> **The future will be different.**
> **But today's feelings will be unchanged.**
> **Tomorrow's readers will feel what we feel today in these poems.**

"Yes," Delun says. "That's it exactly. Art in its physical form can't last forever. But the feelings that art creates in our hearts—that lasts through the ages." His eyes flame with fervor. "I don't know what the future holds for us. But I don't need elegant calligraphy to remember how it feels to be with you right now, in this moment."

Emotion clogs my throat, and I touch his cheek. "Delun, art has always spoken to me and touched me in a way nothing else could. But what I feel for you . . ." For once, I have no words. Delun makes me feel the way a bold curve of a perfectly executed calligraphy stroke does. My ancestress's face, carved in stone. The sweep of bright ink on parchment paper. He is living and breathing art.

But he doesn't seem to need me to say all that to understand. His mouth lowers to mine, and all coherent thoughts but one flee my head.

No matter what the future brings, my feelings for Delun will never change.

CHAPTER NINETEEN

Two days later, I'm exhausted and barely able to stay awake in class. Unlike Delun, Yawen, Rong, and the others, I didn't camp out overnight in Tiananmen Square. But I couldn't sleep at all last night because I was thinking about my friends.

As soon as school is over, I head over to Tiananmen Square, heart beating with anxiety the entire way. Today is May 15, exactly one month since the Tiananmen Square protest started and also the day of Soviet Union leader Mikhail Gorbachev's visit. The protesters have refused to clear out of the square, where Gorbachev is supposed to be welcomed. And now we're all wondering what the government will do. Will it remove us by force? Surely not in front of hundreds of international reporters here to cover the historical summit between China and the Soviet Union.

"Lei!" Delun calls out.

I rush into his arms. "Any word?" Tension spirals up my spine.

"We just heard," he says. "The welcome for Gorbachev has been changed. It won't be at Tiananmen Square."

"Where then?" I ask, unsure of what that means.

"The president and foreign minister met Gorbachev at the airport instead. It's a huge embarrassment for the government." Delun doesn't sound too happy about it.

"That's good," I say. "We made our voices heard and let the world know that we're serious about fighting for freedom from authoritarianism." But I know it's not that simple. Embarrassing the Communist Party is always a risky strategy.

And Delun looks troubled. "I think the situation has just gotten more, not less, complicated." His jaw sets. "I heard that the *World Economic Herald* in Shanghai has been shut down. For being sympathetic to us."

"What?" My breath goes short. The Communist Party letting the *Herald* report about the protests in a fair way was a major sign of government control relaxing. It's a very bad sign that the party is now targeting the paper. Then I remember my father's manipulation of the *People's Daily*'s coverage, his fury at the article Mrs. Liu wrote for the *Beijing Mirror*, and his rant against the lack of restrictions on all these independent newspapers. Ice forms in my blood. Could he have something to do with this new crackdown on the press?

"Hey." Delun squeezes my arm. "It's not all bad. A group of students from Hong Kong just showed up today to support us. *They* still have freedom of the press. When they go back home, they'll tell the world the truth about what's happening here."

I nod, trying to focus on the positive. "And with the China-Soviet summit beginning, at least Rong can start eating again."

Delun shakes his head. "Rong and the others plan to continue the hunger strike until the summit is over in four days."

Damn. Yawen has been looking pale and shaky lately, like *she's* the one on a hunger strike. I'd really hoped that Rong would call it quits, but he seems committed to seeing the hunger strike through to the bitter end. I start scanning the crowd for Yawen and Rong.

Delun notices me searching for our friends. "Yawen took Rong aside to yell at him."

That sounds about right. I lean against Delun and blow out my breath. "When will this be over?" I wonder if the hunger strike is worth it, and I know he's thinking the same thing.

His arm snakes around me, and we stare in silence at the people chanting and holding aloft a huge picture of Gorbachev.

"I don't know," he says at last.

One day after the end of the hunger strike, I'm back at Tiananmen Square. Rong is on campus, recovering as well as can be expected after a week of starvation, and Yawen is with him, so it's just Delun and me today.

After we succeeded in disrupting Gorbachev's mid-May visit five days ago, the movement swelled to unimaginable numbers. Yesterday's rally drew over a million people, and General Secretary Zhao himself came to give a speech. True, he pleaded with us to end the protests—but why would we stop when we finally have the government's attention? Today, we're in a celebratory mood as we march across the square shouting slogans against the government that's determined to stop us.

A sudden commotion interrupts my thoughts and makes my heart thump in fear. I can't help but remember that Ba was at a meeting last night and that he came back late, grim-faced. He wouldn't tell me what it was about, but now I'm suddenly terrified it had to do with the protests. Fortunately, Ba still doesn't know I'm involved.

"Delun! Delun!" someone shouts.

The marchers clear a path for a wild-eyed young man who comes to a panting halt in front of Delun. Blood streams from a cut on his cheek. It's Bo from the student union.

"What is it?" Delun asks, only a slight twitch of his fingers betraying his anxiety.

"Premier Li," Bo gasps. "He's declared martial law. Delun, troops are coming into Beijing right now."

My pulse throbs painfully. This is worse than I imagined. Now I know what Ba's secret meeting last night was about. I should have pressed Ba for information. But I had been worried about raising my father's suspicions by questioning him too much.

Delun turns to me as if he had read my mind. "Lei, can you find out—"

Bo interrupts him. "She won't be able to get through," he says. "Protesters are forming barricades of buses, trucks, and their bodies to keep the troops from advancing." He puts a hand on his cheek. "But they keep coming. The people and the soldiers—everyone is headed here."

Already, I can see more people flooding the square and questions being shouted and answered.

"What's happening?"

"Citizens are trying to stop the troops, but they're pushing on!"

"The soldiers are clubbing protesters who are in the way!"

"They're armed with assault rifles!"

"That's outrageous! Wait until I get my hands on those soldiers!"

Delun grimaces and doesn't waste time on more questions. "Bo, go to the first aid station and see to that cut before you pass out. Tell them to prepare for the possibility of more injuries. Lei, instruct the other peacekeepers to assign each new arrival to a station and make sure that they stay orderly. The last thing we need is panic and chaos." He strides away to find a bullhorn and make a speech.

Even as fear flutters in my throat, I'm proud of Delun's cool competence. Which is more than I can say for myself. I've volunteered to be a peacekeeper, and normally I'm good at it, but right now, I can't remember what I'm supposed to do. My body is shaking, and I'm holding on to my composure by a thread. Numbness wraps around me. How is it possible that the government is sending in military troops against its own people? None of this seems real.

Get it together, Lei. My spine stiffens. Delun has his job, and I have mine. I pass along Delun's instructions to the peacekeepers, and then I organize volunteers to pass out towels and bottles of water to the crowd in preparation for tear gas. *Towels and water won't do any good against assault rifles.* But the important thing is to give people something to do and a sense of control, even if it's an illusion. That's why I keep passing out towels and water, making sure that I give a smile or word of encouragement to everyone I see.

Hours later, Delun finds me. "How are you doing?"

"Where are the foreign reporters?" I ask grimly. "They were here during the hunger strikes. Why aren't they here now?"

"They've been ordered to stop reporting," Delun replies. "Our Chinese news has gone off air too. Premier Li has ordered a news blackout."

"So we're on our own?"

He shakes his head. "There are local reporters sympathetic to our cause, and the people are on our side. Today, it was ordinary citizens slashing the tires of troop trucks with cooking knives and using their bodies as barricades to stop the military from advancing on us. And they succeeded. The trucks have turned back."

"Is it over then?" But even as I ask, I know the answer. The old men afraid of revolution have declared war. And they will not retreat.

Delun hugs me close. "You should leave," he says, "before it gets worse."

"No." I may be quaking down to my shoes, but it has never occurred to me, not even for a minute, to abandon Delun and the others. "It will be all right." I hug him back. "The leaders in the party will listen to us eventually. You said it yourself. The people are on our side."

All I hear for a moment is his ragged breathing. At last he says, "That will just make the party more desperate."

And more dangerous.

CHAPTER TWENTY

I'm standing with Delun, Yawen, Rong, and Bo, looking at a trash-filled Tiananmen Square with students milling around aimlessly. Gloom hangs like a heavy fog over the square. It's been a week since martial law was declared, and we've never been more dispirited. The stench of urine from the overflowing port-a-potties certainly doesn't help.

My parents would throw a fit if they knew where I was now. Luckily, they still think I'm studying with a tutor for the Gaokao or going on dates with Qiang.

"The government is waiting us out," Delun says grimly. "They think we're going to give up and leave."

"Are they wrong to think that?" Bo asks, hefting his rolled-up sleeping bag onto his shoulders. "I'm tired of camping out in this filth! Our leaders have abandoned us—I heard rumors that some are planning to seek refuge in Hong Kong!"

My eyes fly to Delun in surprise. "I didn't know that."

"I'm not going anywhere," he says reassuringly, giving my hand a squeeze.

But he didn't have to tell me that. I already know he'd never leave us.

"I've heard those rumors too," Yawen says. "Delun, I know you won't abandon us, but it's hard to keep going when other leaders are making plans to flee!"

Delun's eyes cloud over. "I know. We need something to reenergize the movement."

"Another hunger strike?" Rong asks. How can he even consider it? His cheeks are still hollow from the *last* one.

"No!" Yawen says forcefully, and for once Rong doesn't argue with her. "Anything but that!"

A pang hits me. There has been talk of a second hunger strike, but none of us wants to see Rong go through that again. Yes, the hunger strike did galvanize the protesters and get us the world's attention. But surveying the ragged tents and exhausted faces around me, I can't help thinking that more deprivation and loss isn't the answer.

We need something beautiful, something to bring us together again.

My eyes land on the blank space on the Monument to the People's Heroes, where the large portrait of Hu Yaobang had been propped. It was removed at some point, and nothing has replaced it. Like the two blank spaces on the walls of my family's basement. That gallery and those two missing portraits have fired up my passions and inspired me in a way that nothing else has. My heart stutters with a revelation.

Art. We need art.

"I have an idea," I say.

I realize this might not be my best idea as we walk onto the campus of the Central Academy of Fine Arts.

"This is a stupid idea!" Bo grumbles loudly.

"It's a brilliant idea," Delun says firmly, spearing Bo with a sharp look. Then he smiles at me. "Leave it to you to see that what we need is art."

"It will give us something to rally around." I speak with more confidence than I feel, but I'm not about to let Bo see any weakness on my part.

Bo mumbles something, and I catch only a few phrases like "artsy nonsense" and "Who does she think she is?"

I raise my voice to drown him out. "Of course, those who lack *imagination*," I say sweetly, "wouldn't understand."

Bo scowls at me and then glances at Delun like he's supposed to chastise me or something.

But Delun just says to me with quiet pride, "Your imagination and creativity are going to bring our movement back to life, Lei."

Bo looks like he wants to barf in his mouth, but for once, he keeps his opinions to himself.

I wish our little delegation didn't include Bo, but he invited himself along, and I couldn't come up with a reason to exclude him. Other than the fact that he's an asshole.

We reach the sculpture building, and a side door opens.

"Hi, Lei!" Heng says cheerfully. "I'm glad you called. I have a bunch of sculpture students here, and we're all dying to hear about this proposal you told me about!" Heng and I have stayed in contact by phone since we first met at Hu Yaobang's memorial rally, but she doesn't go regularly to the demonstrations at Tiananmen Square, so we haven't seen each other in person since our first meeting.

I grin at her. "Thanks for agreeing to meet with us!"

She ushers us into a large studio with various tubs of mysterious materials, scarred work surfaces, and an array of tools. There, she introduces us to fifteen or so other students who gather around us as we enter. They are mostly young men, all of them sharp-eyed and full of eager energy. They start shooting questions at us right away.

"If you want something like the oil painting of Hu Yaobang, why not talk to the painters?"

"The painters? Bah! What can they do? These people want a statue of Hu. I'll put money on it."

"You? You have no money to bet with!"

Heng shakes her head. "Sorry," she says to me, but there's an exasperated fondness in her voice that shows me that this kind of banter is usual among the artists. "Listen up!" she calls out. "My friend Lei is here with representatives of the student movement, and they need our help. So let's hear them out."

"OK," she says, turning back to me, "what can we do for you?"

"We *do* want a statue," I say, "but not of Hu. Something bigger than one person. A symbol. An ideal." I pause, groping for words to describe what I envision.

Bo snorts. "An ideal. Are we going to ask them to sculpt a cloud or something?"

Delun's mouth tightens, and he gives Bo a warning look. "It will need to be fast," he says, turning to Heng and the other sculptors. "Like Lei says, we need a symbol to remind the people what we're fighting for. They've lost faith, and we have to act quickly to restore it. That's why we want to hold a massive demonstration in three days, and we'd like to unveil the statue then."

"Three days?" a student asks incredulously. "That's impossible!"

"As impossible as taking a comprehensive practical art exam in *two* days?" I counter. "You all did that to get into this institute, and you had to be the best to get in. You can do this."

"But that was small scale and had set parameters!" another student says.

I have a response for this too. "So now you get to create your own art—not alone and in competition with each other like the entrance exams, but in true collaboration, working together."

There are murmurs of interest now. Their imagination has been caught.

Worry lines form around Heng's mouth. "But materials for a statue will cost money. Where are we going to get that kind of funding so quickly?"

Delun and I exchange glances. "Are you sure about this?" he murmurs.

"Definitely." It's true that the funding for this project will make a sizable dent in even *my* bank account, but that's not why my face heats up. This will seem like a fortune to someone like Delun, who grew up in a poor village. Bo is certainly giving me a glare of contempt. But Delun's eyes are free of judgment. Taking courage, I pull out an envelope from my purse and hand it to Heng. "There's eight thousand renminbi in there. That should cover the cost of materials."

Her mouth falls open. "That will *definitely* be enough." Then her mouth snaps shut, and she asks warily, "How big of a statue are you thinking?"

"Big," I say. "As big as you can make it."

"Visible from every corner of the square," Delun adds.

I expect there to be grumbling from the sculptors at that, but I should have known better. Instantly, the ideas start flying, fast as hummingbirds.

"It will have to be light enough to build here and then transport to Tiananmen Square."

"What about foam plastic for the structure and then plaster over it?"

"I have a studio practice exercise that we can adapt into a small-scale model."

"We can mark it off in sections and use the measurements for the large-scale statue!"

"But what, exactly, are we making?" one student asks.

Bo breaks in. "A couple of days ago, students in Shanghai carried a replica of the Statue of Liberty in a protest march." He had been standing near the door, watching the proceedings from a distance, but now he strides forward, his voice loud and confident. "That's what you should do: a big-ass Statue of Liberty!"

Heng is already shaking her head. "No! We're not going to copy an existing statue. We're artists, not forgers!"

I think of the foreigner at Club Flash who mocked us for what he thought was a cheap copy of American nightlife. That's the last thing I want . . . but there is something about a woman lifting a torch into the sky that tugs at my heart. I remember the realization I had, standing in Club Flash among the crowd of young people determined to make something uniquely ours. That nightclub wasn't a cheap copy. It was a new hybrid forged from our desire and communal creative energy.

"Besides," Delun adds, "we don't want a symbol for our movement that will seem so blatantly pro-America. Or pro-capitalist."

"What's wrong with that?" Bo demands. "Isn't that what we want? American open market?"

"I'm too much of a socialist at heart to want the kind of Western capitalism where the rich make money off the backs of the poor." Delun smiles dryly. "Open market may help those in Beijing, but it won't help people in rural villages like my hometown." Then he claps Bo lightly on the shoulder. "We are a movement of many voices and many opinions, my brother, and we might not always agree. But that is our strength. That is socialism."

Grudgingly, Bo says, "I suppose you're right. A statue of Hu, then."

I glower at him. Didn't he hear me nix that idea already?

Delun glances at me. "Lei was clear about why the statue shouldn't just commemorate one person, and I agree with her."

That's why Delun is a born leader. His tempered responses. His peacekeeping wisdom. Me? Not so much. But if he is cool reason, then I am fire and instinct. And we need both if we're going to win this battle.

"What we need," I say clearly, "is a statue that represents the best of socialism—the bringing together of many voices. Our strength, as Delun says. Not the Statue of Liberty exactly—I agree with that." Conviction burns in my gut. "But it should be a woman."

"Why?" Bo begins indignantly, but the sculptors are already talking again.

"Yes, a woman!" Heng says. "The mother of the revolution!"

"The practice model I was thinking of is a man," another student says, "but we can make the face and form feminine."

"What should we use as a model for a female face and form?"

"Not a Western model like the Statue of Liberty. Classical female Buddha statues?"

"No. That's too bourgeois. It would look like a statue you'd buy in a tourist shop catering to rich Westerners!"

Eek. I can't help but think of the small stone statue in my basement—the model for the Grand Vairocana Buddha in Longmen Grottoes, made in Empress Wu's image. Yeah, I'm definitely not going to suggest my ancestor as a template for a symbol of a democratic revolution. She was, after all, a monarch who created her own dynasty. That would *not* go over well in a room full of anti-imperialist dissidents.

"Something that represents the people!" another student says. "A worker. Like the stainless steel statue of a collective farm woman by that Russian sculptor, Vera Mukhina."

"Too derivative!"

As the sculptors argue with one another, a formless idea begins to take shape and rise to the surface, taking my breath away.

But then cold reality seeps in. If I speak, it will be clear to everyone that I've come among them as an imposter. What do I know about that heavenly inspiration that great artists experience? As I told Delun at the Lanting Pavilion, all I do is make copies of superior art. And as Heng said, these students are *artists, not forgers.*

Then I remember what Delun said to me. *Art in its physical form can't last forever. But the feelings that art creates in our hearts—that lasts through the ages.*

That is what we're doing here. Not to make an enduring physical work with aesthetic merit. That was never why I loved Wu Zetian's art.

Don't forget who you are. Keeper of an artistic dynasty that has caused great sacrifice on the part of every one of its guardians. That's how Jun sees it, and maybe my mother too. But that's not what I see. I see the power of art to inspire belief and heroism. That's why I love my ancestress's legacy.

I think again of Empress Wu's statue in the Longmen Grottoes, a grandiose masterpiece evoking awe through the ages. My heart stops as I'm filled with a towering vision.

For a breathless, transcendent moment, I can see her in my mind: strength, justice, peace, and love incarnate. Liberty holding a torch with *both* hands, because the work of peace is hard. The strong face and body of a collective farmer woman. Guan Yin, Goddess of Mercy, in flowing white robes. Wu Zetian, who made her image into a Buddhist stone deity to fight Confucian patriarchal strictures against women's power.

Our statue will be all of these women. Not a copy but a collective.

Delun speaks into my ear, making me jump in surprise. "I know that look," he says. "You have an idea, Lei."

I shake my head. "I'm not an artist," I whisper. "Who am I to tell them what to do?"

"Lei, you *are* an artist." His voice is low and intense, as if he can make me believe through the sheer force of his conviction. "Your vision is necessary." He straightens up and looks at me with utter faith shining in his eyes. "Tell us your idea."

I'm filled with so much love for him that my body trembles. His belief is all I need. My chin lifts, and I make eye contact with these brilliant artists, who are my comrades. My doubt is gone. I see an ideal made real, immortal and burning gloriously bright through the night.

"A goddess," I say. "The Goddess of Democracy."

We put up the Goddess of Democracy in Tiananmen Square three days later.

Some of the demonstrators have linked arms and formed a ring around the statue as the artists put on the finishing touches. We brought her in her preassembled parts last night and constructed her literally overnight. Ten meters of white plaster over wire and plastic foam, facing the portrait of Mao Zedong that hangs at the Gate of Heavenly Peace that Tiananmen Square is named after.

She is exactly how I envisioned her. Her face is earthly and mortal, and her body is strong, made for work. Her sturdy bones are draped in flowing white robes—a hint of divinity from myth and folklore, an allusion to our past. But the torch she holds aloft in both hands will light our way into the dim future.

She brings tears to my eyes.

The students are breaking down some of the scaffolding they used to assemble her when Heng comes to my side. "She's beautiful." Her face is pale and there are dark circles under her eyes, but she's smiling. Of course, she must be tired. She and the other students worked in shifts around the clock to finish the statue in time.

"We're going to unveil her soon," I say, stretching stiff arms in the midday sun. I wasn't much help with the actual construction, but I did what I could, mixing plaster and running errands. "Are you going to stay for that or go back to campus to sleep?"

"Oh, I'll stay for the unveiling ceremony." She hesitates and says, "But I don't think I'll come back after that."

My eyebrows rise in surprise. "Why not?" I gesture past the protective ring surrounding the statue. Tens of thousands had poured into the square last night to watch the statue being assembled. And now there are hundreds of thousands waiting for her to be unveiled—more people than I've seen in weeks. There is an air of celebration, with people singing and cheering us on to remove the veil (which is just two pieces of red and blue cloth over her face, because that's all the covering we could gather on short notice). "The people have been reenergized," I say. "It's just as we hoped."

Heng is no longer smiling and looks even more tired. "Lei, you should know . . . the college suddenly canceled permission to use school trucks to transport the pieces of the statue from the campus to Tiananmen Square. The State Security Bureau said that any truck driver involved would lose his license. That's why we had to hire carts at the last minute." Her eyes lower. "There are rumors that party officials are angry about what we've done, more so than anyone expected. It might be a good idea if the makers of the statue keep a low profile."

My skin prickles with worry. "I think you're right." None of the artists have taken credit for the statue, preferring to view the work as a collective effort, and I hope their anonymity will be some protection against the backlash.

I know full well how dangerous art can be. "Stay away from Tiananmen until the country's leaders finally listen to us and take our demands seriously," I tell her softly. "When this is over, we can celebrate our victory."

Her eyes brighten a little. "That will be a great day." She sighs as a muffled curse floats over to us from one of the art students. "I'd better check on that before they break her."

"Not likely. You all built her so she can't easily be dismantled by government officials." They'd have to destroy her completely to take her down. Emotion stabs at my heart. At the unveiling ceremony, a statement will be read. It will say that the physical statue isn't meant to last forever, but that the Goddess of Democracy *will* live forever. I believe that. Even if the statue is destroyed, she will endure as art is meant to endure—in our hearts.

After Heng leaves, I look for Delun, but I don't have to go far because he is walking toward me.

"Lei," he says with a smile, "you did this, you know."

When he reaches me, I wrap my arms around him and lean against his wiry body with Heng's words of warning still echoing in my head. "We are going to win, aren't we?"

Any response Delun could have made is interrupted by a great cheer from the crowd.

Someone is making his way through the crowd, which parts quickly to open a path. It's a young man in his twenties, and he's trailed by a few people carrying speakers, sound equipment, and a guitar case. The man stops to address the demonstrators standing guard over the statue. The ring breaks and lets him in. The artists stop their work and start cheering too, pumping their fists in the air.

"Is that . . . ?" I ask in disbelief.

"The rock star who sang the hit song that's now the anthem of our protests?" Delun laughs at the expression on my face. "Yes, that's him."

I whirl on him. "You knew he was coming today?!"

He nods. "I knew, but I wanted to surprise you." A teasing smile crosses his face. "If I introduce you to him, should I be worried that you'll leave me for a famous singer?"

"You can *introduce* us?" I'm practically screaming in excitement now. This rock star, whose concerts I've always wanted to attend, is here *now*, performing for the protesters? I must be dreaming.

The first strains of the song blast through the air, and the square is filled with screams of joy that the singer's soaring voice pierces with raw emotion. Everywhere, there are uplifted arms and rapt faces. Feet move to the rhythm of the song, and many start dancing and singing along. For a moment, we are not just revolutionaries. We are any group of celebratory young people, full of life and joy.

The lines about a poor boy imploring his love to leave with him make a lump form in my throat. I can't understand why the girl is so unmoved by the boy's pouring out his heart to her. Just like I can't understand why our pleas to our country's leaders are being ignored. We just want to be heard. And we are using our bodies, our music, and our art to make them listen.

"That's your answer," Delun tells me, shouting over the music.

I'm startled out of my thoughts. "The answer to what?" I yell back.

"To whether we're going to win," he says. "The people are celebrating. The Goddess of Democracy has been built. Even if we have nothing else, we have this moment. We have already won."

I know what he means.

We have nothing but moments. This peace blooming in my heart. This great love I feel for Delun and everyone in the square. That is what we are fighting for.

CHAPTER TWENTY-ONE

Two days after the Goddess of Democracy is unveiled, Ba comes home late again.

Ma, Jun, and I are lingering over dinner when he comes home after nine o'clock, and I drop my chopsticks at the sound of his heavy footsteps. My stomach clenches. A bad day at the Politburo means nothing good for the protesters.

It's the first day of June, and by some accounts there are a million of us now—students and other citizens. If the declaration of martial law two weeks ago was meant to quash the movement for good, then it failed. Spectacularly. And I can't help thinking the Goddess of Democracy has a lot to do with that. The people have an ideal to rally around now. The state-run *People's Daily* just published an editorial about the statue and how she must not be allowed into the "sacred" square. It's clear that the nation's leaders are frightened. Our symbol of strong, deified womanhood intruding into the sacred space of male power is their worst nightmare.

But despite withering op-eds against the Goddess of Democracy and government propaganda depicting peaceful protesters as violent young thugs bent upon destruction, sympathy for the demonstrations has only grown. The foreign press is at Tiananmen Square every day now, and all eyes are on China. Some of the more independent Chinese newspapers are printing stories supportive of the protesters, only to be brutally suppressed by a panicked Politburo.

To say things are tense is an understatement.

Without a word, Ba sits down and starts filling his plate with stir-fried green beans and ginger poached bass. Jun silently rises to get him a bowl of rice from the rice cooker in the kitchen. When she returns with the full bowl, he grunts his thanks.

Ma gazes worriedly at him. "Is the fish warm enough? I can heat it up for you."

He doesn't reply.

Surprise steals through me. Ba has been taciturn and grumpy in the three weeks since the student hunger strike began, embarrassing the government in front of the world, but he's never flat-out ignored Ma. In fact, I've *never* seen him be rude to Ma. Anxiety shoots through me. This is more than a rough day at the office.

Ma's mouth flattens. "Or you can just sit there while we tiptoe around your bad temper."

"I'm sorry, Mei." Ba looks at her and then drops his eyes. "I don't know how to tell you this."

Jun and I exchange surprised looks across the table. Because this is another first for Ba—uncertainty in his ability to solve any problem.

Ma stands up from her end of the table and goes to Ba's side. "Whatever it is, Shen, we will take care of it together."

"I killed a news story today," he says heavily.

A news article sympathetic to the protesters? My body goes hot and cold, and for a moment, anger at my father sweeps through me. But no, that can't be it. He wouldn't have any qualms about killing a news story about the demonstrations at Tiananmen Square.

"A story?" Ma asks, turning pale.

"The *Beijing Mirror*. An article by Liu Yuan."

Ma's hand goes to her throat. Jun gasps softly.

"What did she have to say?" I demand.

Ba looks at me as if he's just remembered my presence. Then he slams a fist down on the table. "It's those damn protesters with all their calls for freedom of speech! Now any crazy person thinks they're entitled to vent to the press!"

I'm about to launch into a defense of the movement . . . but then I see the cunning look in Ba's eyes and realize that he's trying to distract me by drawing me into our usual debates.

"What did Mrs. Liu write about?" I ask again.

Ma, still pale, starts to sway on her feet.

"Ma!" Shock freezes me in place.

But Jun acts quickly. She leaps up and helps Ma sit down before Ba has a chance to do anything but shove his chair back in alarm. Slowly, Ba sits back down, but his eyes stay glued to her.

Ma reaches out a shaky hand to him. "Is this about what happened to Peng?"

"Yes, that's it. She's after me because of what she thinks I did to her husband." He clasps her hand in his. "It's just the same thing as always."

"Liar." Her face regains some color. "No newspaper would print such stale rumors about you, especially ones coming from a nobody like her."

Panic is making me sweat now. *What does Mrs. Liu know, and why would anyone be interested?*

"Tell me the truth, Shen." Ma pins him with a steady gaze. "Does Liu Yuan know *my* secret?"

My heart stops. Ma has only one secret, and it's the one I'm going to inherit and guard with everything I have. That would be newsworthy, all right—the wife of a high-ranking Communist Party official hoarding imperial wealth beyond imagining. Art that could have easily gotten her killed just twenty years ago at the height of the Cultural Revolution. In fact, Empress Wu's legacy could still get all of us in serious trouble, especially since there happens to be a student revolution taking place. One that's calling out officials in the Communist Party for corruption and hypocrisy. Mrs. Liu chose her timing well.

There is a long, agonizing silence before Ba replies at last. "She suspects. The story was mostly wild accusations about how I turned my back on Peng when we were both Red Guards, but that's too common a tale to interest anyone." He takes a long breath. "But she wouldn't dare go after me unless she had proof of something that would bring me down. And that's what she wrote—that she has solid evidence that I'm hiding something big. And she promised to reveal it soon."

A chill has taken over my body. Ba doesn't have to explain the rest. He can kill this story and the next. But if Mrs. Liu has evidence of the priceless dynasty art we're hiding, then someone in the Politburo will get wind of it—and then it will all be over.

But what proof could she possibly have?

"Girls, leave us, please," Ma says. "Your ba and I need to talk."

I want to argue that this concerns us too and that we should be allowed to stay, except Jun and I need to talk too.

We flee upstairs, and Jun is the one who pulls me into her room. "What are we going to do?" she wails.

I'm ready with an answer. "Go see Yanlin tomorrow. Find out what 'proof' his mother has."

She nods. "And then what?"

My voice is flinty. "Then we figure out how to stop her."

Everyone seems to have a mission the next day, and they all have to do with Mrs. Liu.

Ba is back at the office to root out any trouble from Mrs. Liu. Ma is having dinner with Mrs. Xu, the biggest gossip in her charity organization, to see what she knows. Jun is going to an extra tutoring session. Since it's just a few weeks before the Gaokao, my parents don't question Jun's seeing her tutor on a Friday night. What she's really doing, of course, is meeting with Yanlin to get information about his mother.

That just leaves me. And I have my own mission. If Mrs. Liu is smart enough to use the student uprisings to further her vendetta with my family, there's no reason she'll stop with the *Beijing Mirror*. She'll go to the student leaders as well. That means I have to get to Delun before she does.

I find myself almost running to the Beijing University campus building where Delun and the other students are likely to be. My heart is beating fast with fear of the worst-case scenario. The legacy of Wu Zetian's art puts my family in danger from both the government and the student activists. If Mrs. Liu reveals our secret, we'll be seen as hoarding decadent art and living off the backs of the people. No one will understand the history or importance of that art. The government will see my father as a counterrevolutionary—it could strip him of his position and imprison him. And the students will see him as a symbol of an oppressive, corrupt government—they could drag us all out of our home to be beaten on the street while they burn down all our secret art. Bitterly, I reflect that Mrs. Liu is sure to find poetic justice in setting a modern-day Red Guard against my father.

Don't get carried away by your imagination, Lei. My worst-case scenario is also the *least likely* scenario. My father has reached a high level in the Politburo, so it's entirely possible he could weather even a scandal of this magnitude. And I know Delun and the other student leaders. They would never perpetuate the violence and murders that the Red Guard did more than twenty years ago. But all the reassurances I tell myself disappear into thin air when I see the person emerging from the student hall just as I reach it.

Mrs. Liu.

She stops short when she sees me. "You're one of Mei's daughters. You look just like her." Her voice drips with disdain. *Mei's* daughter—not *Shen's*.

Anger soon replaces my surprise at her presence. "What do you have against my mother?" The newspaper story may have been about my father, but it's clear that the person she really hates is my mother. It makes no sense, considering that my father was part of the Red Guard, who did all those terrible things to her husband.

"Is everything OK?" a quiet voice asks. Delun has come out of the building and is walking toward us.

Mrs. Liu glances at Delun and then back at me, her eyes knowing. "For that young man's sake, I hope you're not like your mother," she says to me in a low, vicious voice. "*She* was a woman who could always get men to do anything for her. Even if it meant throwing away their lives and honor for her."

What the hell does that mean? Despite myself, a chill runs down my spine.

Mrs. Liu leaves without a backward glance, and despite all I still need to find out, I let her go. I'm not frightened easily, but that woman scares the shit out of me.

Delun reaches me and takes my hand. "You're as cold as ice, Lei."

"What did she tell you?" My voice is shaking.

He hesitates and then says, "She said your father is one of the Politburo members who has sided with Premier Li and is arguing for the use of force to stop the protests." *That, unfortunately, may very well be true.* I desperately want to deny it, but I can't lie to Delun.

"What else?" I can barely force the words out through my constricted throat.

I expect him to press me about my father, but he doesn't. Instead, he says, very gently, "She's writing a story about your family and that you're keeping something incriminating in your house. Something that will eliminate your father as a dangerous voice in the Politburo against us."

"Did she say what it is?" My heart feels like it's going to burst with fear.

"No, but she wants—" He stops and swallows hard. "She wants us to raid your house and find it."

Sweat drips down my face, and my skin grows clammy and cold. For the first time in my life, I feel like I'm about to faint.

Delun grips my arm. "Lei, we all refused. None of us would dream of doing such a thing, no matter who your father is or what he's done. You've been fighting at our side for this long—do you think we'd betray you?"

Tears sting my eyes. "All of you? Really?"

"Yes. Yawen and Rong, of course. Even Bo. We didn't even need to debate over our decision—it was unanimous."

I let out an unsteady laugh. "That must be a first." Relief starts to seep into me.

But his face is still grave. "Mrs. Liu didn't seem worried by our refusal. She said that she didn't really need us to raid your home."

Because she already has the proof she needs to destroy our family. My light-headed fear returns. "Delun, I . . ."

"Lei, I know there are things you're not telling me."

Of course he knows. And now Delun will tell me that he can't be with a girl he can't trust. Anxiety eats away at my insides.

"It's OK." He cups my face in his palm. "You don't have to tell me anything you don't want to."

My breath eases. "That's it? You're not going to ask questions or demand explanations?"

"You'll tell me when you're ready."

That's what Jun said about Yanlin. She said that Yanlin would tell her what his mother has against ours when he was ready. Now, the same patience I found maddening in my sister is what I'm grateful for in Delun. Except the time for waiting is over. It doesn't matter if Yanlin tells Jun what he knows—I have to act now to save my family and the inheritance we guard.

I've been silent too long, and Delun drops his hand. My face feels cold without the warmth of his skin against mine. For a long beat, I just stare at him—his brilliant, angular face and his long, lean body filled with quiet power and heat. I might not be willing to depend on Yanlin or the strength of his feelings for Jun, but I can depend on Delun. "I think I'm in big trouble." I sound calm, but panic is thundering through my ears. "Or at least my family is."

He looks at me with concern. "Can I help?"

I step into his arms and place my cheek against his chest, where the slow beat of his heart reassures me. "After what Mrs. Liu told you about my father, how can you be so willing to help us?"

"Of course I'll do anything I can." He kisses me tenderly—so different from our usual passionate stolen kisses—but something strong and hot still jolts through me. "It's you."

Mrs. Liu had warned me about being the kind of woman that men would do anything for. But I don't care about other men. I care only about Delun. And what does that bitter woman know of what's between the two of us?

I deepen the kiss until I'm panting with need and hope and misgiving. His heart, beneath my splayed fingers, is no longer slow, but fast and erratic.

At last he pulls away from me, his breath ragged. "I love you, Lei. You know that, don't you?"

My whole body is filled with an intense, burning joy. "Yes, but it's nice to hear."

He cups my cheek tenderly. "You are my gong zhu."

An unfamiliar weight presses on my heart. "I love you too."

That's when I remember what my mother said after she named me heir to Empress Wu's art. *I trusted your father to help me protect our secret, and that's why I married him.*

Delun is not the man either of my parents would want for me. But none of that matters. Delun is who *I* want. The man I choose. I can trust him with my life.

And he will help me protect my greatest secret.

CHAPTER TWENTY-TWO

"What are we doing here again?" Delun asks.

My hands shake as I unlock our front door. It's only eight o'clock. The rest of my family won't be back for at least another hour, so it's not fear of discovery that's making me nervous. It's the magnitude of what I'm about to do. "I have something to show you."

He doesn't ask any more questions as I lead him into the wide foyer of our mansion and past the living room filled with plush furniture and silk pillows. His eyes grow rounder and rounder with each marker of my family's wealth. The gold accents. The fancy stereo system with blinking lights and big speakers in the media room. The fact that we even *have* a media room.

Already, I'm regretting my decision.

I'm tempted to turn to Delun and say, *Just kidding! I have nothing to show you. Why don't we make out on the velvet couch?*

Delun must sense my panic, because he brushes a strand of sweaty hair from my cheek and says softly, "We don't have to do anything you don't want to do."

Oh hell. He thinks I brought him here to *sleep* with him. My cheeks warm. It's not like I've never thought about sex with Delun. I think about it all the time. Whenever he touches me, I always imagine more.

But not in the middle of a potential family crisis. And definitely not in my parents' home. "Uh, Delun? I think you might have gotten the wrong idea."

Now it's his turn to redden. "Right. Sorry, I didn't mean to assume . . ." His words trail off in confusion.

Cute as Delun is when he's stammering, we don't have time for this. "Come with me." I grab his arm and lead him into the library and come to a stop in front of the secret panel in the wall. "Remember when I said my family is in big trouble?"

"Yes. And I meant what I said. I'll do whatever I can to help."

I shake my head. "You can't make that promise unless you know what it is that we're hiding."

His eyes widen. He finally realizes why I brought him here.

I inhale deeply. "But you can't tell anyone what I'm about to show you. It would ruin us if word got out."

"This is why Mrs. Liu wanted the protesters to raid your house, isn't it?" His mouth sets. "Don't worry. That will never happen. And I'll keep your secret—whatever it is. I promise."

I believe him. Delun would never betray me. But will he stay with me when he finds out who I am? My stomach churns at the thought of losing him. *No more stalling.* The choice is clear: Let fear stop me as it has so many times before, or take a leap of faith. *I can't love Delun without trusting him.*

I know what I have to do. Hands shaking, I try to extract the key, but the chain around my neck tangles with the gold necklace of my jade pendant, and it takes me a moment to detangle the key.

Delun reaches for the pendant, and despite everything, heat rushes into me at his nearness. " 'Mei,' " he says, reading the character carved into the jade.

"Jun has one with the character for 'jie.' " My voice quivers.

"You two must be very close," he says, "to wear pendants that form the word 'jiemei.' " *Sisters.*

"Of course we are." My heart rises into my throat at the thought of what Jun would do if she knew what I was up to. "We're jiemei, after all." Then I unlock the panel in the wall and push the button.

The bookcase slides open to reveal the hidden stairs.

Delun's jaw drops. "What—what is this?" he stammers.

"Follow me." My spine is stiff with determination. I've made up my mind, and I'll see this through to the bitter end.

Our footsteps echo into the quiet of the gallery and then fade away as we come to a stop in front of the statue of Wu Zetian.

Delun's face is slack with shock as he points to the statue. "Is that . . . No, it can't be."

"It is," I say. "Empress Wu Zetian of the Tang dynasty and her own Wu Zhou dynasty." My heart beats furiously as I gesture to the art on the walls and in glass cases. "This is her art collection, passed down to Princess Taiping and again and again from daughter to daughter through the centuries . . . until it has come down to me, Wu Zetian's descendant and heir."

He's completely silent, and my skin prickles in agonizing anticipation of his reaction. Now he understands what I am asking him to protect. And no matter what I might mean to him, it might be too much to ask.

"You're not afraid of dangerous women, remember?"

He tears his gaze away from the statue and swallows hard. "I think I was trying to impress you when I said that." His eyes swivel back to the statue. "It was foolish of me, wasn't it? To underestimate the power and danger a woman might present?"

"Foolish," I echo, my heart dropping. "So are you talking about Wu Zetian, or me?"

He turns to me, face unreadable. "Are you a dangerous woman?"

"Yes." I'm barely breathing now. "You know what it means if this gets out. I'm the daughter of a party official hoarding dynastic art. Everyone involved with our secret would be in danger from the government. And for you, it would be even worse. You could even risk your standing in the protest movement."

"And what about you? The heiress of the Wu Zhou dynasty has been protesting against authoritarianism and elitism for months, and you're worried about me?" A small, hard smile flashes across his face. "I'm not afraid *of* you. I'm afraid *for* you."

My pulse races as I register the admiration, mixed with worry, in his eyes. Maybe there's hope for us yet.

Then all the blood in my body freezes at the sound of footsteps on the stairs.

"Lei?" Jun calls out. "I need to talk to you—" Her words are cut off by the sight of Delun. She comes to a dead stop on the stairs and turns pale.

Oh hell. "Jun," I say weakly, "I can explain."

Delun murmurs, "I should go." He hesitates and then whispers in my ear, "I won't tell. Don't worry."

I grab his arm, wishing we had finished our conversation so I would know where we stand. "I'll see you tomorrow afternoon at the Meridian Gate," I whisper back. The entrance to the Forbidden City is where we've met before to snatch some alone time before going to Tiananmen Square.

He nods and then goes up the stairs, saying hello to Jun as he passes her.

She doesn't respond, but she does squeeze herself to the edge of the stairs to keep as much distance between them as possible. Not a good sign.

My sister and I stare at each other in silence until Delun disappears from sight. Jun comes the rest of the way down the stairs, but she still says nothing.

Fear is dragging at my breath, but when have I ever been afraid of *Jun*? "He won't tell anyone," I say, pleading inwardly for her to understand. "I trust him."

She just peers at me with dark, fathomless eyes.

Sweat is making my back damp now. "I had to tell him. Mrs. Liu went to the leaders of the protest. She wanted their help in finding out our secret. Delun convinced the others to turn her down."

"And how do you know that she went to the student leaders?"

Oh shit. That's right—I'd promised Jun that I would give up my involvement with the movement. And stop seeing Delun.

"You lied to me." There's a hard glitter in her eyes.

A lump forms in my throat. "I'm so sorry. I meant to keep my promise, and I did . . . for a while. But the protest is important!"

"You've been seeing Delun." She takes a step toward me, and if it had been anyone but my sister, the expression on her face would be downright scary. "You lied about that too. Were the dates with Qiang and your tutoring sessions just a cover so you could sneak around with a revolutionary who threatens our family?"

Anger rises in me. "I'm not the only one who's dating someone our parents would disapprove of!" It's a low blow, but I'm too mad to fight fair. "Did Yanlin even tell you what his mother is up to?"

Red splotches appear on her cheeks. "Yanlin promised that he'll stop her from writing about us."

Mrs. Liu's tight, bitter expression flashes through my mind. She sure didn't seem like she was planning to stop anytime soon when I last saw her, trying to instigate a student raid on our family. "And you believed him?" *Whoa. Slow down, Lei.* Implying that her boyfriend is lying to her probably isn't the best way to defuse the tension between us. Plus, it's not fair to Yanlin. At least he's trying.

Jun's face grows stony. "I haven't forgotten how dangerous his mother is."

My anger simmers down. My sister and I are in the same impossible situation. "Jun, please understand—I love Delun like you love Yanlin. And like you, I'm choosing to trust the boy I love despite the danger."

"Love?" She sounds like she's struggling with tears. "That's so like you, Lei. You think you can have whatever you want and damn the consequences. You can call it love, but it's just selfishness!"

This is so staggeringly unfair that my breath whooshes out of me and I'm unable to respond. How could my sister say such awful things about me?

Then her face suddenly crumples and tears stream down her cheeks. "I broke up with Yanlin."

"What?" I gape at her in shock, my resentment forgotten. This must be why she's back so early from her date.

"He wanted to tell his parents about us." Her voice is scarily toneless. "He said his mother would stop trying to write about us if she knew that I was . . . the girl he loves . . ." Her words trail off, and her voice comes alive with pain. "But I knew that would make his mother come down even harder on our family."

"But, Jun, you love Yanlin! You could have figured something out. Why did you have to break up with him?"

"How can you stand here in the middle of Wu Zetian's art and ask me that? Whether Yanlin believes it or not, his mother is dangerous to us. And so is Delun."

"He's not." My whole body is numb in the face of my sister's fierceness, but this much I know: Delun would never harm me or my family.

"I gave up the boy I love to keep our family's secret safe, but you?" Her face is cold. "You brought Delun here and told him everything. Because you're in *love*." She practically spits out the last word.

Hurt sweeps through me even though I understand why my sister is upset. She was strong enough to give up Yanlin, and she sees my refusal to give up Delun as weakness. *I just have to convince her otherwise.* "I didn't bring him here because of some lovesick whim! I brought him here because he can help us."

"Oh, Lei, don't you see?" Her face softens. "You'll get bored with him like you do with all your flirtations and dump him for someone shiny and new. And what do you think he'll do after you break his heart? He'll use our secret against you. You have to break up with him now, before he gets too attached and has a reason to hate you."

"You're wrong." My voice is steely. "Wrong about Delun and wrong about me. There is nothing that will make him turn against me and betray our secret. And there is no one else for me but Delun."

"You refuse to give him up?"

I promised Jun before that I'd give up Delun—and I had broken that promise. This time, I won't make a promise I can't keep. "That's right. I refuse."

Her face shutters down. "Then our mother was wrong to entrust our inheritance to you."

My heart freezes. This can't be happening. *Who is this girl staring at me so coldly? That can't be my sister.* I'm still reeling from her words when she turns and walks back up the stairs, leaving me in the lonely splendor of the art around me.

My chest is exploding with the pain of a thousand land mines. What do I do now? The only thing I can do when I am this shattered and lost. My vision blurry with tears, I stumble around display cases and statues, my hip catching the solid edge of a table and shooting a sharp ache through my body. At last, I reach the place I always go for inspiration and answers: the wall of three poems.

The last poem, heavy with sorrow, fits my mood exactly. Jun and I have never had a fight like this before, and I still don't know what hit me. I want something to echo the emptiness left in the wake of that bruising elemental storm.

Sun. Skies. Earth. Shining. These characters in the poem are four of the fifteen characters that Empress Wu changed during her reign, except they have reverted to their original forms, which means the poem was written after Wu Zetian's death. There's only one way the poem could have ended up in this collection.

It must have been written and placed here by the daughter who inherited this imperial legacy, Princess Taiping. My ancestress who passed on the art inherited from her mother to her daughters all down the ages, keeping a forgotten dynasty alive. But what filled Princess Taiping with such sadness? Throat tight with emotion, I start to read the poem out loud:

The sun has set below the border of mountains.
Even the skies weep and water the dusty earth.
I am alone with my tears and the silent stone.

I can't go on. My body is racked with grief, and I'm sobbing over the rift between me and my sister. The poem has always had the feel of prophecy to it, and now it feels like a prophecy of tragedy, weighing down my heart with the unknown future.

CHAPTER TWENTY-THREE

The next afternoon, I'm supposed to meet Delun at the Meridian Gate, but Jun spikes my plans just as I'm about to leave the house.

"Remember that you're going to help me study for the Gaokao today," she says.

I'd promised Jun no such thing, but how am I supposed to say anything with Ma beaming at us like that and Ba nodding in approval?

Annoyance tightens my neck muscles into knots, but I go with Jun into the library, where we take our places across from each other at a sturdy wood table. She's left me with no other choice. She'd better not expect me to help her study for real.

But Jun doesn't say a word to me. Instead, she calmly takes out her notebook and starts reading.

After a solid hour of glaring at her while she silently reviews her notes, I've had enough. Worms of anxiety are eating through my stomach. I need to meet Delun before he decides I'm not coming. I put a book in my backpack, and then I leave the library.

Jun follows me out, of course. "Where are you going?"

Our parents look up from the couch in the living room where they're watching TV.

"Done studying already?" Ma asks.

"The Gaokao is important to your future," Ba says. "You can't afford to take it lightly."

Tamping down rising frustration, I reply as calmly as I can. "I promised Chunhua I'd meet her to return a book I borrowed. She needs it to study for the Gaokao."

Jun glowers at me with suspicion, but she doesn't call me out in front of our parents. I guess that's the best I can hope for. "You'll be back as soon as you return the book, right?" she asks pointedly.

I bare my teeth at her. "Yes. I'll be right back." But I have no intention at all of keeping my word.

There's nothing now but mistrust and broken promises between my sister and me.

By the time I get to the Meridian Gate, I'm in a panic about how late I am. The entrance to the Forbidden City isn't nearly as crowded as usual, which makes sense since it does face Tiananmen Square, after all. And skirmishes between the army and protesters have been breaking out all day, so even the most intrepid tourist is thinking twice about getting anywhere near Tiananmen Square today. But even though there are fewer people here, I still don't see Delun. *Did he decide not to wait?* I desperately need to talk to him and find out how he feels about me and my secret.

"Lei!" Delun steps away from the crowd and waves me over. As soon as I reach him, he gathers me into his arms. "I was worried you weren't coming."

"I'm sorry I'm late!" I say breathlessly. "It was hard for me to get out of the house with Jun watching my every move."

"I thought your sister would convince you not to see me anymore." There's a thread of fear in his voice.

"She tried." My chest aches at the thought of Jun. "But I refused to give you up."

His heart beats faster against my cheek. "So you're not here to say goodbye?" His voice rumbles low and hard into my chest, but I can't tell if it's relief I hear in his question or something else.

I've refused to give up Delun—but what has *he* decided? I've gone against my family and my duty as the guardian of Empress

Wu's art. Not only by falling for a revolutionary who stands against everything I'm hiding, but by believing in those same revolutionary values. But Delun has his own conflicts and responsibilities. He is a leader in the protest movement that my father is trying to take down. I'm as dangerous to him as he is to me.

I stumble backward out of his arms. What he said to me outside of Maxim's on our disastrous first date flashes through my memory. *I should walk away from this. For both our sakes.*

My breath catches painfully in my throat. "No. Not goodbye," I say. "Not unless you want to walk away from this." *Now that you know who I am.*

His eyes burn like fire. "Never," he says. "I'll never walk away again." Then he's holding me again so tightly that it feels like he'll never let me go. "I love you, Lei."

My breath is coming in short and jagged spurts. And it's not because of how hard I'm being held. It's because of the pure joy spreading through me. "I love you too," I say fiercely. "And I'm not walking away from you either. No matter what."

"And I'll help you guard your secret," he says. He must notice how tightly he's holding me because he lets go. "What do you need from me?"

His question douses my happiness, sending chills through my body. "Nothing yet." Hopefully, Yanlin will keep his promise to stop his mother. Except that seems like a lot to expect from a boy who's just had his heart broken by my sister. "But if I need you—if my family is in trouble—will you stand by my side? Will you use your position in the student movement to help us?"

"Yes." He grips my hands. "I'll do anything I can to help you."

Suddenly, I remember what Mrs. Liu said to me yesterday evening. *For that young man's sake, I hope you're not like your mother.* Disquiet fills my body. But no—I'm being ridiculous. I would never risk Delun's life. And the thought that my mother was some kind of vampy femme fatale—it's so ludicrous that it's not even worth thinking about. But Mrs. Liu's words cling to me as if she had cast a malevolent curse upon me. "And I'll do the same. Whatever I can do to help you and the other students, I'll do it. I promise."

Delun smiles, but it fades as he looks toward Tiananmen Square. "I need to get back," he says. "There have been some reports of tear gas being used on protesters. I should go and keep an eye on things."

My stomach twinges with anxiety. "What do you think is happening?"

His eyes darken. "I wish I knew."

That's when my body goes cold with premonition. Ba wouldn't tell us why he came home even later than usual last night. And the last time Ba attended a secret late-night Politburo meeting, the government declared martial law and military troops came into Beijing the next day.

"Delun, I think it's big." I clutch his hands hard. "And I think my father might know what's happening."

"I hope you're wrong," he says seriously, "but I have a feeling you're not."

"I can try to find out what my father knows."

He's already shaking his head. "He might figure out that you're involved with us if you ask too many questions."

He's right, but I ignore the way my heart races at the risk I'm about to take. "Maybe it's time I stopped hiding my involvement then."

"Lei, are you sure?"

Gently, I free my hands from his grip. "You said that you'd do anything you could to help me. How can I do any less for you and the others?"

Delun is silent for a moment, looking at me with stark emotion in his eyes. "I'm afraid of what will happen when you go back home," he says at last.

I stare at him in surprise. *He's* the one who's heading back to the powder keg at Tiananmen Square. Not me. "Why are you afraid?"

"I'm afraid your family will talk you into giving me up," he says, "and they wouldn't be wrong. This situation is getting more dangerous every day."

"And we need to know exactly how dangerous it will get," I say. "That's where I come in."

"Fine." He takes a breath. "But when you get back home, you should stay there. I'll call you later, and you can tell me what you find out."

"That might be too late. If I can get my father to tell me what we need to know, I'll come right to Tiananmen Square." He looks like he's going to argue with me, so I add, "There's no use trying to talk me out of it. You're just wasting time."

He sighs. "I know I can't change your mind. You're too stubborn."

I smile at him. "I'll be back as soon as I can. Be careful."

"I will." He pulls me to him and kisses me like he'll never see me again.

My eyes drift shut as I breathe him in, one hand clenched in his hair and the other roaming the corded muscles in his back. The heat of our parting kiss scorches me with an intensity I feel down to my toes.

I just wish it didn't seem like we were always saying goodbye.

CHAPTER TWENTY-FOUR

My whole family is waiting for me in the living room when I get home.

I hover in the entryway, and a tendril of fear unfurls in my heart. Ma is sitting on the gray velvet couch, looking wan and pale. Ba's eyebrows are drawn over burning eyes, and he's perched stiffly on the edge of his armchair.

But it's Jun who scares me the most.

She's next to Ma on the couch, and her whole body is tense with guilt. *No. She couldn't have.* My sister would never betray me. But an awful sensation slithers through my stomach.

"Lei, come in and sit down." My father's emotions are tightly leashed, and I can't tell what he's thinking.

I advance farther into the living room, but I don't sit down. The back of my neck is slick with sweat now. I'm clinging to the belief that Jun is still on my side . . . and I desperately don't want to be wrong.

Ma puts a hand on Jun's shoulder. "Tell Lei what you told us."

My heart falls like a burning meteor.

"I told them everything." My sister drops her gaze. "They know about Delun. The protests. How you showed him our secret." Misery chokes her voice. "I had to tell them."

Pain explodes in my body. *So this is what it feels like to be betrayed by the person closest in the world to me.*

"Nothing to say for yourself?" Ba's face is stony.

I manage to unlock my throat from its paralysis. "You know that

I've always believed in the students' cause," I say. "Free speech. Economic policies that create equity."

"Don't lie to me!" His fist crashes down on the arm of his chair, making us all jump. "You got involved with the protests because of that counterrevolutionary dissident!"

"It's not like that." I take a steadying breath. "And you don't know Delun. He would never turn against me."

"How could you be so stupid? You, of all people—to be drawn in by the seductive words of a dangerous radical and used against your own family!"

Shock sends me reeling. Never in my life has Ba spoken to me with such contempt.

"That's enough, Shen," Ma says. Then she turns to me. "Lei, this young man you're seeing could jeopardize everything our family has fought so hard to protect."

I'm not the only one who had a secret and dangerous relationship. I glance at Jun, but she won't meet my eyes. The urge to blurt out her secret creeps over me. But I don't. It doesn't matter if my sister has let me down—I still won't turn on her. "I understand why you're upset, Ma, but Delun won't do anything to expose us. In fact, he can help us. Mrs. Liu"—now I'm the one who's avoiding Jun's eyes—"is trying to use the protesters against us, but Delun won't let her."

"And you'd trust this radical before you'd trust me?" Ba demands.

"No, that's not what I meant!" Panic rises in my chest. *This is all going so wrong.* Maybe I shouldn't have lied to my parents about Delun and the protests. But the realization is too late. Because everything has blown up in my face.

"I can protect my family without the help of your hooligan boyfriend!" he shouts. Then he whirls on Jun. "And I don't need the help of *your* young man either."

"Yes, Ba." She looks at me at last. "I told them about Yanlin too. That it's over now and that I made a mistake." Her eyes beg me to understand.

I'll never understand what Jun did. But it does make me feel marginally better that she hadn't ratted me out without also confessing about Yanlin.

Now my family is looking at me in expectant silence—and it dawns on me that they're waiting for me to say that *Delun* was a mistake and that it's over between us. But I can't. My stomach turns into hardened stone. *I won't.*

"Give him up." Ba's voice is hard. "If you want to stay a part of this family."

Fear rips through me. *He's bluffing.* Ba would never kick me out of the family—would he? Shakily, I turn to Ma.

Her face is pale but resolute. "I chose you to inherit the art from Empress Wu, our ancestress, because I believed you loved her art and would guard it with everything you have. But if you can't give up this young man, then you are not the daughter who should inherit our legacy."

Something hard clogs my throat. I found out only recently that I would officially inherit Wu Zetian's art, but in my heart, it's always been mine. Never in a million years could I have imagined that I would have to choose between the art I love . . . or Delun.

"Jun, you've met Delun." I'm throwing all pride to the wind and pleading with my sister now. She's my last hope, thin as it is. "Please tell them that he's nothing like they imagine. That he'll never be a threat to any of us!"

She takes a breath, and for one shining moment, I think she's going to fight for me. But then she says, "I'm sorry." Her voice is faint, and her eyes squeeze shut like she's blocking out the sight of my face. "I can't support you in this."

"Jun . . ." But I don't know what else to say. My twin has always had my back, and there's a gaping hole in my body now that she's abandoned me.

"Lei, please." Ma's the one who's begging now. "Just promise you won't see this boy again, and everything will go back to the way it was." Her eyes are wet. "You were meant to be the guardian of Empress Wu's art. Don't throw that away for an infatuation with a boy you barely know."

"Don't make me choose between Delun and my family. What I feel for him isn't a schoolgirl crush." My voice is so cold that I barely recognize it as my own.

"You *are* a schoolgirl." Ba sounds like he's striving for patience. "You're still young and you've made a mistake, but your mother is right. It's not too late to put this behind you."

"We're your family, and we love you," Ma adds.

A wild mix of feelings whirls through me. I'm being torn apart by my desire to fix things with my family *and* stay true to Delun. Icy rage rises in me. It's not fair that they're making me choose between them and the boy I love. "Ma, you were about my age when you fell in love with Ba."

She glances at my father. "That was different."

"It doesn't seem all that different," I say, fighting for calmness. "He was a revolutionary, and you trusted him with the secret of Empress Wu's legacy."

"And I justified her faith!" he shouts. "Your reckless friends know nothing about what it means to protect what you love! They are children playing at being revolutionaries, and you will get hurt if you put your faith in them!"

"Just like your *best friend* got hurt when he put his faith in you?" Heat sweeps through my body. I've lost all control over my anger, and I don't care. "Mrs. Liu's husband was a Red Guard like you were during the Cultural Revolution. Why didn't you help *him*?"

The color drains out of Ba's face, and Ma gasps. Jun looks worriedly toward our parents.

Then all the pieces fall together, hitting me with the force of a tsunami.

Mrs. Liu doesn't want revenge on us because of my father's failure to help her husband. She wants revenge because of my father's feelings for my mother. Because of what Ba did out of love. *She was a woman who could always get men to do anything for her. Even if it meant throwing away their lives and honor for her.*

I stare at my parents with horror seeping into my numb body. "Did Mr. Liu get too close to our secret? Did you set the Red Guard on him, Ba?"

He meets my gaze without flinching. "I had to undermine his credibility before he made an accusation about your mother!" he says fiercely.

Jun draws her knees to her chest. There's a stunned expression on her face. Ma wraps her in a hug, and a sharp envy shoots through me at their closeness.

"So you had him beaten and imprisoned on the off chance that he knew Ma's secret?" A cold lump sits in my gut.

"I didn't know that would happen." His face loosens with the memory of an old regret. "Peng was one of us. I didn't expect the Red Guard to be so merciless."

Strangely, I believe him. "You did what you had to do to protect our family." My shock and anger are fading, replaced with a desperate desire to make my family understand me. "And I'm doing the same thing." I turn to Ma. "I trusted Delun with our secret so he can help me protect it. Like you did with Ba."

"Lei," Ma says, "I know you mean well—"

"No!" Ba's hands are clenched by his sides. "Mei, we'll lose her if we let her go down this path!"

Fear flashes across Ma's face and she falls silent.

"Lei, please listen to them." Tears are streaming down Jun's face.

The last thing I've ever wanted was to cause pain to my family. *All you have to do is give up Delun.* But it's more than just that. I believe in what the students are fighting for. Am I willing to turn my back on them just because my family doesn't trust my choices? But how can I let my family down?

Ba turns to me. "I'm not just trying to protect your mother's secret." He reaches out a hand to me. "I'm trying to protect *you*. That boy is dangerous. Those protests he's dragged you into are dangerous. You have to give it all up *now*."

I've failed to make them understand, and now I have to choose. Agony knifes through my chest. *You know what you have to do.* "I will do everything possible for this family." Tears sting my eyes. My decision is made—and it is shattering my heart. "But if you make me choose, I will choose him and my belief in the movement. I love Delun, and I will stand by him and the others."

"You would be throwing your life away for nothing!" Fury sweeps over Ba's face. "Those protests are over! Do you hear me?"

"What do you mean?" Fear grips me, and icy rivulets of sweat snake down my back. This is why I came back: to find out what is going to happen. "You know something! *What do you know?*" I scream the last question at him.

He gazes at me with a calm more chilling than his anger was. "It all ends tonight, Lei. Thousands of troops have been sent to take Tiananmen Square and our city back by any means necessary. If the protesters resist . . . they will be crushed. That's why you can't go back to the square."

Delun is in Tiananmen Square.

"After tonight, your terrorist friends will no longer be a threat to the government. Or to you." Then he must see what's in my face, because he half rises from his chair.

Panic throbbing through my body, I turn and run.

"She'll be killed!" Ma screams. "Stop her!"

I hear a thud and glance over my shoulder to see Ma on the ground and Ba and Jun rushing over to her. *Ma!* Fear shoots through me. But I can't stop and check on her.

"Lei, wait!" Jun cries, one hand stretched out to me even as she kneels next to Ma. For the first time in my life, I refuse to listen to my big sister.

Wrenching open the front door, I dash into the night, racked with guilt and worry over Ma. But the terror bursting my heart is stronger. I have to get to Tiananmen Square. I have to warn Delun and the others of what's coming.

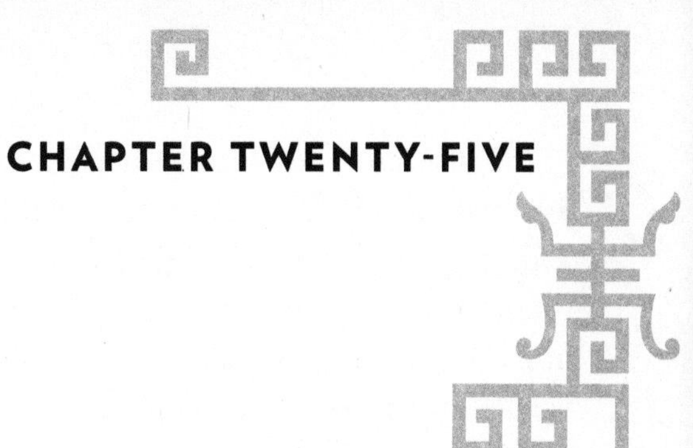

CHAPTER TWENTY-FIVE

I'm too late.

The streets are filled with overturned military vehicles on fire and people brandishing rocks and broken bottles, trying to slow down the People's Liberation Army as it advances on Tiananmen Square. It's already begun. My spine tingles with dread.

It's nearly dark when I stumble into Tiananmen Square with my heart in my throat. Long shadows creep over the ground, and the evening air slices through the thin sleeves of my blouse. I shiver in cold and fear. The protesters have set up a barricade of trucks around the perimeter, and they're starting to link arms to form a human barrier against the onslaught that is coming.

This can't be happening. But it *is* happening, and I don't have time to stand around in shock. I have to find Delun.

There are thousands who have made their way to the square, and everyone is agitated as they trade stories of what they've seen.

"One old woman waved a butcher's knife at the soldiers and told them that they should be ashamed of themselves."

"An army truck crashed right through a barricade, injuring a man!"

"But people are pouring into the streets in support of us!"

Despite the feeling of impending doom, no one is stampeding in panic. Delun and the other student leaders are doing a good job of maintaining calm and order. For now.

Anxiety pulsing through me, I make my way through the masses to the Monument to the People's Heroes. I hope Delun, Yawen, and Rong are there.

But when I see Delun at last, I barely recognize him. His face is streaked in grime and sweat, and his eyes are narrowed in ferocious concentration as he gives commands to restock the first aid stations and reinforce the barricades. He doesn't seem like a political science college student anymore; he seems like a revolutionary leader under siege.

I clear my throat. "Delun."

He whips around, and his eyes light up when he catches sight of me. And just like that, he's the boy I love again. "Lei!"

I run to him, and he holds me hard against his body. Abruptly, he releases me. "You shouldn't have come back! It's too dangerous."

"I told you I was coming back with information." He starts to speak, but I interrupt him. "We don't have time for this! Armed troops have been sent to take back Tiananmen Square by force. This time, they won't stop."

Someone gasps, and I turn to see Yawen with her hand over her mouth.

Rong is by her side. Thankfully, he didn't participate in the second hunger strike, but he's still too thin and pale from the first one. But his voice is as loud and confident as usual. "We'll stop them! They'll see how strong we are!"

"Rong," Delun says, "they will come armed. We have nothing but rocks."

"What do we do then?" I ask.

Delun rubs a hand tiredly over his face. "We try to reason with them, see if we can come to a peaceful resolution." His expression goes bleak. "And we hope that the government isn't crazy enough to go to war against its own people."

"What if they *do* attack us?" Yawen asks in an uncharacteristically small voice. "Shouldn't we be evacuating?"

"Admit defeat?" Rong asks incredulously. "No way!"

"It's not up to you, knucklehead!" Yawen retorts with her usual spirit.

"But the other leaders will agree with Rong," Delun says grimly, "and the protesters will follow their example."

"Do you mean that everyone will stay even if they know what's coming?" My voice rises in disbelief.

He just looks at me with sadness in his eyes. "And what will you do if I tell you to leave and go back to the safety of your home?"

OK, I see his point. I swallow hard. "I'd stay with you. No matter what."

"I need you to listen, Lei," he says urgently. "The soldiers will have orders to arrest the student leaders, not the daughter of a high-ranking party official. If they arrest me, there's nothing you can do to help me. You'll only get in deeper trouble with your father. In fact, you should leave before things get worse."

My mouth sets. "You know me better than that." I'm not going to abandon him and the others because I'm worried about what Ba thinks. My parents have already threatened to cut me off. What else can they do to me?

"I do, and that's why I'm not asking you to leave now," he says. "But if you're going to stay, you need to promise me something."

"What?" I ask.

"That you'll leave if I ask you to."

A lump forms in my throat. "I promise," I say reluctantly. It's not a promise I'd ever wanted to make to him.

Delun bows his head as if he's carrying the weight of all these thousands of lives. "Then we will stay," he says heavily.

My neck muscles tighten in response. I brush a finger along the tense line of his jaw. "We'll get through this together." *This* is the promise I wanted to make to him.

For a long moment, we stand still and close, both of us trying to read the future in the constellation of each other's eyes.

It all goes to hell at about one in the morning.

Bullets and screams tear through the night, rooting me to the ground in paralyzed fear. Soldiers are shooting live rounds of ammunition at us. They are shooting people in the back as they flee. The air crackles with fire and smoke, and everyone is shouting and running, and there is blood on the stones.

"Lei," Delun shouts, "you have to move!"

But I can't. The noise and the rumble of tanks fade out, and my vision blurs. Yawen is saying something to Rong, and he responds, but I can't take in what they're saying. Numbing fear fills me. We all need to get out of here.

But I still can't move. Because a truck filled with military personnel is implacably advancing toward the Goddess of Democracy. My gorge rises. *They can't.* But of course they can.

And they do.

In what seems like slow motion, they plow right into her. And she—indomitable goddess—falls and falls . . . and there is still no sound as she breaks upon the hard ground. My heart plummets into the endless deep as men leap from the truck and start attacking her with crowbars, reducing her beautiful face into white dust and her strong body into shards.

Delun is also watching the destruction of the Goddess of Democracy with a face like stone. Then he picks up a megaphone and starts shouting into it.

With an awful jolt of understanding, I realize that he won't abandon his post until everyone else is safe. And with that realization, sound comes rushing back into the world.

"Everyone leave the square, but don't trample your comrades," Delun shouts, the muscles in his neck corded with tension. "Help the wounded!"

"Rong! Come back, you idiot!" Yawen suddenly yells.

Terror rushes through me as I whirl around to see Rong running straight for a tank with a rock in his hand.

I know I should do something to stop him, but my body is frozen in dread.

Rong throws it with a triumphant yell. "Take that, murderers!" The rock clangs against the tank and doesn't even make a dent.

Then, shock blazing through my brain, I see an advancing soldier lift his rifle and take aim at Rong.

No. Oh please, no. My mind can't register the horror of this moment. The tanks, the soldiers pounding the Goddess of Democracy into dust, the fleeing students—everything seems to stop. Like the whole world is holding its breath.

Then there's a sharp crack, and Rong crumples to the ground.

My body explodes with pain, and I know this memory will play on an endless loop in my nightmares for the rest of my life.

Yawen's screams fill the night.

She sprints toward his still body, and abruptly, I come out of my shock. "Yawen! No!" I run over to where she has collapsed over Rong's body. His chest is a bloody mess, and my heart falls into an abyss. *He's really dead.*

And I can't even let my friend grieve. "Yawen, we have to get out of here!" I tug at her arm, but she won't budge. The tanks and the soldiers are getting closer. We'll be crushed or shot if we stay here. Cold fear sits in my gut.

"We can't leave him here!" She's sobbing and covering his lifeless, blood-soaked body with her own.

Then Delun is by our side. "There's nothing you can do for him now, Yawen!" He lifts her to her feet and says sharply, "Rong would want you to live. So you have to leave. Understand? It's what he would want."

Quickly, I sling her arm around my shoulders and clasp her around her waist. Her body is limp and racked with sobs, but she doesn't resist me. Delun is someone people listen to. *Good.* Because I'll drag her out of here if I have to.

"Go," he says to me. "Get her to safety."

"What about you?" Panic is choking the breath out of me. "I won't leave you!"

"You have to," he says, touching my face gently. "You promised. And I need you to live."

Then he whirls around, putting his body between me and the tanks. He lifts the megaphone. "I am Chuang Delun, a leader of the student movement!" he shouts. "Come and arrest me if you want!"

No! My heart thuds in frantic fear. Delun is sacrificing himself to buy us time to escape. *I can't leave him.* But Yawen, slick with Rong's blood and her own sweat, is starting to slide from my grasp. She's a breath away from running back to Rong's body. I have to get her out now. Choking on a sob, I tighten my hold on her and take one last look at Delun.

He's dropped the megaphone and is facing the tank with his arms outspread. The tank has ground to a halt. Sharp and tempered relief floods me. At least they aren't planning to run him over or shoot him. Because they'd rather arrest and make an example of him.

Delun looks over his shoulder at me. *Go,* he mouths. *I love you.*

Pain stabs my chest. Knowing he can't hear me over the machine-gun fire and shrieks of terror, I whisper, "I love you too."

Then I shoulder Yawen's weight and stumble away as fast as I can.

We're surrounded by others with their own burdens of bloody, limping friends who are moaning in pain. But there are also those who are shoving and fleeing the square without heed for anyone else. This is the stampede Delun was trying to prevent.

Then, before my horrified eyes, a girl is shot in the arm, blood spraying everywhere. She trips over broken rubble and falls, disappearing beneath a mass of people, still screaming for help. My stomach goes queasy with dread. Before I know it, I'm slipping free from Yawen.

"Keep going," I say urgently. "I'll catch up."

Yawen's eyes are unfocused, but when I give her a tiny shove to propel forward, she keeps going. Not as fast as I'd like, but at least she's moving.

I sprint toward the injured girl, pushing past a stream of people and shouting, "Stop it! Help that girl!"

Someone's elbow catches me in the face and I stumble. I flail my arms frantically to regain my footing, and my pulse speeds up crazily. If I fall, it will be me getting trampled. Another fleeing person bumps into me. Suddenly, I'm losing my balance and toppling. Panic claws at my chest as I topple headfirst toward the hard stone ground.

And then darkness closes over me.

Luoyang, Seventh Century

Taiping's pulse quickens with nerves as a palace maid opens the doors. She and her mother drink tea and talk in her chambers every day. But today is different. *I have to keep my promise to Wan'er and break off the engagement that my mother arranged.*

Her heart rate accelerates. The empress is a woman whom no one crosses. Not even Taiping, her only daughter and favorite child. To go against her is a risk only the most foolhardy would take. Just ask Empress Consort Wang and Consort Xiao, who schemed against her. But you'll have to ask their ghosts, because those two ladies are dead now. Her mother had them executed for the murder of her infant daughter.

Some say it was a trumped-up charge and that the empress is still haunted by their wrongful deaths. They say that the empress insisted on moving the seat of power from the main capital of Chang'an to the eastern capital of Luoyang to escape the ghosts of her late rivals. The rumors are wrong. Taiping does think her mother is haunted, but not by Wang and Xiao. Taiping's older sister was murdered at the palace in Chang'an. It's *her* ghost that still haunts the empress.

Mother smiles at Taiping's entrance. "My dear daughter, this is the part of the day that I always look forward to."

"Me too." It's true. Her elder brothers pay their sparse visits to their mother as a matter of duty, but Taiping loves the time she gets to spend with her mother. Her eyes wander to the walls of her mother's sitting room. This is where the empress, proud patron of women artists, displays the art she commissions. Taiping's portrait—and Si's—will end up here soon. Then Taiping frowns. There are two new framed poems on the walls. She moves closer and sees that they are the ones that Wan'er and Si wrote for her ill-conceived contest. "Why do you have *her* poem?" Taiping asks.

"I've always collected the work of gifted poets," the empress answers calmly, even though she must know what Taiping is really asking. *Why is Si so high in your esteem?*

"Si's poetry isn't exactly on the same level as Wan'er's."

"How would you know?" Mother says with a touch of impatience in her voice. "You've never had much interest in poetry." *Or aptitude for poetry, or any other kind of art.* She doesn't say it out loud. Not now or ever—but Taiping knows it's what she must think.

She flushes, and a deep heat sinks into her skin. It's a terrible thing to be the untalented daughter of an empress who loves art. "You're right," she says humbly. There are few people more qualified to evaluate poetry than Wan'er and her mother. If they both find value in Si's poetry, then Taiping must be missing something. "Wan'er told me that Si used all fifteen characters you rewrote." Making an effort to keep her voice even, she says, "Wan'er said it was clever." It *was* clever, to ingratiate herself with her mother by using the language she created.

The empress gives her a sharp look. "You think I'm blinded by flattery, don't you?"

Taiping's face heats. The truth is that despite her mother's and Wan'er's praise, she just sees the gimmicky scribblings of an untalented girl.

Her mother's face softens, and she gestures for Taiping to take a seat across from her on a silk-cushioned stool. "Si's poem broke all the rules of the lüshi form. I know that. But for too long, no one has challenged the idea that the *only* poems considered to be good are the ones that follow the strict conventions created and popularized by men centuries ago." She smiles. "Even Wan'er doesn't try to break the rules in her poetry. She just became better than the men at following them. But Si—she made up her own rules. *That's* what I admire about her poem."

Taiping's eyes drop to her hands. "I see." And she does. Her mother's world of talented artists will always be a world that Taiping will need explained to her, a world that she will never quite understand. Yet, all this art will be hers one day. She will be the one who will inherit and keep her mother's legacy alive.

Dismissing the palace maid after their tea is poured, the empress says, "Let's not talk about poetry anymore. I'd rather know what you've been up to."

Other than organizing a contest to embarrass your new court talent and alienating my lover, you mean? But the thought of Wan'er reminds her of what she needs to do. She takes a sip of fragrant chrysanthemum tea to wash away the dry anxiety in her throat. "I have something to ask you."

The empress raises an eyebrow. "Oh? What is it?"

"I want to break off my engagement."

"That sounds more like a demand than a request," she says icily.

Taiping's palms grow damp. "I didn't mean it to come off as a demand. I just want—"

"I know what you want. And it's impossible."

"Why is it impossible?" she asks. "You built me a Taoist temple, named it after me, and appointed me its abbess to avoid an unwanted engagement! What's so different this time?" Taiping's body jitters as she waits for her mother's reply.

"You want too many things." The empress's voice is hard. "One day, you'll learn that you can't have everything."

"All I want," Taiping says, fighting tears, "is to get out of this marriage."

"That's not true." Her mother presses her hand to her forehead. "You want Wan'er."

"How—how did you know?" she stammers.

"I spent much of my life as an imperial concubine and then as a Buddhist nun," her mother says dryly. "I'm no stranger to love between women."

"Then you'll let us be together?" Hope rises in her heart. "You'll free me from this engagement and let me be the abbess at Taiping Temple in truth and not just in name?"

"This is what I meant when I said that you want the impossible." Her mouth thins. "Did you think that you could just break your engagement and live happily ever after with Wan'er at Taiping Temple?"

Taiping is silent, because that's *exactly* what she had thought.

"That's a silly hope," the empress says coldly, "and you should know better. Wan'er is too necessary to me. I can't maintain my power without her, and I certainly can't let her run off to a Taoist temple with my errant daughter."

Anger seethes in Taiping, and she jumps to her feet. Apparently, her mother doesn't need *her*. She just needs Wan'er with her cleverness and gifts in statecraft. "So power is all that matters to you!"

The empress remains unmoved. "No, that's not all that matters. But power is important. Wan'er would be the first to agree with me. Do you really think she'd give up her position as imperial secretary to run away with you and become a nun?"

Her assessment of Wan'er cuts Taiping to the heart, especially since she's right. "You won't even give Wan'er a chance to decide for herself! Why can't you let us both go?" she pleads.

Her mother's expression hardens. "You grew up in this court of intrigue and danger, and despite your current behavior, you're generally not a fool," she says. "You know that I'm in a precarious position, ruling without the title of Huangdi. The title of Yellow Emperor belongs to your father, and I am merely empress consort. I need Wan'er at my right hand to stay ahead of my political enemies who would cut me down if they could."

"Your enemies are the ones who should worry," Taiping says, and her mother smiles.

But Taiping's not done.

"I've heard the rumors and know exactly how little protection the title of empress consort has." Her heart pounds with her own daring. This is the most she has ever hinted about what she knows about the late Empress Consort Wang's fate.

The smile is wiped off her mother's face. "Tread carefully, daughter."

"Why?" she asks, a thick knot forming in her chest. "Because you might be as merciless to your own daughter as you are to your enemies?"

Her mother turns pale as death. "What have you heard?"

"That it was *you* who killed your own baby." As soon as the words are out of Taiping's mouth, shame twists her gut. Of course she doesn't believe it. It's just the sick feeling of marrying a man she doesn't love and losing Wan'er that made her want to hurt her mother.

And judging from the horror-stricken look on her mother's face, it looks like she has succeeded.

"You can't possibly believe that," the empress whispers.

"I don't." Tears sting her eyes. "Of course I don't believe you did it."

Taiping can't even say it again—the rumor that her mother killed Taiping's older sister to frame Empress Consort Wang for murder. She's sobbing as she throws herself into her mother's arms.

"I'm sorry! I didn't mean it!" *Curses take every lady who has ever whispered that poisonous tale into my ear.*

"Is this all because I won't let you run off with Wan'er?" the empress asks heavily.

Sniffling, Taiping tries to lift her head so she won't stain the silk of her mother's gown with her tears, but the empress pulls her back and nestles her against her shoulder. "I'm sorry," Taiping says again.

"I told you," her mother says, "what you want is impossible." She pulls away from her. "But I will give you a choice. That much I can do for my daughter."

A faint hope glows in Taiping's heart. "What choice?"

"You may leave to take on your abbess role at Taiping Temple . . ."

Joy fills her—only to be dashed by her mother's next words.

". . . but without Wan'er."

"And my other choice?" Her voice is dull with disappointment. She wants Taiping Temple so badly that she burns for it—a desire matched only by what she feels for Wan'er. "Marry my cousin so you can have another political alliance?"

"Not a political alliance for *me*. This marriage would be for *you*. So you can build power."

Taiping stares at her mother with her mouth open. "What do you mean?"

The empress rises and opens the door swiftly, glancing in the hallway before shutting the door again, making sure that it is closed all the way. Even then, she comes close to her daughter and lowers her voice. "I did not scheme and fight for power all these years to hand the empire over to one of my indolent, weak sons to rule."

Taiping's heart beats in terror . . . and excitement. It isn't exactly treason to speak this way, since none of her brothers is emperor. Not yet. *And maybe not ever.*

The empress steps away from her to walk over to a tall black lacquered cabinet inlaid with jade and unlocks it with a key around her neck. She tucks the key back beneath her robes and then pulls the cabinet doors open. Inside is a small stone Buddha statue . . . with the empress's face.

"What is that?" Taiping asks, puzzled.

"An enduring ideal," she replies. "A way to battle the men still clinging to the patriarchal teachings of Confucius." Her voice is soft with hope.

Taiping still doesn't understand, but her mother closes the cabinet doors and locks them without further explanation.

Then she comes back to Taiping and leans down to her ear, speaking fast and low. "Your father is ill. I don't like it, but it's a fact.

When he dies, I will take the throne and begin a new dynasty in my own name. And after I die"—her eyes meet Taiping's—"I want the throne to go to my daughter, who is most like me."

Her mind whirls with what her mother is telling her. This is more than she ever dreamed of. Wan'er and her, someday ruling the empire together. This would be enough power to satisfy even her beloved. And then cold reality splashes down on her wild thoughts. There's a catch to what her mother is offering her. "I would have to marry my cousin. And give up Wan'er."

"You've known all your life that royalty do not marry for love. We marry for political advantage. And you'll need every advantage you can get if you want to become Huangdi in my footsteps." She sounds very sure, given that *she's* not even the regent in her own right. Yet . . . Taiping has no doubt that she will become Huangdi. That's how strong her mother is.

But questions boil up in her. Could Taiping really inherit a dynasty in her mother's name? Is she strong enough to rule? Is the regency what she wants? *Or do I want the quiet peace of a Taoist temple?*

Her mother sits back down at the table. "For royalty, marriage is a convenience," she remarks. "It's not unheard of for a royal lady to take a lover outside of marriage as long as she is discreet. She wouldn't want any question of the legitimacy of her heirs—which won't be a concern for you." She sips her tea, which is probably cold by now. "There are some practical benefits to having another woman as a lover."

"We are not . . ." Taiping begins before remembering how useless denials would be. All lies that her worldly mother wouldn't believe anyway. Then what the empress said hits her, and her breath goes short. "Wait. Do you mean that I *don't* have to give up Wan'er?"

"One way or the other, you'll have to give up something." Her eyes are sad.

Taiping Temple. Girls giggling behind reed curtains. Cool rooms filled with scrolls. Taiping had dreamed of stealing kisses with Wan'er and reading poems together there. The temple would feel empty without Wan'er. But can she give her hand and body in marriage to a near stranger and stay in this palace full of whispers and conspiracies?

"I wish I could give you everything you want," her mother says, "but I can't. The most I can do is give my daughter this choice between peace and power." She beckons to her, and Taiping kneels at her feet. Tenderly, the empress lays her hand on Taiping's cheek. "I'll give you time to make your decision. It is not an easy one."

No, it is not. Peace or power. Safety or love. As her mother said, one way or another, she will have to sacrifice something.

CHAPTER TWENTY-SIX

Beijing, 1989

My eyes are crusty and every bone in my body aches when I wake up to the sound of whispered voices and bright lights. Gradually, my family's anxious faces come into focus. *Where am I?* The last thing I remember is the hard ground meeting my face—so why am I now lying on a soft bed in what looks like a hospital ward?

"She's awake!" Jun exclaims.

"Thank the heavens!" Relief is palpable in Ma's voice.

My own relief floods me. Ma seems to have recovered.

Ba moves closer to my side. "Lei, can you hear us?"

It's Ba's voice that jolts me to full consciousness. "Delun!" If anyone knows what happened to him, it would be my father. I grab his hand. "Where is Delun?" I ask, trying to tamp down the full-on panic taking over my body.

His face tenses up, although he doesn't let go of my hand. "I've been too busy making sure you're taken care of to worry about the hoodlum who dragged you into this mess."

"That wasn't his fault!" If anyone, it's the fault of his buddies in the Politburo. But it won't do me any good to throw accusations at my father now—I need him too much to alienate him. I need his help to find Delun. "Please, Ba." Tears wet my cheeks, and I clutch his hand harder. "Use your connections to find him."

"You were at Tiananmen Square," he says grimly, "and you saw what happened. You will need to prepare yourself for the worst."

"But Delun gave himself up to be arrested!" My voice climbs in fear. "They wouldn't kill him, would they?"

"I don't know." He stares down at me with an unreadable look on his face.

Part of me wants to fling myself into his arms for the comfort he's always given me. But fear of losing Delun makes me ache with a terrible pain. So I pull my hand away from Ba's and ignore the hurt flashing over his face. I'm no longer a little girl with blind faith in my father. "Find out," I say tightly. "No matter what, I want to know."

Before he can answer, Ma hurries to the bed and lays a blanket from my bedroom over me.

A pang of guilt hits me for leaving her after she collapsed. "Ma, I'm so sorry—"

"Hush, child. There's nothing to be sorry for, and I'm fine," she says. "But you've been unconscious for a day."

A day? My mind fills with the horror of all that could have happened while I was safe in this hospital bed.

"We were so worried," Jun adds, her face scrunched up like she's going to burst into tears.

"Oh?" Logically, I know my sister had nothing to do with the bloodbath at Tiananmen Square. But every time I think of her telling my parents about Delun, I go cold with anger.

Ma looks between us in concern. Then she tucks the blanket neatly around my shoulders. "You'll make yourself worse if you work yourself into a frenzy, Lei."

Frenzy? She hasn't seen me in a frenzy yet. I bolt up in bed and instantly feel a rush of dizziness. "Tell me what happened, Ba." Whatever his faults, sugarcoating the truth has never been one of them.

"It was a massacre," he says bluntly.

Jun gasps, but I don't even turn to look at her. I clench the blanket in my fists, and a sick feeling overtakes me. I'm remembering the flare of assault rifles and the blood and the screams. *Yes, I knew that already.* "How many were killed?" I whisper, foreboding creeping coldly over me.

"Official accounts say it was a hundred or so."

That could mean that thousands died. My stomach churns.

"I didn't expect . . ." Ba presses his mouth tight. That's the closest he'll ever come to criticizing his comrades—despite any horror that might be lurking in his secret soul.

"I was with friends." I'm fighting to stay focused, but with every passing second, the fear in my chest threatens to burst out. "I need to know if they survived." *Yawen.* I'm filled with shame because this is the first time I've thought of her since waking up from unconsciousness.

"I'll find out," he says with a sigh.

Rage burns in me. Because he's acting as if I'm asking for nothing but a new dress. Like my need to find my friends is an irresponsible whim. But I tamp down my anger. I can't let Delun and Yawen down. And as for Rong—it's too late. Sorrow bursts in my heart. "There was a boy . . . a friend. He was killed." My throat is clogged with emotion. "Can you see that his body gets to his family?"

"The government is planning to cremate the dead and bury the ashes in a mass grave," Ba says in a matter-of-fact voice, "but I'll see what I can do."

How can he be so calm when he's talking about cremation and mass graves? But even with grief and fury storming in my heart, I match my father's icy control. "The last time I saw my friend Yawen, she was alive. If she survived, what will happen to her?"

"If your friend Yawen wasn't a student leader and has been arrested, she could be released . . . if she has the right connections." *Meaning that Ba can secure her release. Unless she's been killed.*

I struggle to breathe past a wave of fresh pain. I'll have to follow up on this. But first . . . "And Delun? What will happen to him?" My heart beats fast with fear. I saw him give himself up. I know he was arrested.

"Your Delun *is* one of the leaders of this insurrection," he says slowly and deliberately, as if he wants me to understand the seriousness of what he's saying. "If he hasn't already been arrested, he will be. The government is tracking down all the student leaders who have escaped arrest."

Despair swells over me at his words. Even if Delun is alive, I've lost him.

"Your father will do his best to help your friends," Ma says soothingly.

I'm not as sure. "Will you?" I look directly into Ba's eyes, hoping beyond hope that I'm wrong about my father. "Will you get Delun out?"

He meets my eyes with a hard expression on his face. "It would cost me my position in the Politburo to help him escape arrest or set him free."

That means Ba can help—but won't. His betrayal hurts more than I could have imagined. Helpless fury sweeps through me. "How can you worry about your reputation when it's Delun's life at stake?" I demand. "You know what can happen to him!" Labor camp. Torture. Execution.

"It's my reputation that has protected this family for decades! I won't throw it away for one reckless boy!"

My throat aches with agonizing frustration. "But—"

"Forget him," Ba says roughly. "You still have the Gaokao to worry about. It's in just over a week."

"The Gaokao?" I ask incredulously. "You expect me to take a test when my friends have been murdered and arrested?" My head feels like an avalanche has crushed my skull, I'm sore to my bones, and I'm on the verge of collapsing in tears. I can't even contemplate dragging my aching head and heart out of this bed. How can I possibly endure a grueling exam that lasts two days?

"Lei just regained consciousness! Surely she doesn't need to take it so soon," Ma says, a worried pucker in her forehead. "We can get her a medical exemption to take it later."

"On what grounds?" Ba asks sharply. "For getting injured during an illegal protest? It was all I could do to convince the authorities that she was just an innocent bystander. But if she doesn't take the Gaokao when it's scheduled, it will look bad."

"I don't care how it looks," I say dully. "In fact, I don't care about the Gaokao." That's not completely true, but it's hard to care about my future when my present has been blown to pieces.

"It's the only way you can get into college!" Jun says, visibly shocked.

Ma covers her mouth with a shaking hand. "Lei, what about your dreams?"

But Ba doesn't seem concerned. "In return for your taking the Gaokao," he says calmly, "I will secure Yawen's release if she's been arrested. It may be possible that I can commute Delun's sentence as well."

Go to hell. But I think of Yawen's loud laughter and how she was the first person to accept me into the student movement. *You can join us! Anyone who can take my boyfriend down a notch gets my respect.* Memories of Yawen with Rong feel like a blow to the heart. I can't let her rot in prison alone with her grief. And there's Delun. My jaw tenses. Making a perfunctory attempt on the Gaokao is a small price to pay for the chance of saving him from death and torture. "Fine," I say through gritted teeth. "I'll take the Gaokao."

Ba's eyebrows slant down. "And you will need to score well on the Gaokao. High enough to get into a tier-one school."

I gape at him. There are only two tier-one schools—Beijing University and Tsinghua University—so their Gaokao cutoffs are notoriously high. Yes, I've always wanted to go to Beijing University, and I've done well on the practice tests I've taken, but there's never a guarantee of making the cutoff. Pinning my friends' fates on that kind of score is ridiculous. And besides . . . "What about the admission quotas against women?"

He shrugs. "I'll take care of that."

I wince. He means that he'll pull strings as he always does. I can't turn a blind eye to my father's corruption anymore, even when it benefits me. Especially when it benefits me.

"Just make sure you get a tier-one score," he says. Just like that—as if what he's demanding is easy.

Ba can't be serious. But a sinking feeling in my gut tells me that he is. "The Gaokao is over a week away, and scores won't be published for weeks after that!" I can't wait that long to find out what happened to Delun and Yawen.

"I'll be able to know the exam results right away," he says. "In any case, I don't think I'll be able to get any information on your friends in less than a week." A muscle twitches in his face. "Everything has been rather . . . chaotic."

"The government batters us with propaganda against peaceful protesters, and the military attacks its own people. Thousands of students are dead or imprisoned for their beliefs. And now a witch hunt begins for the survivors." My voice is chilly. "Chaotic is one way of putting it. But it's good you have your priorities straight—me, getting a good score on the Gaokao."

I think my father is going to get defensive and yell. Instead, an emotion that might be remorse flashes over his face. "Whether I agreed with it or not, the party decided on this course—and it won't waver. It's out of my control. The only thing still within my power is to make sure that your part in this insurrection doesn't destroy your future. That's my priority." Quietly, he says, "And there's something else. You must promise never to see or speak to them or anyone associated with the protests again."

My heart goes cold. I'd rather he had yelled and cursed me out. "What?" I ask numbly.

"You might think I'm being harsh." He rubs his chest as if he's trying to get rid of a deep ache. "But I just want what's best for you. A high score on the Gaokao will get you into the best colleges and help you realize all your dreams. But you have to cut ties with associations that will only hold you back. Your mother has always wanted to pass on her legacy to you. And I want the same." He touches my face tenderly. "Imagine what you can be. Your mother chose *you* to be the guardian of Empress Wu's art."

It's the first time he's openly acknowledged my mother's choice for me to inherit Wu Zetian's art, and out of the corner of my eye, I see Jun flinch ever so slightly. So she does mind after all.

"You could also be the first female Communist Party official," Ba says.

Nausea makes my stomach swim. "I don't want that." The very thought of having anything to do with the party that murdered my friends repulses me.

"I suppose I saw that coming." He sighs. "Fine. You don't have to join the party. But we still want you to have everything you've ever dreamed of."

My dreams have changed.

When I'm silent, he continues. "You'll go to Beijing University in the fall and study art history, and you can put this tragedy behind you."

He's delusional. Anger pounds through me. *How can I go to the campus where I met Delun without thinking of him every moment?* My anger dims, and my body aches under an onslaught of fresh sorrow. It's not just my friends and my present life I've lost. My future is gone too.

I don't want the life of power and prestige my parents are offering. Not if it means stepping over the bodies of my friends, with the blood still staining the stones in Tiananmen Square. But that's not the choice my father is giving me. He wants to put my feet on the path that I once desired with all my heart. And all I have to do is give up my friends. My heart twists. Give them up in order to save them. That's what I have to do.

"It's the right decision," my mother says softly.

It's the only option they've given me. There was never any real choice—not with the lives of Delun and Yawen in the balance. "All right." I'm struggling to speak . . . to breathe. It feels as if my lungs have been ripped out and I'm somehow supposed to keep living. "I promise."

Then I catch a glimpse of my sister's face. She's gone pale, and there's a blank expression in her eyes. It's the way she looked when our mother first announced that I would be inheriting Wu Zetian's legacy.

No one expects Jun to score high enough on the Gaokao to get into the best colleges. They aren't offering *her* the chance to take my mother's place as keeper of a secret inheritance or my father's place in the precarious ranks of government. A cold trickle of premonition works its way down my spine.

For the first time, I wonder what it would be like to be the sister who isn't offered a choice for her future. As dangerous as it might be.

Then Jun blinks as if she's coming out of a trance. She walks over to my bed and unfastens the gold chain around her neck. My eyebrows draw together, but then she hands me the pendant, and I see the character carved into the jade is "mei." My confusion grows. This is *my* pendant.

"Mei Mei," she says, using a childhood endearment she almost never uses anymore. "I wanted to wear our necklaces together," she explains, her voice catching. "Jiemei. Sisters. I . . . thought it would bring you luck and that you would wake up if I held my little sister to my heart."

A lump forms in my throat as I grip the smooth jade, still warm from my sister's body heat. Maybe I haven't lost Jun after all. Maybe my jie jie is still looking after me.

CHAPTER TWENTY-SEVEN

My family hovers anxiously while a doctor asks me questions to test my cognitive functions. I answer them impatiently and wish my family would leave so I can ask questions of my own.

At last, the doctor says that other than a concussion and some scrapes and bruises, I seem to be in good health, but they'll need to keep me for a day or two to monitor my condition. It's only then that my family leaves with promises to visit tomorrow.

A nurse stays in the room to take my vitals, and as she leans forward with a thermometer, I grab her arm.

"Where's the nearest phone?" Of course Ba's made sure there's no phone in my room. Or TV. I can still see the empty brackets on the wall where a TV should be.

A startled expression flashes across her face. "There's a pay phone in the lobby, but you're not supposed to leave the room."

That's pretty much what I expected. "Fine." I let go of her arm and tamp down my irritation. "Can you get me a newspaper then?" I'm desperate to find out *some* information, even if it's just the official party line.

The nurse, an older woman around my mom's age, shakes her head. "I'm not allowed to give you a newspaper." She looks at me with questions in her eyes. "I'm sorry, I don't know why."

It's obvious she wants me to explain the mystery of why I'm forbidden to have a phone, TV, or newspaper, but I'm not in the mood to satisfy her curiosity. I lean forward and lower my voice. "What happened in Tiananmen Square? Are the injured being treated here? How many—"

"I have no idea." Her face has whitened, and the thermometer dangles from her hand as if forgotten. Then she visibly pulls herself together. "I need to take your temperature."

She's scared. Why? It's not my father, because she doesn't even know why my access to news has been restricted. But it's clear that the nurse won't answer my questions, so I let her put the thermometer in my mouth. As I clamp my lips around the cool glass, I try to think of a way to get past her defenses.

When she finishes taking my temperature, I make my voice as friendly as possible. "So, how long have you been a nurse?"

She records my temperature on my chart. "A while," she says, avoiding my eyes. *OK, this is not going to be easy.*

An orderly who looks like he's in his late twenties wheels a meal cart into my room. "Lunchtime," he says cheerfully.

I straighten up in bed at the sight of a new potential informant. "Do you know anything about Tiananmen Square?" I ask, not wasting time with polite formalities.

The friendly look on his face disappears at once, and he casts an uneasy glance at the nurse, who pauses on her way out of the room. "No," he says, looking back at me. "I don't know anything." His voice is flat.

Why won't anyone talk about Tiananmen Square?

The nurse leaves, and the orderly places a covered dish on the hospital table and swings the table over my bed.

"Please," I say urgently. "If you know anything, tell me. I had friends in Tiananmen Square, and I need to know what happened to them."

His face furrows. Then he looks around quickly and whispers, "Look, everyone is afraid. People were brought in with their legs crushed from tanks and gunshot wounds. It was like a war." He hesitates, and fear leaks into his voice as he continues. "But the doctors and hospital staff who speak out in anger or talk to foreign reporters are being arrested. So now we keep our mouths shut and just do our job."

My whole body goes cold. "How many . . . ?" I swallow hard. "How many do you think died?"

"The news says it was a hundred, but it's more than that." His eyes are somber. "I'd say thousands."

Horror shudders through me. All those bright young people—my friends and comrades—shot dead and crushed by tanks. My throat tight, I say, "So the news is reporting on the protests? That must mean the news blackout is over. What are they saying about Tiananmen?" My voice is hard with anger. "Are they telling the world that the government sent in troops and tanks to murder peaceful, unarmed students demonstrating for freedom?"

He licks his lips nervously. "Let me give you some advice, miss. You're in our best hospital suite, so I'm guessing you have major party connections. But if you say things like that, even *your* status might not be enough to keep you out of trouble." A sympathetic look comes into his eyes. "The only news we're getting is state-run, and they're saying the military was sent in to put down a small insurrection. Anyone who says differently is being interrogated and possibly arrested." He places utensils next to the metal dome covering my meal. "So I'd be careful if I were you."

I don't move to touch my lunch after he leaves. Hot tears build up behind my eyes, and I finally give in to the grief tearing at my heart. Shoving aside the hospital table, I bury my head in my knees and sob uncontrollably. It's too late to be careful.

I've already lost everything.

Why do I need to stay in the hospital so long? The doctor said they needed to keep me here only for a couple of days at the most, but it's already been *five* days. And every time I ask why I haven't been discharged yet, the nurses and doctors say it's just a "precaution." Of course they mean they don't want to piss off a high-ranking Communist Party official. Ma and Jun are just as evasive. But I know Ba was the one who made the call to keep me at the hospital for longer than necessary. And I'm not even able to confront him about it.

That one is my fault. When Ma and Jun came on the second day of my hospital stay to drop off Gaokao study materials, I told them that visits from Ba would "delay my recovery." I guess he took me at my word because he hasn't visited again.

Without anything else to do, I resume studying for the Gaokao, but I find myself staring in blank confusion at math problems that I used to solve easily or struggling to remember key historical facts buried in the foggy recesses of my brain.

Physically, I've recovered. But my nights are haunted by visions of Rong's bloody body and his sightless eyes, and I haven't been sleeping well. Stress, depression, and exhaustion don't exactly make for a winning combo when it comes to taking the Gaokao.

But I keep taking (and inevitably bombing) the practice tests. It's not like there's anything else to do in the hellish monotony of the hospital. I'm allowed supervised walks on the hospital grounds, but that's the only time I can leave my room. And even worse than my enforced physical inactivity is the blockade on the news. I don't see the sympathetic orderly again, and no one else will talk to me about what happened to the other protesters. They just look at me with scared eyes and refuse to answer my questions.

Nine days after my arrival, I return home from the hospital.

Have my friends and comrades been wiped out of the country's memory? Now that I'm finally home, I have to find out what happened to them.

"I'm fine," I say impatiently to Ma and Jun as they try to follow me into my bedroom. "I just need to be alone." So I can make desperate phone calls to Delun's and Yawen's dorms to see if their roommates know anything.

Ma and Jun exchange looks, and Ma says, "We'll let you rest, but we're here if you need anything."

"OK." But what I need is information, and they can't, or *won't,* give me that. As for Ba . . . I'm so furious about his part in the massacre that I don't know how I can ever speak to him again. Maybe he doesn't quite agree with what happened, but he didn't try to stop it either. And I can't forgive him for that. I'm glad he's at work and didn't come with Ma and Jun to bring me home.

Ba probably let me come home only because the Gaokao is tomorrow. My hunch is that he kept me in the hospital so its built-in security would keep me from fleeing. He didn't have to bother. I'm not going anywhere until I take the Gaokao. Anxiety worms into my stomach. My mind is still too full of grief for the focus required to get a tier-one score and fulfill my end of the bargain with my father. Right now, I'll be lucky to get a second- or third-tier score. I just have to hope that Delun and Yawen have both escaped arrest and are out there somewhere safe.

Ma kisses me on the forehead. I know she means well and that she wants so desperately for things to be back the way they were. That's probably why she stood by Ba's side and didn't say a word to support me when he coldly bargained with me to give up my friends. The spot where she kissed me burns like an acid splash. Ma wants to believe she can rewind time and turn me into her carefree, fun-loving daughter again—by taking away the life I chose.

But she's wrong. There's no returning to the person I once was.

My mother massages her temples. "I think I'll go lie down too."

A twinge of concern touches me. A headache again? I haven't forgotten that she fainted the night I ran from home to join the movement's last stand in Tiananmen Square. But I just can't muster the energy to ask if she's OK, so I let her leave.

Jun lingers behind. "Are you sure you don't want to talk?"

There was always a nurse or orderly coming in or out of my room at the hospital when Jun came to visit, so we haven't had a chance to really talk. And actually . . . I'm not ready for a heart-to-heart with my sister yet. She *did* betray me by telling our parents about Delun and my involvement with the protests.

"I don't want to talk right now." I suppose I can't forgive Jun yet.

Her face falls, and a pang of regret shoots through my heart. But as soon as she leaves, I slam the door shut and race to my phone.

But when I reach my nightstand, my phone is missing. Did it fall off? Heart racing in panic, I drop to my knees and peer under my bed and check behind the nightstand. No phone. In fact, the phone jack behind the nightstand has been covered with a smooth beige plastic plate. And the cardboard box under the bed where I kept old copies of newspapers is also gone.

I leap to my feet so quickly the blood rushes from my head. Frantically, I scan my room. My small TV is missing too. My mind races. Yawen and my other friends only have the number to my private line—and that's been cut off. Now they have no way to reach me. And I can't get news about them either, assuming that the press is even allowed to report on what happened in Tiananmen more than a week ago. My stomach clenches in anger.

Now I know why Ba kept me in the hospital so long. He needed time to make my home into a prison.

I run out of my room and down the hall, yelling, "Jun!"

Her bedroom door opens at once. "Lei, what's wrong?" she asks, her face filled with alarm.

I push past her and go directly to her nightstand where her phone should be, but it's also missing. I whirl to face her. "Don't tell me you're on lockdown too."

"Not exactly." Her cheeks are tinged with red. "Ba didn't know if I could . . . stand up to you." Meaning that Ba didn't trust her to say no to me if I asked to use her phone.

I dash out of her room and run down the stairs. He can't stop me from using another phone in the house, can he?

"Ba took out all the phones!" Jun calls after me. "There's one in his office and one in Ma and Ba's bedroom, but that's it. And both those rooms are being kept locked."

I come to an abrupt stop on the stairs and turn around. "That's a little extreme, don't you think?" But should I expect anything less from the father who threatened to disown me if I went to the protests? Yes, it was a bluff, but the fact that he even made the threat hurts.

She descends the stairs so that she's just one step above me. "They're just trying to keep you safe."

I don't trust myself not to scream at her, so I hurtle down the stairs with Jun behind me. If the phones are out of the question, then I can at least get the news.

But when I get to the media room, I find that there's a new TV cabinet and, no surprise, it's locked. Frustration bubbles up in me. It's a sure bet that there won't be a scrap of newspaper to be found in the whole house.

I glare at Jun, who's followed me into the media room. "How is Ba going to keep the news from me when I go to college?"

She just stares down at her feet.

I go to the cabinet and bend to examine the lock. There's a small keyhole on the handle. I straighten and study Jun with narrowed eyes. "I don't suppose you know where the key is, do you?"

She looks up. "No."

Satisfaction courses through me. One benefit of being a twin is that I can always tell when Jun is lying. "Really? No idea, huh?" Slowly, I pace around the room and keep an eye on her. "It would be pretty inconvenient for Ba to carry around the key since he's not home all that much. What would happen if you or Ma wanted to watch a soap opera or something?"

She doesn't respond, but when I pass a replica of a Ming dynasty vase, she touches the end of her braid. *Gotcha!* I stop moving around the room and reach inside the vase; my fingers touch cold metal. The key.

Jun gasps. "How did you know?"

"Come on, Jun. When could you ever hide anything from me?"

I don't wait for an answer. I'm already fitting the key into the lock and swinging open the door of the cabinet.

"Lei, I don't think you should do this."

"Don't worry," I say bitterly. "I won't tell Ba that you were the one who told me where the key was."

"But I wasn't . . . I didn't!"

I spare a glance at her, and she's clutching her hands together. "Then you have nothing to worry about," I say as I press the power button on the TV and change the channel to the news station.

An image of a male news anchor comes onto the screen. The female anchor who usually presents the news with him is conspicuously missing. "What happened to the other news anchor?" I ask out loud.

"She was suspended," Jun replies, "for seeming sympathetic to the protesters."

Shock pours through me. "What did she say?"

"It was more *how* she reported on the troops coming into Tiananmen Square. She wore black during the broadcast, and her voice seemed somber."

"That's *it*? They suspended her for *that*?" How could a nationally famous news broadcaster lose her job for something so small? My skin crawls.

I've come out of the hospital into a new and much scarier world. One where people are too afraid to speak the truth and punished for the slightest human compassion. Sadness jabs my heart. Not too long ago, my friends and I had hoped that we were on the verge of a more open and free China—but that seems like a distant dream now.

"This is what I was trying to tell you," Jun says earnestly. "It's dangerous for everyone who was involved at Tiananmen and even those who are sympathetic. That's why Ma and Ba are making you cut all contact with the protesters."

Before I can respond, the male anchor on the screen says, "And now for breaking news. Police are looking for the counterrevolutionary student leaders of the riot at Tiananmen Square."

My heart hammers into my throat. *Delun.* If he hasn't been arrested, they'll be looking for him.

Then faces and names come onto the screen. The news anchor, in voice-over, keeps talking. "These are the twenty-one most wanted leaders. If anyone has information about these dangerous individuals, call this hotline immediately."

Tuning out his voice, I frantically scan the names and faces. They're all vaguely familiar to me. But I don't see Delun. If he's not on the most wanted list, then he must have been arrested.

Suddenly feeling weak, I stumble backward until my legs hit the couch. Bonelessly, I collapse onto it. My last hopes that Delun is free crumble into dust. But if he's in prison, why isn't the government bragging about its capture of one of the most prominent leaders?

Then an idea so fragile that I hardly dare to think it blooms in my head. Does Ba have something to do with this silence? Is this part of his deal with me to commute Delun's sentence if I score high enough on the Gaokao? Maybe even laying the groundwork to free Delun . . .

Jun walks over to the TV and turns it off. "Lei, are you OK?"

I barely hear her question. My body is hardening with iron resolve. I have to ace the Gaokao tomorrow. Delun and Yawen are both depending on me.

CHAPTER TWENTY-EIGHT

Jun and I come back from one of the many testing centers in Beijing, completely worn out from the last day of the Gaokao. Each of the two days consisted of nine hours of intense questions, but the biggest question wasn't on the exam. It's the one gnawing at my insides. *Will I do well enough for Ba to keep his end of the bargain and help Delun and Yawen?* Under the fire of my determination, it did feel like my old focus and ease with the test had come back. But nothing is ever certain with the Gaokao.

"How do you think you did?" Jun asks brightly as we take off our shoes and place them on the shoe rack in the entryway. She's still pretending that everything is normal.

I have no interest in playing along. I shrug and move into the living room without answering. At this point, we're barely on speaking terms. But that doesn't keep her from trying to connect with me.

"Those English grammar problems were so hard! I couldn't figure out when I was supposed to choose the simple past tense or the past perfect tense. What's the difference again?"

"It's too late now," I snap. "The test is over, and now we have to wait."

Her face folds in on itself, and I feel bad. She did what she thought was best by telling our parents about Delun and my involvement in the protests. I might be able to forgive her eventually, but not just yet.

"Ma," I yell, running up the stairs. "Where are you?"

Ba won't be home yet, but maybe he's called. Maybe he told our mother how I did on the Gaokao.

Jun follows me, and we find our mother in bed with the lights off in her room. Another migraine. She's been getting them daily ever since I came home from the hospital. Despite everything else pressing down on me, I worry about Ma.

She smiles at us wanly from beneath the covers of her bed. "How did the test go?"

"Fine," Jun says brightly.

"OK, I guess." I don't have the heart to ask if Ba had called. Besides, Ma would've told us if he had.

"We should let you get some rest," Jun says, and Ma doesn't protest, so we tiptoe out.

Jun trails me down the hall to my room, and I spin around to confront her. "So, now you're spying on me?"

She takes a step backward. "I'm not spying on you!"

"Then why do you keep following me around?"

"I just want to talk. Lei, can we please make up? I'm so sorry for everything."

Despite myself, my heart thaws. I want my sister back.

Before I can answer, a voice rings out from the bottom of the stairs. "I'm home!"

It's Ba. Forgetting all about my sister, I race down the stairs with my heart beating in fear and anticipation. Jun, naturally, follows at a more sedate pace.

"Do you know my Gaokao score?" I demand breathlessly. It's the first time I've spoken to him in over a week, and it causes me almost physical pain to speak to him now.

"Come into the living room." Then he smiles.

Surely the smile is a good sign? My stomach sickens to know that my friends' lives are dependent on his goodwill. Tamping down my anxiety, I enter the living room. By now, Jun has joined us. We usually sit together on the love seat, but this time, she takes the love seat while I sit on the curved velvet couch by myself.

Ba sits in an armchair, setting his briefcase down at his feet. "Congratulations, Lei. You got a tier-one score!"

It's what I wanted, but my stomach twists. Because the reason I want such a high score is different now. It's not admission to Beijing University that I want so badly. It's Delun and Yawen's safety.

"I've already put the fifty thousand in your bank account."

I gape at him for a second before remembering his financial incentive. *Like I care about the money.*

"You did well too," he says to Jun. "Second tier. Twenty thousand for you."

Her eyes darken, but she says mildly enough, "Thank you, Ba. I'm glad—"

"Then you'll help my friends?" I demand, talking over Jun. I don't care about her score on the Gaokao. Not when Delun's and Yawen's lives are at stake.

Jun presses her lips tightly together, and a muscle twitches in her cheek.

He opens his briefcase, extracting a long envelope. "I had absolute faith in you." Then he comes over and hands it to me. "That's why I've already secured your friend's release."

Impatiently, I tear it open and take out two sheets of paper. One is a copy of release papers for Yawen, signed by Ba and dated two days ago. The other is the confirmation of release, also dated two days ago. My heart hurts. Does Yawen know how she got out? Has she been calling me since her release and wondering why I'm not picking up?

But I have a more pressing concern right now. "What about Delun?" My hands are clammy with dread. "Did you find out what happened to him?"

Ba's face turns grave. "I'm sorry, Lei."

My mind shoves futilely at the horror descending on me like a cold fog, but I'm powerless to stop what's coming.

Then he says three words that pierce me to the heart. "Delun is dead."

Suddenly, I'm choking on tears and fighting to breathe. "He can't be! I saw him arrested!" *But did I?* I saw Delun give himself up, and I saw the tank stop. And then I was running for my life with Yawen and didn't see what happened. I never should have left him. A terrible emptiness overwhelms me.

"He was executed for insurrection against the government."

Pain stabs through the numbness wrapped around my body. "No!" I shout, my throat raw with denial. My head feels light, and for a moment, I think I'm going to faint. "I want to see him."

"I'm afraid that's impossible," Ba says. "The bodies of the executed were cremated and put into a mass grave."

"Then how do you know he's dead?" Desperately, I cling to any small chance that Delun might still be alive.

"I saw his body before it was cremated." He holds up a hand against my next question. "Jun identified the body."

My throat goes taut as I turn to her. "But you've been taking the Gaokao with me all day."

She looks away from me, and it's Ba who answers. "Your sister came with me to identify the body right after we left you in the hospital."

My whole body tenses with grief and fury. "Do you mean," I say in a deathly quiet voice, "that you've known for *over a week* that Delun was dead?" Sick nausea swirls in my stomach.

"You had the Gaokao to take."

I stare at him blankly, and then I understand. He didn't want my boyfriend's *death* to distract me from a stupid test. I make myself look at Jun, even as the muscles in my chest clench against this new betrayal. "You went with Ba. You knew too."

She stares into her lap and doesn't answer.

Ba exhales heavily. "Lei—"

No. I can't believe that Delun is really gone. "I don't believe you!" The tendons in my neck strain taut.

"I saw the order for his execution," Ba says.

The blood drains from my face, leaving me chilled to the bone. "You saw the order?" A storm of rage rises in me. "You could have stopped his execution! *Why didn't you?*"

He stays silent.

No, it's too horrible. I can't believe that just a couple of days ago, I thought my father might be secretly clearing the way to secure Delun's release.

To go from such hope to such despair is agonizing.

Grief strikes my body like a rain of bullets. *Delun is gone.* And my father is too. If he is truly the monster that let my love be murdered, then he is not the person I knew and loved. Flailing under the grief drowning me, I grasp on to a single thought. *Jun.*

Gasping in pain, I whirl to face my sister. "Is this true?" Tears batter the back of my eyes. "Did you see Delun when I didn't even get a chance . . ." *To hold him. To see his face one last time.* My lungs burn in pain, and I'm seized with a vicious need to make her admit to her betrayal. "Have the guts to say it to my face, Jun!" I scream.

She looks up at that, her face strained and pale. "I did," she whispers. "I saw Delun dead." And then her hand steals up to the end of her braid. Just a touch—not a tug.

The world snaps back into focus, and my chest grows tight with hope to see her telltale nervous gesture. Could Jun be lying? *Delun might still be alive.* Then despair crashes down on me again. *No.* I'm just grasping at straws.

There's no way Jun would tell me a lie this devastating.

The doorbell rings suddenly, its loud peal jarring in the tense quiet of the living room.

Jun stands up immediately. "I'll get it."

I barely notice her leaving. My heart is caught in a vise of sorrow and denial. I'm being a fool, but I can't let go of my conviction that Delun isn't dead. Ba just isn't capable of such cruelty. Except what else would I call condoning the mass murder of thousands? What is that if not cruel?

"I know this is hard, Lei," Ba says gently, "but you need to live your life."

"You let Delun die," I say. "You took my life away, and I will never forgive you for that." My voice is leached of all emotion. I'm done screaming and crying. I'm done talking to him. I can't even *look* at him.

But before I turn my head away, I see him suck in his breath like he's in physical pain. *Good.* I can't possibly hurt him as much as he has hurt me. But I'll take what I can get.

Jun comes back into the living room. "It was a salesperson." She tugs the end of her braid.

I frown. This time, she's lying for sure. But why? Suspicion snakes around my heart. She's hiding something. I stand so quickly that Jun's startled eyes meet mine.

"Lei . . ."

Ignoring her, I bolt up the stairs to my room, my heart pounding with a nameless instinct. Once I get into my room, I race to the window that looks out over the front driveway. I'm just in time to see a figure disappear out of sight. Even from this distance, I'd recognize those broad shoulders and that blunt haircut anywhere.

Yawen.

What was she doing here? Did she decide to come to my home when she couldn't reach me by phone?

The sound of Jun's footsteps on the stairs makes me whirl around. I need to get the truth about Yawen's presence here out of my sister.

I yank my door open and come face-to-face with Jun. The twin I thought I knew as well as my own heart. Disappointment and rage pulse hotly behind my eyes.

"Lei," she says, "I'm so sorry that Delun is dead."

How dare she speak his name? Agony threatens to swallow me. Is there any chance that Delun is still alive? And if he's dead . . . did he have a last message for me? Even the painful knowledge of his last hours would be better than this terrible blankness in my heart.

Yawen. She might know what happened to Delun.

Something that's not quite hope flutters in my chest. It's a reason to live. I push through my breathless hurt and force myself to think. I can't ask Jun about Yawen because then she'll tell Ba, and he'll stop me from seeing her.

"What are you doing?" Jun tries to peer behind me into my room.

"Nothing." I know better than to confide in her now.

She gives me a sharp look. If I can tell when my twin is lying, then she can tell when I am too. "You know," she says, her voice empty of emotion, "they give you everything, and it's not fair for you to throw it all away."

The hell with it. She doesn't deserve anything from me. I slam the door in her shocked face. And then I begin to plan.

CHAPTER TWENTY-NINE

At breakfast the next day, I wait with bated breath until our parents leave the house before pushing my chair away from the dining table. This is the first day that Ma has left the house since I came home from the hospital, and I'm going to take full advantage of the absence of both parents, who seem to be ready to relax their surveillance now that the Gaokao is over.

All I have to do is get past my sister.

"I'm going to visit Beijing University today." If I can't call Yawen, then I need to see her in person.

Jun freezes with her chopsticks halfway to her mouth.

Come on, Jun. She knows Yawen is a student at Beijing University. I'm giving her the perfect opening to come clean and tell me about Yawen's visit yesterday. My body tenses in anticipation. If my sister can give me just *one* truth, then I can start to forgive her.

"Lei, you know you're not supposed to contact . . ." She puts the chopsticks down and struggles with her wording, but she doesn't seem to be able to say Yawen's name. "Any of the protesters."

My heart aches with disappointment. Why do I keep hoping, when all she does is let me down? "I'm not planning to see anyone," I say, a challenging tone in my voice. "I'm just checking out my future college." *Call me out on my lie. I dare you.*

"I'll go with you then."

To spy on me and report to our parents, no doubt. "Why?" And because I'm still burning with resentment, I add nastily, "It's not like *you're* going to college there."

Jun looks like I've struck her.

My stomach tightens. Not too long ago, I would have never dreamed I could be so awful to my twin sister. But that was before she ratted me out to our parents and lied about Yawen coming to see me.

I leave without another word to Jun.

A pang hits my heart when I step foot on campus. This is where I first met Delun. But I don't go to the meeting halls where we spent so many hours.

I head to Yawen's dormitory. The campus is eerily quiet for late afternoon. There is a sense of grief that blankets the campus like an invisible fog. The few people I see are unsmiling and silent as they rush to whatever class they're going to. The pain in my body grows as I wonder how many of the students here have been killed or arrested or gone on the run. If Delun is still alive, maybe he's one of those in hiding.

But I know he isn't. If he had escaped arrest, his name and face would be on the most wanted list. Besides, he would never leave without telling me goodbye.

The halls of Yawen's dorm are deserted. I thought about calling her from a pay phone before coming here, but in the end, I just wanted to see her in person. I swallow nervously before knocking on her door. *Please, please be here.*

The door opens, and Yawen is actually standing before me. Thank heavens. Emotion clogs my throat. But my relief is short-lived.

She scowls at me. "What are you doing here?"

My head spins with bewilderment. "I'm—I'm here to see you," I stammer.

"You have some nerve coming here after what you said to me!"

Foreboding creeps down my spine. "Yawen, I haven't spoken with you since we got separated at Tiananmen Square." After Rong was murdered before our eyes. And after Delun surrendered to give us the chance to escape. My chest tightens in memory.

"Bullshit!" she yells. "You came to see me in prison right after I was arrested, and you didn't ask how I was doing . . . or . . . even say anything about Rong. It's like you forgot what happened to him."

Prison? The awful suspicion in the pit of my stomach is growing stronger. "I could never forget about what happened to Rong," I say shakily, "and I've been so worried about you and Delun. I was knocked unconscious at Tiananmen Square and woke up in a hospital a day later. I wasn't discharged until a few days ago, and I haven't been able to call or get away to see you. I haven't spoken to you until right now!"

"Do you think I'm stupid?" She laughs, a harsh, cawing sound. "I guess I am. Because I had convinced myself that you didn't mean what you said to me at the prison—that you never wanted to see me again. And I thought that maybe you were the one who got me out of there." Her face crumples with terrible suddenness. "But when I came to your house yesterday, you threatened to call the police and have me arrested if I ever tried to contact you again."

My stomach drops. *Jun.* I can see her now, hand on one hip and a sly smile on her face, looking exactly like me. I'm surprised that she turned out to be so eerily good at passing for me. Even more surprised now that I know what she used her talent for. "That wasn't me." I take a breath. "That was my twin sister."

Yawen's chin lifts, though her eyes sparkle with tears. "Yeah, right. I've met her. She's nothing like you."

"Yawen, you *know* me." My heart is a hot mass of pain, bursting with everything I want to say. *I was by your side when Rong died. I dragged you away when you would have stayed to die with him. I left Delun behind to get you out of that damned, bloody square.* "Do you really think I'd turn my back on you when you're heartbroken by Rong's death?"

She's silent for a moment, and then hope flares into her face. She flings herself into my embrace, and we're both sobbing in each other's arms. It's the first time that this tangled, heavy ball of messy grief in my chest has started to ease in days.

"Do you know what happened to Delun?" I ask when I'm able to breathe again. "Was he arrested with you?" But I can't ask the most frightening question: *Is he dead?*

"He wasn't with those of us arrested and taken to the local police precinct," she says, "but I heard that the leaders were being held somewhere else."

"Where?" Urgency makes my voice sharp.

She shakes her head. "I don't know."

"Are they . . ." My heart thumping hard, I make myself finish the question. ". . . executing student leaders?"

Yawen throws me a startled look. "I've heard stories about mass executions," she says sadly, "but not of the student leaders. The government doesn't want to make martyrs out of them."

I stare at her in growing horror. A yawning suspicion stretches out before me. There's only one reason Delun would have been executed if the other student leaders weren't.

My father.

Faintness overtakes me. What if Ba didn't just see Delun's execution order? What if he signed it? *No.* My father couldn't have possibly turned my plea to save Delun into a death sentence. I have to believe he is still alive. I have to have faith that my father wouldn't be so cruel as to murder the boy I love. And it shouldn't be difficult to believe this. But it is.

Yawen looks at me in understanding. "I'm sorry," she says. "I haven't even invited you inside." Gently, she pulls me into her room.

Even with numb dread weighing on me, I register the smallness of the room crowded with bunk beds with thin mattresses. This spare, utilitarian room that houses eight students is smaller than my room at home.

Then I catch sight of a half-filled box and an open suitcase. "You're going somewhere?" Yawen was supposed to graduate from college this year, and graduation is just a couple of weeks away.

"Yes," she says shortly. "I can't stay here. Too many memories." Tears rise in her eyes. "I see him everywhere."

"Oh, Yawen." My heart aches because I see Delun everywhere too. "I'm so sorry."

She sniffles and wipes her face with the back of her hand. "There's nothing worth staying here for, anyway. The rumor is that those of us graduating this year will have a harder time finding jobs in Beijing or getting into graduate school. We're all suspected of participating in the protests whether or not we actually did."

I think of Heng and the other artists, and feel a tightening in my chest. I hope their futures haven't been destroyed by their part in the protest. At least Heng had the forethought to stay away from Tiananmen Square after the unveiling of the short-lived Goddess of Democracy. I couldn't bear the death of one more friend. "This is so wrong."

Yawen just nods tiredly.

"Where will you go then?" I ask in a small voice, thinking of how lonely it will be on campus without her . . . and only ghost memories of Delun and my friends to keep me company.

"Back home to Shanghai, I suppose. Rong was from there too. I want to be there for his funeral." She takes a shuddering breath. "His family told me that his body has been sent back."

"I'm glad my father kept his word about that at least," I say bitterly.

"It *was* you then," she says. "You got your father to use his contacts to get me out of prison."

"Yes, but he made me promise to cut off all contact with you and the others in exchange." Sadness wells up in me. "I can't even go to Rong's funeral," I realize.

"We wouldn't even have a body to mourn without you."

There isn't really anything to say after that, and we fall silent.

Then Yawen starts as if coming out of a reverie. "Oh, I almost forgot." She goes to a small dresser and opens a drawer, taking out an envelope. "The police gave me this when they let me out of jail." She hands me the envelope. "I guess your father was serious about getting me out of your life."

Mystified, I open it. It's a permit to enter Hong Kong from mainland China. I almost drop it in shock. These are nearly impossible to get. And every student leader on the run from the long reach of the Chinese government is desperately trying to get to Hong Kong. "Yawen, do you know what this is?"

"Yes." She meets my eyes steadily. "But I'm not going to Hong Kong, so I don't need it."

I had thought that she would jump at the chance to leave, especially after all her talk about being blacklisted for jobs and the devastating memories of Rong. "Why not? This could be your chance for a better future outside of mainland China."

"I didn't join the movement because I wanted a better future for *myself*," Yawen says. "And neither did Rong, Delun, or you. We joined because we want a better China." Her lip quivers. "Rong died for his love of our country. How can I abandon what he loved—what he died for?" She gestures to the paper in my hand. "Please take that with you. I don't want to be tempted to use it."

I nod, too choked up to speak. The paper catches on my clumsy fingers before I manage to slide it back into the envelope and put it into my purse. I understand why Yawen doesn't want to go to capitalist Hong Kong. Like Yawen, I'm a patriot. I believe in my country's communist ideals of equality and our fight against Western imperialism. Despite the Chinese propaganda painting us as anti-communist, capitalist-loving terrorists, I love my country too. Even if my heart is buried somewhere in an unmarked mass grave with Delun, I can't imagine leaving my homeland either.

Yawen is staring at me, but then she gives me a small smile. "Sorry. It's just . . . your sister really did look and act exactly like you."

"You really didn't suspect at all?"

She shakes her head. "No. Obviously, I knew you had a twin, but it never even occurred to me that it wasn't you."

It's disquieting that Jun was able to pass for me so easily. And even more troubling is *why* she did it. It's beyond time for my sister and me to have a reckoning. But first, I have a friend to think of.

Yawen and I say goodbye and hug, clinging to each other for a long moment before reluctantly letting go. I tell myself that Shanghai isn't that far away and there will be many opportunities to meet again.

But when I leave, I can't shake the inexplicable feeling that this is the last time I will see my friend.

CHAPTER THIRTY

When I get home, I go into my room, sit at my writing desk, and stare at the hard truth without blinking. There are only two possibilities: My father is telling the truth and Delun is dead, possibly by his orders, or my father lied and Delun is still alive. Either way, my father has betrayed me. I close my eyes and run through all the evidence in my head piece by piece, but there's no logical way to discover the truth.

If Delun were really dead, I'd know it. I'd feel despair in every molecule of my body, and it would feel as if I'd died too. But that's not how I feel. A conviction that he still lives thrums through my soul. That means I have to find him. Determination hardens in my body.

But how? I can confront Ba, but that might just make him decide to kill off Delun for real. And if I find Delun, then what? I have no way to get him out of prison without my father's help, and hell will freeze over before Ba throws away his career to release a convicted counterrevolutionary.

I gaze listlessly at the piles of paper on my desk, and then in a fit of helpless frustration, I shove the neat piles off the desk. Paper flies everywhere—one even floats to land gently over my latest attempt at re-creating the portrait of Princess Taiping. A sea of calligraphy covers the floor, and I'm overcome with remorse. I haven't touched that portrait in weeks. Art and poetry were once my ruling passions, and I've just literally swept them aside.

Kneeling on the floor, I start to gather up my copies of Tang dynasty poetry. And then I freeze. I have never been a good artist.

But I'm surrounded by evidence of what I *am* good at. I'm a damn good forger.

Heart in my throat, I leave the poetry on the floor and pick up the purse I'd tossed onto my sofa. I extract the entry permit Yawen gave me and then take the copy of her prison release paper from my nightstand.

A crazy plan is taking shape, and my pulse races with my own daring as I sink onto my sofa and open the two envelopes. I run my eyes over both documents. Ba made sure that Jun and I had state-of-the-art computers, so the forms won't be hard to replicate with my desktop publishing software and inkjet printer. The signatures, including my father's on the release papers, also won't be difficult to forge. The hardest part will be the official stamps on the documents. But I've had enough practice with re-creating Wu Zetian's imperial seal that I think I can manage a fair copy of these.

I walk over to my writing desk and take out my calligraphy brushes and red ink. Time to find out if I'm a good enough forger to save Delun.

I've got it. Dazed, I look at the copies of the prison release form and the entry permit to Hong Kong. They look identical to the ones my father procured for Yawen. As I suspected, copying the seals was the hardest, but they look authentic. The entry permits are issued by the Chinese Consulate General, and I've made extra copies of these since there are still student protesters in hiding who might need them. I'm not sure how to get them into the right hands, but Delun can help with that. I just have to find him first—which is easier said than done. A wave of hopelessness washes over me. If he's still alive, he could have been sent to any of the prison labor camps scattered across the country. And there are a *lot* of them.

There's another problem. Even if I do find Delun, securing his release from prison means using my father's signature. That will get Ba in a ton of trouble. Angrily, I push this thought away. I don't care. All I want is to find Delun alive and make sure he stays that way. Everyone else can be damned.

But I can't hold on to this unforgiving hardness. Deep down inside, I understand the choice I will have to make. If I use the release form, and forge my father's signature, to free Delun, I will be betraying my family. Ba's position in the Communist Party is the only thing standing between my family and the accusations that Yanlin's mother plans to level against us. And it's a sure bet that the government will be suspicious of my father's apparent release of a criminal counter-revolutionary leader. Ba could lose his power to protect us. We could lose all the safety and peace that my parents have fought so hard to give us. And it would be all my fault. A cold lump forms in my stomach. *Delun or my family.* It's an impossible choice.

A knock comes at my door, and I yell out, "Just a minute!" Hastily, I gather up the scattered poems on my floor and dump them over the forged papers on my desk to cover up what I'm doing. Then I grab a book at random and sit on the sofa.

"OK, come in," I call out.

I think it's going to be Jun, but instead, Ma walks in.

Wariness crawls up my spine. "Hello," I say stiffly. I haven't forgotten that she threatened to take away my inheritance if I refused to give up Delun and the protest. And then I turned around and fled to Tiananmen Square on the night of the massacre. Is she here to tell me I've lost Wu Zetian's art?

She sits down next to me. "I want to talk to you about your sister."

"What about Jun?" Maybe Ma isn't here to take away my inheritance. I'm surprised to find that there's relief under the hard layers of resentment in my gut.

"Forgive her," Ma says gently. "She only revealed your secrets because she was worried about your safety." Her eyes cloud over.

"And it turns out she had good reason to be afraid. We're lucky you're alive."

My mother doesn't understand how much it hurts to survive when Delun is missing and Rong is dead. And thousands of others are missing or dead. Am I supposed to just forget them? "Jun was just afraid for herself, not for me." My heart is heavy. I've lost so much . . . but my sister turning against me is just too much to bear.

"She was afraid for all of us," Ma corrects me gently.

Because Jun thought I had betrayed them by showing Delun the art we hide. My sister was guarding our heritage—the same thing I was doing by asking Delun for help. Not that Ma sees it that way. In a small voice, I ask, "Do you forgive me, Ma? For revealing *your* secrets?"

Sadness crosses her face. "Mrs. Liu was coming after our family, and you hoped your young man would protect us. I understand. You thought you were doing the right thing."

The tension in my chest eases a little. "Am I still the guardian of Wu Zetian's art?"

"Yes," she says firmly.

It's not enough to make up for all the deaths and my fear for Delun. But reconfirming my guardianship of the art does feel like a missing piece reattaching itself inside me. "Thank you."

"No need to thank me." Her eyes slide away from mine. "You're not the only guardian who once trusted the wrong person."

Delun wasn't the wrong person. But then I hear what she's saying. "Ma," I say, my thoughts tumbling in confusion, "I thought you said Ba was the right person to trust and that was why you married him."

"Of course." She hesitates, and then her hand slides across the heavy silk of my sofa. "Do you know why I chose you to be the guardian of Wu Zetian's art?"

Over Jun. My heart beats faster in anticipation. "Why?" I whisper.

"Because your jie jie is just like me."

Surprise clogs my throat. "Isn't that a *good* thing?"

Ma seems to struggle for words. "All I'm saying is that if it ever came down to a choice between the art we protect and our family, Jun wouldn't hesitate to sacrifice the art for our family. She wouldn't try to find a way to save both." She touches my cheek. "You would. That was what you were trying to do. That's why you are the right choice to be the keeper of Empress Wu's dynasty. You will be a better guardian than I was."

My heart overflows with emotion. "Ma . . ." I don't know what to say, but I try anyway. "It wasn't your fault that the paintings were stolen."

She hardly seems to be listening to me. She's staring into the distance as if she's reliving a long-ago memory. "You will learn from your mistakes as I did."

My stomach drops. She still thinks it was all a mistake. Trusting in Delun. Fighting for a world where we don't have to hide our legacy.

That's when I finally understand.

I will never change her mind. Ma will never let me share Empress Wu's art with the world.

Her gaze returns to me, steady and unblinking. "I forgive you, Lei."

My jaw sets because I know what she's saying. "I'm not ready to forgive Jun."

She sighs. "You are so much like your father."

Like Ba? Anger burns in me. "I'm nothing like him." It wasn't too long ago when I would have been proud to be compared with him. But that was before he destroyed my world.

"You both have strong feelings of justice and what is right and wrong. You love fiercely and protect those you love. Those are good things." Ma pulls me toward her and kisses the top of my head. "But you both expect so much of the people you love. People will let you down, even those you love. And you have to forgive them, Lei. Or else you will be haunted by regret—like your father."

I don't know who Ba loved and could not forgive, but he doesn't exactly strike me as someone *haunted by regret*. But despite all that he's done, he's not the only one I can't forgive. It's Jun too. My twin, my other half—the one person I thought I could trust to the ends of the earth.

"Talk to your sister," Ma urges. "The two of you used to be so close. I'd hate to see your anger come between you."

I stay stubbornly silent and pull away from her. It's not *my* anger that is at fault—it's *her* deception. Every time I've tried to forgive Jun, she hands me another lie like a poisoned fruit.

Ma peers at me in worry. At last, she pats my knee. "There should be peace between sisters," she says sadly before leaving me alone.

Once she's gone, I have to blink away tears. I want to fix things with my sister, but I don't know if we'll ever regain what we've lost. If I can get Delun back, I might begin to forgive Jun, but if he's dead . . . No. I can't think that way. Angrily, I wipe my eyes, go to my desk, and start flinging sheets of poetry aside to unearth the documents I had painstakingly forged. And then I catch a glimpse of three lines from a poem. The poem I always believed would tell me who the mysterious lady in the painting was.

Peace and shining beauty are gone.
The long-ago choice weighs heavy on my heart.
Yet, I would not give up love for peace.

Long ago, Princess Taiping, the subject of one of the missing portraits, wrote those words. Like me, she had a choice to make. She also lived in an era of danger—and in a country on the cusp of revolution. And like me, my ancestress did not give up love for peace.

Maybe my choice is the same.

There are many kinds of love and many kinds of peace. That's why the word "peace" is written with a different character each of the two times it's used in this poem. The kind of peace that my family wants is a secret safely hidden in a dangerous time. The peace I want is a world where we no longer have to hide our secret. My family has always been torn between the choice of love and peace.

Jun gave up Yanlin to guard our secret—she chose peace over love. My mother chose love first and then peace. *You're not the only guardian who once trusted the wrong person.* My family—they all regret the love they gave up.

I don't know what Princess Taiping had to choose between, but at least she was not haunted by the love she gave up. I will make the same choice as my ancestress. I won't choose the kind of peace Ma and Jun have chosen.

But can I forgive my family for trying to force me into the same choice they've made?

My mother's voice comes into my head again. *People will let you down, even those you love. And you have to forgive them, Lei. Or else you will be haunted by regret—like your father.* But if my father regrets anything he's done to me, then I can't see it. My heart flares in pain as I remember him telling me about the massacre with barely a flinch and confessing to Delun's murder with those chilly, dispassionate eyes. For my father, regret seems to be an old ghost that no longer has any power over him.

And that's when the pieces click together. Horror steals my breath away. No. It can't be. But the insidious thoughts keep scrabbling at my mind. My father didn't just refuse to help the boy I love—he felt the need to make him disappear. *What if this wasn't the first time?*

What if Ba didn't just turn his back on his old friend in the Red Guard? What if he was the one to *cause* Mr. Liu's downfall?

You don't get that cold and that hard without bartering with your soul at least once before. Whatever price my father paid for his uneasy peace, he's paid it before.

I've always known this poem holds the key to a mystery.

It's just not the mystery I thought it would be. A shudder overtakes my body even as my path opens up before me with dizzying clarity.

I won't give up the boy I love *or* the family I love. That's an impossible choice. But if there's a way to save Delun without abandoning my family to the danger they face, then my choice is clear. This poem hasn't helped me figure out who the second lady was. But now I know what happened to those missing paintings and how to get back the lost image of Princess Taiping, my ancestress.

And knowing that, I know what I must do to save my family.

CHAPTER THIRTY-ONE

The next day, my hair is in a braid and I'm wearing a pastel-pink chiffon dress. I wipe my sweaty palms on the skirt of the dress before I remember that it's not mine. Jun's going to kill me for getting sweat stains on her favorite dress. *Well, I'm about to give her a lot more to be mad about than messing up her dress.* I'm standing outside an apartment unit with grime caked onto the gray stucco siding. Steeling my nerves, I ring the doorbell.

There's the sound of footsteps, and then Yanlin opens the door. His mouth falls open in shock. "Jun? What are you doing here?"

I rehearsed it a hundred times before leaving my house. A nervous smile. Regret for breaking up with him. And, oh yeah, asking for one teeny favor. But my voice is frozen in my throat.

The look on Yanlin's face is so . . . *hopeful.* And I keep seeing Jun's empty eyes when she told me that she had broken up with Yanlin. I just can't do it. I can't break both of their hearts all over again. "I'm Lei, not Jun."

"Oh." The eagerness drains from his expression. "I thought . . . never mind." With studied casualness, he asks, "Did Jun send you?"

"No. She doesn't know I'm here." My stomach twists in pity, and I feel like I've just kicked a puppy, eager for any small scrap I can give.

"Oh," he says again.

I fidget awkwardly, mind racing. Now what? My plan hinged on Yanlin thinking I was Jun. Will he be willing to do this for me—Lei? It's not like I can just come out and *ask* him. But in the end, that's exactly what I do. Taking a deep breath, I say, "I need to see your father."

Confusion comes over Yanlin's face. "My father?"

"Yes." I jitter in place. "Um, your mother isn't home, is she?" No need to elaborate on why I don't want to run into the woman who wants to take down my family.

"She's at work." His shoulders straighten. "At her new job, that is."

"New job?" I stare at him, hardly daring to hope. Did Yanlin really fulfill his promise to stop his mother from writing damaging stories about our family? Even after Jun dumped him?

"Yeah. I, uh, convinced her that a career as a journalist for a tabloid won't give her the status she wants." He smiles wryly. "I may have given my mother the idea that she'll rise in stature when the business I'm starting after graduation becomes successful. Not that I'm likely to get rich." His expression turns bleak. "I guess that's why your sister broke up with me."

"She told you that?" I ask, shocked.

"Not exactly, but it was pretty clear that she didn't want to date a poor student with no future."

My heart twinges, but it's not like I can tell him the real reason Jun broke up with him. To break the tense silence, I ask randomly, "What kind of business are you going into?"

He reddens. "I'm opening a clothing store, actually."

Ah. That explains the beautiful clothes Yanlin and his mother wore to crash a high-society fundraiser. He has a better chance at getting rich than he thinks.

"But you didn't come here to talk about my future plans," he says. "You wanted to see my father."

"Is he home?"

Yanlin peers steadily at me. "Yes."

I was pretty sure he would be. After all, Yanlin had said that the damage inflicted by the Red Guard had made his father an invalid.

"I don't suppose you want to explain what's going on?" His voice is dry as tinder, like he already knows my answer.

"I can't. But trust me, it's important." Anxiously, I twirl the end of my braid.

His gaze is drawn by the gesture, and I quickly drop my hand from my hair. I'd copied Jun's nervous habit without conscious thought. "Sorry," I mutter, though I don't know what, exactly, I'm apologizing for. Maybe for reminding him of the girl he still loves.

"Does this have anything to do with what happened at Tiananmen Square?" he asks gently. "I heard that Delun is missing."

"Yes." My voice cracks. I'm not lying. Everything that has led to this moment started with Delun.

Yanlin holds the door wide for me. "Come in." His eyes are dark with sympathy.

Relief floods me. "Thank you."

He leads me into a small living room and invites me to sit on a worn couch. "Wait here, please." He hesitates and adds, "I was very sorry to hear about Delun. And the other protesters, of course. If there's anything I can do to help, just let me know."

Tears well up in my eyes. My sister was a fool to give him up. "Thank you."

He gives me a nod and then leaves.

I look around the apartment as Yanlin gets his father. The furniture, though old, looks comfortable, and the place is scrupulously clean. It's a nice home, but for a woman like Mrs. Liu, who craves admittance to the upper echelons of society, it can't possibly be enough.

Yanlin returns soon, aiding a frail man using a cane. Mr. Liu must be around the same age as my parents, but he looks much older.

"So you are Mei and Shen's daughter," Mr. Liu says as his son settles him into an armchair across from me.

"Yes." My throat grows dry. If I'm right about him, he can't be happy to see me. But he seems more curious than angry about my presence.

"Do you need me to stay, Ba?" Yanlin asks.

"No, no!" Mr. Liu waves him away.

Yanlin gives us both an anxious look. "I'll be in the kitchen if you need me." Then he leaves, and I'm left staring at his father with no idea of how to proceed.

"Well, girl," he says, "what do you want from me?"

That's pretty direct, but I can be blunt too. My heart flutters with nerves. "I want what you took from my family."

He barks out a laugh. "What makes you think I have anything of yours?"

At least it's not a denial. "Your wife said that our family destroyed you." I take a deep breath. "I think my father reported you to the Red Guard for anti-communist beliefs, and then they raided your home like so many others."

"You think you've got it all figured, don't you?" he says coolly.

"I'm not done." I lift my chin. I've got to see this all the way through, even if I'm wrong. "Even if Ba reported you to the Red Guard on suspicion of being a counterrevolutionary, it shouldn't have gotten you sent to a labor camp. You were a Red Guard like him, after all." There's a tremor in his frame, and I don't know if it's from a memory of fear or illness, but I press on. "It doesn't make sense—unless they searched your home and found something."

I meet his eyes square on, trying to hide the clammy chill creeping over my skin. Because I'm about to take a big risk. As big as running off to Tiananmen Square on the eve of a massacre. "There are few things dangerous enough to take down a Red Guard during the height of the Cultural Revolution." My heart slams against my ribs. "But two Tang dynasty paintings would do the trick."

He's silent for a long moment, and I quietly start to hyperventilate. *Shit. Oh shit.* I've just shown my hand to my family's age-old enemy. And for what? A hunch that's about to blow up in my face.

"Let's say you're correct," he says at last, face impassive. "In that case, the Red Guard would have burned the paintings. So—I repeat—what makes you think I have them?"

Because in my bones I know—with the same fierce conviction that keeps me believing that Delun is alive—that the portrait of my ancestress still exists. But I can't explain that to Mr. Liu, so I say, "Your wife is trying to destroy us." I try to slow my breathing, but my nerves make me talk too fast, my words jumbling together. "She hates my mother and says she has proof that my father betrayed you, and she wants to reveal—"

"Breathe, girl," he says dryly, "before you pass out." As I gulp for air, he says, "I suppose you have a theory for how those paintings got into my home?"

That's when my stomach drops. Because I *do* have a theory. One that I can't think about without feeling sick. "There's a reason your wife is so bent on revenge." I hope with all my soul that Mrs. Liu is wrong. That *I'm* wrong. "She thinks my father planted the paintings in your home." The words twist sourly in my mouth.

"Why do you think he would have done that?" There's still no glimmer of emotion in his face.

My feelings are a painful, tangled mess in my gut. "To protect my mother, who showed those paintings to you, thinking you would help her guard her secret." I make myself say each word slowly and clearly. "But you didn't, did you?"

His hands clasp tightly together. Emotion at last.

At first, I think he isn't going to answer, but then he says, "I was stubbornly committed to the anti-imperialist ideals of the Cultural Revolution. Mei . . ." His gaze drops to his clenched hands. "She trusted me. Shen was in love with her too, but Mei chose *me*. She loved me, and I betrayed her."

"What happened?" It comes out as a tense whisper. So, I was right. Mr. Liu *was* who Ma meant when she said she had trusted the wrong person.

He bends over slowly, joints creaking, and picks up his cane. Is he done with this conversation? But he doesn't attempt to leave. Instead, he folds his hands over the head of the cane and leans forward. "One day, your mother asked me to come over because she had something to show me. Then she took me to her room and showed me those two paintings. A lady in yellow, and a lady in red. I knew at once that they were classical imperial paintings. Elitist contraband. I was so shocked . . . I lost my head." Pain flashes in his eyes. "I denounced her as an enemy to the people. I suppose I scared her."

"Yes, she was scared," I say tightly. No wonder Ma freaked out when Jun told her that I had shown Delun, a revolutionary student leader, our secret art. Delun would never betray me, but Ma wouldn't understand that. She was burned too badly once before. Then why would she trust another Red Guard after Mr. Liu turned on her? I ask the question out loud. "Ma went to my father because she was afraid you'd expose her. Why did she go to him? He was a Red Guard too."

"Shen was . . . never as committed to the ideals of the Cultural Revolution as I was," he says slowly, "but he was committed to your mother. He stepped aside when she chose me first, but he never stopped loving her. Mei must have known that—just as she must have known your father wouldn't betray her." He bows his head. "As I did."

Ma always said that she married Ba because she trusted him with our secret, but I never realized he was her second choice. Sadness pierces my heart. Years ago, this man in front of me, a fanatic Red Guard, betrayed my mother, prompting her to turn to the man who ultimately vindicated her trust. But my mother's safety had come at a terrible price—the two paintings from our inheritance. Did Ba take them without her knowledge? How could she have forgiven him for such a betrayal? I shiver as I take in the harsh lines of pain scored into Mr. Liu's face. And there was another price: My father had to betray his best friend.

"I was young," he says, as if it's an explanation for what he did.

I'm young. And so is Delun. Rong was young too—as were the thousands in Tiananmen Square who were killed or arrested for their beliefs. But none of us turned against our own people the way the Red

Guard did. "Would you have done it? Reported my mother to the Red Guard if my father hadn't framed you first with those paintings?"

His eyebrows draw down as he peers at me. "So you believe that's what happened? That your father took the paintings to frame me?" He shakes his head. "Those portraits were your mother's greatest treasures."

Good—he doesn't seem to know about the *rest* of the art. Mrs. Liu's attempts to instigate a raid on our house must have been a shot in the dark.

"If you believe that, then you don't know my old friend at all."

Wait. Is he implying that my father *didn't* take the paintings? "How the hell did the portraits end up at your house for the Red Guard to find if my father didn't plant them there to frame you?"

"I told Mei those paintings were dangerous. I swear I just wanted to protect her! But she wouldn't give them up." A sheen of sweat forms on his forehead, and he wipes it off. "So I told her I'd report her if she didn't give me the paintings. It was a lie, but she believed me. I got the paintings, but I lost her love and trust."

My breath stutters in shock. I thought the paintings were *stolen*. Never in a million years could I have imagined that Ma had willingly parted with them. How could anyone who was entrusted with the safety of Wu Zetian's legacy have done such a thing? No, I don't believe it. Then I remember what she said to me. *You will be a better guardian than I was.*

All those years of guilt weren't because the paintings were stolen under her watch. It was because she had given them up.

Mr. Liu interrupts my tortured thoughts. "Your father came to see me and tried to convince me to return the paintings. I should have listened and given them back to Mei. Or at least promised that I would never report her."

"Why didn't you?" He could have saved us all a world of trouble if only he had returned those paintings and promised to keep our secret.

Mr. Liu laughs, but there's no mirth in it. "I was too angry. Mei had told Shen about the paintings. That meant she trusted him. And that she had chosen him. I had lost the love of my life and couldn't admit that I had lost her to the better man. For your mother's sake, your father vowed to leave the Red Guard. And he kept his word—right after he reported me to them." His mouth sets. "As it turns out, it was good timing. Shen stayed in the Communist Party, rising to power and escaping the later backlash against the Red Guard, while I rotted for years in a labor camp."

I can't shake off the weight that has fallen over this room, the tragedy that took place years before I was born. Then I remember why I came here. "But your wife says she has evidence of our family's corruption that can destroy us. Is it the paintings?" I'm breathless with fear. What if I'm wrong and the paintings were actually destroyed during the Cultural Revolution? But no. The way Mrs. Liu made those threats—I'm certain she has something to back it up. "And why does your wife hate us so much if my ba didn't actually frame you?"

Anger storms over his face. "He didn't frame me, but he *did* report me, knowing I had those paintings. And he and your mother both knew the paintings would be destroyed if the Red Guard found them. So what makes you think I still have them?"

Grief numbs my body. *Ma let Empress Wu's art be destroyed out of fear.* And it wasn't even necessary. Mr. Liu wasn't ever going to report her. I know that now.

I might have already lost Delun. The hope of those paintings was all I had left. The pain of my loss flares up, burning away numbness, but I try to make my voice gentle. "I'm sorry to have bothered you, Mr. Liu. I'll leave now."

"Wait." He closes his eyes, and when he opens them again, they're filmy with tears. "Yuan had always loved me, but I didn't know it. Not until I was finally freed from the labor camp, and she was waiting for me. I was honest with her—that I would always love Mei."

Unexpected sympathy for Mrs. Liu creeps into my heart. How devastating it would be to know that the love of your life was in love with someone else.

"Yuan always knew she was my second choice," he says sadly, "and that was my fault. I have many regrets. One of the biggest is telling my wife what I had done for your mother."

Suddenly, I remember what Mrs. Liu told me. *I hope you're not like your mother. She was a woman who could always get men to do anything for her. Even if it meant throwing away their lives and honor for her.* I thought Mrs. Liu had meant my father. But I was wrong. She meant her husband, who lost everything in his misguided attempt to protect the woman he would always love. A woman who destroyed him. No wonder Mrs. Liu hates Ma.

"But you must understand—I grew to love my wife. She gave up a life of privilege to marry me, a man with no prospects. I won't hurt Yuan. And it *will* hurt her if I give you what you want."

I almost choke on the hope that rushes up into my throat. "Do you mean that you have the paintings? That they weren't destroyed?" My heart pounds furiously in the silence that follows my question, but at last, he speaks.

"Yes."

I lean forward and almost fall off the worn couch in my eagerness. "Give them back to me. Please."

"I told you." His chin juts forward. "I can't. My wife wouldn't understand if I gave what I paid for in blood to the family who condemned me. She would take it as proof that I will never love her as much as I love your mother. I couldn't do that to her."

"Then don't tell her you gave me the paintings," I say, forming my resolve as I speak. "Tell her that I stole them."

He stares at me in disbelief. "Do you know what you're saying? What if my wife reports you to the police for theft?"

"Then she'll have to tell them that you, a former member of the Red Guard, have been hoarding Tang dynasty art for the past twenty years," I retort. "I don't think that's very likely, do you?"

"She could still make things hard for your family, accuse them of harboring a criminal."

Fear tightens into a hard knot in my stomach. "She can't blame my family if I disappear tonight with the paintings."

He snorts. "You have no reason to take such a drastic action."

"You'd be surprised at my reasons." Bitterness hits the back of my throat. But he's right. I won't leave Beijing. Not until I know where to go from here—not until I know where Delun is.

Mr. Liu peers at me more closely. "That's right," he says. "Yanlin told me about you. Your young man was a leader in the student protests. Did he come out of that massacre all right?"

I swallow hard. "He was arrested." Suddenly, I want to tell Mr. Liu everything. Maybe because he once stared down the horrors that Delun is facing—and survived them. "My father says he was executed."

"Doubtful," he says darkly. "The party likes to keep its opposition leaders alive."

My heart clenches around the fear I can't escape. "My father was the one who had Delun executed."

"He has that power, yes," Mr. Liu says, "but you should have more faith in your father. Shen could have had *me* executed. For a long time, I was too angry to be fair to him, but anger is a bitter companion, and over the years, I have come to admit that my old friend only set the Red Guard on me because he thought I was going to expose your mother." He thumps his cane on the floor. "*And* he let me live—despite the danger he thought I was to Mei."

Maybe Ba let Delun live too. My heart pounds with painful hope.

Acidly, Mr. Liu adds, "Although Shen didn't lift a finger to help me when I was thrown into the prison reserved for the most notorious political dissidents."

My gaze sharpens on Mr. Liu, and my body freezes with the chill of knowledge. A Red Guard who had betrayed the Communist Party would be classified as a dangerous criminal of the Cultural Revolution—never mind that the party itself was responsible for the extremist violence committed in its name. And Delun, if he's alive, is being held by that same government, deathly afraid of the monsters it's created. Except this time, the only monsters are its own reflections. "Where were you imprisoned?" I whisper.

Understanding dawns on his face. "You've been looking for him, haven't you?" At my shaky nod, he says gently, "I was imprisoned at Qincheng. But you knew that already."

Qincheng Prison. The infamous maximum-security prison labor camp reserved for the greatest threats against the government. And that's where Delun might be. Despair squeezes my heart. If he is there, how can I get him out?

"I can't help you with your young man," Mr. Liu says with that same gentleness, "but I can give you back what is yours." He raises his voice: "Yanlin! Come in here, please."

Yanlin appears so quickly that he must have been on alert for his father's summons.

"Get the painting," Mr. Liu says. "You know the one I mean. And don't say a word to your mother about this."

I'm dazed with all the revelations of the past hour, but this pierces my shell-shocked brain. *You know the one I mean.* "*One* painting?" Sorrow clogs my throat.

Yanlin says quietly, "I'll go get it." He leaves the room with purpose in his stride.

"About that," Mr. Liu says heavily, "I should tell you that one of the paintings was destroyed—burned by the Red Guard. But they didn't find the other one. That's why I still have it."

I nod, too numb to speak. It shouldn't matter so much after the massacre in Tiananmen Square, after Rong's death and Delun's imprisonment. But I still grieve over the painting of the unknown woman. Because I'm sure it's the one that was destroyed and the one of Princess Taiping survived. I can't explain the connection I've always felt to the princess—a gifted poet who wrote about her world with such grief and love—but I've always known, to the marrow of my bones, that a likeness of my ancestress must still exist in the world.

And there's no likeness of Princess Taiping other than the painting that Empress Wu's descendants have guarded over the ages. *Embroidered yellow dress. Blunt fingers plucking the strings of a zither.* I've listened to my mother's descriptions and have tried to re-create my ancestress so many times that I can almost see her in my mind. Almost, but not quite. Now, I will finally be able to see her.

Yanlin returns with a flat crate with a handle.

He starts to pry the crate open, but I stop him. "Are you OK with this?" I ask. "You know your father is going to give me the painting, right?"

He smiles. "It belongs to you," he says simply. Then he carefully opens the crate to reveal layers of foam packing. "Do you want to do the honors?" he asks me.

"Yes." I'm shaking with anticipation as I put on the white cotton gloves that I had stashed in my purse just in case. I kneel on the floor and slowly fold back the foam like I'm unswaddling an infant. My breath catches at the first glimpse of brilliant color . . . and then my breath leaves me altogether.

Because it's the wrong color.

A lady in a red dress and blue-green sash stares back at me. *Not* Princess Taiping. It's the unknown woman.

At first, all I feel is betrayed anger. Where is the portrait of my ancestress that I was so certain still exists in the world?

And then I really look at her. The woman seated before the blank parchment has a certain stillness on her face. It is the look of someone who sees the future. I think of the poem, of the two different characters for "peace." My lungs constrict as I gulp in air and understanding. *Holy shit.*

I know who she is.

CHAPTER THIRTY-TWO

The next hour passes in a dreamlike fog. I feel like an actor in a play, like it's not really me taking the steps toward an irrevocable decision. I stash the crate in a train station locker, the last place I thought I'd be storing priceless Tang dynasty art. Then I go to my bank and calmly withdraw all the money in my account. Thanks to my parents' generous allowance and Ba's Gaokao bribe money, it's a lot. More than most people in China make in a lifetime, and definitely enough to start anew with Delun . . . if I can save him.

I'm standing at the exit of the bank, my oversized purse weighed down with a ridiculous amount of cash, when the awful reality hits me. My body goes weak all over, and I start trembling uncontrollably. *I can't do this.* But there are two terrible roads ahead of me, and I must choose one of them.

I have the painting that Mrs. Liu will think I've stolen. Reporting me to the police will mean confessing her complicity in hoarding illicit art, but who knows what she will do out of unthinking rage and jealousy? Bringing this painting home might damn my family. My mother made the choice once to let the paintings be destroyed in order to save her family. What if she makes that choice again? My stomach sickens to think of getting back one of the missing paintings only for it to be destroyed.

But no. Ma wouldn't do that. She's learned from her mistakes. I think back to what she said right before she announced that *I* would inherit Empress Wu's art. *We keep this gallery secret because our job is to protect our family* and *the art—something I failed to do because I didn't value what I guarded enough. You must understand that in order to avoid my failure.*

Is that why she made me the guardian of our legacy? Because she knew that I would never sacrifice Wu Zetian's art? But suddenly . . . I'm not sure. Now that the portrait is in my possession, I understand the decision my mother had to make. This painting could destroy my family. But I can't bear to give it up, especially now that I might know who this mystery lady is. I also have a good guess about where Delun is, and I have the forged papers that will free him. But using them will condemn my father.

I need to leave—for everyone's sake. My stomach churns in agony. How can I leave the only home I've ever known? Yet . . . the other choice is unthinkable. I could give up the painting if I had to, even though it would hurt as much as losing a limb. But I can't give up Delun.

Jun. The thought of my sister bursts into my thoughts. It's madness to pin my hopes on her after she's betrayed me time and time again. But she is still my twin, my other half. Deep down inside, a faint voice tries to get my attention. *If Delun is alive, that means she lied to you.*

Stubbornly, I argue with that terrible, insidious voice. Jun was only trying to protect me. She'll be on my side now that I've gotten back one of the missing paintings. She'll see what I'm willing to do to guard our legacy. Ma too.

Maybe Jun and Ma can help me convince Ba to get Delun released. If anyone can figure out a way to free a convicted counterrevolutionary leader without jeopardizing his standing in the Politburo, it's my father. Desperate hope shakes me to my core. If Jun and Ma stand by me, we can convince my father together. *Everything will work out. I won't have to leave home.*

This is the only truth I can allow myself to believe.

I'm standing in front of my closet, throwing clothes haphazardly into my duffel bag and hoping with all my heart that my preparations are unnecessary, so I'm barely paying attention to what I'm tossing into my bag. A sequined sapphire top. A pair of denim overalls. A black tulle skirt—the one I was wearing when I first met Delun.

My body freezes as I'm flooded with memories of that night. Bittersweet pain overwhelms me as I remember the way his face came to life when we first made eye contact—and then the storm of electricity that rose between us. *Please be alive, my love. I'm coming for you.*

That's how Jun finds me, sobbing into the scratchy fabric of the skirt pressed into my face.

"Lei, what's wrong?" she asks, alarm in her expression.

I must have been so lost in thought that I didn't hear her knock. But . . . *what's wrong?* Seriously? What does she *think* is wrong when, for all I know, my boyfriend is dead, and my comrades have been massacred or arrested or are running for their lives?

But then I remember how badly I need her.

"Jun. I was going to look for you after I finished . . . um . . ." *Packing, in case I need to run away from home?* Yeah—no. There's no good way to finish that sentence. Sniffling, I drop the skirt into the bag and wipe my nose on the sleeve of my purple tie-dyed shirt. I've already taken off the dress I "borrowed" from her. "We need to talk."

She collapses onto my silk sofa like her legs won't support her anymore. Her face is tense with wariness. "OK."

I stay standing and rub my hands nervously on my jeans. "I have to tell you what I did."

"Your hair is in a braid," she says suddenly.

Why is she fixating on my hair, of all things? "Jun, I'm trying to tell you . . ." I trail off when I realize she's not looking at me.

She's staring at the pink dress I flung onto the bed in my haste to get out of my sister's clothes. Slowly, her eyes swivel back to me. "You went to see Yanlin."

Dammit! "It's not what you think." I yank out my hairband, freeing my hair from its unaccustomed braid. "I did go to Yanlin's house, but I didn't pretend to be you. I mean, I thought about it, but I didn't go through with it."

She doesn't seem to hear me. "Did you do it for revenge?" Her face is mottled with the kind of anger I never thought to see in my sweet sister.

"You mean because you let Yawen think that you were me? Of course not!" How can she think I'd impersonate her for revenge? "But it was still a shitty thing for you to do." I'd be chewing her out for that if I didn't have the more pressing matter of getting her on my side so we can save Delun.

Relief flits over her face before her expression turns to one of contrition. "Lei, I'm so sorry for that. Ba told me that he'd have your friend arrested again if I let her see you."

"Oh." I shiver. I hadn't thought about how I might be endangering Yawen by going to see her. "You should have told me."

"I know. It was a stupid thing to keep from you, but you were already so mad at me. Can you forgive me?"

There should be peace between sisters, my mother said, and I didn't think I could forgive Jun, but maybe Ma is right. I exhale slowly. "Yes." It was easier than I thought it would be, and a tiny fraction of my despair bleeds away.

Jun smiles, but there's a telltale crease in her forehead. "I still don't know why you went to see Yanlin dressed like me."

Now is the time to tell her about the painting. But there's something nagging at me. *She's afraid.* I know my sister, and as crazy as it seems, she's scared to death. But of what? I stare at her, an easy smile on her face that would fool almost anyone. Who knew that Jun could be that good of an actress? A sick feeling grows in my stomach. *No.* She couldn't have. But it all makes awful sense. Jun pretended to be me to drive Yawen away. Her first thought was that I was trying to fool Yanlin out of revenge. My breath is choked with horror. "You pretended to be me."

Jun pales. "Yes, when I fooled Yawen into thinking I was you."

"No," I say, sick to my stomach. I remember Jun returning my necklace to me after telling me that she wore it as a good luck charm so I would get better. *Dear sister, what a liar you've become.* Conviction solidifies in me as my world shatters around me. "I mean when you fooled Delun."

She shrinks away from whatever she sees in my face, her body curling deeper into the yellow silk couch. "What do you mean?" she asks faintly.

"You asked me if I had impersonated you. And you asked if I had done it out of revenge." Bitterness throbs through me. "What did you think I had done, Jun? Fooled Yanlin into believing that you never loved him? Is that what you did to Delun . . . make him believe that I never loved him?" My nails dig into my palms, and my heart hammers so hard against my chest that it hurts. "Think carefully before you answer, Jie Jie. And don't forget that I can *always* tell when you are lying." I take a deep breath. "Did you go see Delun in Qincheng Prison and pretend to be me?"

Her eyes are wide with fear. "Yes."

Relief sweeps through me. *Delun is alive.* But the aftermath of my fierce exultation is a cold emptiness. "You knew that he was still alive." My voice is hard with all the pain and anger I had tried to let go of. "You *knew,* and you let me believe the boy I love was *dead.* And you let him rot in jail believing that I had abandoned him!"

"I had to," she cries out. "It was because of him that you almost died! Ba said we all had to keep him away from you."

"Does Ma know what you did?" My voice cracks. I can't bear it if Ma also knew Delun was alive and kept it from me.

"We all knew," she says simply, completely unaware that she has just burned down my last hopes.

They all knew. My whole family tried to take Delun away from me. I stalk over to Jun, and her eyes widen. "What did you tell him?" I snarl, looming over her.

She swallows, and the slender column of her throat trembles. "That I . . . you . . . didn't want to see him again." Color bleeds back into her face. "It's what you should have done if you cared about your own family and the secret we guard."

"Don't you dare." My anger is a still, terrible void. *You have no idea what I have done for our family, Jun.* But it's not just the painting that has sealed my fate. Delun is wasting away in prison, thinking that I've forsaken him. Because of my sister. I don't know why I can't forgive this betrayal when I forgave all her other ones. Maybe it's that I now know what it feels like when everyone I love has betrayed me. And this must be what Delun thinks I've done.

I know what I have to do.

With shaking fingers, I unclasp the necklace around my neck and pull a snarl of gold and steel ball chain over my head. The key clinks against the pendant as I drop them both into Jun's lap. The key to Wu Zetian's art gallery. The character for "younger sister" carved into green jade. Gifts I had dreamed of passing on to my future daughter. Past and future hopelessly tangled together in my sister's lap. "You can have it all. I won't pass on such a curse to my daughter."

Tears spring into Jun's eyes as she touches the key and the pendant. "You can't do this."

Later, I will remember this moment, and it will hurt beyond bearing. But for now, all I feel is a dull ache in my heart. "You'll get what you've always wanted. To be the guardian of Wu Zetian's art. To be our parents' greatest pride." I wish I had never underestimated Jun's ambition. Qiang was right after all. I never knew my own sister.

"That's not fair," she says, her voice trembling.

I turn away from her and pick up my duffel and my hobo purse. If only Jun hadn't taken this last thing from me, I could have forgiven her for everything else. She can have the rest of it, the art and even our parents' pride. But I will never forgive her for stealing Delun's faith in me. "Goodbye, Jie Jie."

Her hand reaches up to touch her own pendant, carved with the character "jie." But it's not until I'm halfway down the stairs that she realizes I'm serious. She races after me, stumbling over her feet. For once, she's not moving at a sedate, ladylike pace. "Lei!" she wails with raw desperation. "I'm sorry! Please don't go!"

Peace between sisters is impossible now.

My heart ripping to shreds, I turn to Jun. "I'm leaving," I say with deathly calm. "You'll never see me again. And if I have a daughter, she will never step foot in Beijing."

Then I leave.

CHAPTER THIRTY-THREE

My throat is tight with anxiety as I pace around Qincheng Prison's antechamber. The forged papers have been submitted, the bribes have been paid, and a hired car is sitting outside. All I can do now is wait and hope.

Mainly, I hope Ba hasn't figured out what I'm up to. I came here right after leaving home, but Jun will have called him to rat me out one last time. *Please let me be one step ahead of my father.* If so, it will be the first time. My stomach wrenches to think of everything I could lose.

At least I didn't tell Jun about the forged papers. Or about the "stolen" painting. In retrospect, I've left quite a bit of illegal activity in my wake. The police are just as likely to throw *me* in prison as they are to release Delun. My palms grow sweaty. As the daughter of a high-ranking official, will I get preferential treatment? Maybe they'll let me make dolls in my private cell like Madame Mao so I can escape the hard labor of the prison camp.

Steps sound down the corridor. I stop pacing at once, and my breath catches at the crushing hope that hits my body. Even though I still have to explain to Delun that Jun tricked him and that I never abandoned him, all my muscles strain toward the closed door. Every risk I've taken and everything I've left behind will be worth it, if only I can save the boy I love.

The door opens. It's Delun.

I don't even glance at the prison guard next to him. I'm launching myself at Delun before I remember all the reasons he has to hate me.

But his arms come around me, and he's holding me tight, murmuring "Lei, Lei" over and over again into my hair.

The guard coughs, and I remember where I am. "Right," I say, stepping back. Now that I look at him carefully, I'm struck by the sharpness of Delun's cheeks and the dark circles beneath his eyes, stark against the paleness of his skin. A tremor snakes through my body. What have they done to him?

"Let's get out of here," I say grimly.

He nods with equal grimness.

"Just a moment," the guard says, sending my heart plummeting. *Now what?* He goes over to a desk with a phone and picks up the receiver. "I need to check with my superior."

Asshole. Is he really going to accept my bribe and then turn around to report me to his superior?

Delun and I exchange nervous glances, and sweat drips from my forehead. *Please don't let his superior be someone who works for my father.* It would be heartbreaking to get this far and lose Delun now.

"Yes, sir," the guard is saying on the phone. "The release papers look legit, but the thing is . . ." He glances at me. "The girl who came to get the prisoner is just a kid." He listens for a moment and then picks up my forged release paper. "The signature is . . . Sung Shen Yi. Isn't that the same official who sent the prisoner here in the first place?"

So my father *was* the one who put Delun in this prison camp. Anger slams into my body.

"Understood, sir." The guard sets down the receiver. "You're free to go," he says.

Relief bursts into me, and I'm barely able to stay upright. Shakily, I thank the guard, half expecting him to slap me with another round of paperwork and bureaucratic tape, but he simply leads us out of the waiting room and to the exit.

Delun and I are silent as we leave the prison and walk toward the hired car. Anyone could be listening. I can't quite believe that the forged papers actually worked, though I'm sure the bribes helped too.

It's not until we're safely in the back seat of the hired car with the soundproof barrier raised between us and the driver that I can breathe at last. The car is turning onto the road leading us away from the prison, but Delun is still looking out the window at the gray stone gate fading out of sight.

"Are you OK?" I ask, and then kick myself for such a stupid question. The movement he poured his heart and soul into has ended in blood and with countless comrades dead. He's been in a prison labor camp for nearly two weeks. *Oh, and there's the part where he thinks I visited him in prison just to tell him that I never wanted to see him again.*

"I'll be OK." He turns back to me and attempts a smile. It's a little weak but genuine. "Thanks to you, Lei. You got me out."

He doesn't seem to be holding a grudge against me, but I can't put it off any longer. "It wasn't me!" I blurt out.

Confusion spreads over his face. "You weren't the one to get me out?"

"No, *that* was me." I'm probably just making this all worse. I take a ragged breath. "I mean that I didn't come to see you when you first got arrested. I wasn't the one who told you that I never want to see you again."

"I know," he says calmly. "It was your sister."

I gape at him. "You *know*? How?" Even Yawen didn't suspect that Jun was pretending to be me. "Do you mean that Jun didn't wear my pendant?"

"The one with 'mei' carved in jade?" he asks. "Yes, she wore it outside her shirt so I would be sure to see it."

"Then how—"

"I know you, Lei. Pendant or no pendant, I knew it wasn't you."

A great weight lifts from my chest. It had hurt to think of Delun alone and captive with the pain of my betrayal. A tear tracks down my cheek.

He reaches out tenderly to wipe it away. "From the first time I saw you, I recognized your strength and heart. No one can imitate that. You're my warrior princess. And I'd know you anywhere."

I smile shakily. "Hardly a princess anymore. I've left home, given up my inheritance, and I'm going to Hong Kong with you."

Alarm sparks into his eyes. "You can't leave your family because of me!"

"I've made my choice." I tap the soundproof barrier to test it, but the driver doesn't turn around or make any indication that he can hear me. Then I tell Delun about the forged papers and the *teeniest* chance that there might be an arrest warrant for me for the theft of a priceless Tang dynasty painting. "So I can't go back. Not right away."

Delun looks stunned. At last, he swallows hard and asks, "Can't your father smooth this over? Revoke the arrest warrant, if there is one out on you, and justify my release?"

"Probably," I say dryly, "but the last time my father tried to fix my life for me, it ended up with you in a labor camp and me believing you were dead."

"I would have ended up here anyway." Pain flashes across his face.

"Delun, listen," I say urgently. "I forged extra release papers, and I can make more. If we go to Hong Kong, we can contact our allies there and help get others out."

He opens his mouth and then closes it again. I can tell he's torn between his desire to help the protesters and his worry for me. "You're right that the Hong Kong students will organize to get the Beijing student leaders to safety," he says, reluctance in his voice. "They were planning something even before the . . ." He takes a breath before continuing. "The massacre. They were calling their plan Operation Yellowbird. And your papers could help."

"Then we'll go to Hong Kong and join Operation Yellowbird," I say, firmly tamping down the panic flooding my body at the thought of leaving Beijing.

"But your father! If he finds out you forged his signature to help others escape, you might not be able to come back yourself." His gaze narrows on me. "I can't let you lose everything you care for. Empress Wu's art, Beijing University, your inheritance, your family—you can't give it all up!"

"I withdrew enough money from my bank account to live on for a long time, there are universities in Hong Kong, and I'm taking one of the paintings with me." I tick off an answer to all his objections except for the last one. My family. "So, you see, I'm not losing everything I care about." I cup his face with trembling fingers. "But even if it meant losing everything, I would still choose you, my love, over any art and over all the money in the world."

Fire blazes in his eyes, and then he's reaching for me. We kiss with all the pent-up, frantic hope and fear of the past two weeks, and my hands lock tight in the small of his back as desire floods my body. I never want to lose him again.

Delun pulls away first, breathing hard. "But your family," he says.

My stomach goes cold. I can leave the money and status without a backward glance, and I can even give up Wu Zetian's art, as much as that would hurt. The thought of losing my family feels like a hot poker stabbing my heart.

My mother's words pop into my head. *If it ever came down to a choice between the art we protect and our family, Jun wouldn't hesitate to sacrifice the art for our family. She wouldn't try to find a way to save both. You would . . . That's why you are the right choice to be the keeper of Empress Wu's dynasty.*

If I went back home with the painting, Jun might burn it herself and think she was saving us. Ba would destroy Delun and think he was saving us. And Ma . . . she would let it all happen.

But *I* can't let it happen.

I can't give up the art *and* Delun. But maybe I don't have to give up my family either. I have to believe that is what Ma meant. That she chose me to be the keeper of the dynasty because I can do what she couldn't: save Wu Zetian's dynasty and the people I love without sacrificing one for the other.

"It's not forever," I say with more confidence than I feel. "Once the dust settles, they'll look for me in Hong Kong."

Ba will find out that I forged his signature on Delun's release papers, and he'll guess that I forged travel documents to Hong Kong as well. My father isn't stupid. He knows me well. Ba will know that I want to come back home. They all will. Ma and Jun too.

But I can't help but think of the last thing I said to my sister. *You'll never see me again.* My heart twists in pain.

I hope those words don't turn into a terrible prophecy.

Luoyang, Seventh Century

The last person Taiping expects to see outside her mother's imperial chambers is Si. "What are you doing here?" Inwardly, she winces at the undertone of accusation in her voice. She knows what Wan'er would say. *You don't need to be jealous of Si! You're the imperial princess, and she's just a nun who writes poetry that happened to catch your mother's eye.*

Si bows her head. "The empress summoned me."

"Oh." Taiping is at least an hour early for tea with her mother. But she's been going stir-crazy just pacing her chambers and getting more and more anxious. The week her mother had given her is up, and she has to make her choice *now*, even if she doesn't know what her choice will be. Peace at Taiping Temple. Or love at the imperial court. *Maybe I can put off the decision a little longer.* "I'll come back later then."

Si raises her head, and her eyes widen. "I couldn't possibly take precedence over you, Princess." She's already turning to leave. "Of course you should be first to see the empress."

"Wait," Taiping says.

Si eyes her warily. "Yes, Princess?"

"Do you know why the empress asked to see you?" Taiping tells herself that it's just idle curiosity and that she's not still driven by envy. But she can't help but wonder if her mother is about to make a daring move.

"Yes."

When Taiping realizes that Si isn't going to say more, she tamps down her irritation and asks, "Well, why then?" If Mother really is going to make a bid to become Huangdi, she will need all the political support she can get. She's already started by giving Wan'er, her imperial secretary, power second only to her own. Taiping knows how her mother thinks. Her next move will be appointing a loyal imperial court poet. Wan'er's grandfather once held that high position of political influence . . . before he was executed for treason against the empress. Mother will make sure the next imperial court poet is someone she can trust. And since she's already appointed Wan'er to an even greater position . . .

"The empress is offering me a choice for my future," Si says reluctantly, "and I'm here to give her my decision."

Looks like Si is going to be the first female imperial court poet. It doesn't upset Taiping as much as she thought it would. After all, her mother isn't just consolidating power for her own sake. One day, Wan'er and Si will be Taiping's political allies too. But it all depends on the choice Taiping makes today. Her stomach writhes with indecision, but the smile she gives Si is genuine. "Congratulations. It is an honor to be offered a future by the empress."

"A great honor," she agrees, her body going even more stiff, "but it's a difficult decision."

Why would a nobody like Si hesitate at the chance to become the imperial poet? But like any high court position, it comes with danger. Just ask Wan'er's grandfather. Maybe Si is smarter than I give her credit for. "I hope you make the right choice. I have a difficult choice of my own to make."

Her smile is startled but sweet. "Thank you, Princess. Good luck with your decision too."

Si leaves, and Taiping is alone and standing before the ornate wooden door of her mother's chambers. Who would have thought that she and Si would both be given a choice to make by her mother? But, of course, the choices of a princess and a nun are very different.

She inhales much-needed breath and courage as she lifts her hand to knock. The time has come to choose between peace and love. And she knows what she will choose.

Despite the character "ping" in her name that means "peace," there can be no peace for her. Not without Wan'er. So she will give up the temple named after her. She will stay in this dangerous imperial court and walk this path of fire with Wan'er and her mother. They will wrest power from the men who hoard their wealth and influence. Or they will die trying. Her heart trembles in her chest as if a shroud over the future had lifted briefly. There will be no peace for any of them.

I choose love.

Suburb of Chicago, 2001

Delun comes into my study, bouncing little Gemma. "I think she's hungry again." He lifts her up and sniffs her bottom. "Um, maybe I should change her before you feed her."

"Thanks." I smile at the sight of my baby daughter gurgling and butting her head against my husband's chest. A fierce joy wells up in me. No matter what I had to give up, it was worth it to find this happiness. "I'm just finishing up something, but it won't take long."

"OK," he says cheerfully. Tucking the baby against his shoulder, he makes his way to her bedroom, and I can hear him cooing a little nonsense song. "Xiao bao bei, little treasure, little gem, Gemma."

Gemma. The American name that Delun gave our daughter is beautiful. I gave our daughter her Chinese name: Jun. Maybe I shouldn't have, because I can't bear to call her by my sister's name. Still, Gemma should have some connection to my lost family. A wave of grief washes over me.

Nothing turned out as I had hoped it would. In the eight years Delun and I spent in Hong Kong, my family never tried to find me. Year after year, my hope dwindled. And when we boarded the plane to come to the United States in 1997, right before Hong Kong reverted back to Chinese control, I knew I had lost my family for good.

Even when I agreed with Delun that we should change our last name from Chuang to Huang, I knew it didn't matter. We have nothing to fear from my family. They won't be coming after me. Because they don't want me back.

It still hurts. Sometimes I wake up in the middle of the night and think that it was all a nightmare: Rong's death, Jun's betrayal, and the loss of my family. Would they want to know that I've become the art director at a museum? Or that Delun is a political science professor? Most of all, would they want to know Gemma? My daughter will never inherit the legacy that should have been hers. Many times, I've wanted to write to Jun. There are a million things I've longed to say. *Let me come back. Our daughters were supposed to inherit together. I miss you so much.*

Again, I open the creased blue airmail letter I received a year ago. There's not much to it, but that doesn't stop me from reading it over and over.

Dear Lei,
Jun just gave birth to our beautiful daughter. She doesn't know I'm writing to you, but I thought you should know.
All my best,
Qiang

Reading the letter is always bittersweet. On the one hand, it's news of my sister, and on the other hand, it's proof that Jun could have easily found me at any time—but didn't.

I reach for the picture of Gemma and flip it over. Then I just stare at the blank white space. What do I write? Even after all these years, I harbor too much confused hurt and longing to convey in words. I don't have the poetry of my ancestors to express what is in my heart. All I know is that my memories are haunted by the love and hope my twin sister and I shared. I'm desperate for her to remember what we once were to each other, but I don't know how to tell her that. I take a breath and write, *I do not forget.*

It's not enough. I know it isn't. But if my sister knows me as well as she once did, she will understand. She will hear the words I can't write.

I do not forget the times we huddled in bed and laughed in secret past bedtime. I do not forget how you braided my hair like yours whenever I asked. I do not forget that we kept trying to re-create Mrs. Wan's famous mooncakes, but they always ended up too sweet, not sweet enough, under-done, or dry as dust, but it didn't matter because we knew we'd make the perfect mooncake someday. I do not forget that you were once my other half—and I yours. I do not forget that you loved me. I do not forget that I love you still.

It hurts too much to remember.

Before I can change my mind, I slip the photo of Gemma into an envelope and write Jun's address on it. I don't put a return address on it. If she wants to write me back, she can get Qiang to find my address.

My hand reaches up to my throat in the habitual motion I've made a hundred times. And every time, I feel a jolt of pain to find the jade pendant missing. Another thing I can't give Gemma.

I look up at the portrait of the lady in the red dress hanging on my wall.

She would understand.

If she's who I think she is, she has known both great loss and love. But unlike me, she had the words for what was in her heart. Her eyes are dark and knowing as she bends over the blank parchment, brush poised to write her poetry.

As I've always known, the answer to the mystery of the unknown lady was in the last poem. I think again of the two different characters for "peace" in the poem. The first "peace" was written with the character "ping." That must mean Princess Taiping; her name meant "Great Peace." And then there's "shining beauty." There are two people this could mean, but I think it refers to Wu Zetian, whose personal name was Zhao, "to shine." Less likely (but possible) is that "shining beauty" refers to Lady Shangguan Wan'er, who held the title Consort of Shining Countenance.

But this poem wasn't written by Shangguan, or even by Taiping as I had once thought.

The poem was written by the lady in red, whose eyes are filled with the same loss that looks back at me in the mirror. And the second "peace" in the poem gave me the clue to who she is. That "peace" was written with the character "an."

Yet, I would not give up love for peace.

Or it could be read as

Yet, I would not give up love for *An*.

It's curious that Wu Zetian posthumously gave her murdered eldest daughter a name that also meant "peace."

Princess Si of *An*ding.

Did the princess refuse to give up love for her royal name? I'll never know. Just as I'll never know how or why her death was faked or how she ended up having her portrait painted in full court regalia. Or what her relationship with her sister, Princess Taiping, was like.

All I know is that there is no mention of Princess Si of Anding in the imperial records except of her infanticide.

But she survived. She lived to become the keeper of the dynasty.

And she lived to become my ancestress. Because Wu Zetian's art was passed down from daughter to daughter. So if Si of Anding wrote and placed this poem among the art she inherited, then she, and not Taiping, is the daughter I'm descended from.

I would love to know her story.

But for now, it is enough that I have this one last remnant of my family legacy to pass on to my daughter. I can only hope that Gemma will someday inherit a world where she can share the lost princess's portrait, as I have always hoped to do with all of Empress Wu's art.

Delun comes back into the room. "All nice and clean!" He tickles Gemma under the chin as she gurgles in delight. "Here you go, Gong Zhu," he says, passing her to me.

I smile to hear my love's nickname for me. "Thank you." Although I gave up my privileged life of secret royalty many years ago, to Delun I will always be a princess.

I cradle Gemma in my arms and revel in her baby softness against my skin. One day, I will tell her about her legacy, but that's a long way off. A pang hits my chest.

It's strange—when I became a mother myself, I inherited all Ma's fears. At times, I wonder what happened to that headstrong girl who fought for a revolution. But when I hold Gemma like this, I feel a rush of fierce protectiveness, and I know that I am stronger than ever. Strong enough to guard the most precious things in my life.

Gemma and Delun, my two great loves—I will choose them over and over again. There is deep pain in my soul but no regret. How can I regret what I could not have done differently?

I think Si of Anding must have felt the same.

I look down at Gemma, and my throat tightens with love. When she becomes old enough to understand what I am saying, I will lock away the poem written by her ancestress in the silence of my heart.

But for now, I softly speak the words of my daughter's legacy like a lullaby.

The sun has set below the border of mountains.
Even the skies weep and water the dusty earth.
I am alone with my tears and the silent stone.
Peace and shining beauty are gone.
The long-ago choice weighs heavy on my heart.
Yet, I would not give up love for peace.
Watch through the ages, beloved ones.
The dynasty is given to my daughters.

A NOTE FROM THE AUTHOR

Dear Reader,

When I first introduced Lei in *Heiress Apparently*, I knew that book two of the Daughters of the Dynasty series would be her story. But *Her Rebel Highness* turned out to be a hard book to write! Of course, it was always going to be a challenge to write about something as complex and fraught as the Tiananmen Square protest and its tragic aftermath. But I had no idea how emotional a journey writing this book would be.

I still remember my horror and shock as I watched the live TV images of the Tiananmen Square massacre. I was about Lei's age, and like her, I had been fired up by the youth activist movement taking place in the country of my parents' birth. And then the unthinkable happened. The tanks rolled into the square and soldiers opened fire on civilians. It was June 4, 1989.

It might seem strange to write a YA novel about a topic as serious as this. But young adulthood is the age many of us come into our activism. There is nothing quite like those burgeoning conversations about equity and justice, and I wanted to capture that energy. I also wanted to celebrate youthful hopes, dreams, and passion—and isn't that the heart of any YA novel?

I tried my best to maintain historical accuracy in *Her Rebel Highness*, but I did take some liberties. Most notably, I changed the age difference between Princess Taiping and her older sister. In reality they were probably a dozen years apart in age, but I condensed it to a couple of years. There were also some minor tweaks

I made to the timeline of the 1989 events, like changing the dates of the Gaokao (National College Entrance Examination) from July to June 1989 and moving up the opening of the first Beijing nightclub (and it was more a bar than a nightclub) by a year or so. Although this is a fictional story and Lei, Delun, and the other characters are not meant to be real-life people, I wanted to depict this historical moment with the care and respect it deserves. I hope that I succeeded.

In my author's note for *Heiress Apparently*, I shared my feelings about writing during a surge of anti-Asian hatred and violence. Sadly, this was still true as I wrote the second book in the Daughters of the Dynasty series. If anything, things have only gotten worse.

It was also jarring to write *Her Rebel Highness* at a time when peaceful Black Lives Matter protesters have been met by tear gas, Tasers, and armed National Guard. And yet, when violent insurgents stormed the U.S. Capitol with the intent to harm our government representatives and overthrow a democratic election, maiming and killing Capitol police in the process, they were met with words of praise and support from some of our leaders. Those in power encouraged violence against their political enemies, called for crackdowns on freedom of the press, dismissed media stories sympathetic to BLM demonstrations as "fake news," and threatened military force against unarmed civilians. All of this seemed chillingly familiar.

In fact, I had to constantly remind myself that I was *not* writing a contemporary novel set in the United States, but rather a novel set more than three decades ago in China. My point is that it would be overly simplistic to think of China as an innately backward, repressive country. As recent events in the United States have shown, democracy is fragile. And as Lei, Delun, and their friends have shown, democracy is worth fighting for.

My father gave me some advice on the publication of *Heiress Apparently*. What he said was this: "You are a good writer, a very good writer. Your mother and I are very proud of you, but if you don't mind, I have a few suggestions for you. Avoid political views. Some readers may or may not like the writer's political view."

Sorry, Ba. It's good advice. But some stories need to be told.

Readers, whether or not you like my political views, I hope you enjoyed Lei's story. Thank you for reading *Her Rebel Highness*!

ACKNOWLEDGMENTS

I want to thank my editor, Anne Heltzel, for her amazing insights and wholehearted support of this book. Thank you to Mercedes deBellard for the beautiful cover art, and big thanks to Laura Bernier, Jessica Gotz, and everyone at Amulet Books. *Her Rebel Highness* owes so much to all of you.

I am, of course, forever grateful for my agents, Christa Heschke and Daniele Hunter. They really are the best, and I am so lucky to be represented by them.

Thank you to Christina Scheuer for her encouragement and brilliance. Her suggestions and uncanny ability to ask the perfect questions helped me immensely. You are magic, my friend.

My belated thanks to Christine Bryant for her helpful insights during a lovely and memorable conversation at a Seattle bar when I was just starting to write *Heiress Apparently*. Thanks also to Melissa Grinley and Terri Chung for their continual support, and a huge thank you to my parents; my brother, David; and all my family. My heart is full of appreciation for you all.

As always, my husband, Joel, deserves my thanks for his steadfast encouragement *and* for putting together all the furniture in my backyard writing shed. Much love and appreciation to you, Joel!

I am grateful to Kieran, my seven-year-old, for sharing his funny and heartfelt fanfiction about the world of *Minecraft* and the adventures of Pusheen the Cat. Recently, he asked me how he can become an author when he grows up. I told him to keep writing the stories he wants to write. "OK, I will!" he replied—easy as that. His joy inspires me, and I can't wait to read more of his wonderful stories.

I am also grateful to Liam, my eleven-year-old, for telling all his teachers, classmates, classmates' parents, his school librarian, doctor, dentist—and basically everyone he has met—to buy my books. Liam also told me that "It's not enough to be your beta reader. I want to be your alpha prime reader." I'm still not entirely sure what that means, but he's the best alpha prime reader I could ask for.

I love you both so much, Liam and Kieran.

Finally, although there can be only one alpha prime reader (and that position has been taken), my heartfelt gratitude goes out to all of you, my readers.